THE HIGH PRICE OF LONELINESS

BY EDWARD GRAY

Inspired By Real Life Events

A Note From Edward Gray, Author: To My

READERS

"Why I Had To Write This Book"

First and foremost, thank you for the gift of your time to read The High Price of Loneliness. Perhaps the highest honor I have ever received is that of having a reader come and turn these pages together. It is my greatest hope that you will fall in love again and never wish to let go. But first, I feel called to reveal why I had to write this book.

The romance genre took a dark and sexy turn beginning with the Fifty Shades of Grey series, which was so successful, it launched a tidal wave of authors rushing to join the trend. However, many such authors have little, if any, actual experience with the subject matter. Now, a dark and dangerous mold has been cast, with most of the writing about the Romance Erotica BDSM world being a poor representation of the actual lifestyle.

Are you familiar with the staggering statistic of the orgasm gap? Can you believe that almost half of all women don't experience the sexual pleasure they desire? Shocking, isn't it?

Millions of women have now been seeking a Dominant to come into their lives. They yearn for a 'real man' who is a powerful take-charge leader with a hint of danger, willing to raze the world to protect his woman. This sometimes means a Dominant who can take charge inside and outside the bedroom. Maybe if we indulge some of these primal desires and fantasies (safely, of course), we can come out emotionally and sexually satisfied.

Why me? I have lived in this world my entire adult life after discovering I was a Dominant in my early college days. Decades later, when the books about this lifestyle became global sensations, there was an outpouring from within the BDSM–Tantra–Kink community that said universally, the books are nothing like the real thing. Yes, there is a large and very active community for this lifestyle in the real world, and we talk and compare notes often.

In writing this book, I will dispel the misconceptions and inaccuracies that dilute the BDSM–Tantra–Kink lifestyle. You will not see the common tropes, such as the protagonist, who is a victim of early abuse, or extreme sexual encounters that leave the characters somehow broken or in intense pain. On the contrary, you will see the primal drives and desires embedded in all of us that drive millions to explore this world. While the line between pain and pleasure may be thin, it is crossed using consent and communication. Any Master-level Dominant or anyone in this lifestyle will tell you that consent, deep trust, and understanding are core pillars that ensure you and your partner are having safe but mind-blowing sex.

As you embark on this journey, I urge you to lose yourself in the plot. Learn from the characters but also enjoy the experience. This book is not an instruction manual, but you can take away many lessons to spice up your sex life. Like Angelica, try Orgasm Meditation and see how it works for you. And if you are a man and you're curious about the Two Rules, try it out step by step for yourself, and see how it brings pleasure to your partner like never before. If you love the characters and the book in general, I ask that you leave an honest review. With your help and support, we can expand the community of readers, and you can help someone else, just like you, discover this story and the real essence of what draws so many to this lifestyle. Some lucky reviewers will also get special bonus content, including sexy "homework assignments." If you have read the book, you already know these will have you reeling in pleasure. Thank you for taking the time to read this personal message. Now, let's get started!

Edward Gray, Author

BONUS CONTENT

Curated Digital Experiences For My Readers

If you would be so kind as to take a moment to send me a screenshot of your honest review, I would like to send you a personal "thank you." It will include amazing **bonus content,** including videos and curated digital experiences to help bring this story to life, especially for you. Plus, you will receive access to my "Reading Room," where I personally read selected chapters with the emphasis on the "Author's Pen." Sometimes, it's not just what you say but how you say it. Also, you will discover a few "behind the scenes" insights into the real-life inspirations behind the story. Thank you for reading this personal note. *Now, let's get started.*

Contents

CHAPTER ONE

The Blind Date

Angelica Hart took a deep breath and closed her eyes to feel the breeze that moistened her body with saltwater from Sarasota Bay. She loved to come and watch the sun go down and walk in the shallows as she felt the waves rush over her feet and ankles. Since she was a little girl, she had been doing this, and it still felt good to her. She liked watching the luxurious superyachts cruising by and had always imagined what that must feel like. Watching the lifestyle on those yachts seemed like a faraway dream, like a fantasy world. But she still liked squinting her eyes and imagining what a day in that life might be like.

"Oh damn! I'm going to be late!" she said aloud, quickly returning to her car. It was time to rush home and get ready, but first, she took one last glance at the beautiful bay loaded with boats for the sunset. *I will text him*, she thought. But that was bad manners, especially for an arranged "blind date," as she sped out of the parking lot on Siesta Key Beach. Her mind raced, thinking of ways she could save a few minutes here and there to get ready quickly. *I hate blind dates*, she thought. *Perhaps this evening will be different from the others*.

Angelica texted him that she was running a few minutes late, to which he replied promptly, "Already on my way to pick you up."

"Damn," she scowled at herself as the stress kept building. She seemed to be catching every red light on the way home as she thought, *why does this always happen to me?*

The stress was replacing the blissful calm she had felt just minutes ago at her favorite beach. She finally pulled into her driveway and dashed inside to get ready.

"I must not keep being late." She recited this mantra aloud, hoping to retrain herself and stop this persistent habit.

She hurried into her bathroom, and only five minutes into getting ready, her date texted, "Just pulling in your driveway now. Let me know when you are ready."

Angelica slipped into her favorite red cocktail dress. It showed just enough legs and curves to gain a bit of forgiveness for keeping him waiting. She raced to brush her long blonde hair and then touch up her makeup and lipstick, but now her heart was racing a bit. *Perhaps this first date would be different ... even unique?* She'd thought about a magical first glance and powerful first touch since she was little. But somehow, the real thing never seemed to measure up to the ones she had imagined. And how she could imagine!

The doorbell rang, and she grabbed her small purse and phone. This evening could change everything.

Her blind date was at the door wearing a white shirt and a dark jacket with a European-style ponytail. His hair was slick and oiled back, and she felt he was a good bit older than in the photo he had texted her. *Not exactly a "catfish" date*, she thought, but she had discovered that many people she met online might not exactly be "as represented" when they finally met. It was him, all right, just a slightly aged version of the photo he had shared—so, best not to say anything.

"Sorry to keep you waiting," Angelica said softly.

His eyes sparkled as he drank in her legs and curves moving under her red dress. "No problem at all—it was well worth the wait for a babe like you!"

Angelica silently groaned at his greeting, thinking, *A babe like you?* Not exactly the words she had hoped her Prince Charming would have used. Sometimes it's almost a relief when you are on a first date, and you just know—this person is not "the one." Then you can just relax and enjoy the dinner or the movie or whatever the plans were—because you know you're not going to want to see them again. But she had always been taught to "be polite."

She could feel his eyes checking her out as they walked to his BMW. When they reached his car, he got in the driver's side without opening her door for her. *Another sign*, she thought. *Where have all the gentlemen gone? Doesn't anyone know how to treat a lady on a date anymore? Opening the door just shows respect and courtesy. Plus, it shows how she can expect to be treated in the future, and it certainly wasn't going to be like a princess with this one.*

The drive to the restaurant was a monologue, with her date talking about himself and bragging about his wealth. He mainly spoke of what he owned or what he had bought. On and on, the endless ego show went. But he was not alone—there had been a series of men with money that never seemed to stop talking about their "stuff." It was a complete turnoff and sometimes seemed to be never-ending in Sarasota. So many wealthy people so eager to flaunt what they could buy. She couldn't care less and just found it mostly annoying.

Miles away, Edward Gray sipped a Taste of Diamonds champagne while observing his breath flowing deep down and up through his lungs. It was not just another casual day for him. Gray was far from the typical man you would see or walk past daily in Sarasota.

He was a successful CEO who had built his life from humble beginnings—and which he never forgot. He held the power to make almost anything happen and liked to do things one of two times, either "now or right now."

Gray was well-known in Florida for his philanthropy in supporting numerous worthy causes, but often anonymously. Being a man in his position in life, and with his striking good looks, Edward never failed to capture the attention of young and mature ladies wherever he showed up. He was one of the most handsome and eligible bachelors women yearned to lock their lips with and explore further, if possible. But he was elusive, a mysterious man with class and always with his own unique exquisite taste.

"Mr. Gray, you have a phone call waiting," one of the staff said, walking toward him.

Gray replied, without looking up, "Not just now, Jacob. I need to head out. Ask them to ring me back in about ten minutes once I'm in the car."

Edward had a true calling for the passionate things in life. He always embraced his nature for who he was and what he believed in. Most of all, Edward loved making a difference, and his companies always served a mission that attracted great people to come work, stay, and succeed. But then Gray also enjoyed sensual pleasures, particularly in a seductive manner that most men would not dare.

Tonight, he wore a pitch-black tuxedo, leaving the first few buttons open and letting a few strands of chest hair out. Edward got into the back seat of the black Cadillac Escalade, and his driver handed him a folio of papers to review for his upcoming phone call. His phone rang almost immediately as he answered, "Thanks for calling me back. I just needed a few minutes to get on my way."

After giving instructions and answering a few business questions, the SUV arrived at one of his favorite restaurants. He marched straight in and sat in the reserved section at the bar.

"Where are you?" Gray said into the phone while running his eyes across the tables in the restaurant. But his voice froze when he saw a gorgeous woman with long flowing blonde hair gracefully walking into the restaurant. She wore a low-cut scarlet red silk dress with a deep side seam slit. Her shimmering tanned leg flashed a slight peek with each stride as she elegantly glided through the room, accompanied by her date. Gray told his caller, "Never mind, take your time."

As Angelica walked, her eyes caught Edward's familiar gaze, and he thought, *Have we met before?* An electrifying sensation pierced his body at the flash of her gaze into his. She walked onward to a table, just a short distance away from Gray's seat at the bar, and gracefully slid into her booth seated across from her ponytail date.

Edward recalled that they had seen one another a few times around the small but very affluent town of Sarasota, but they had never actually met. They had shared a few flirting glances previously, but this night was different, and he could not take his eyes off her graceful energy.

Why haven't I talked to her before? he wondered as he switched his seat to have a better look at her. *And who's this guy she's with?* He looked at her date who was no match for her. He was beneath her level. Edward couldn't help but stare at her stunning body with perfect curves. He looked at her well-toned, shimmering thighs, and his urge was to take a bite of her gorgeous drop-dead body wrapped up in the sheer silk dress. Her stunning face and figure were tormenting his mind, and he could not let that woman sit with another guy who had no chance of matching up to her level. Glancing momentarily at her date, he seemed a good bit older than her, and his hair was tied up in a ponytail. Edward thought, *He looks boring. But I see fire inside of her, and he's just an average guy*, shaking his head and returning all his attention to her.

I'm not going to let this opportunity slip away, Gray thought as he silently activated his horny beast mode. He carefully observed her facial expressions while waiting for his friends to show up for their guys' happy hour night. She seemed bored and slipped a couple of straight gazes at Edward as he sipped his cocktail. Every time she looked at him, she bit her lower lip softly and stunned him with her smile.

A waiter approached their table, carrying a tray of salads and soups for another party, and paused briefly to let them know he would be with them shortly. Her date then abruptly got up and walked to the men's restroom, leaving her alone at the table. Edward recognized the momentary opportunity that had just presented itself.

Once again, he saw her gorgeous almond-shaped eyes glance at him, which he considered an invitation to approach her. He wanted to be quick and direct, already knowing what he had to say. Edward confidently walked the few fateful steps to her table and sat in her date's now empty seat directly across from her. She looked up, quite surprised by his forward advance. "I want you to get rid of this guy…and come back here to meet me," he said, his voice deep and sexy.

Angelica looked into Gray's deep blue eyes, gazing intensely into hers. No one had ever approached her this directly before—especially when she was already on a date. She stammered, a little flustered.

"Who are you?" she asked with just a hint of a smile. Angelica felt her heart racing still surprised by Gray's unexpected and straightforward approach.

As she heard his invitation again, she felt he was beckoning her as he leaned in slightly and urged her almost in a quiet whisper now, "I said... get rid of this boring guy and come back here to meet me."

The tension was building as her heart raced and she found herself drawn to his great charm and charisma, like a compelling magnet. At a momentary loss for words, she said simply, "Well then," and laughed, showing off her perfect smile.

He yearned to compete for her sole attention and added, "That's quite the ponytail your date has on top of his head." Angelica picked up her glass of wine. Gray asked with a playful grin on his face, "Doesn't it look like a pulled-out horse tail?"

Angelica laughed as she added, "I don't know what to say. The poor horse, I guess!" She laughed so hard that she accidentally spilled a bit of wine on her partially revealed breasts. She suddenly felt embarrassed by her spill, but Edward, always the gentleman, came to her rescue and quickly pulled out a linen handkerchief and handed it to her. Feeling relieved to have his help, she slowly wiped the dripping wine off her feminine curves. She bit her lips hard and tried to contain her excitement as she felt his eyes watching her brush the wine from her *décolletage*. Feeling embarrassed in a seductive way, she returned his monogrammed handkerchief, and said demurely, "Thank you."

He nodded graciously and replied with a disarming smile, "What else are these for if not to rescue a princess?" His last few words were her favorite.

The initial ice between them had quickly melted, and they were already exchanging playful laughs as they became more comfortable. But just as quickly, the friendly smile on her face changed to one of concern, and she looked anxiously over Gray's shoulder. He heard footsteps approaching from behind and realized that her date must be returning to the table after taking a long break from his gorgeous date. As Edward leaned forward to her one last time, he urged, "Don't forget what I have told you. Remember my request, and might I ask your name?" as he stood up from the table.

She whispered hurriedly, "Angelica."

Gray now addressed Angelica's date, impatiently standing, waiting to regain his seat at the table.

"My apologies. I didn't realize that anyone was sitting here," Gray said, covering his intrusion. Then, motioning to Angelica, he added, "She's far too beautiful and charming to be left alone. Please pardon the interruption and allow me to send you each a glass of beautiful champagne. Enjoy your evening." He left the table, returned to the bar, and called the waiter.

Gray gestured to Angelica and her dowdy date and requested, "Please be so kind as to serve each of them a glass of Dom Perignon champagne and put it on my check."

Meanwhile, Angelica's date did not utter a single word to

Gray, even though he seemed as if he was close to bursting out with rage. But now he chose to take his frustration out on her, as he was rattled and angry and was furiously lashing out at her.

"I leave for five minutes, and you're already giggling with another man?" he spewed at her with a ferocious glare.

During the few minutes it took for the waiter to deliver the champagne, Gray watched over Angelica protectively from the bar as she rolled her eyes in disbelief. After all, she was innocent. It was not her fault that she stunned the restaurant with her beauty and graceful presence. It was not her fault that her boring date with a pulled-out horse tail couldn't handle her charm and poise. Edward smiled, secretly delighted, as he watched the collapse of his competition. *He should have known better than to leave a woman like her alone.*

Finally, the ponytail said, "I won't have dinner here now. Let's go somewhere else."

Edward heard a few words of their heated argument in between and saw her shaking her head in despair. He lacked the backbone to turn to Gray and take revenge; instead, he lashed out at the waiter. "Bring the bill," he roared, aggressively stirring his drink and muttering words to himself. As the waiter approached him, he threw the credit card across the floor.

This guy is just a horse's tail, Edward thought with a slight smile. After quite the display of histrionics, the ponytail left the restaurant with Angelica in tow. Edward patiently remained and waited at the bar, watching the entrance and hoping for her to return to him.

Suddenly, Edward remembered his friends who planned to meet him there for happy hour, and he immediately pulled out his mobile. He called them to explain. "Let's call it off for tonight. Something urgently important has come up," Gray said to his disappointed but understanding friends on the call. He remained steadfastly waiting and watching the door for her return.

Hours went by, and Mr. Gray kept stroking his cocktail glass in a circular motion hoping to see Angelica's smile walking through the door again. He kept replaying their conversation in his mind. He was sure that he had made his invitation clear—*Come back here to meet me.*

The hour was getting late, and only a few tables were left having dinner in the grand restaurant. A few were emptying the last of their wine bottles or finishing desserts here and there. But the atmosphere was winding down and getting later as they went. Finally, at almost 10 o'clock, she walked back through the restaurant door. When she saw Edward still waiting for her at the bar, a huge smile beamed across her face as she glided across the room. Edward's heart sang, *It's her!* He felt his adrenaline pumping when she walked directly to him.

She watched his face and saw the huge look of relief that she finally showed up despite the unpleasant incident earlier. She watched him rise, as a gentleman, to walk over and greet her, and she loved how tall he was. His voice was deep and sexy as he leaned into her ear and said, "I'm so glad you returned."

She squeezed into him gently for a brief hug. "Hello." She loved the feel of his masculine chest.

The restaurant manager stopped by to greet them. "Good evening, but we will be closing shortly," adding, "This is the last call for the bar."

Angelica smiled at him with a simple shrug. "Just one drink, then."

Edward pulled out a bar stool for her and she slid into it gracefully. "So, here we are finally, free from all the horse crap." His voice was heart-meltingly deep.

Angelica shook her head in disbelief. "That guy was so damn childish. Did you see the way he lashed out at me?"

Smiling into her beautiful eyes, he nodded as he replied in a confident but comforting voice, "You deserved better, and I knew it from the moment you walked in. Would you like to grab a late bite with me somewhere else?"

Angelica found Edward charming and incredibly attractive, but it was getting late, so she said warmly, "I'm not hungry but thank you. Perhaps we could make plans for another night?" She smiled into his dreamy blue eyes.

"Absolutely!" he replied but with a thoughtful look on his face. "Just curious, why did you take so long to come back? I was waiting for you for hours." He reached over and gently pulled her bar stool a bit closer to his.

Feeling the ease with which he moved her next to him, she complimented, "Oh, you are so strong." Reaching over and touching his muscular biceps, she smiled admiringly into his eyes.

Gray wasn't ready to change the subject. "Thank you kindly, but you didn't answer my question."

She continued to look at him as she licked her dark red lips, as they opened to answer his question. She thought to herself, *Phew, he's blazing hot!*

Angelica felt an intense tingling sensation running across her body. She answered gently, "I felt very turned off by the way my date behaved, and there was no way I was going to have dinner with him. Then, afterward, I wasn't sure if I felt comfortable coming back here to meet you alone." Her voice was beginning to tremble as she gathered the strength to keep looking him in the eyes. She continued, "I called some friends, and everyone seems to know who you are. You're quite famous here in Sarasota."

She looked down. "Then, I Googled you, and all the news articles about you went on for pages," she whispered in a low voice as he smiled slightly back at her. She watched as Edward responded to the accolades with humility and a total lack of hubris, very much unlike her ill-fated last date.

"Trust me, being famous has pros and cons," he said thoughtfully.

She continued, "I don't like walking into a place at night alone, so I gave it some thought before driving all the way back here."

"The restaurant is closing soon anyway. The least I can do as a gentleman is walk you to your car," Edward offered, nodding his head encouragingly.

Angelica liked the respectful way he spoke to her, the way he made her feel special. Now, as they left the restaurant together, she explained, while pointing towards the corner of the parking lot, "My car is over there." Gray offered her his arm to hold on to as she walked across the dark asphalt in her heels. Another gold star, she thought. Perhaps there are still some real gentlemen left in the world.

She drove a passion-red convertible Nissan Z sports car, and as they slowly walked together, Edward nonchalantly asked, "Would you mind giving me a lift to my car? My friends all left to go elsewhere for dinner, and I planned to ride with them, but I wanted to wait, in case ..."

As Gray paused with a moment of silence, Angelica interjected, "In case I returned?" smiling as she blushed at once.

He smiled warmly and nodded as he confirmed her guess, "Of course."

Angelica was happy to give him a lift. "Where is your car parked?"

She felt him hesitate ever so slightly before he replied, "My car..." Gray repeated the line and looked into her gaze, "is at home," he said with a charming smile.

Angelica laughed with her playful eyes. "Oh, you are smooth!" Which, apparently, Gray took as his cue to walk around to the passenger door and get in beside her. He had a confident and easy way about him that made her feel comfortable. She had returned to meet him, and now they were together at last, at least for the ride to his home with Edward's eyes admiring Angelica's beautiful smile and captivatingly stunning figure all the while.

"I can give directions to my home. It's right on the water on Longboat Key."

She perked up with a coy look on her face. Little did he know, Angelica was way ahead of him. "Oh, I already know where you live, Mr. Gray. My friends told me all about you, so I looked you up and drove by your home before coming back to meet you," she retorted with a smirk.

She saw him off balance, for the first and last time that evening as he replied, "I'm flattered, I think..." clearly surprised by her unexpected research. But sure enough, Angelica started up the horses under the hood of her red Nissan Z and made all the correct turns, unassisted by Gray, heading straight to his oceanfront estate.

They turned to head across the arched bridge connecting Sarasota to the barrier islands of Lido and Longboat Key. "So, what would you have done if you had returned to the restaurant, and I was no longer there? After all, it had been quite a while."

Angelica glanced over to him and flashed a playful smile, then revealed yet another of her secrets. "Well, I thought about that before driving all the way back there. So, I called the restaurant and asked the hostess if a very distinguished and handsome fellow might still be sitting at the bar by himself. She said yes and told me she thought you had been there waiting for someone for quite some time. So, I felt that coming by for one drink was the least I could do. I didn't want to leave you there pining away for me." She looked at him playfully as she pulled right into his circular driveway.

Edward was smiling at her differently now with newfound respect that she was "not just a pretty face," as he admitted, "OK, I'm impressed."

"Would you care to come in for a few minutes?" he asked politely, knowing they had just met.

Angelica hesitated. "Edward, it's getting late. I really should get going."

Gray's deep voice guided her ever-so-gently forward. "Just for a bit. I give you my word that I'm a perfect gentleman. One hundred percent guaranteed."

Angelica hesitated and then nodded, "OK, but just for a bit." They both got out of her flame-red convertible and walked across the drive as he retrieved his keys. Gray opened one of the two substantial, arched wooden doors set in the front glass wall of his home. The door opened inward, revealing a massive, vaulted ceiling living room. The centerpiece was the vast wall of glass across the back of the oceanfront estate. She smiled, seeing the Gulf of Mexico at night across the beautifully lit infinity pool.

"Come and sit with me," Edward encouraged as he walked over to one of the two white leather couches in the great room. As they sat down, she felt his eyes gazing slowly from hers down to her exposed neck and across the upper curve of her breasts. She took a deep breath as his gaze plummeted down to her small waist and beautiful hips and finally down to her gorgeous legs before slowly returning back to gaze into her eyes once again. Her heart was racing with nervous energy as he finally spoke. "Pardon me, Angelica. It is just so rare to see so much beauty in one person," he apologized after poring over every inch of her with his calm, powerful eyes.

"Thank you for the compliment, Edward," she said shakily, biting her lip softly as she hoped her voice didn't give away her real attraction to him. This was the one she had fantasized about since she was a little girl, and she didn't want to mess this up.

Edward poured her a glass of beautiful wine and handed it to her. "Careful with this one—not to spill again." He smiled into her eyes as she took the crystal glass. As they sat in the living room facing the gorgeous ocean view, his arm gracefully circled behind her, and his fingers softly began stroking her shoulder as they talked. Edward said openly and candidly, "I'm not going to sleep with you tonight. I don't 'dance' on a first date or meeting—ever."

Looking right into Edward's eyes, she replied, "Who said I was going to sleep with you either?" She smiled broadly, relieved that the conversation was finally out in the open. Her mind raced excitedly that Gray was already thinking of her that way.

She heard Edward's tone shift a bit more seriously, and he hesitated before speaking as he told her, "Angelica, there is something you should know about me. I may not be right for you or what you are looking for, and I would rather be open and upfront."

Her smile faded a bit as she asked with hesitation, "Edward, tell me more about what you mean…exactly?" Her facial expression and body language now seemed a bit confused.

Edward leaned back and paused before he explained with a slight grin, "Well, you see, I have certain drives—certain preferences and appetites that may not be for you. You could say…I like a bit of 'kink in my coffee.'"

The easy and natural smile finally returned to Angelica's eyes, and she immediately responded, "That's not necessarily a bad thing at all!"

Edward gave fair warning of what might lay just around the corner. "Well, before you jump to the next level, you should know, for example, that I have a Red Playroom here at home—which comes complete with two rules. You may not find it to be your cup of tea."

Angelica felt her blood racing and her adrenaline coursing with excitement, hearing Edward's deep and sexy voice guiding her gently forward. Her better judgment was trying to press the "pause button" but with no such luck. She heard her voice asking, "What are the two rules?" all the while, thinking quietly to herself, as her mind was wandering—and wondering, *What was this Red Playroom?* but she dared not ask, at least not yet.

CHAPTER TWO
The Two Rules

Looking into Edward's gaze, Angelica felt powerfully drawn to his masculine energy. But she felt a mixture of both nervousness and excitement to hear the answer to her question, about his "two rules." Were they about to cross a line from which there was no safe return? Her eyes were pleading with Edward to share some things that were very personal.

She could see Edward thinking carefully, as he knew full well, that once delivered, they could not be unsaid. He began slowly. "Since you asked, let me start by answering you in the least intimidating way that I can, to explain the two rules. If we decide to pursue this powerful attraction, that we both are feeling, further, Angelica, then whenever we are in the Red Playroom, Rule Number One is: You may never have me inside of you."

Angelica heard his words but did not believe her ears. Surely, she had misunderstood him. She blurted in surprise, "What?"

Angelica's face said it all, so Gray quickly continued, adding, "Unless…" (she would soon learn there is always an "unless"). With quite a different meaning set in this newly added context, he repeated for emphasis, "Unless you are already climaxing very, very hard."

Angelica's mind, now racing with all the implications of Rule Number One sat silently as she processed what this tectonic shift might mean for her frustrated experience with intimacy. She found herself listening ever more closely as his deep voice continued to draw her into this new world. "You see Angelica, if you think about it for a moment, most boys that you have been with, and I use the word 'boys' intentionally here, most likely have already figured out how to easily please themselves." He paused, then continued, "But they may not have invested the time … and energy to truly discover all the different ways to please their woman. All the different ways that can make your body shake like a leaf. Do you know that feeling right before you climax? When your core is just trembling? When you are just at the edge…" His voice trailed off.

Angelica's mind was still stuck on the part that "most boys have learned how to please themselves." But she dared not answer his last question. Embarrassed at her only true answer, she had no words to explain her dire dilemma. "Maybe, I think so," she muttered softly, looking shyly down at her hands.

She was relieved to hear him continue, so she would not have to elaborate. "Well, when you commit yourself to one Dominant male energy in your life, who truly understands this lifestyle, he takes ownership of that journey to complete joy for his submissive. And, over time, you get to a place where you can quickly and easily get to that state—each and every time, and often repeatedly. But that is the point that brings us to Rule Number Two, which is the catch."

Angelica still kept her personal dilemma with her sexuality a secret, as he now led her to door number two. She asked with interest and a bit of intrigue, "Ok, Edward, I'll bite. What then, is Rule Number Two?"

What she heard next was beyond unexpected. It floored her. His words came tumbling out slowly for dramatic effect. "Rule Number Two says you are not allowed to climax."

Interrupting him instantly, she retorted, "What! Then what is the point?" with a face that was unmistakably disappointed. This had not been part of her childhood dream of being "swept away" by her prince in a blissful escape from earth to heaven. She looked intently into Edward's face for some sign, seeking some sense of purpose to this painful point. The feeling rolled full circle as she saw the sly smile of the magician about to do his "great reveal." The secret was about to be shown to her, it appeared, as she temporarily suspended her first instinct, to now listen to the finale.

Gray added the all-important, "Unless." (There was that darn "unless" again.) He repeated for its full effect, "Unless you ask for…permission first."

Angelica liked this more fully refined version far better but now quickly pivoted in her thinking. Seeking to corner Gray on his purpose, she wanted to know his reason for Rule Number Two. Challenging him with a coy smile, she asked, "So, Rule Number Two is so you feel you have control over me, right?"

A slight knowing smile crept onto Edward's face, as he paused to reflect on her question, but then took on a different tone as he went deeper, bringing her with him as he guided her further down the rabbit hole.

"Perhaps a little, but the real reason for Rule Number Two is quite something else altogether. Rule Number Two is about our desire for forbidden fruit. Remember when you were little, maybe 5 or 6 years old, during the holidays, and Mom, Dad, or Grandma told you, "Angelica, you can't have any of those special cookies. Those are for company tomorrow night," Gray smiled as he continued the story. "Oh, my god, you were just 5 years old. What was in those special cookies? Now, you just couldn't stop thinking about them. You probably even had the thought cross your mind— I'm going to have to sneak one of those cookies later when no one is looking!" He finished with a charming smile: "Forbidden fruit. We all want—what we can't have."

Angelica nodded and said, "I can see that."

Gray leaned into her ear and added, "So moments ago, your subconscious mind just heard that you are not allowed to climax. Without permission, that is. The real purpose of Rule Number Two is to create that secret desire for what is forbidden. And it will help you get there faster, more times, and harder—than ever before."

Angelica's mind was racing. Should she tell Edward about her issues? How could she explain that she had never had that type of climax before, at least not with a partner? She thought she might have had some little ones—sort of—by herself, but she was never a hundred percent sure, and she certainly never talked about it with a man before.

She didn't want to lose Edward's passionate attention; his gaze, the way he looked at her, and the way it made her feel. If she said something, would he judge her and lose interest? She now worried that perhaps she was not enough for him—with all that he wanted from a partner.

But there was something about the way Edward spoke to her, the way he made her feel comfortable, she just felt she should take the risk. Perhaps, it was now or never. Angelica summoned some courage to share her worry. "May I ask a question, Edward?"

His voice was calm. "You may ask anything of me."

She swallowed hard and finally let it out, "Well, what if I can't? I mean, what if I'm not able to 'get there' with your Rule Number Two? What would that mean?"

Gray gently and calmly replied, "You mean to climax, Angelica? Have a complete and full orgasm experience?"

Angelica looked down from the steady gaze of his eyes for the first time as she mumbled, "Yes." She hated looking away but felt uncomfortable with her question. She had always felt uncomfortable talking about it with a man—so she just never did.

Edward's warm and gentle hand cupped Angelica's chin—to lift her gaze back to his. He marveled at how baby soft her skin felt. "Perfect," he said aloud.

Confused by his response, she felt compelled to ask, "How is that perfect? That I have trouble in that department?" she retorted with a puzzled look on her face.

Edward smiled, still softly caressing her cheek, touching the baby-soft hair framing her face. Looking into Angelica's eyes, he explained, "No, not that of course. Just your skin is so—perfect. Soft. Supple. It feels amazing to the touch," he said smiling into her eyes.

Angelica felt her face flush, looking into his amazing blue eyes, and hearing his gentle compliment completely changed her state of mind to lean into him before the real relief came next. Gray elaborated, "As far as your concerns about reaching a climax, that would never be your worry again. I can guarantee you, 100%—unless you have had a car accident or trauma where there is major physical, nerve, or internal damage, you absolutely, positively can have wonderful, full orgasms. You just need the right partner and a bit of time and patience to help you get into the right head space."

Angelica was more than a bit intrigued. Could this be the answer to her greatest ache? Her greatest worry about her feminine energy? Her worth as a partner? "What do you mean?" She gravitated toward his eyes unblinkingly this time.

She felt Edward's warm hand run across her shoulder and neck gently for one reassuring squeeze and connection before he explained, "It's 100% mental not physical. It always has been, and always will be. Today, everyone is busy. Everyone is stressed. Lots to do with careers to juggle and busy schedules to keep, and it is very common to feel the way you do, Angelica. I'm sure you have female friends with the same issue if they just felt comfortable talking about it."

Angelica nodded. "Yes. We all talk about it a lot and several of my friends are just like me. Sometimes we just fake it for our husbands or boyfriends, quite frankly, so they don't feel bad."

Gray nodded at her words knowingly and, looking deep into Angelica's eyes, he said, "What I am offering you is a completely new type of sexual experience. But first, you must trust yourself and your partner to 'let go.' To forget worries about the past or future and be completely, totally immersed in the moment. In fact, that is the primary purpose of the Red Playroom. It takes us both out of our everyday 'busy' minds and energy. It helps to create an entirely sensual world when you are ready—to explore and be open to focusing just on this moment. Right now. You will discover the amazing feminine energy that has always been right there inside of you. Perhaps waiting for just the right opportunity to feel completely safe and free."

She thought about the idea and confessed, "The Red Playroom idea is a bit intimidating. I would be scared, I think."

He nodded knowingly, as he smiled and moved closer to her slightly. "If you were completely comfortable—if you trusted me, and just me alone, no one else for some time—I could train you, your mind, body, and spirit, Angelica, to let go and to have an incredible climax every time as you have never experienced before."

She felt both hopeful excitement mixed with "sounds too good to be true" running through her mind. How could it be this easy? And why doesn't everyone know about this? So, she asked simply, "Are you sure it could work for someone like me? How do you know for sure?"

Edward's eyes smiled into hers. "I can show you the path to feeling 100% in the moment and, with it—a complete and total release—and eventually, perhaps something called a full-body energy orgasm. And you will take that ability with you for the rest of your life. There is a name for this practice, and it is highly effective in the hands of those trained and skilled in this art. It is called 'OM,' short for orgasm meditation. Have you ever heard of it before?" he asked.

Angelica's mind raced with the possibilities. "No, I don't think so."

"I would encourage you to Google it. You will discover you are not alone, and this has worked for tens of thousands of women all around the world. And, with trust, time, and practice, I can show you how to reach that peak each time, and eventually, you may have an orgasm lasting for up to fifteen minutes long."

Angelica had been listening intently to everything Edward had been telling her with a bit of newfound hope and curiosity, up to this point. But when she heard him describe a fifteen-minute climax, her face turned to one of total skepticism. Perhaps like the first time you heard a friend say they had seen a UFO. She blurted out, "What? How is that even possible? That would be hard to even imagine!"

"You would not be the first or last to feel that way about OM, but I guarantee you—you will feel a transformation not just in your sex life but in every area. When we are centered and happy, healthy, and balanced, life just works better. We are happier. We are more fulfilled and want to serve others more. But when we are frustrated, when there is scarcity, stress, or worry, that spills over into all those other areas of life as well."

Angelica's mind was now racing with the possibilities. With a tiny bit of hope, she added, "Well, I will look it up online like you suggested." Her face was alive with curiosity now.

Gray's deep voice spoke with confidence as he leaned back into the couch, pausing before he said, "Ultimately, here is the question you must answer for yourself: Which do you choose? Light or dark? Hope or despair? It is completely up to you. All I am offering is to show you the path. If you accept my invitation, there is still my core requirement. You would just have to agree to my two rules."

Angelica smiled at his handsome face as she was intrigued by all the possibilities. "Well, it seems like I don't have much to lose and lots to gain if even half of what you said is true. But it is getting late Edward, and I should be going. I have to work in the morning."

Gray rose slowly and helped Angelica stand as well. He pulled her close, feeling her full breasts press against his chest for the first time. Taking her chin and cheek in his hand again, he pulled her full lips to his, and they kissed softly, slowly, and then more passionately. Angelica's heart raced as she felt his powerful, muscular body pressing into her. She looked at him with a seductive glance. "So, is this when you would like to show me this Red Playroom, Edward?" she said smiling while still pressing fully against him.

His deep blue eyes still smiled into hers as he said, "No, Angelica, as I told you earlier. I never 'dance' on a first date or meeting. Not ever. But I will walk you to your car, if you feel ok to drive home safely?"

Her heart was still beating hard as they walked through his arched front doors. Arms around each other's waist, he guided her to her car. She smiled when Edward opened her door for her, like a gentleman for his princess and pulled her close for one more kiss goodnight. "Here is my card Angelica, with all my numbers. Drive safely, and please text me to let me know when you are home. Ok?"

She didn't want this magical connection with him to end, so she kissed his cheek and whispered, "When will I see you again?"

She looked into his gaze to see his eyes smiling as he replied, "I will call you for a proper date, the moment you text me that you are home safely. How is that?"

Angelica gazed, more than just a little smitten, into his eyes as she wondered if this was the one she had been dreaming of since she was a little girl. Her mind raced as she thought, "Could it really be him finally?" Her heart was racing just to be near him. Her one-word answer to his question would be her first of many tests to find the truth.

"Promise?" she asked, looking closely at his face. Gray nodded yes with a reassuring smile.

CHAPTER THREE

The Phantom

Angelica's drive home was like a blur. Her mind was whirling thinking about what had just happened. She was excited about the possibilities—and especially about seeing Edward again. It was like a dream come true. Is this why no one else had ever measured up to her imagination? How could she have dreamed of what it would feel like to meet a man like Edward Gray? She realized she was speeding on her way home because her heart and adrenaline were racing. Her excitement had manifested itself into the wind flowing through her long blonde hair, but wisely she decided to ease off on the gas pedal. She simply couldn't wait to get home and text Edward, hoping for his phone call already. As she parked in her much more modest driveway, still sitting in her car, she texted him, "I'm home safe now…"

Her phone rang almost immediately. "Hello!" she answered a bit too anxiously.

His deep warm voice caused her to want to curl up with her phone in the car for a bit, just to hear him. It felt like a warm blanket around her as he said, "I am glad you are home safe. Where are you exactly now, Angelica?"

She grinned as she confessed, "Well if you must know, I'm still sitting in my car. I texted you as soon as I got home, just as you asked."

She heard his next compliment come wafting through her phone, keeping her blissful energy rolling. "Good girl, I like that you are so coachable and followed my instructions," Gray encouraged her. "You get a gold star every time you do that, Angelica."

Playing off his energy, she kept the intrigue going just a bit teasing playfully, "Oh really? And what do I get if I collect a lot of gold stars?"

But her face changed when she heard Gray answer in his deep, gravelly voice. "You get everything you can imagine. A new world will open, but first, you must show me you can be a good girl and follow all my instructions. You will quickly learn that I will only ask you for things that are completely in your best interest— or ours together."

Angelica liked the sound of this new game with Edward and asked with purpose this time, "Ok. I'm in! What would you like me to do next?"

She heard Gray's voice go even deeper, and in his most sexy and slow tone, he said, "I want you—to go inside. Undress for me and get ready for bed. Do all the normal things you do when you are winding down for the day, and then text me as soon as your head is on your pillow. Would you do that for me, Angelica?"

She was already getting out of her car to rush inside as the eager answer came, "Yes, of course."

Angelica heard his deep voice add, what would become, a secret key in their adventure, "One last thing, Angelica. When I ask you to do something for me, something that you are completely comfortable with, I would like it very much if you would agree to answer me with, 'Yes, sir.' Do you think you could do this for me?"

She thought about his request before responding. Compared to things other men had asked of her, and how she had often been treated, this seemed like a fairly minor request. But she paused momentarily, before she finally took a step into Gray's world, saying, "Yes, sir" in her soft and playful voice.

"Excellent. When you say that, it is a sign of respect. And when someone treats you with great respect, it is natural to want to return the favor to them as well. And together, we start building deeper trust. But real trust takes time. Don't you agree?"

"Yes, sir. Everything you've told me tonight makes sense and feels right. I'll text you from bed in just a few minutes," she said sweetly. Angelica raced inside to get ready. She wanted the next call with Edward, and she could hardly wait until she was ready for bed. She wanted more of Edward's dreamy, sexy voice on the phone.

She had never hurried so fast to get ready for bed in her life. Brushing her teeth, turning off the lights, undressing, and leaving clothes and shoes wherever handy—she was in bed with her heart pumping hard in just a few minutes.

Finally, it was time to text Edward. "My head is on the pillow—waiting for you..." it read. But this time her phone didn't ring right away. She waited. Her toes started "tapping" up and down, waiting and waiting for Edward to call. Her mind started to fill with doubts and worries. Had he gotten busy on another phone call? Had he lost interest in her already? Why didn't he call her back right away like when she texted from the car? A million questions were running through her mind. Then she started worrying and hoped everything was ok with Edward, when the phone finally rang.

Angelica answered the phone and said, "I've been waiting for you."

There was a pause of silence on the phone before his deep voice asked, "Are you in bed like I asked, Angelica?"

She blurted out quickly, "Yes, I was waiting for you." She tried not to let her frustration from having to wait a few minutes for his call be detectable, but no such luck.

Gray asked with his sure, steady confidence oozing through the phone, "Were you a bit… anxious waiting, Angelica?"

Her mind now turned inward, reflecting on her impatience as she felt the purpose of his question. "Maybe just a little…" she confessed.

She was surprised by his answer. "Good," he said. "That is useful energy sometimes. But you must learn to control your anxious mind, Angelica. You will discover that absolute certainty gets rid of almost all of those negative and wasted emotions."

She could listen to his voice all night. With her head now on her pillow, she got more comfortable under the sheets, and she egged him on to tell her more. "What do you mean by 'certainty?'" She leaned in, drinking in her bedtime call from Gray, to hear his story.

His dreamy voice explained, "It is one of the four primal needs in every human. The need for certainty is number one. But when we humans get enough of it, then we want to shake things up. We want some variety and excitement, and that often is the start of our conflicts."

Instead of counting sheep, Angelica found herself in bed counting primal needs as Edward shared them. She asked him to give her the others, injecting, "That's the first two. You said there were four."

Angelica waited for more as he continued, "Well, number three is love and connection. But if you are human and have lived for a while, you probably have fallen in love before and have been hurt. Almost everyone has had this experience, so that's how we learn to build 'walls' around our hearts for protection—so that doesn't happen again, or at least not to a level we can't handle. Building those walls is the skill I am best at, but that also numbs us from what is possible."

Angelica thought about it before asking, but felt cozy hearing Edward talk into the night and risked it, "Why do you do that? Build those walls, that is." She waited for the reply that never came.

After a bit of a pause, he simply continued with, "Lastly, at number four is significance."

Edward continued, back on a roll perhaps to cover Angelica's unanswered question about the walls he so expertly builds. "Well, for example, many women meet a guy whom they like a lot but may not truly love deeply. But some believe if they marry and have children with him, they will gain numbers 3 and 4: Total unconditional love and babies and children to whom 'Mother' is the most significant human in the world. But even that doesn't last forever. Just wait until they turn into teenagers. Maybe that's why we love our pets so much," he said laughing. "They will give us unconditional love no matter how things are going at work or even if you're having a bad hair day or whatever. All they want is our love and attention."

Angelica thought of people she knew growing up and examples just like Edward had described. She just hadn't heard them framed up quite this way before. She added, "Yes. That's true, I think, now that you describe it that way. Is that how you look at the world, Edward? Do you always psychoanalyze people?" Angelica giggled softly into her phone.

Edward paused before answering her question, then shared, "When I meet people—whether it is business or personal—I do make it a point to observe and try to discover what is most important to someone. What drives them."

Seeing the opportunity to bring the conversation back to their night together, she couldn't resist asking, "Oh, and which of those four primal drives do you think motivate me?" Angelica smiled, anxious to see if Mr. Gray was as smart as he sounded.

There was a short pause over the phone. She imagined she could hear Edward breathing as she waited to hear how he saw her. "Well, I would like you to ask me again after we have spent more time together, but my first impression of you tells me your number one highest value is love and connection." Then he added the all-important headline, "You are a romantic."

Angelica's eyes opened a bit wider hearing him accurately describe her heart. "What makes you say that?"

Gray paused before continuing, "Because of your eyes. When you returned to the restaurant late tonight to find me still there, waiting for the princess to return after hours had gone by, your eyes lit up like it was a test to see if I would wait that long for you. And when you saw me still there waiting just for one more chance to see you, it filled you up inside."

Angelica asked in amazement, "How could you tell that? Are you a mind reader?"

Gray said in the deepest register of his voice, "No, I could just feel your energy from across the room. Then, when we kissed, I could feel both your softness and your passion. So, I knew, with certainty, that you are a romantic. Angelica, your number one value—I am guessing—is love."

She felt her heart racing as she lay there in bed. She would never be able to fall asleep now that adrenaline was coursing through her. Edward had seen her from across the room on a date with another when he intervened. But now, she discovered, here was a man who really saw her. A dozen thoughts were now competing for her attention as she paused before asking, "So, what does that mean? And what about you?"

Edward's deep voice guided her slowly. "All this in time," he shared. "But I will tell you now that keeping you and your heart safe will be my biggest responsibility. I don't ever want to hurt you or let you down. I have no sad stories in my life, Angelica, and I don't want to create any with you."

Angelica nodded into this last revelation as she agreed, "I've had enough of those already." She paused, thinking about some of the pain in her past relationships. Somehow, they all seemed to follow the same pattern, eventually.

But that thought was happily interrupted by his voice again. "If you decide to take this chance with me, if you do this and are truly mine and no one else's, then, and only then, can I protect us both. It is that dangerous place in the middle where we have one foot on the boat and one foot on the dock where we are most apt to fall and get hurt. Let's talk more about this in person when I see you on a real date, which was the promise I made to you when we kissed goodnight."

Angelica smiled, "Oh, so you remembered!"

"Yes, a first promise made, and it is now being kept. When may I see you again, Kitten?" Edward asked with a flair of his charm. Her face beamed with a broad smile hearing his question.

"First of all, I love the nickname 'Kitten,'" she cooed. "And, as far as a date night, were you thinking Friday or Saturday?" she asked, not wanting to appear too anxious.

She loved his reply which came barreling back across the phone without delay. "There is no way I want to wait that long. I was thinking of tomorrow. Are you available for lunch or dinner?"

Angelica's heart was pumping with excitement again. *He can't wait to see me!* she thought to herself. "Dinner tomorrow night would be great," she said, trying to sound cool and calm and collected.

She heard only the confident voice of a man who knows what he wants in his reply. "I will pick you up at 7 p.m. Wear heels. I am taking you somewhere very nice," Gray said. Smiling into the phone, her mind was racing again, already starting to think of what to wear for him, as she heard him say, "Good night, Angelica. I hope you have amazing dreams."

As Angelica answered, "Goodnight," a moment of silence went by before a click ended their call. Now that she was alone and it was safe, she was overcome with energy—kicking both of her legs under the sheet up and down, giggling the entire time for a while. Magic!

The next day took forever to pass. She looked at the clock more than every hour, waiting for seven o'clock and her date with Edward. Why didn't she accept the lunch invite? When finally, it was 4 p.m., she started getting ready early. There was no way she would be a minute late for this date. *What a difference just one day can make*, she thought. But it wasn't just a different day. It was the feeling of being the center of his powerful attention. A man who could have anything or probably almost anyone he wanted—chose her.

It was a mix of nervous energy and excitement as she started getting ready. She picked out several of her favorite outfits and shoes. Especially the shoes, of course, as Mr. Gray requested that she wear heels, since he was taking her somewhere nice. He didn't say where—perhaps that was part of his mystery and charm. But he was a man who knew what he wanted and was clear about it. And he was making plans for them! No one else had ever spoken to her the way he did, so confident and clear, but with a calm and powerful voice. She could listen to him for hours.

Tonight was going to be big, and she was curious if Gray would take her back to his home and let her see his Red Playroom. Her mind raced, thinking of what that might be like. What did he have in store for her? She finally picked a black cocktail dress that was elegant but did show off her curves. He had already seen her in red the night before, so definitely the black dress and stiletto heels with red bottoms. Just a touch of red as a reminder of the night before. Perfect!

Could she stop pacing and watching the clock? At six-thirty, she was looking out the window waiting anxiously for Gray's car when her phone rang, and it was him! "Good evening, Ms. Hart."

Her energy was bubbling over, and she responded smiling through the phone, "I'm so glad you called, and I'm so excited to see you. Are you on your way?"

She waited anxiously to hear him confirm, hoping he wasn't canceling or rescheduling at the last minute. That had happened to her more than once before, and it would simply kill her if that happened with him, of all people.

She smiled with huge relief when she heard, "Of course, I'm just leaving now, but I wanted to suggest you bring a light sweater in case it gets cool this evening."

"But it's Florida. It's rarely sweater weather here."

Edward gave her a bit of a sneak preview of his plans. "Yes. I agree. But I'm taking you to the theater after dinner, and sometimes it gets a bit cool there."

Understanding his plans better now, she asked, "Oh, we're going to the movies?"

The answer she received made her eyes widen. "No," Gray countered, "Not exactly. I'm taking you to the Performing Arts Center. I'm a season member with box seats for all their shows. I thought you might enjoy it. Bring a wrap, Kitten, and I'll see you soon."

The Performing Arts Center. She had heard about it often but had not been since her high school class trip years ago. How exciting and sophisticated, being whisked out to dinner and an elegant evening! She quickly checked her dress again. Was she dressed up enough for something this fancy? *Oh, shoot, there's no time to change again—he is on his way.* Her heart was racing as she touched up her makeup one last time and grabbed her smallest purse and a light black sweater wrap that was very soft. Her only cashmere had been a gift from her grandmother years ago. She still missed her grandmother and had only worn her sweater once before, to keep it safe, but always loved how soft it felt.

When her doorbell rang just a few minutes later, it was all she could do to not run through the house to greet Edward. Smiling and a little breathless, she opened the door to see him in a black suit and tie with roses and a gift box with a giant bow.

Edward smiled, as he presented the treasures he had brought her, saying, "For you, my lady. May I help you put these inside before we go?"

She beamed but said, "Oh my, don't look at my house. I wasn't expecting company!"

"No worries, just take the flowers first, and I will wait here. Put these somewhere special, so they will be the last thing you see when you go to bed tonight and the first thing when you wake up in the morning," he requested.

Angelica, relieved not to have her messy home discovered by Edward's discerning eyes, gushed, "I know just the place for them," smiling broadly as she went. She took the gorgeous roses, mixed with orchids, baby's breath, and lush greenery in a heavy crystal vase, from Edward. She whisked them away to her bedroom and placed them just in front of her dresser's big mirror. The reflection appeared to double the size of the already huge flower arrangement. Amazing!

No one had ever shown up for a date with her like this before, dressed to the nines with flowers and a gift! Her heart was still racing when she returned to Edward, still patiently waiting at her door with the other gift in hand. He said with a slight smile, "This you get to open in the car, but not until later—on our way back home." He understood the power of anticipation, which might keep Angelica wondering.

He offered her his free arm, as a gentleman, and walked her to the driveway. But, oddly enough, she noticed that Gray had left his car at the foot of the drive near the street. Thinking this odd, she smiled at her date, and asked, "Do you always like to park far away, Edward? Perhaps in case you change your mind and need to make a quick getaway?" Angelica laughed as she poked fun at yet another of his eccentricities.

He smiled warmly at her ribbing, but he nodded at the car with a bit of a surprise for her in store. "No. Just this once. It's a new feature, actually, and I wanted to try it out." They paused at the top of the driveway for just a moment while Edward pressed the 'Summon' button on his key fob for his black Tesla X. The electric smart SUV started itself and slowly drove up the driveway to pick them up with no one inside. The work of self-driving car innovation. Incredible!

Another click of the key fob opened the doors, and Gray escorted Angelica to her beautiful white leather seat. He guided her in and said, "You are the first to ever ride in this with me. I hope you don't mind if I play with the technology just a bit. It's fun, don't you think?"

"Ok. I'm impressed, Edward. But much more with you—than with the car—just so you know." Angelica smiled gazing into his piercing blue eyes. Off to dinner they went with the car in the self-driving mode so Edward could pay more attention to his date. They both had their flirt engine on, and it wasn't hard to tell that the natural attraction between them was sweeping them forward, like a force you just couldn't resist—so why try?

They arrived at one of the premier restaurants in Sarasota, Michael's On East, where the valet took over the car. Michael's was well known for delivering exquisite food with service to match. The owner was a very good friend of Edward's. Nothing like a "home court advantage" when you want to impress a date. Gray was greeted by almost everyone, including the owner, and it was easy to see he was a "regular" at Michael's.

Angelica loved the VIP attention and confessed to Edward, "I've heard so much about this place. I've always wanted to try it sometime. Thank you for bringing me here!"

The host led them to an elegant circular fanback booth that was plum colored and felt opulent, where they were seated. Dinner was phenomenal, and they talked nonstop, easily getting to know one another. The evening seemed to fly by, until it was time for the theatre, and Edward said they needed to go.

She saw the opportunity for a bit of good-natured fun, so she simply had to ask, "Won't they hold the start of the show for you, Edward, if you tell them we are running a bit late?" Angelica smiled and teased, poking a bit of fun at her wealthy and powerful date as she linked arms with him. Gray shook his head, smiling at her brand of humor, and off they went.

It was packed at the Performing Arts Center. Edward described the show to her. "Everyone who loves theatre loves *Phantom of the Opera*, whether it is your first or many times seeing it."

Her heart was racing with excitement about seeing the show together, as Angelica chimed in, "Oh, it will be my first time, and I'm so excited!"

She looked into his deep gaze as he said, "I hope you love it, and if so, there are many more experiences I would like to share with you, Angelica." Gray smiled still looking deep into her eyes for a bit longer to deliver the well-intended double meaning.

The usher took them to the center box on the balcony, where they had premier seating. Edward nodded and said a distant hello to several theatergoers who knew him from the Sarasota social scene. The curtain went up, and the house lights went dark. The show was brilliant, and the music was a powerful and emotional roller-coaster, telling the story of a mad composer who falls in love with an innocent, naïve soprano singer named Christine. It was the perfect aphrodisiac for an ending to the evening that Angelica had been hoping for all day. Actually, much longer than just today. She had dreamt of being courted and wined and dined and treated like a fairy-tale princess for as long as she could remember. She didn't want to wake up and discover that this was all a dream.

Then applause. Loud applause as everyone rose to give the cast and crew a standing ovation, and Angelica snapped back to the present moment and stood next to Edward to join the rousing cheers. Edward's arm encircled her waist and pulled her gently to his side as they—and a few thousand others—moved through the theatre to exit the grand Performing Arts Center.

The valet had Edward's car stationed nearby as they approached, so they and only a handful of other patron theatergoers had a quick and easy exit. Meanwhile, Angelica observed, almost everyone else would have to wait in quite a long line for their cars.

The black Tesla X whisked them silently and quickly onto the main road and towards home. As they went, Angelica could not stop talking about the show. "I cried I don't know how many times. It was so, so unbelievably beautiful. I just loved it, and I would love to see it again now that I know the story! Thank you for bringing me. It just doesn't quite say enough. I really appreciate this, Edward—more than you know."

She looked up into Edward's handsome face now lit only by the dash lights of their SUV. Secretly, she had stolen a few admiring glances of him during the show in the theatre. She had been torn between the passion and power of the show, *Phantom of the Opera*, and who she was seeing it with. Both had made her heart pound all evening.

"Seeing you this happy is thanks enough, Kitten. I had hoped you would like it, at least. Not everyone reacts to the theatre and opera the same. Most people can grow to appreciate opera over time. But a few have an immediate and very emotional reaction to it like you did tonight. And for them, it will always be a part of their soul."

Angelica simply sighed as they drove away and began, "Edward, are we ...?"

She paused, hesitant to ask what was on her mind. Sensing this, he asked, "What, Kitten?"

She continued, "Are we going to your place and the Red Playroom now? I thought about you and all that you said last night and... I think I am open to exploring that with you. But only if you want to."

He drove silently but engaged his Tesla's self-driving mode so he could turn to her, then replied, "Before we go much further, Angelica, remember your gift from earlier this evening?" Edward handed the red gift with a sparkly red bow to Angelica.

She received the package replying, "Everything has been so exciting all evening. I guess I completely forgot about this until now."

Edward smiled and nodded approvingly, "That's refreshing and a good sign, actually. Open it please, as we go, if you don't mind."

She said, "Of course!" Angelica took great care opening the beautifully wrapped red box. Inside was the largest box of Godiva chocolates she had ever seen. Plus, there was a large bone-ivory colored envelope with a red wax seal with a large letter "G," for Gray she assumed, stamped across the fold.

Not wanting to disturb the special-looking wax seal, she asked, "What's this?"

Gray instructed her, "It is for you and your eyes only, Angelica. Please go ahead and squeeze to lift the seal. It should come open for you easily." She was even more intrigued now, hearing "for her eyes only." What could it be?

The seal opened just as Edward predicted, and inside, she pulled out several pages of a document labeled "CONFIDENTIALITY AGREEMENT."

As she held the pages in her hand, she heard Edward's voice explain, "I would like you to take this home with you, Angelica, and read it over carefully for me. If you have any questions, I am happy to discuss them with you tomorrow or whenever you are ready."

She was a bit confused to say the least. Her mind was already racing to take the leap into Edward's arms and his bed, but he gave her paperwork instead. This seemed more than a bit eccentric to her, but she asked hesitantly, "I see, so, what does it mean?"

Gray's deep voice explained, "It means whatever happens between us is private. You've heard of 'The Vegas Rule?' What happens in Vegas…" He paused for her interpretation.

"Stays in Vegas," Angelica finished his sentence for him.

Edward nodded as he continued, "Before we can begin exploring the Red Playroom and all the different levels of your discovery and training, it is important to me that you sign the Confidentiality Agreement. So, for tonight, I am taking you home. But it was nothing less than phenomenal spending the evening with you." Gray smiled broadly—looking into her eyes as the self-driving car turned down her street.

Angelica was a bit disappointed. She had been secretly aching to explore Edward's muscular body. She felt him pressed against her the first night when they kissed. And, after all that he said and knew about how to take her to new levels. All those deep dark desires put on hold, for now, left her disappointed about the waiting.

She sighed quietly, resigned to waiting. Waiting to be swept away by this powerful attraction she felt aching inside like never before.

CHAPTER FOUR
The Power of OM

As the Tesla parked itself smoothly, Angelica heard, "Please wait. Allow me to come open your door for you."

She smiled seeing how Edward always treated her with such respect when they were going out and thought, *I could get very used to this*. He opened her door and offered his hand to help her gracefully step out. As his strong but gentle power lifted her to his side, she asked, "If I read it tonight—may I call you if I have questions?"

She felt him slipping his arm comfortably again around her waist on their walk to her front door. He leaned into her ear to reply, "Save the questions for tomorrow." Angelica pulled her house keys out of her purse, and Gray said, "Allow me?" As she nodded once and let go, he took the keys gently from her to do the honors.

As her front door opened widely, Angelica cooed, "Thank you for the best first date ever." She turned to face Edward and he wrapped his arms around her, pulling her to his chest as he lifted her easily off her feet and then carried her inside. Angelica's heart was racing as Gray closed the door behind them. Only a momentary distraction before he pressed her up against the wall by the front door, kissing her passionately.

Angelica was an amazing kisser, as he knew from before, and he wanted more of that divine connection. They kissed deeply. As her full soft lips were roaming his, she felt him gently pulling her lower lip into his mouth to softly suckle. Her blood raced as she felt his hungry mouth move down to her neck.

With his powerful muscular arms, Edward slowly turned Angelica around to face the wall. She felt him move her long blonde hair away with one hand saying, "I want the back of your neck." He kissed her gently, his fingertips tracing the outline of her spine down her backless black dress. Goose bumps broke out on Angelica almost everywhere. She arched her back like a cat to press back against Edward. She wanted to feel how hard and excited he was. He responded by pressing his thick, rock-hard manhood into her gently, then turned her back to face him for one more deep kiss from her beautiful full lips.

Her heart racing wildly, she felt her blood surging and an ache so deep inside her as she pleaded, "I want you so badly, Edward."

He replied, "You will have me fully, but not until you are ready, Angelica."

She did not want to be denied. She urged him with her eyes, and her voice trembled, "But I *am* ready!"

"No." He responded, "First, I must help you discover how to climax fully. I don't want our first time, or anytime we are together—to just be for my pleasure. I need you to have that experience, and you deserve to know what you've been missing."

"Enlighten me then. I am yours if you'll take me there," she pleaded.

Gray gazed deeply into her pleading eyes, with his now full of temptation. She felt a rush of relief to hear his answer. "All right, but what I can offer you tonight is a very different kind of sexual experience, Angelica. One where I will remain fully clothed, and the focus and energy will be completely and totally on you and you alone. Do you understand?"

Her mind raced trying to envision what she just heard. But without hesitation, her words flowed, saying, "I'm not sure, but ok." Angelica nodded; anxious and intrigued.

She watched Gray lock the front door behind them and then turned to say, "Take me to your room." She smiled and led Edward by the hand to her bedroom, now filled with the fragrance of beautiful flowers. In the center was Angelica's king-size bed with a soft white comforter.

She heard his deep, sexy voice guide her, "We need a blanket and lots of pillows. The more, the better."

Her inner curiosity spoke next, asking, "Ok, but why?" as she retrieved a blanket from the closet shelf.

"You will see. First, we will need to build a 'nest' for you out of the pillows and blanket in the center of your bed. Like this," Gray said as he started arranging pillows in a star shape with the blanket at the side.

She looked into his eyes, asking eagerly, "What do you need me to do?"

He smiled warmly into her anxious eyes and asked, "Do you have a very comfortable robe? Something soft would be ideal. Not lingerie. Just something warm and comfy you could put on?"

Angelica answered, "Yes, I'll be right back," as she hurried to her master bath to change. As she slipped into her soft pink house terry robe, she thought, *This was not like anything or anyone she had known. A bit different—well, more like very different.*

She heard Gray's voice say, "I'm heading to your kitchen to wash my hands. I will be right back."

When she returned in pink, the room was now softly lit. Edward had made himself at home turning all the lights off except one small lamp in the corner. Escorting her, Edward said, "Come lay on your bed and let's get you comfortable first." As Angelica climbed onto the bed, her robe opened just a bit, revealing a glimpse that she wore nothing underneath.

"Excellent," he said. "Now, come lay in the center with your head on your favorite pillow." As she moved to the middle, she felt his warm hands position her knees slightly open, each on their own pillow, and then draped the blanket over her gently. As the gaze of his deep blue eyes returned to her, he said, "Do you feel comfortable, Angelica?"

She smiled from her cozy nest of pillows and blankets. "Yes, I feel all comfy like you just tucked me in for the night." Then reaching for his face, she stroked his cheek adding, "You make me feel ... totally safe."

He looked deeply into her eyes and spoke to her in the lower register of his voice, "You will always be safe when you are with me, Angelica. It takes time to build real trust, but you will see that taking care of you is my first principle. Now close your eyes for a moment, and just listen to my voice."

Feeling comfortable in her nest of pillows and blankets, she said softly, "Ok, and just so you know, I love your deep reassuring voice."

He instructed her slowly, "For the next 15 minutes, I want you to let go of everything in your past. Let go of traumas or disappointments or anything that holds all of us back sometimes.

Let go of everything in your busy day or things you have to do tomorrow. I just want you to feel and be fully present in this moment." His voice was calm and hypnotic. "All I will do for the next 15 minutes is to very softly and gently stroke you. Touching you softly with just the tip of my finger. Is that okay with you?" he asked, seeking consent for all things regarding intimacy.

As she lay in her warm robe, hearing his words, her busy active mind spoke out, "Yes. But what do I need to do?"

He leaned into her and said, "You don't have to do anything except breathe, relax, and feel your amazing body. Let your energy just flow naturally." His guidance continued. "I may ask you a question or two about how I am stroking you. Such as, would you like it a bit softer? Or would you like it to be a bit harder? Feel free to answer yes, no, or any way you would like, but no matter what the answer is, I will thank you for the feedback. There is no wrong answer ever." He paused before asking her gently, "Ok so far, Angelica?"

Seeking to visualize what he had in mind, she was playing the movie of the scene, in her head, as he described it. She said, "Yes, but may I ask a question?" He nodded yes. "Why would you want to do this for me? What is in it for you, Edward?" Angelica asked curiously. No man had ever thought about her pleasure, much less wanting to dedicate 15 minutes exclusively to her needs before, especially if it wasn't going to lead to having sex with her in the end.

Her answer came in his delicious sounding reply. "Your exquisite pleasure is my greatest reward, Angelica," Edward said with confidence. "It will make me feel like King Kong to know that I can guide you this way," he said. "But before we begin, I want to remind you about my two rules. Most of all, Rule Number Two, if you recall, says you are not allowed to climax without permission," he instructed her. "So, would you practice your words for me—just in case you start to feel all trembly inside and you feel the beginnings of an orgasm? You should ask permission by saying, "Please, sir, may I cum?" Gray asked, "Would you try that for me, Angelica, just in case you need to ask?"

Her mind was filled with doubt. She had never reached a climax with anyone, and only little ones, so she thought, by herself. Asking for permission was not the problem she was worried about. Ever needing to ask was more of her personal and very private dilemma. But Angelica went along with his request, saying softly, "Please, sir, may I cum?" Immediately her face flushed, a bit embarrassed to be asking that out loud.

Immediately she saw Gray's warm smile and heard his praise, "Good girl. Thank you for doing that, Kitten. Now, try it once more, a little louder this time, just to make sure you don't forget your words, especially if you are excited, and the adrenaline is pumping through your whole body."

She felt the words roll off more easily the second time as "please, sir, may I cum?" came across her lips loud and clear. Angelica felt a little surprised to hear those words coming out of her in her full voice this time, especially since she was asking permission to visit a world she had barely, if ever, experienced.

His deep voice rewarded her again. "Great job! I am proud of you, Angelica." Gray encouraged her gently, "Now, just take a deep breath and hold it for five seconds." She felt her chest rise under her pink robe as she took a very deep breath. She focused on his voice now, as he guided her again by saying, "Good. Now exhale slowly for five seconds."

Angelica closed her eyes as she complied again, and as all the air left her body, Edward leaned into her ear in a quiet, deeper voice and whispered, "Very good. Now repeat that two more times for me." She continued her deep breathing, and with it, she felt more and more relaxed listening to his voice and letting her mind clear and drift into his energy.

Edward asked slowly in a meditative voice, "How are you feeling now, Angelica?"

A hint of a smile crept across her lips as she said softly, "Relaxed but also a little excited."

"Good answer. You are doing very well. Now I am going to position you with your legs a bit more open, so I may touch and stroke you gently. But I want to make sure that you are in a very comfortable position, ok?"

"Yes," she replied as Edward's strong hands opened her thighs wider apart but still partially draped under her soft blanket, pillows still under her knees supporting her.

Edward paused to ask, "How does that feel so far, Angelica?"

Relaxed in her new nest of pillows and blankets, she replied, "Everything feels good."

Edward placed the palm of his hand over her fully exposed mound and just held it there warm and steady with only a slight bit of pressure. He could feel that she was already creamy and moist with excitement just from talking and listening to his steady voice.

He mentored her, "Just breathe and feel, sweetheart. You don't have to do anything. Just be with me in this moment." And with that, Edward began stroking with just the tip of his finger. This was a very soft touch and the most delicate of gentle stroking. It felt as tender as if he was gently brushing something from her eyelash.

She took a deep breath, instantly responding to the energy she was feeling and moaned gently, "Ahhhhhh!"

Edward's deep voice asked calmly, "Is anything hurting, Angelica?"

She whispered intently, "No, not at all—keep going."

"Thank you," he replied, while steadily, slowly, and gently stroking her most delicate lips, tracing lightly across her most sensitive pleasure spot. Her body flowed with the response, and he stroked a bit faster.

After a minute or two, he asked, "Would you like a softer pressure?"

Her heart was racing and along with her rapid breathing, her "No" was pushed out quickly.

"Thank you," Edward replied, adding, "Your delicate lips are changing color to pink and coral. You look beautiful."

She thought, *No one else has ever talked to me this way. Or even bothered to pay attention or seemed to care how I felt.* Her breathing was coming harder and faster now. So, intuitively, feeling her energy, Edward increased the speed and pressure of his strokes ever so slightly. Rhythmically, steadily, over, and over.

Angelica cried out softly. Blissful joy and energy were building inside as she had never experienced before. She felt like electricity was starting to spark inside her rushing over her entire body. All the while Edward continued stroking—now with a bit more fervor and energy. Angelica's voice cried out, "Oh, my god!"

as she felt her core starting to tremble. Her legs were twitching as she cried out, "It is happening! Oh my—Please!"

Gray's voice demanded, "Please, what?" still stroking her intensely now.

She arched her back, knees stretching as wide apart as she could open herself to beg, "Please, can I cum?"

He released her finally. "Yes, you may cum just one time," he said in a loud commanding voice, as he stroked her firmly now with intensity.

Angelica was completely locked up, as though her entire body was in a fit of seizure. It was so intense it was almost too much to endure. As she climaxed with waves rolling through her, over and over and over again, she cried out, "Ahhhhhhhhh! Oh, Oh, Oh…Shit!"

Locked momentarily in a silent world, unable to speak, but still gripping the blanket tightly in her hands, she felt Edward finally stop stroking. He placed the palm of his hand over her mound again, holding it there with a calming steady pressure to help guide her back down to recover. He could still feel her trembling and the occasional aftershock still as she convulsed lightly in his hand. Angelica cried softly. Sobbing just a bit, she heard his deep voice ask quietly, "Is everything ok, Angelica? Are you hurting anywhere?"

She cried more loudly now. She sniffled and tried to catch her breath before saying, "No. Everything is ok. I've just never … I've never felt that before. Ever!" Angelica exhaled hard, trying to talk, and then gulping air in. "Not with anyone."

His reassuring voice calmed her gently and slowly back down. "Shhhhh," Gray whispered. "Shhhh. Just breathe, Angelica.

It's ok. It's totally normal to feel this way. Just take a deep breath and try and hold it for me. I am right here with you."

As he closed her thighs back to their starting position, he covered her completely now with the blanket. Stroking her forehead and hair to comfort her, he asked, "How are you feeling?"

She took a deep breath before speaking and then gazed into his eyes as she replied, "That was *amazing*. More than amazing! I don't have any words to explain." Angelica stumbled to put into words what she was feeling.

She felt Edward lay next to her as he asked, "Can you turn toward me, and just put your head on my shoulder for a bit?" As she turned toward Edward, she kissed him softly on the cheek and then nestled her head into his chest, wrapping her knee over him. She felt almost like they were snuggled up as if to watch a movie together. "Perfect. Now, just rest and lay here with me for a while, ok?" he said.

Angelica exhaled like the wind was leaving her soul. "This is like … heaven," she said softly and sweetly, wrapped around him.

Gray asked gently and with a softness in his voice, "When we are together—this will always be a safe place to say how you feel. You can tell me anything. Open and honest communication is the only way we grow and learn. So, I would like to know one or two things we just did that you liked and would like more of next time, and … maybe one or two things that you would like a bit less of?"

Her mind was still floating in the afterglow of her most powerful release ever. There was no list of things for improvement, only the soft pink energy left inside of her. But her favorite part of Edward's question was that it was about "next time." The thought of that made her heart smile. She said only, "Everything. I liked everything, and I wouldn't change a thing next time."

Edward gently squeezed her in his arms and reassured her, "It is ok to share anything you don't like. I am a confident man and won't be defensive or take it personally. What I mean is it won't hurt my ego if you give me feedback or suggestions. This is a safe place to share anything."

Angelica insisted with an urgency to make Edward believe her this time, "No. It was simply amazing. I still don't have the words to explain, but don't change a thing, please."

She heard him finally relax into her words now as he replied, "Thank you for sharing that, of course. But I also want to thank you for being so open and free with me tonight. Thank you for your trust." She felt his fingers streaming through her long blonde hair softly as he continued, "This is extremely personal and our most intimate space, Angelica. So, most of all— thank you for choosing me."

She wanted him to know what this was like for her and how he made her feel. But the bright white light inside her came rushing out, simply as a sigh of relief. "I am so glad I came back to the restaurant last night—and now all of this!" Angelica said with genuine happiness. She was glowing from head to toe, as she made her next request. "Will you sleep with me? Stay with me tonight, Edward?" she asked.

She looked into his deep blue eyes smiling at her slightly, as he replied, "Not tonight, Kitten." She felt him lean over and kiss her softly on the forehead. Stroking her baby-soft hair tenderly. "Just lay here and rest. I will lock your front door and check it to make sure you are safe and secure on my way out." As she felt him start to rise from her bed, he added, "Have sweet dreams, and I will call you tomorrow afternoon."

Angelica pulled him close to her for one more hug before he was gone, holding on tightly. She felt—like she would never want to let go.

CHAPTER FIVE

The Telephone Date

Angelica overslept. She hadn't slept that deep and hard in ages and was still comfy lying in bed, experiencing that feeling when you need to get up, but it still feels good and cozy laying there halfway between asleep and awake. She looked at the time and said out loud, "Oh, crap!" A wave of stress flowed through her as she would now have to rush to be on time for work. She crawled slowly out of the still-warm bed to make her way to the shower, stripping off her pink robe from the night before—smiling as she remembered Edward's voice and touch—even though she had to hurry now.

Stress looming over her, from the pressure of running late, seemed to be a frequent visitor with Angelica, but she welcomed the hot shower streaming over her body. She leaned back, feeling the jets pounding down on her soft skin. She loved the feel of it. Next, her back got a turn under the torrents of water streaming down her spine and legs.

The bathroom was getting steamy now from the hot shower with mirrors fogging, and she turned the water off sooner than she would have preferred. She needed to quickly dry off and finish getting ready. She liked the feel of the towel on her skin, and with a second towel, she wrapped her hair—Carmen Miranda style—to help gently dry it.

She chose a conservative outfit for the property management office where she worked. A straight black skirt and silver blouse for her day answering calls from tenants and the occasional sales prospect. She was good with people, but it seemed there were a hundred details to handle, and never enough time to get everything done. It was something of a one-person office most days, so she really hated being late as that would mean no one answering the phones.

She rushed out the door to hop in her convertible. Not the fancy self-driving type like her dreamy date with Edward the night before. As she sped off to the office, her foot pushed on the gas, and she could feel the few miles to work click by.

Meanwhile, Edward had important business in Washington, D.C., and was already on the way to his morning flight out of Rectrix, one of the private jet terminals at Sarasota airport. He wanted to message Angelica before leaving, so he texted her with, *Good morning, Kitten. Big business in Washington, D.C., today and will return home tomorrow. Would you be available for a phone date this evening? If so, I have a homework assignment for you—if you don't mind. Edward.*

Angelica smiled while reading his message, amused by the word "homework." What kind of "homework assignment" is he talking about? She hadn't done homework in years. She was sad about him leaving Sarasota—even for a day or two. But she was excited that he wanted a phone date with her that night. She texted back promptly, *Of course! I would love a phone date. Just let me know what time works with your busy schedule. Have a safe flight,* she replied.

Edward texted moments later with, *After our business dinner—by about 8 o'clock at the latest, I should be back in my hotel room. I will text you before I call.* Gray added, *Wheels up. Bye, for now, Kitten.* And he was gone.

Angelica parked and ran in to unlock the office and start her day, which would often fly by. Nonstop calls, projects, and problems to fix. Her workday typically didn't include time for a real lunch break. She would usually just grab a bite, when she could, between calls. It was exhausting most days, and this turned out to be one of them.

Not quite a thousand miles away, about 2 hours by jet, Gray wrapped up his negotiations for the week with a business dinner at The Palm Steakhouse which included lots of handshakes and welcoming new partners in a business that would keep him involved in Washington, D.C., back and forth, for a few years to come. He particularly loved the downtown area and the beautiful, impressive architecture and monuments of D.C., especially lit up at night. As he headed back to his hotel after dinner, he texted Angelica, *Deal wrapped up in Washington and heading back to my hotel now. I will try phoning you up in about 30 minutes.* She saw the screen on her phone light up and then smiled reading his message. Her heart raced with excitement for her phone date with Edward. She loved his deep voice, how he spoke to her, but most of all, being at the center of his very intense attention.

She started getting ready for Edward's call, so nothing else would distract her. Turning a few lights down, she poured herself a glass of white wine. Pinot Grigio was one of her favorites.

She kept watching the clock—counting the minutes before Edward would call. Full of anticipation, she could hardly wait for her phone to ring. Finally, the screen of her phone lit up again, with another text asking, *May I call you now?*

She grabbed her phone eagerly to respond as quickly as she could, *Yes, please!* She smiled to see one last playful text from Edward. *Ring, Ring,* it read. Her phone began ringing instantly with her caller ID displaying "Gray Global Enterprises." She answered in her most charming and enthusiastic voice, "Well, hello Mr. Gray!"

His deep voice was full of playful energy. "How is my gorgeous and amazing woman feeling this evening?"

She didn't want to ask him, but her mind was already racing with the possibilities. *Did he just say—in a roundabout way—that I am his woman* now?

But her welcoming words said simply, "I am doing great, especially now that you called, and I get to hear your dreamy voice for our phone date! Actually, I don't think I have ever had an official *phone date* before."

She leaned into Edward's voice to hear every nuance of his reply. "Well, if something is important to you, you should make time and schedule it. Hearing your voice today was— important to me. And, being that I'm about a thousand miles away right now, a 'phone date' it is." Angelica beamed as he sounded like a man on a mission. And, most of all, *she* was that important mission.

"Well, I have to admit, I like that you said our call was important to you."

Edward's voice now added a bit of a flirting smile saying, "You *are* important, Angelica. And I do have an important question for you. Being a man, we are almost always 'visual.' I hope you don't mind me asking—but, what are you wearing today? I want to get the mental picture of you in my mind while we are talking."

Angelica blushed at the flirty question. She felt a slight rush come over her, being at the center of his very male attention, as she answered, "Of course! Nothing too special, but I'm still wearing what I wore to work today, a straight black skirt, just above the knee, and a silver silk blouse with tiny black polka dots on it. It is very elegant looking," she shared.

Wanting the details to complete the picture, he asked, "What about your shoes, please?"

"Oh, those black heels came off the minute I got home. Just my bare feet right now—if you must know," she laughed lightly.

Edward was growing a bit bolder as he continued his voir dire of Angelica, "Excellent, and where are you exactly? What room are you in, as we are talking, Ms. Hart?"

She took a deep breath and spoke in a sexy lower tone, getting her flirt on for Edward, "I'm lying on the bed—right where we were together last night. Drinking a glass of white wine," she said in her most intimate and inviting voice, hoping Edward would wish he was there with her.

"And what kind of white wine are we drinking this evening?"

Angelica smiled, holding her glass up to look at the light gold color of the wine and said, "Santa Margarita, Pinot Grigio. It is in an ice-cold frozen glass I keep at the ready in my freezer."

Hearing the sultry shift in her voice and energy, Edward felt encouraged to push further, adding, "And, if I may ask, Kitten, what are you wearing *underneath* that very proper office outfit?"

She felt her heart race as her adrenaline coursed through her. How she ached hearing his sexy voice ask her that while separated by distance so far away that night. She took a deep breath before answering, "Well, I could tell you, but it would be a lot more fun for me to show you if you were here with me, Edward." She paused to smile and giggle softly into the phone, before adding, "And what about you? What is my Mr. Gray wearing this evening?"

Gray, feeling the focus moving to him for a bit, paused to take a deep breath, subtly shifting his voice a bit deeper to reply, "I'm still in a midnight blue suit from business meetings, with a white linen shirt. But the tie and shoes came off when I got back to my hotel room. Then I poured myself a Cognac, just before calling you."

Angelica closed her eyes hearing his dreamy voice describe the image forming in her mind. She ran the fingers of her free hand through her long hair listening to him paint the picture for her. She smiled as he added, "Right now I'm in the living room of my hotel suite looking at the view of downtown D.C. But next, I'm heading to the bedroom to 'join you,' so to speak. Wouldn't it be more romantic if we were both in bed for our phone date?"

She imagined him looking dreamy and powerful in his midnight blue suit, holding his Cognac in one hand and his phone in the other. She responded, oozing with romance twinkling in her mind, "Yes, I love that idea. So, tell me, how was your day, dear?" She had been waiting all day to ask Edward that iconic line.

He replied briefly, "The business was good. Our deal closed, but that was but a formality. We've been working on it for almost a year now. And I also signed a lease on a nice rental here for one year. It's a penthouse apartment with a view of the entire skyline of Washington, D.C., with giant oversized windows. I'd love to show it to you sometime."

Her mind raced. *What did she just hear?* She could feel her blood surging with the thought of losing Edward to D.C. as she asked with alarm, "What? Are you moving?"

Gray explained, "No. Not at all. It's just that when I buy a company, it's a long-term commitment. Specifically, if it requires my involvement in leading its growth, I prefer to have a comfortable second home there. A place where I can keep a few clothes and toiletries. Plus, I like to get a home office set up the way I need it, so I can travel light. And it feels a bit more like a home away from home when I'm there rather than staying at hotels all the time. Just my personal preference and way of doing things. I'm not leaving you or Sarasota—to be sure."

Angelica had felt a momentary panic about losing her newfound connection with him. But Edward's words made her fear magically fade away now. She felt relieved. "Oh good. I was worried there for a moment that you were moving away when we were just getting to know each other."

He now turned his energy and focus back to her to ask, "May I ask you, Kitten, how did you sleep last night after I left?" Gray asked with a more sensual tone—inferring after their OM session.

"Oh, my god," Angelica confessed. "I slept so hard. I don't think I even moved all night. In fact, I overslept this morning and had to race to get to work on time."

She heard Edward's encouraging and supportive reply, "That's good. Your body probably was overdue to catch up on some well-deserved sleep. Did you like our first OM session, sweetheart?" he asked gently.

All day at the office, Angelica had thought about their date last night, and especially being in bed with Edward. How he had made her feel. How he had touched her, moved her physically, mentally, and emotionally like never before in her life. Having a day to reflect on what had happened, she wanted to share and said, "Yes! It was beyond amazing. It was like you were reading my mind and knew just what I was feeling. It was a first for me. Never like that before—not ever—have I been able to really let go with anyone."

Edward's deep voice guided her further, "Well, it won't always be the same, Kitten. Some times will be more intense than others. Some may even be much greater or smaller. And all of that is completely normal. Totally ok. What was great last night was that you allowed me to guide your mind to be totally present in that moment and to be free and relaxed and simply feel. That was the gift you gave us both last night."

Angelica purred, "I still felt so relaxed this morning when I woke up. I felt—different."

Edward's voice was clearly smiling through the phone, as he said, "I'm very glad to hear you say that. Thank you for sharing, but that now brings us to your homework assignment. If you are still open to hearing about it?"

Angelica felt her energy rising at the sound of this, asking, "Yes, I am a bit intrigued … What is it exactly?"

Gray shifted his voice to his deepest register, speaking quietly and intimately, "I want you… to go change into your pink robe, the soft one you wore last night when we were together. Would you do that for me, Angelica?"

She smiled instantly at the intimate sound of how this homework assignment was beginning, as she said willingly and easily, "Yes, of course."

"Just lay the phone down and I'll wait for you here."

She whispered urgently, not to keep him waiting, "I'll hurry. Be *right* back." Angelica unbuttoned her blouse as she walked briskly to her bathroom. Off came the black skirt with that thin, tight, skinny zipper in the back that often got stuck, but not tonight, thankfully. She removed her white lacey bra and panties taking care to lay them on a clean towel on the bathroom counter. They were her favorite, and she wanted them to stay safe and dry. She slipped her baby soft pink robe on again, as she had done for Edward just the night before, and she quickly returned to the bedroom to pick up her phone. "OK, I'm back and I'm wearing the pink robe from last night, just as you requested," she said eagerly.

She then heard Edward's playful confession, "I was imagining you undressing for me and was enjoying how you looked in my mind," his seductive tone coming through loud and clear to her.

She smiled as she reported, "I'm back in bed—just as before. What's next?"

She waited with eager anticipation for his voice to direct her. She felt more open with him than anyone ever before. But now, she was on pins and needles waiting to hear the next step unfold. "Now, Angelica, I want you to do something for me—if you are open to it. I would like to help you to retrace all we did last night together, but this time using *your* fingertip, not mine. I would like to guide you and encourage you with just my voice. Would you be willing to trust me again tonight?"

Angelica paused for just a moment. A bit shy by nature, her first impulse was it might be uncomfortable doing this over the phone. But Edward's voice was pulling her forward somehow. She hesitated slightly before saying shyly, "Yes, I'm willing to try. It's just…I've never done *anything* like this over the phone before."

Edward's reassurance was ever present, a steady deep anchor for her feminine energy. So, she simply loved it when he said, "It's OK. I will be with you every step of the way." She agreed, smiling a bit this time, softly whispering, "OK."

She welcomed Edward's encouraging voice, guiding her forward with, "Perfect. Now the first thing I would like you to do for me is to push the speakerphone button on your cell, and lay it next to you on the pillow, so your hands are free. One less thing to think about. Would you do that for me, Kitten?" Angelica found the speakerphone button and laid the phone on the pillow, near her ear as he asked, and smiled sheepishly, saying, "Yes, I'm ready."

Edward continued with her homework instructions. "Excellent. Next, I want to remind you of my two rules, and in particular, Rule Number Two, which says, "You are not allowed to climax unless what?"

She well remembered the struggle with Rule Number Two from the night before. How simple it had sounded until she was actually in the moment. Then it had been difficult to think coherently, much less, speak. But nevertheless, she certainly remembered the answer he was seeking. She replied, "Unless I ask for permission first."

Gray praised her for remembering his rules. "Good girl! Before we begin with your homework, it is time to clear your mind from the day and all the things of your busy life. Let's start by taking a *deep* breath. Inhale for five seconds, and then hold it for a bit. Can you do that for me?"

She breathed in deeply and slowly, while Gray counted to five, and then held her breath as he again counted aloud for her. "Now breathe out completely for five seconds." She exhaled to the rhythm of his deep voice. Metering her body tempo to the sound of him, the deep breathing continued as he counted for her again and again. She heard his relaxing and hypnotic voice guiding and encouraging her, listening only to his steady, sexy voice each time.

"Great job. Next, I want you to stretch and relax even more deeply. First, let's start by stretching your legs, feet, and toes, pointing them toward the bottom of the bed as though you were trying to grow them longer magically. Feel your energy flow into your legs as you stretch, stretch, stretch. Good. Now completely relax your legs. Let all the energy go out of them like light beams shooting out of your toes. Completely relaxed in your legs now, they may even feel light as though they could float upwards. Very good," he encouraged.

Next, she followed Gray's voice instructing her to stretch, tighten, and release her core, then shoulders, arms—even head and neck before finishing with, "Now take a deep breath and let it out right away, free flowing from here forward. Do you feel a bit more relaxed now than when we started?" his deep voice asked.

"Yes. Your voice is very soothing," Angelica said quietly. "I could listen to you do that for hours or drift off to sleep; it's so relaxing."

She listened closely as his voice took her onto the next level of her homework, just ahead, saying, "Thank you. I enjoy being the voice in your ear right now. Next, I want you to position your pillows and blankets, if you can recall, just the way we did last night. Put one pillow under each knee for support, with your knees just a bit open and apart. Your favorite pillow supports your head and neck, and then let's finish by covering you with a soft blanket. OK?"

Angelica, following his instructions, set up her own "nest" with pillows and blankets, just like the night before. But she said longingly, "OK. Everything is just like last night—except you are not here next to me. And I miss your magical touch, Edward."

She waited to hear his response to her longing words, which came flowing back to her ear with, "My sweetest Kitten, you have all my energy and attention focused 100% on you. I am there with you right now—even as we speak," his voice reassured her.

"Now, close your eyes, and gently take all ten fingers of both hands and very, very softly touch your face. Let your breathing slow and deepen as you explore, barely touching the skin. Very lightly touch your eyelid with your fingertip and lightly stroke it once or twice. Feel how softly you can stroke it and remember this pressure. Now slowly trace your jawline and down your beautiful neck. With just a couple of fingers on each hand, trace your collarbone and feel that little hollow spot. Next, slowly find your way down to your breasts. Explore them first with just the soft palm of your hands, feeling how you harden and bud up against the softness of your palm. Now stroke them gently with your fingertips and squeeze and pluck the nipples gently. Feel them lengthen and bud harder in response to your touch. Encircling and cupping, lift your breasts very gently once before slowly sliding further downward. As your hands glide across your tummy, search until you land on both of your hips."

He encouraged her gently, saying, "You are doing very good, Angelica. Now open both of your knees just a bit wider for me, and trace the inside of your thighs with just your fingertips. You may find the apex of your center and come close to your delicate clitoris, lightly grazing it, softly touching it for just a second as if by accident. Imagine my hands brushing against you accidentally on purpose."

Angelica's breathing was getting deeper as she responded to Gray's voice and the magical feeling of touch he was guiding. "Next, take only the palm of your left hand and place it gently on your smooth mound, and just hold it there for a moment." She did and felt a little surprised that she was completely wet; moist and flowing with her own excitement.

She heard his knowing voice from miles away wanting to share her discovery. "How are you feeling right now at this moment?"

She eagerly confessed to him right away, "I was surprised. I am ... well, I am wetter right now than I have ever felt when I am alone."

What she didn't say aloud was the ache she felt inside. How she wanted him. More than just his touch and his fingertips. How she fantasized all day wanting his full measure inside of her. His voice continued as her mind raced with anticipation of more, hearing, "Good. You are doing great, and your body is responding in a natural and healthy way. Next, I want you to take just the index finger of your left hand and stroke your clit up and down only. No circular motions, just upward and just slightly to the left from your viewpoint and then downward with the very tip of your index finger, over and over for me. You may explore the thicker pad of your finger for more full contact, or you may wish to explore faster strokes to increase energy and tension. Also, if you wish, try longer, slower strokes for more steady and calmer energy, but all of it is good. And it will be as though I was right there with you. Will you do that for me, Angelica?"

She whispered her reply as her fingers began stroking slowly at first, "Yes, I will."

Edward heard her breathing harder and faster, sometimes with little gasps and noises intertwined with her breathing, so he instructed her, "Now remember your rules, Angelica. Don't climax without permission. Otherwise, you may get into big trouble with Mr. Gray. Do you understand?" he added with a bit of seriousness mixed with playful energy.

She managed to get out as she was stroking faster and breathing harder, "Yes, sir—OK. But I'm not sure if I can get there by myself. May I use a little toy that I have? It is just a little vibrating silver egg."

His deep and sexy voice replied, "Of course. Get the egg and come right back to this same position."

Angelica reached over to her nightstand opening the top drawer. "I'm back. I didn't even have to get out of bed."

Gray heard the sound of a soft vibration on the speakerphone and guided her, "Now let the egg do much of the work for you. Gently stroke up and to the left."

"Uh-huh," she murmured. "Uh-huh," again louder this time. "Oh. Oh!" She quickened with intensity, almost immediately reaching the top of her wave when she cried out, "Please, sir…" Breathing hard, she gasped once. Please, may I cum?" she begged him.

"You want to climax already for me?" Gray asked quickly.

"Yes! Yes, please," she said as her body ached with the pent-up wave inside her.

"OK, you may cum just one time," he released her finally.

Wave after wave after wave of energy rolled across her, almost like the night before. She pressed her egg against her moist mound gently but with urgency feeling electricity all through her body. Rushing and tingling with an intensity she had never felt when she was alone, it continued again and once more again. So much so, it was almost overwhelming, and she finally moved the toy away from her and just collapsed, breathing... long and deep.

Lying there in total silence, she finally heard his voice checking on her, "Is... everything OK?" Gray's voice inquired still next to her on the pillow.

She was still reeling from the waves of energy that had rushed through her. Once again, Edward had led her to a powerful peak—now leaving her empty and drained. She murmured softly, "Yes. Everything is... amazing. Yet again, with you."

She felt his energy watching over her from afar and smiled hearing his voice once more encouraging her. "I am very proud of you. I felt like I was part of your journey, even though I am far away tonight. Thank you for trusting me again, Kitten, and I hope you liked your homework assignment tonight," Edward said with confident but humble encouragement in his voice.

"You are incredible, Edward. How can you do that to me with just your voice—when you aren't even here with me?" she gushed, heaping praise and admiration on him from every inch of her body and soul. She was feeling her bliss and wanted to give it all back to him.

"It wasn't me, Kitten." Edward explained, "It was almost 100% you. You have always had that ability locked inside of you. It is a part of you. Your feminine energy is now and will always be available to you. You just have to know how to access it. I was simply there to help guide you a bit."

She loved that Edward was confident but not cocky or arrogant about his masculine energy. He was always so sure of himself. He is a man who knows what he wants and goes after it like the night they met in the restaurant. He saw her out on a miserable date with the wrong guy and simply rescued her that night. And he did that again, in a different way just now. She gushed, "You were amazing!" her voice emotional as she said the words.

Edward's deep voice wanted to probe further, saying, "Thank you. But I would like to ask you to share with me, if you don't mind, what were a couple of things that you most liked about your homework tonight? And what might there have been that you would prefer less of next time?" Gray asked with real interest and a bit of earnestness in his voice.

"I liked it all. Everything," Angelica said instantly. When you first told me what the homework assignment was, I wasn't sure this would even be possible with you so far away and over the phone. But, then last night, you touched me in a way that unleashed something inside of me. For the first time I could see what all the fuss was about. I never knew orgasms could feel this way or that my body could have wave after wave of bliss. You did more with just one fingertip than any other man has ever been able to, even using their whole body. And now, tonight, you've done it again— without even touching me! Oh, my god!" She was swirling with emotions. *Is this what it means when you find your soul mate?* she thought to herself.

Angelica pointed out the most important part to her, saying, "Most of all, I feel safe with you, Edward. Everything you do. Everything you say and how you say it makes me feel safe and secure," she confided in him.

She heard the rasp of his deep male voice speak slowly and with intent, adding, "You will always be safe with me, Angelica. You will see that over time. I'm glad you feel that way. It is very important to me. Now, I want you to get a good night's sleep. I have a 4 a.m. start in the morning and should be back in Sarasota by midday."

Angelica asked eagerly, "Will I see you tomorrow?"

Gray said in a friendly, fair, but firm tone, "If you sign your Confidentiality Agreement, then I am willing to continue your training. That is, if you would like to do so."

Her reply came without hesitation, "Of course, I want to continue!" She laughed at the question just a bit.

He replied with a smile in his voice, "Good answer. I will text you when we land tomorrow. Now be a good girl and get a good night's sleep. You are going to need your rest the next time I see you," Edward said turning his flirt engine back on one last time.

She replied playfully, hoping to tease Edward into sharing more details of his plans for her next experience with him. "Oh? Is that so? Am I finally going to get to see your Red Playroom?"

He said with a deep and sober warning in his voice, "Perhaps. But be careful what you wish for, Angelica." His admonition had the intended effect.

She said much more softly and tenderly, "Good night, Edward."

Their phone date ended with the sound of Edward saying, "Sweet dreams," followed by the click of the phone, leaving her body floating on the nest of pillows and blankets and her mind drifting in the afterglow wondering what might be in store for her next.

Angelica slept deeply again for the second night in a row. She woke early, stretching like a big cat—a bit surprised at herself for waking this early. *Perhaps this is what happens when you get plenty of great sleep*, she thought, smiling at a new day and feeling blissfully happy. Peaceful.

She took one of those deep breaths Edward had taught her and held it momentarily.

Last night was incredible with Edward's deep voice guiding me in my ear, she thought to herself. She discovered yet another blissful byproduct of her OM session with Edward was waking up early and still feeling this inner glow. *What an excellent way to start the morning without racing to the shower, running out of the door, and being late again*, she thought as she headed to the kitchen to make coffee. She said out loud, "I should do this more often," as she put the Keurig coffee cartridge in the machine. She even used the 60 seconds while the coffee was brewing to put away a few dishes and straighten the kitchen. "I'm feeling pretty productive this morning!" she smiled, giving herself a rare compliment. Angelica couldn't help but wonder if Edward would be proud of her for getting up so early after two nights in a row of deep and restful sleep. All of this was caused in no small part by their OM sessions with his incredible energy and sexy voice in her ear.

He had told Angelica that it was almost 100% her that caused the OM experience to end so blissfully, but she knew better. She thought she might never feel that way again with anyone if she were not with Edward.

Her Keurig hissed its final time at her, and the coffee was ready. She loved the way coffee smelled, almost more than drinking it. There is something so comforting about holding a warm mug in your hand or even close to your chest—warming you while the aroma drifts up for your nose to enjoy.

She brought it to her master bath to savor while preparing for the day ahead. Today, she was a morning person.

Gray was wrapping up an early business breakfast with the new team in D.C. His driver picked him up in a black Suburban SUV, a beast of a vehicle, and headed straight to the plane. They would be flying out of Manassas Regional Jetport, where many of the private jets connect in and out of the Washington metro area, and it was a beautiful morning for it so far.

Edward texted Angelica and said simply, *Dinner this evening? My place.*

Her heart raced when she saw the early morning message from him. She was still moist from the shower and drying with the towel, but now she was beaming with smiles. She grabbed her phone to reply, *Yes. I'd love to! What time do you want me there?*

Gray replied, *7 p.m., please.*

Would you like me to bring anything? Angelica offered thoughtfully.

Just you and that beautiful smile of yours, Kitten, he replied.

She finished getting ready for work and was out the door in the best mood. *I can't remember starting the day feeling so great with everything going my way like this*, she thought to herself. *And tonight, dinner with, of all people, **The** Edward Gray at his home. Oh my!*

What might this lead to tonight? Would it end with the mysterious Red Playroom she had been so curious about? A man in his position must have many options with women, but for the past few days, she had clearly been at the center of all his attention. She loved that feeling. It was intoxicating.

She felt she would do almost anything for him to keep this feeling going forward. What would he ask of her next? But whatever it was she was excited for the next step in the journey to unfold.

She parked her red sports car at the office and arrived almost fifteen minutes early, giving her a nice and easy start to the morning. She made a second cup of coffee and thought, *This will be an amazing day!* That her mind kept returning to the evening planned to follow was, of course, the most exciting part.

Tenants and repairmen called throughout the day as she clicked off all the property management jobs that needed tending to. More than once, people commented on what a great mood she was in today. Not that she was usually grumpy. She wasn't, but she felt this energy inside her all the time that was just overflowing with people on the phone. She kept looking at the clock throughout the day—counting down the hours to 5 p.m. so she could race home to prepare for her evening with Mr. Gray. She had been thinking for hours about what to wear that evening and going through a mental inventory of all her favorite options. She didn't want to wear something over the top as they were staying in. But she wanted his attention and energy to be fully on her. She knew just what to pull from her closet. It was almost too much excitement—she could hardly stand it. And finally, it was time.

She flew home in her red convertible. Speeding, yet again, was one of her personality flaws. But this time, it was justified. She could hardly wait to prepare for this evening's dinner with Edward. As she arrived back home, she was floating up her driveway. She almost skipped up her walkway to her front door like when she was five with excitement. She dropped her keys in the bowl by the front door and went straight to the kitchen for one little glass of her favorite white wine. It was always a good idea, she thought, to have a "dressing drink" while getting ready for the evening. Then off to raid her closet and lay out everything she would wear for Edward. She loved this part.

First, she selected her soft, off-white, bone-colored gauze pants that hung perfectly from her hip bones. They looked like they might slip and fall off, but fortunately, they never did. And the matching mid-drift but long-sleeved top. It looked like something Barbara Eden would wear on the TV show, *I Dream of Jeanie*. She loved that look. She added a gold belt with tiny seashells that dangled with matching earrings, but she went back and forth on matching heels or flat sandals. *Hmmm, white or gold?* She was torn.

She got in the steamy shower to get ready with her ensemble lying across the bed, beckoning her to come and try them all on, but only when she showered and finished her hair and makeup. No need to risk getting anything on the beautiful off-white dream outfit before it was almost time to leave.

Gray was home having their gourmet dinner prepared by a few different chefs and then delivered. He was an amateur gourmet chef himself but loved having the best in town preparing dishes that he already knew would be amazing. Everything was being prepared and delivered to his home to delight Angelica. He'd had a busy day and he wanted to simply plate the food with a beautiful presentation and be able to focus on his special guest.

He carefully thought about this evening and texted Angelica, *I'm looking very much forward to seeing you. Please remember to bring the Confidentiality Agreement if you can.*

She replied, *Of course. I won't forget.* Admittedly, she hadn't thought of that all day, so she took the envelope with the fancy red wax seal from the kitchen countertop where it had been sitting and placed it on top of the bowl holding her car keys so she could not forget and leave it.

She finished getting ready and decided to wear the gold sandals to match her belt, plus a tiny gold purse. Finally, she felt put together for the evening with Edward and grabbed her keys and the important-looking envelope, and away she went.

Longboat Key is home to some of the most beautiful multi-million-dollar homes in the area, and for a view of the ocean—there is none better. It was just time for sunset in Sarasota, so the drive across the Ringling Bridge to St Armand's Circle was gorgeous. The sky was orange as the sun ball had just touched the ocean marking the beginning of a magical night ahead.

Angelica made the one right turn heading up to Longboat Key for her date with destiny. She parked in Edward's driveway—only for the second time—but it already felt like they had built a closeness and bond. She was excited but comfortable already somehow with him. Using her rearview mirror, she checked her lips and eyes one last time before ringing his bell.

Edward was impressed with her being right on time—7 o'clock on the dot, to be precise.

He opened the door holding a gin and tonic, wearing a comfortable Tommy Bahama shirt and slacks with open chocolate leather sandals. She was instantly relieved that she had picked the right outfit to wear. "How was your drive out to the Key?"

"It is always so beautiful coming over the bridge, but tonight I saw the sun setting right as I was on the bridge's peak. It was so gorgeous!" she beamed.

"As are you tonight," he admired. "Please come in, and may I offer you a cocktail or a glass of wine?"

Angelica glided through his open door smiling at Edward's golden ocean view and said, "Yes. What are you having?"

"I usually start with a Tanqueray Gin and Tonic and then switch to wine with dinner. But we have a full bar and wine cellar. Almost anything you might enjoy is here. So, what would you like?"

"Just a glass of white wine would be fine," she said, walking across his enormous living room to the glass wall facing the Gulf of Mexico. "I just love your view."

"Thank you. Just a moment, and I'll open a special bottle of wine for you," he said, heading to one of the seven-foot-tall wine chillers with wooden pull-out shelves, each loaded with various types of wine and stories.

"Don't go to any trouble for me," Angelica offered politely.

"I know you said you like Santa Margarita Pinot Grigio, which I have several bottles of, but I would like you to try this one instead tonight." Edward emerged holding a bottle of nicely chilled wine and said, "It's Cakebread Cellars Chardonnay. A little bit harder to get a hold of but delicious. I hope you like it."

Edward placed the bottle into a large wooden wine press with a large lever handle that skewered the cork dead center and removed it all in one action. He handed her a heavy crystal wine glass, ice-cold from the chiller, filled about halfway.

"For my princess," said Edward smiling as he handed her the glass along with a monogrammed paper napkin imprinted with "Gray Enterprises."

"Oh, you have your own napkins, I see," Angelica said with a smile as she took the offering.

"For when we host events or cocktail receptions for business. So, I have a few boxes of the napkins and other specialty items left occasionally."

"Oh wow! This is my new favorite white wine ever," Angelica sang out. "What's the name of it again?"

Edward shared the name of the label and said, "Cakebread Cellars."

"Yum!"

Gray motioned for her to join him at the already set dining table. "Please have a seat," he said and gestured to a particular chair for her.

She glided into his formal dining room and followed his suggestion of where to sit, placing herself immediately on his right side.

"Angelica, it would be best if we dispense with the paperwork before dinner or any more wine. Would you be ok with that?"

"Yes. Absolutely."

"Do you have any questions about the Confidentiality Agreement?"

"Not really. What does it say exactly?"

"You mean you haven't read the agreement?" Gray asked, surprised and a bit irritated with Angelica, adding, "You should always read every document before you sign it."

"Well, I don't sign many contracts, probably like you do," she answered.

"Basically, it says that what we do in private is confidential and that neither of us may discuss or disclose anything that happens in private to anyone else. It protects our privacy equally, and my attorney insists on it," Gray grumbled a bit about that last part.

"Well, I'm fine with signing that without reading it. I would never discuss anything that happens between us in private with anyone. Not even my best girlfriend or family. I am a very private person. So that Agreement notwithstanding, is just how I am. Agreement or not, I would operate the same way. So, I am completely comfortable signing it, Edward."

"Point well made, Ms. Hart," Gray said, impressed by how she expressed herself.

He lifted a heavy gold and silver pen from a leather pad and signed both copies of the Agreement and handed them to Angelica. She signed both and folded one copy and placed it under her purse to keep.

"Now, how can I help with dinner?" she inquired, smiling softly.

Gray took her hand gently and lifted it to his mouth, kissing it regally on the back. Angelica smiled more broadly with delight. Butterflies again!

Edward's smile was warmer and more relaxed now with the paperwork out of the way. "Follow me," he said as they returned to the kitchen.

Catering boxes filled the big sub-zero refrigerator, and salads and appetizers were at the ready.

"I cheated just a bit and recruited some help from my favorite chefs around town," he laughed. "I do cook, but I wanted to focus my attention on you, not the kitchen, this evening."

Angelica peeked at the incredible food waiting for them, all beautifully prepared, and smiled. "It all looks amazing and delicious, but that's no surprise with you," she beamed. They each selected an appetizer plus a 1905 Salad from the Columbia Restaurant on St. Armand's Circle and went back to the dining table.

Angelica smiled and said with excitement, "I could make my whole meal just on the 1905 Salad! I just love those!"

"I had them delivered moments before you got here, so they would still be fresh. They are so good," he agreed with a smile.

Both were starving by now, and they took turns sipping white wine, eating, and talking about life in Sarasota. Dinner was salmon covered with delicious seafood stuffing. Still, the pièce de résistance was the rice in a beggar's purse made of banana leaves. Inside was rice with peppers, onions, hominy, and amazing spices steamed inside the bag of leaves delivered piping hot from Selva Grille in downtown Sarasota.

She took one bite of the salmon and smiled. "It's so good!"

"Wait until you try the rice. But be careful, it is still steaming hot."

She carefully peeled open the banana leaves, watching Edward do the same until the ball of rice inside was exposed. Then she dug out a heaping spoonful of the rice mixture, which smelled like heaven, and took her first bite. Her face literally changed to an "out of this world" look with just one bite of the devilishly delicious rice mixture.

"Oh, my god!" she said out loud. "That is amazing. Wow! I have never tasted anything like that."

"I'm so glad you like it," he said, smiling, happy at the delight and pleasure oozing from her voice and visible on her beautiful face. "Next, try this," Edward suggested, combining a bite with the salmon, the crab stuffing, and the aromatic rice and peppers on a large spoon. "Open wide for me, Kitten..." he said, gently leaning into her with his next decadent delivery.

Angelica willingly edged closer to Edward's waiting reach. She closed her eyes trustingly and opened her mouth wide to accept the spoonful of delicious offerings he had prepared just for her.

Edward slid the spoonful slowly into her eager, open, and waiting mouth. But Angelica took control from there, as she slowly, sensuously pulled her full plump lips away from his spoon taking it all in one bite. She wanted Edward to have a sneak preview of the pleasure her lips could provide him with her provocative and sexy mouth. She chewed only once before she moaned, "Mmmmmmmmm...." opening her eyes to find his gaze as they both smiled playfully.

The sensual moment sent both of their already supercharged libidos spiraling upwards as Edward said, "I have something for you, Angelica. I will be right back."

"Leaving me like this, are you, Edward?" she toyed with the Master of the Universe, suddenly flustered with her soft feminine energy.

"I'm not leaving you—I'm just bringing everything to you," he answered as he smiled and walked just a few steps away.

He returned with a black bag with white and red tissue paper billowing out of the top and said, "I ordered this especially for you this evening."

"Aww, thank you. But you didn't need to get me anything. I only came here to be with you," she purred gently.

"Well, truth be told, I ordered this partially for me," Edward confessed smiling. "Please take a look inside."

Angelica pulled the tissue paper out of the way and inside was a clear plastic bag with a zipper. She took it out and opened it. Inside was a long flowing nightgown, floor length, trimmed on the sleeves and around the entire neckline and bottom of the gown in black ostrich feathers. It was stunningly beautiful. She held it up and could see how sheer the black fabric would be over her body.

"Edward, it is so beautiful. I've never worn anything like this before," she blushed.

"I wanted to start building a small wardrobe for when you come to visit me and hoped you wouldn't mind and might even like it," he said with a rare bit of hesitance.

"I love it! And I am so excited you thought of me wearing this!" she said, smiling openly. "I'm so full. Why don't we save the rest of this food and dessert for later, and perhaps you could show me where I might try this on?" she said boldly.

"Well, now that you have signed the Confidentiality Agreement, I can share it with you openly. Bring your new robe in the black bag and come with me, Angelica," Gray said invitingly.

They left the grand dining room and headed across the giant expanse of the living area to a stainless-steel elevator door. They went inside and up to the second level, which had beautiful balconies overlooking the ocean. Edward took her hand in his as he guided Angelica down to the end of a long hallway to a dark wooden door with heavy black iron hinges and fixtures. Gray produced a brass key and inserted it into the locked door.

Before opening the heavy door, Edward gazed into her eyes to remind her, "Angelica, remember, you never have to do anything with me that you do not enthusiastically choose. There is nothing to fear in the Red Playroom—ever," he said reassuringly. The lock clicked open, and Gray opened the large, oversized door.

Inside was dim and subtle red lighting underneath furniture, three unique lamps, and two large round beach-ball size orbs glowing with red light. Gray gave a voice command for music, and the smart room played Enigma's "The Principles of Lust." Angelica saw walls full of shackles, handcuffs, and leather collars everywhere she looked. However, she particularly loved the sheer white material draped over the massive four-poster bed. Each of the large wooden columns on the bed was the thickness of her entire body, with an ironworks canopy suspended above. The bed had a red satin comforter and sheets plus white pillows and blankets made from uber-soft, UGG boots-type material. The ceiling was tiled with antique mirrors with black framing, creating an exquisite look if you were facing upward.

A large red leather bench was at the foot of the bed, and on the far wall of the vast room was a matching set of tall dresser drawers three columns wide. She wondered what was in all of the drawers. A sizeable floor-to-ceiling mirror in a beautiful ornate gold frame reflected the entire room. A gorgeous cocktail drink bar set in a circular metal frame held a large champagne bucket, champagne flutes, and a set of cocktail shakers for fancy stirred drinks. The lower shelf of the cocktail bar was fully stocked with Fiji bottled water.

It was decadent and intimidating, and exciting all at the same time.

"So, what do you do in here, Edward?" she asked bravely. "Is this where you want to tie me up and hurt me?" she said, touching some of the large whips and floggers hanging as art from large wooden and iron hooks on the wall.

"I would only punish you if you misbehave and don't follow the rules, Angelica," he said calmly and quietly. "And there are also rewards and pleasures as well—to incentivize good behavior."

"And how will I know what the rules are?" she said, suddenly feeling shy as she turned toward him.

"Training," Edward offered. "I would like to continue your training here. However, with the added incentive of even greater pleasure and a bit of punishment if needed, you will discover that we have only just started. We can go much deeper, and it can be even more rewarding."

"I've never..." she hesitated. "I've never done anything like this before."

"Understood." Edward nodded with acceptance, adding reassuringly, "Small steps, Angelica. Small steps... are the best way to begin. I would like to invite you to change into your new robe and come join me on the bed just to talk some more about all of this."

She looked around the room—hearing the ethereal, sexy music playing, feeling the wine and the energy from Edward, but felt a bit hesitant.

Feeling this, he assured her, "I will keep you safe—always."

Angelica softened at hearing Edward's deep and assuring voice. "Of course. Where would you like me to change?"

Edward felt relieved to hear her acceptance of this new world. At least for another small step forward, replying with, "The bathroom across the hall is yours, complete with a granite walk-in shower. You may try on your robe there, and I would also like to change and meet you back here in a few minutes," he invited.

"Ok," she heard herself saying as she made her way to "her" new bathroom. Her heart was pumping—blood was racing as she thought, *Did I hear him say that correctly? This is mine?*

CHAPTER SIX

The Blindfold

Angelica went to her new granite and gold bathroom, where Gray had asked her to change, and looked in the mirror at her new floor-length black sheer robe. Its feather-lined elegance looked stunning as she pulled it from the black gift bag for the second time that evening. But this time, she was slipping into it for him to admire. She stripped out of her long sleeve bandolero style top and matching gauze pants and hung them on the elegant velvet hangers behind the bathroom door. She only left her panties on and slipped into the sexy sheer robe.

She looked amazing with her long flowing blonde hair cascading down the back of the sheer robe as she glanced again over her shoulder at the mirror. "Wow! Good things take time— but great things happen—all at once," she said aloud and then wondered, *Is this my moment?* as she turned the bathroom lights down to dim and opened the door heading across the marble-tiled hallway back to the Red Playroom. She glided gracefully to make a perfect appearance for Mr. Gray's eyes to drink in. The results were as she had hoped.

Edward stood silently waiting as she entered his domain. His eyes looked directly into hers and then—languidly traveled down her body across her ample breasts and curvy hips. Slowly his gaze glided down her legs to her feet before he gently lifted them back to her stunning face.

"Beautiful," he said, in his deep and hypnotic voice. "You are simply beautiful, Angelica."

"Thank you," she smiled. She had finally learned how to gracefully take a compliment from men after years of struggling with hearing them.

Gray reached towards her, and she placed her hand in his as he spoke, "Come stand in front of the dresser mirror with me and see how gorgeous you look right at this moment." The dresser held three large red lit candles, which provided a delicious fragrance in the Playroom. She walked with Edward as he positioned her right in front of the mirror with him just behind her. The mirror framed the couple, each looking directly into their reflection of perfection.

Angelica felt safe with Edward, but she could feel her heart racing now with anxious tension as he leaned into her ear to ask quietly, "May I touch you?"

She took a deep breath and calmly said, "Of course."

Gray leaned into her ear once more, but this time he quietly and in his deepest voice said, "Remember, whenever I ask something of you—something that you are completely and enthusiastically okay with, I would like it very much if you would answer me with, "Yes, sir." Would you do that for me, Angelica?"

She understood he was asking for her to speak to him submissively, and rather liked it, replying instantly with, "Yes, sir." It just seemed to roll right off her tongue with a playful smile.

"Excellent! I like the fact that you are so coachable, Angelica. When you show me such great respect, it makes me want to return the favor. Remember I told you before about building trust, and how it takes time to build?"

She liked the way Gray described trust and respect. She was feeling more comfortable already with the gothic style, intimidating Playroom with all its floggers and shackles hanging from the red walls because of how he spoke to her. So, she nodded gently as she responded to him with, "Yes, sir, I agree."

Edward continued forward with the tour of her new world. "Next, on the dresser in front of you is a heavy, round wooden box with a hinged top. Please lift the top and open it. Inside you will discover something very special that I ordered for you for this evening," Gray requested.

Angelica was intrigued to see what else Edward had for her besides the gorgeous robe that she was already wearing. "Yes, sir" came across her lips again as she reached for the lid of the antique round box that was wrapped in embossed leather. As it opened, she discovered a black velvet bag inside.

"Take whatever you find inside the box, Kitten, and open it."

She opened the drawstring on the velvet bag and inside was a beautiful ornate black lace blindfold. She held it up in front of her and could easily see right through it. "It's so beautiful and elegant!" she said smiling.

Edward watched with long-awaited anticipation as she held the blindfold up in front of her view and asked, "Have you ever worn a blindfold before, Angelica?"

The lace felt delicate to her touch. She thought and quickly responded, "No. Never, sir."

Gray wanted her to continue her journey of exploration forward so he coaxed her gently with, "Angelica, you look amazing in the black robe, and I sort of hate the idea of covering your beautiful eyes, but would you be open to trying the lace blindfold on for a minute or two to see how it looks and feels?"

Without any hesitation, she smiled and replied, "Yes, sir. Of course," as she wrapped it gently around her face covering her eyes and began tying it in a bow behind her head. It was a stunning picture in the mirror. Angelica was quite the vision in the sheer, see-through black robe trimmed in black ostrich feathers and now wearing the sexy and elegant, black lace blindfold.

Gray, feeling powerfully aroused by his new submissive's willing response to his every request, grew a bit bolder and said, "Now, place both of your hands on the dresser for balance while wearing your blindfold." She complied, silently placing her hands as he instructed. She felt him leaning into her ear, and again she received her favorite request, "May I ... touch you?"

She gave him permission with her eager, "Yes, sir." She tingled with anticipation, still holding onto the dresser with both hands.

Edward moved her long blonde hair to the side, exposing her elegant, pale white neck. He moved closer, kissing her very softly just behind her ear. Instantly, goose bumps beaded up on her everywhere as Gray's arm reached around her to wrap his large warm hand around her throat. He was not crushing or squeezing but gently, firmly tilted her head backward until it rested on his chest and shoulder. Still kissing her neck and now down to her collarbone, she responded by arching her back. Pressing her heart-shaped derriere against his trousers, she could feel his thickness growing.

Gray momentarily released her neck and slid both of his hands down the length of her arms until his hands rested on top of hers on the dresser.

Next, he lifted her hands up to her throat and chest, gently placing them there and said, "No one knows a woman's body better than she does. So, I would like to ask you to show me... how you like to be touched." With Angelica's hands leading and his hands on top of hers, to feel how she moved, the slow journey downward began. First, their joined hands moved across her full breasts, stopping to circle lightly, lingering and stroking. She moaned softly at the touch before adventuring on and once again downward across her flat abdomen to her hips. Here, Gray paused the journey momentarily to grip her and pull her gently but firmly against him. He was aching to feel her more fully and for her to feel him. She let out a louder moan of anticipation before she resumed her journey of their four hands and continued to their ultimate destination. Her fingertips lightly caressed the "V" of her great delight the last two evenings. She already had experienced how Edward could give her an amazing climax with just his voice, fingers, and energy. Now she ached to feel the fullness of the experience with him. *I would do anything he asked. Anything and everything*, she thought.

Angelica knew that he was aching with anticipation as well. She could feel the thickness of his rock-hard manhood pressing into her as they finished their sensual stroking and touching of her feminine shape. Then, she heard his next request in her ear, "I want you to go to the bed and lie down for me, Angelica. I want to watch you for a moment. I want to take in just a bit how you look right now."

She hated to leave his touch, as she was still pressed against him fully, but said, "Yes, sir." She felt the heat from his eyes on her as she walked slowly, hands out in front of her to feel the corner post of the bed as the lace blindfold partially blocked her vision in the dimly lit Playroom. As she climbed onto the super-king-sized bed, she felt the soft blanket at the foot and cool slippery red satin on her hands and knees as she made her way to the center of the bed.

He watched her every graceful move guiding her forward with, "Thank you, Kitten. Next, I see that you are wearing exquisite panties, but I would like you to lift your hips and slowly, very slowly, remove them for me. I like watching you. Would you do that for me?"

Her heart had been racing ever since he kissed her neck and began touching her at the dresser. But now he wanted her to put on a bit of a show for him, and the thought of being at the center of his attention excited Angelica to new heights. "Yes, sir," she whispered with a deeper, sexier voice than before. She was signaling her readiness and how she ached for him. He wouldn't need the plentiful supply of handcuffs and restraints hanging on all the walls to have her tonight or as often as he desired.

Gray walked to the bed with the slow, deliberate gait of a man who intended to take his time with her. Next, he lay beside her and spoke slowly. "Angelica, you never have to do anything that you do not choose. Do you understand?"

She found it comforting how often he asked for her permission and how he confirmed and reconfirmed that she was comfortable with each step he took in his role as her Dominant. No one had been this attentive to her in her life. She was intoxicated with his voice and her excitement, saying now with growing confidence in her new role as his submissive, "Yes, sir. I know," she replied.

"And, in this room, even though I am the Dominant and you are my submissive, we share the power equally through safe words. Yours are to be 'yellow' and 'red,'" he advised. "We all know what those mean, of course, from driving. 'Yellow' means slow down, or we are getting near the edge of your comfort zone, and 'red' means stop. Stop immediately. Not even one more stroke or action. Understood?"

Angelica smiled, secretly yearning for him to continue exploring her body with his hands, mouth, and more, as she said, "Yes, sir. I understand. And thank you for always making me feel safe when I'm with you."

Gray continued, "Of course. One more thing, when a safe word is used, the only proper response from the Dominant is to say, "Thank you for communicating clearly and openly." In this way, we share the power in this room 50/50 as partners. We just have different roles to play. A Dominant who does not have a submissive who chooses him as their partner has—nothing."

Angelica was thinking about this differently now, hearing how he described the balance of power. It made her feel safer and closer to him even more.

"Do you understand, Angelica?"

"Yes, sir. I do not have to do anything here with you that I do not enthusiastically choose, and my safe words are yellow and red, which I doubt I will ever need in your hands. But they make us 50/50 partners in this room," she repeated back to him.

Gray rose up a bit in the bed, impressed with her recital of the base rules he had explained, offering to her, "Well said, Angelica. I am rather proud of you just now." They both smiled at their first Mentor / Protégé moment.

"One last thing to add," he continued. "Don't forget my two rules. Rule Number One says you may never have me inside of you unless—you are already climaxing fully. And Rule Number Two says you may not climax without asking for…?" He paused for her input to make sure she remembered.

"Permission," Angelica chimed in, already blissfully familiar with the challenge artfully embedded in Rule Number Two. *Right as she was shaking. Right, when it's hard to fully breathe — much less speak*—she was thinking. *It is hard to find the words.*

As if reading her mind, Edward invited, "Let's practice your words for Rule Number Two a time or two, just in case you need them this evening or perhaps need them many, many times. I would like you to practice saying, 'Please, sir, may I cum?' Would you do that for me?"

Angelica's mind was racing thinking about his words, that she might need to ask permission "many, many times" tonight. *Oh, my goodness,* she thought to herself as she happily complied, saying in her quiet voice, "Please, sir, may I cum?"

Edward pushed her forward boldly. "Say it louder," he instructed.

"Please, sir, may I cum?" her full voice repeated, causing her face to flush pink.

"Good girl," he complimented her. "I recall from our telephone date last night that you sometimes like to use a small vibrating toy when you need a release. Yes?" he asked gently and without judgment.

"Yes, sir. Sometimes," she said shyly.

Gray was not insecure with the use of toys if it enhanced her experience and replied, "Excellent," he nodded approvingly. "Have you ever tried the Hitachi Magic Wand before?" he inquired.

"No. I'm not sure what that is exactly," Angelica replied.

Edward left the bed momentarily and walked over to the oversized triple dresser and opened one of the drawers. He produced a long, shrink-wrapped box the length of a loaf of bread from the drawer. He pulled the plastic wrap from the shiny new box and opened it to reveal her first Magic Wand vibrator. Edward handed her the end of the white device and encouraged her to feel it with her hand. It had a small tennis ball-shaped flexible head that was slightly soft to the touch but firm. Next, he turned on the switch for the powerful battery-operated device.

Angelica was already intimidated by the size of the wand—*perhaps the size of her entire forearm*, she thought. But, when Edward turned the power button on, she blurted out, "Wow! It's so strong." Her eyes widened at the thought of the powerful wand being anywhere near her delicate parts.

Gray smiled knowingly but understanding her hesitation still could not resist letting her know, "And that is just on the low of several available speeds," he informed her.

"Oh my gosh…" Angelica said with a bit of doubt creeping into her voice.

"Nothing to worry about. Just wanted you to be familiar with it should you ever want to explore it a bit," Edward consoled her. "It is used in adult videos of late almost exclusively because of the amazing results it can produce."

"Oh, is that so?" she replied with a hint of renewed interest. "Maybe sometime," she said, leaving it open for discussion.

Edward then cleaned the toy with high-quality sanitizing cleaner especially made for sex toys and laid it on a clean white towel on the nightstand. She watched the care he took with anything that might touch her for it to be immaculately clean, even though brand new.

"Now, close your eyes for me," he said softly, "and simply feel." His hands traced from her cheek and jaw down her neck, full of secrets and desires long hidden, awakening now as he caressed her breasts full in the palms of his strong hands. Then, as he stroked with ten fingers across her core to her hips, he lifted and turned her so that her legs opened toward him as he stood beside the bed.

Next, Gray knelt on the floor as if at an altar for a sacred and safe connection to her ultimate source of pleasure. Then, gently opening her knees wide to expose her moist and very delicate lips, he stroked first with gentle fingertips, which she remembered so intently, but then with his talented and knowing tongue.

The feeling of his velvety tongue took her instantly to new levels of energy coursing through her. "Oh!" Angelica cried out one lone syllable at the first touch of Edward's tongue like a perfect ache.

Rhythmically and slowly, he grazed her delicate clitoris to peaks of excitement again and again as he stroked her with just the tips of two fingers circling slowly inside her. His tongue played her masterfully like an orchestra leader, finding all the peaks and valleys of emotion roaring then soothing, then roaring again and again while stroking her G-spot with just an ounce of perfect pressure.

She felt her legs shake and then shake again. Her core quivered as her whole body tightened, and when she knew it was already too late, she begged out loud, "Please..."

Sensing she was long past the point of no return, Gray demanded, "Please, what?" he urged her for more.

"Please, sir…" she mustered.

"Say it louder!" Gray pushed her, edging her closer and closer but not releasing her yet.

"Please, sir, may I cum?!" she finally shouted in blissful agony as her climax was already to full roll.

"Yes. You may cum just one time."

It was as if the dam finally broke, and all the pent-up water pressure that had ever existed inside of her came rushing out all at once. Gushing, literally as she convulsed and locked up, unable to move. Then Gray opened her legs wide and picked up the Magic Wand toy from the nightstand.

"Give me your right hand," he instructed her with urgency.

She complied, reaching towards Edward with her right hand open. He turned on the Magic Wand to low, and the device sprang to life again. He placed it in her hand with the magic vibrating head pointed downward towards her still quivering mound of pleasure. He guided her hand with the toy pulsing hard right to her point of peak excitement and sensitivity.

"Oh, oh, oh!" she moaned loudly at first contact with the toy—right as she was already climaxing. He released her hand to continue unguided so she could adjust the amount of pressure of its touch. And, within just a breath or two, he slid all of his thickness inside of her in one long, deep stroke and just held it still inside her, buried to the bone.

Angelica's back arched hard, and she was locked physically at peak so hard she could not move and could hardly breathe. She could feel the pulsing and vibration of the wand on the outside and having all of him buried deep inside her; reaching all the way to his length buried to her very core. It was pure agony and ecstasy—all at the exact same moment.

She did not want it to end but was unsure if she could stand it for even another moment. So, she finally moved the toy away. Still trembling, the little aftershocks still rumbling through her body, she could not speak. Barely breathing and then gulping the air finally, the first exhale was the hardest.

Gray loved feeling wave after wave of her still trembling around the thickness of his very hard cock. He held still, not moving his hips, at least not yet but just feeling each of her soft trembles. He leaned down and kissed her softly on the lips. She kissed back once, then again. He took her lower lip into his mouth, while the fullness of his length was still buried deep inside her. As their kissing grew more passionate, he began slowly moving his hips with long, slow, deep strokes inside her still. "Oh…" she sighed. "Just a minute." She still needed to recover and gather herself back.

"No," he insisted. "Take me all the way inside you. You can do it." As she opened her bent knees wider, she reached around him and placed her hands on his toned, muscular ass, pulling him into her more profoundly with each stroke.

Hours passed in the Red Playroom, and with them so did every position Angelica could imagine possible played out, along with one very long and much-needed break in the middle of playtime to rest and recover. They drained several of the bottled waters and each other. Angelica lost count of her orgasms at seven or eight—possibly even nine. She couldn't remember how many.

But one thing she remembered quite clearly. Never ever before with anyone else had it felt like this.

She looked at Edward lying on the bed, with his toned, tan swimmer's type body, and smiled as he said to her, "Come lay next to me and rest your head on my shoulder."

Angelica complied, wrapping herself around his side with her knee gently bent and wrapped over his thighs. She could feel his warmth as her head nestled next to his cheek.

They both sighed and took a deep breath, as he asked her, "How do you feel?" He paused. "Anything hurting?"

"No, I feel amazing," she shared with a huge smile looking up at him. "I'm a bit exhausted, but everything is good."

"Excellent. I'm so glad to hear that. You were equal parts nervous and then amazing today, Kitten," he complimented her. "If I may, I would like to ask, what are a few things that you most enjoyed that you would want more of in the future, and … maybe one or two things you would want less of next time?"

She thought about his question for just a moment, but then she simply gushed, "I loved everything! All of it. I wouldn't want to change anything." She smiled and squeezed him with her arm and leg wrapped around him pulling herself gently tighter into him for just a moment and then relaxing again.

"Good. Thank you for sharing, but always know that this is a safe space for you to talk and communicate with me, Angelica. I don't have a fragile ego. I won't take comments or suggestions personally. Real and open communication is key for us to grow and learn together. Does that make sense?"

"Yes. I agree completely," she nodded gently. "But not all men feel that way. If you say something or offer a suggestion, they get angry, or their feelings are hurt."

"Exactly right. But exactly the wrong way to think and feel about honest communication. In life, Angelica, something is either growing or dying whether that is a person, a plant, a business, a relationship—anything. I want to always be on a journey to stretch and grow. So, the only way we can learn and grow together is if we agree we can talk openly, not to be unkind or harsh, but have free and open communication. Is that fair?" he asked her encouragingly.

"That's perfect, and yes, I agree," she said as she smiled and felt safe living in his words and the world he was introducing her to.

"Final question," Gray began as he gently stroked her hair and traced his fingers down her shoulder and back, barely grazing across her skin lightly. "Did you feel comfortable in the Red Playroom? Did you feel safe with me?"

"Yes. Completely. One thousand percent," she instantly reported. "You made me feel totally safe with your voice, how you guided me, and in everything you did, Edward."

"Excellent. That is very important to me, Angelica," Edward added with purposeful intent. "You will always be safe when you are with me, but knowing that and feeling that way grows stronger over time. Thank you for sharing. This lifestyle requires much greater than average communication before, during, and after playtime. I hope you don't mind."

She closed her eyes and drifted off for a bit nestled under the soft blanket and the glow that filled her in Edward's arms. *Bliss*, she thought silently to herself.

CHAPTER SEVEN

The Sugaring

Angelica awoke from a deep sleep in the Red Playroom to discover Edward was gone. No clocks were in the room, so she had no idea how long she had napped. Was it the middle of the night? She got up slowly, put on the sheer robe that Edward had given her, and quietly left to use the bathroom across the hall and then to go find Edward.

Quietly, she walked the long hallway to the kitchen, where she discovered him wearing only his black yoga pants and no shirt. His toned, sculpted body made her think of the famous statue of "David" by Michelangelo. She stood there smiling quietly to drink in the picture of Gray making a snack tray from the refrigerator.

Finally noticing her watching him, he returned her gaze steadily and smiled. "I didn't want to wake you," he explained. "You were deep asleep, so I covered you with the blanket and eased quietly out of bed."

"How long was I sleeping?" she asked yawning, rubbing her eyes and face gently.

Edward replied, "Only about an hour or so. I came back and checked on you once, and you were really out so I just let you sleep. Are you hungry?"

"Yes! I'm starving," she replied, smiling at the invitation.

"I made us a late-night snack tray from our dinner earlier. There was so much good food left untouched."

"I would love some. Dinner was so amazing!" she recalled. "Should I still wear this to eat in?" she said playfully, watching Edward's eyes drink in her sexy shape easily visible through the very sheer material.

Edward smiled and said, "Perhaps I can offer you something more comfortable to change into for a late-night bite. Follow me," he invited her as he took her hand for the walk to the other wing of the house. There in his master suite opened two large-scale dressing rooms lined with elegant clothes of all types.

She marveled at the enormity of his dressing rooms. They were easily as big as her bedroom at home. "Would you prefer a shirt or a robe?" Edward asked, running his hand over a few options for her choosing.

"One of your shirts—definitely," she replied. "How about that one?" she said, pointing to one of the soft white linen long-sleeve shirts she loved seeing him wear.

"Of course," he offered, handing her the hanger.

The robe dropped to the floor as she turned her back to Edward for modesty, for some reason, as she slipped into his long white shirt.

Edward scooped up the feather-adorned sheer robe, placed it on the hanger, and hung it on an ornate gold wall hook. As he was a Virgo, everything had a place in his closet, and everything was in its place. White shirts were all in a neat row, and above them, the blue shirts were in theirs. She noted that even the socks were paired and rolled into perfectly symmetrical balls like so many eggs in a carton in their neat wicker basket in Gray's closet.

"Let's eat outside," he invited, and off to the kitchen they went to retrieve the tray of delicious delights waiting for them. Gray asked, "Would you like another glass of wine or just water?"

"May I have both?" she said smiling.

"Of course." Gray added two of each to the growing tray for them to share.

Outside, they found a pair of chaise lounges with a round table between them perfect for holding the tray, and Gray spoke more seriously as he said, "I would like to discuss something new with you, Angelica. If you don't mind."

"Of course," she replied, digging into the food with eager energy.

Edward broached the new subject with her. "I would like you to let me take care of you, including things like a clothing allowance for when we go out. You may be accompanying me to functions, etc."

She paused for a moment. Caught off guard by his offer, she spoke her first instinct saying, "No. I wouldn't feel comfortable taking money from you, Edward," she sighed, adding, "That would just feel—odd to me."

"Listen. The places we will be going and the kind of clothes I would want you to be wearing are also a reflection of me," he explained. He paused momentarily before adding, "And, no offense, but I don't think your current salary would cover the kind of clothes that I would like you to wear when we go out," Edward pleaded his case.

She listened while sipping more of her wine and retorted, "There is a name for what you are talking about, Edward, and I wouldn't like that to be how you think of me."

Gray paused before replying, "I'm not putting any labels on our arrangement or understanding, Angelica, and no limits on how we might grow and develop as a couple later on. Plus, if two people take care of one another's needs, I see nothing wrong with it, and, quite frankly, it is no one's business but ours anyway. This would be a completely private arrangement. I just want to take care of you and spoil you a bit."

"Well. Let me think about it, Edward. Ok?" she offered. "I'm just not used to the idea."

Edward watched her face and her look of sweet innocence as she was reluctant to accept his generous offer and found himself ever more drawn to her. "Which, quite frankly, Angelica, makes you all the more adorable to me and rare to find," he complimented, smiling as he lifted his glass towards her. "Cheers," he said as they clinked. Little did Angelica grasp just now, but that toast in Edward's mind had sealed their deal.

Angelica woke that morning in Edward's master bedroom. She hadn't even remembered drifting off into her velvety sleep last night. She loved waking up to the soft ocean breeze blowing through the French doors. They opened directly onto that ocean view from the third-floor balcony. It was expansive and beautiful but also so serene and peaceful. She could listen to those ocean waves crashing on the beach forever.

She couldn't remember when she had slept that deeply anywhere but in her own bed. Perhaps it was the combination of her energy being drained repeatedly in Edward's Red Playroom, all the wine she drank, and the sound of the ocean waves rolling steadily all night that had led her to sleep so deeply. But now, she desperately needed coffee.

Angelica went roaming through the spacious, estate-sized home looking for Edward and finally found him outside by the pool having his morning coffee. She walked up, still wearing his white linen shirt, to give him a good morning hug, leaning over him from behind. Edward beamed with the energetic smile of a morning person and reached up to pull her closer. As he did, Angelica whispered playfully, "What does a girl have to do around here to get a cup of that coffee?"

Edward, ever the great host, smiled and said, "Let me help you with that." Together, they made their way to the gourmet kitchen where everything was already prepared. Edward's Keurig coffee machine was surrounded by a rotating rack with every possible flavor of coffee, plus a crystal bowl with packets of every type of sugar and sweetener one could want, with an assortment of creamers to top it off. He showed Angelica where to find the coffee mugs for the future, but she asked, "Do you happen to have a to-go cup instead? I have to hurry off to work soon."

Armed with her coffee, she made her way back to the bathroom where she had changed into the dreamy robe the night before. She quickly did her best to restore her hair and touch up her makeup before leaving him.

It was hard leaving Edward's goodbye embrace in his muscular arms. He held her close at his front door before she had to leave to head home. She didn't want to pressure Edward, but she simply could not resist asking him, "When will I see you again?" She winced inside as the words came out of her, but she had the aching feeling of missing him already, even just as she was about to leave.

Edward's eyes narrowed, as he said more seriously and with intention, "You'll never have to worry about that, Angelica. You are mine now, and I will take care of you like a princess. You will soon see." She gazed deeply into his eyes smiling with equal parts of relief and happiness at the energy in his answer.

As he walked her to her car and kissed her softly one last time that morning, she whispered into his ear, "And I will treat you like my king, Edward." Hearing her parting words, he held her tightly but gently as if possessed by his protective power, one more time.

She looked back up at his expansive home that contained the history and mystery of their first night together in his Red Playroom. Adding to the dream had been waking up in his master bedroom that morning, but now, she finally had to wave goodbye to Edward. She slowly pulled out of his circular driveway in the crisp morning air and onto the Gulf of Mexico Drive to head home. Her mind raced, reliving the night before and all that had happened. She felt her adrenaline flowing and her heart racing as she made her way along the spectacularly scenic drive back to town. She was soaring with newfound energy as she loved the views on each side of her; Sarasota Bay on her left with the early morning skyline of the charming city and the Gulf of Mexico on her right. The wind blew her hair in the open convertible as she cruised slowly and beamed with her morning glow to her modest home back in town.

She hoped his words were genuine and would not be their last. Angelica was a worrier. As it turned out, she would not have to worry for long. As she pulled into her driveway at home to get ready for work, Edward texted, *Home safe?* She smiled, thinking, *Still watching over me protectively, I see.* Somehow that kind of attention from other men she had dated had seemed annoying or bothersome. But not from Edward. She liked being the center of his attention. It felt different than with anyone else she had known.

Yes, sir, she texted her reply, still in "character" from her first training night with Edward as her Dominant and her as his very willing submissive.

Excellent, his message said in return. *I placed an envelope in your purse with an important note. I hope you will be ok with my request, Ms. Hart.*

He rarely used her last name unless he was making an important point and wanted to add a bit of significance. She quickly opened her purse to find her second ivory-colored envelope with a red wax seal embossed with the letter "G." She peeled it open, wondering what it would be this time.

Inside, she opened a card with a handwritten note from Edward, a platinum American Express card in his name, and two more of his business cards.

The note read: *Angelica, I am watching you sleep as I write this note; watching you breathe, drinking in your beauty. I want more… Today, after work, I would like you to do me the honor of shopping for two new outfits. One is to wear to a fancy Tampa event this weekend, and the second is to wear for me only—in the Red Playroom. Would you do this for me, Angelica? If so, you will find my American Express card, and if there are any questions about you using the Amex without me there, hand them my business card and ask them to please call me. One last thing… When you are shopping, please text me a photo or two of the outfits you are considering for the fancy black-tie event; I would like to help make the final choice if you don't mind. But text me photos only for the evening wear. The private outfit I will leave up to you—as I will enjoy the anticipation and then the surprise of seeing what you choose to wear and model for me. Yours, Edward*

The last two words were her favorite. Angelica beamed as she went to shower, her mind racing with anticipation. First of all, she loved that he had watched over her while she slept. That meant far more to her than his American Express card. But shopping for Edward! A first. No man had ever done this for her before. She even loved that he wanted to see photos of the dresses before she chose to gain his input. And, quite frankly, she would be relieved to have his final approval before she spent a fortune on one of those types of dresses. As she showered under the steamy jets of water, washing away all the sins of the long steamy night in his Red Playroom, she wondered about this fancy event in Tampa and envisioned what that might be like—arriving at a black-tie event and socializing on his arm. Exciting did not even begin to describe it. She was giddy with the feeling of anticipation.

Today felt like another new beginning in life at the next level. Time to get downtown and open the office. Work would be a bit of a letdown from the high she had felt all night and this morning because of how Edward made her feel. Angelica could not stop watching the clock all day, waiting for 5 p.m. so she could head out shopping as Edward had requested. She texted him to ask where he would suggest she look for the dress. He recommended Saks Fifth Avenue and told her to ask for Sandra as she was the best person to work with there. It seemed he was a regular customer, and they would take excellent care of her if she dropped his name when she arrived.

Angelica finally wrapped up her workday, which seemed to crawl by. She was simply dying to head out shopping for both of her assignments from Edward. After she went through rush hour traffic, she parked a short distance from the entrance to Saks with her energy thumping. She always loved shopping, but this time it was a different feeling. Armed for the safari with Edward's credit card, she felt both a twinge of guilt and a rush of delight about what lay just ahead in the mall.

The cool air inside Saks Fifth Avenue rushed across her skin as Angelica opened the second set of stainless-steel doors to step into the store and perhaps into a better life. So, she walked with a bit more confidence than usual, armed with his credit card. At the end of the shopping day, she wouldn't have to worry if her card limit could afford what she would be trying on. This was certainly a first for her in a store like this where dresses, bags, and shoes could sell for thousands each. A lady greeted Angelica in the dress department, and she asked for Sandra.

"One moment, let me get her for you," she said politely. Angelica waited until a few minutes later when a very well-dressed and sophisticated-looking woman, several years her senior, came walking over with a bit of a powerful-looking demeanor and said, "Good afternoon, how can I help?"

"I'm Angelica Hart. Edward Gray told me to ask for you," she said sheepishly to Sandra.

"Oh! Edward called me and told me you might be stopping by." Sandra changed instantly to a charming smile and friendly demeanor. "So, tell me, Angelica, what are we shopping for? Where will you be going?"

Angelica felt relieved. Sandra was so engaging now and gave an abundance of welcoming and friendly energy. She shared, "We're going to a special function in Tampa this weekend."

"I see. How exciting! Will it be formal or casual wear?" Sandra asked as she started walking towards the dress collections with Angelica following her lead.

"He said it's black-tie, I think," Angelica said, thinking back to the note from Edward.

"Well, you'll need an evening gown!" Sandra said with an engaging and easy smile, adding, "How fun!"

"Sandra, I'm a little nervous about it. I've never been to something this fancy with anyone like Edward before," she confided, half whispering.

"We will make sure you look amazing, and Edward will be proud to be the lucky one with you, sweetheart. All guys are the same that way. I got you covered—not to worry!" Sandra promised with the voice of experience and a friendly, comforting style that made Angelica feel like she was shopping with a good friend who "just knew" what would be the perfect thing.

Sandra led her to a VIP section with a collection of evening gowns that were equally stunning to try on in front of the triple mirrors, with price tags starting at a few thousand dollars, and that's before you get the matching shoes and elegant handbag to match.

Sandra recommended a sophisticated champagne gold—almost a rich cream color with a light sprinkling of aurora borealis crystals—for a touch of bling and sparkle, but not overdone. It was stunning on Angelica. Sandra held up some matching earrings, the perfect finishing touch in the mirror.

Next was a black sequined gown that was a good bit flashier and completely backless. Finally, the gold chain on the smallest black sequin bag you have ever seen had sexy written all over it.

"Oh, my, Sandra. I love them all, but the first two you had me try on, the champagne gold and then the black sequin one, are my favorites, but they are so expensive. I just don't feel right asking for them."

"Mr. Gray told me you might say something like that, Angelica. Not to worry, both of these are well within the budget he suggested, even with shoes and accessories. Which is your favorite?"

Angelica hesitated and bit her lower lip for just a moment to think and stress just a bit. "Edward asked me to send him a photo of the dresses before making a final decision. Let's take a photo of them hanging by the mirrors, side by side, and get him to pick. Ok?"

"Of course! That's a great idea, actually," Sandra replied enthusiastically.

The two new friends had fun posing and photographing the dresses in a few ways, showing the backless look of the black dress and the close-up detail of each. Angelica texted the best ones to Edward for his input. She included a clear photo of the price tag for each.

"Any feedback from Mr. Gray?" Sandra queried.

"Not yet," Angelica muttered softly, rechecking her phone.

"Let's look at shoes next while we wait. What size are you, dear? A seven, maybe seven and a half?" Sandra asked as they walked one section over.

"How did you know that?" Angelica asked.

"It's my job to know," Sandra said, smiling as they both chuckled, wandering into the dangerous gravitational pull of the shoe department. While they fitted Angelica with designer options for each dress from Jimmy Choo, Christian Louboutin, and Prada, her head was swimming. She had never dreamt of spending this much on shoes, but what girl wouldn't want at least one pair of designer heels in her closet for special occasions? She could feel her blood surging as she tried them on.

Sandra said, "These designers just seem to know how to accentuate a woman's feet and make your leg line look longer and more elegant, don't they?"

"Yes. I just love them!" Angelica confessed.

Her phone buzzed with a text from Gray, and the message simply said, *Get them both.* Angelica showed Sandra, and they both smiled in giddy excitement. Would you like a glass of wine," Sandra offered her, "while we wrap all these up for you?"

"Yes. Absolutely!" Angelica said with her adrenaline still pumping at the surprising text from Edward. Her head was still spinning.

Sandra gave Angelica her business card as they finished up at the register and told her, "Anytime you need something, even if it is small or you just want to browse, call or text me, and I'll make sure to be available whenever it is convenient for you to stop by."

Angelica held the thick high-quality business card for just a moment looking at it before putting it in a special pocket in her purse. No questions were asked when she presented Mr. Gray's Platinum American Express card since he had already called Sandra about the shopping spree. The charges combined were well into the five figures, and the credit card sailed through. "Would you like the receipt in your bag?" Sandra asked.

Angelica, still stunned at the total on the register, hesitated and then managed a simple, "Yes. That will be fine."

"Is there anything else I can do for you today?" Sandra asked before they parted.

"Oh, yes," Angelica responded, remembering the second part of her shopping assignment. "I need to get some lingerie. Something irresistible for this weekend. What would you suggest?"

"Oh, that's another department, but I will call my friend Elise who runs that area of Saks. She is excellent to work with and will take great care of you."

The two left the evening wear and shoe department with Angelica carrying her bags and boxes proudly like trophies from a shopping safari and headed over to meet Elise, who was more of Angelica's age.

"Elise, I have a guest who needs your assistance—a very special guest. This is Angelica Hart."

"Hello, Angelica!" flowed Elise's voice with a soft French accent.

"I will leave you in great hands, Angelica. Elise will take good care of you," Sandra said, giving her a quick one-arm hug as she left for the next customer.

Angelica turned to Elise to begin again, "So, I need some elegant lingerie. Something nice to wear for someone exceptional," she said with growing confidence now. She remembered how Edward wanted to be surprised by this part of the request, and she wanted to make sure he was pleased.

"Oh, the way you describe this to me suddenly becomes very simple: Agent Provocateur or Dolce Gabbana. Either way, you cannot go wrong," purred the French accent from Elise. "What colors are your favorite to wear?" They started examining the delicate lace and satins from some of the world's finest lingerie brands.

Elise guided her in such a friendly and helpful way after the VIP introduction from Sandra and poured options across the wooden table for her to select and then try on. Angelica did not realize that lingerie could cost thousands of dollars also—for a single piece.

She was not supposed to text Edward photos of the lingerie, but perhaps the prices? Should she get his okay before spending even more? She decided to keep the cost more moderate on the lingerie after spending so much on dresses, shoes, and accessories.

Elise was very accommodating, and it still was much more than she had ever spent on lingerie. But a couple of the pieces she thought he would absolutely love on her in the Red Playroom. With no questions about using Edward's card, Elise rang her up again, given Sandra's special introduction.

This was the next level of shopping with essentially an unlimited budget, treatment that she was unused to. She realized she was more than just a bit out of her element in his world. Walking to her car, she carried all the bags and boxes from Saks Fifth Avenue, turned a few heads in the parking lot, and filled her backseat. She put the top up on her convertible, not wanting anything to happen to her new treasures on the drive home.

She pulled out and texted Edward, "I just left the store. May I call you?"

Her phone rang almost immediately. "Hello, Edward?" she answered as she pulled out of the parking lot.

"Yes. How did it go with your shopping assignment?" Gray asked her.

"Oh my gosh, everything is so beautiful! But it was so expensive. I don't know what to say," she stammered a bit.

She heard his deep reassuring voice come soothingly through her phone, "It's okay. It is for an exceptional event, and there will be other opportunities to wear them. I will be proud to see you in them," he explained.

"Well, 'thank you' doesn't seem quite enough to say to you right now, Edward. No one has ever done this for me before. Ever." Angelica could feel the emotion in her voice rising as she spoke and was worried he would hear her tearing up.

"It is my absolute pleasure, Angelica," he assured her with gracious and kind energy in his voice. "Did you do both parts of the shopping assignment for me?"

Her energy switched to a more joyful and flirty place inside her, knowing that this part of the assignment was a bit more for his pleasure and enjoyment, and she responded enthusiastically, "Yes, I did! I think you will just love what I have to show you." She teased playfully, "When would you like me to model them for you?"

Gray's energy shifted to a more serious tone, "I like to do things one of two times—either now or right now, Ms. Hart."

"I can head there right now," Angelica said smiling, her heart beating at the thought of seeing him again.

"Excellent. Plus, I think this evening is the perfect time to continue your training if you are open to that, Kitten."

"I am open to anything with you, Edward. I trust you," she said softly, her heart filled with hope. Edward ended the call with, "Drive safely. I will be here waiting for the princess."

CHAPTER EIGHT
The Fashion Show

The drive back to Gray's oceanfront estate felt different. She wasn't sure how to feel about all the shopping and the "spoiling" he had showered on her today. Who wouldn't be happy and excited with a dream shopping spree? But Angelica felt torn between a bit of guilt about spending so much and, on the other hand, excitement for him to see her in those dresses. Would he see her as more glamorous and exciting for a man like him? She was now feeling a bit intimidated by all this and feeling that she was way out of his league.

But then, looking over in the passenger seat at the elegantly wrapped boxes holding the new sexy lingerie that Edward asked her to "surprise" him with—she smiled. She hoped he would love it as much as she did. How could he not? It was gorgeous and sexy and showed off all the feminine curves he was drawn to when they first met.

The moment of truth was about to arrive soon. Angelica texted him, *Pulling in now.*

Her red sports car, once again, glided slowly into Gray's circular driveway, loaded with trophies from the evening's shopping spree at Saks. As the front door to the palatial estate opened, so did Angelica's car door. As she gracefully stepped out of her car, her long tanned leg reached out to touch the ground, revealing her shimmering soft skin for Edward's viewing. She waved to him briefly, her smile beaming with excitement. Then she turned and bent over fully to retrieve the rest of the bags and boxes from the back seat.

Edward feasted his hungry eyes on her beautiful heart-shaped derriere. Knowing full well he would be watching her every move, she caught him enjoying the show when she turned to face him and caught him eyeing her. "I have a lot to show you, Edward," she said, looking right into his eyes as she held up the many shopping bags in both hands.

"I'm very much looking forward to seeing everything, Angelica," Edward said with intent. "Now get up these stairs and inside, young lady," he added playfully. His mind was racing with his vision for the hours that lay just ahead.

As Angelica reached his side at the front door, she could smell his delicious cologne. He always smelled so good, and it made her melt. Gray was holding a glass of red wine, wearing his casual Florida shorts, sandals, and Tommy Bahama summer shirt with a casual elegance that he pulled off with ease. She kissed his cheek softly and whispered, "How can I thank you for all that you do for me?" Her cheek and lips lingered near his ear, their skin barely touching one another.

Gray's arm encircled her waist, and he pulled her inside the entrance and pressed fully against her. "I think you may have an idea or two of the answers to your question," Gray said, smiling with a playful but definitely mischievous look on his face and added, "I think you are in big trouble, once again, this evening, Ms. Hart." He closed the large arched front door behind them and clicked the lock shut tight.

"I like that kind of trouble with you, Mr. Gray," Angelica said playfully. "Can I show you the dresses for this weekend?" she added with girlish excitement. She could hardly wait to pull everything out on the couch to show Edward the beautiful new wardrobe he had sponsored.

"Not just yet, Kitten," Edward replied. "I want the full experience. First, let me pour you a glass of your favorite white wine. And then, we will take all your new clothes to the guest suite just off the main living room. You can use that as sort of your dressing area for this evening's fashion show. Then, I want to watch you do a proper entrance in each of the new outfits."

"I love that!" Angelica blurted with excitement at getting to showcase the dresses for Edward. "I mean, yes, sir," she amended.

"Good answer," Edward said as he helped Angelica take the bags and boxes full of treasures to the guest suite, where they laid everything carefully across the bed. The guest room suite had its own connected bath and a view of the infinity pool looking out over the Gulf of Mexico, newly dark just after sunset.

In his deep sexy voice, he invited her to the wine bar and said, "Perfect. Now let's get you that wine and you can come back to get things organized in here."

Angelica told the story of her entire shopping experience including how Sandra had greeted her so warmly and treated her like such a VIP. "Thank you for calling Sandra ahead of my shopping trip today, Edward." That was very thoughtful of you, and she was so nice to me."

"Of course. And Sandra is truly knowledgeable. I knew she would help you find just the perfect thing for this weekend's special event."

"Yes. She was great! And she knew all about the event in Tampa. She said it is a fundraiser for Tampa Children's Hospital. I didn't even know that. Sandra said a lot of people from Sarasota were going. It sounds so exciting!" Angelica gushed as Edward opened a fresh bottle of Chardonnay for her. "What are you drinking this evening, Edward?"

"I was in the mood for red, so Pinot Noir for me, but I will be careful not to spill any droplets on the new evening gowns. Promise," he said and smiled. "Now, off you go to change for the first of the fashion shows. I will be waiting in the living room in my favorite chair facing the princess as she grandly enters the room."

Angelica was racing inside. Her blood was rushing with excitement to wear the most beautiful dresses she had ever owned and to walk like a model for Edward. She was actually more relieved that Edward was being so gracious and was not upset, in the least, at how much she had spent on shopping. He seemed almost as excited about seeing her try them on for him as she was.

The living room where Edward would be waiting for her was beyond grand. It was a massive room with an expansive Gulf view. It would be quite a showplace for her to model for him. Romantic music from Celine Dion began streaming throughout the smart home to set the mood while she changed.

"Now, which dress to model first—the champagne gold or the black sequin backless dress?" she said quietly to herself. Definitely the softer, more elegant champagne to begin, she decided. The black sequin backless dress looked too much like liquid sex the moment you see it. She thought, *He will never let me leave to model the other one if I wear that one first*, and laughed to herself.

She stripped down to her undies to begin the transformation from everyday Angelica to Cinderella, who was ready for the ball. The bathroom had a full-length mirror and plenty of countertop space for the earrings and shoes etc., so she made this into her makeshift dressing room. She loved the elegant earrings and the Christian Louboutin shoes that they had picked for this outfit. They were so beautiful. She thought her heart might leap out of her. She was so excited about the moment just ahead—the grand reveal for Edward's eyes only.

Angelica knew he was waiting for her, but she took one more moment to look at herself now, in full gala wear from head to toe in the mirror. She felt a wave of emotion over more than just wearing new clothes. *This was how Edward wanted to see her*, she thought. This is how Edward wanted her to see herself. It moved her in some strange way to know that he knew how this might make her feel. She wiped one, then a second tear from her eyes, shaking her head a bit to stop it.

She took a deep breath and headed to do the runway modeling show just for him.

Edward was waiting somewhat patiently in a large, oversized leather chair at the center of the living room. She saw him facing her, full on, as she opened the guest suite door. She was relieved to see his eyes widen and his smile broaden, as she revealed the elegant champagne gold gown with a plunging neckline in the front. It was the first of the two high-fashion evening selections for his eyes to take in. She took two timid steps forward and paused for his first response. "What do you think?" she asked hopefully.

"You look very beautiful. Elegant," Edward assured her. "Now, walk for me," he instructed, with his eyes locked on the curves inside the gown. Edward smiled his encouragement for Angelica. This time she moved with more confidence, encouraged by his words. She walked directly towards him, with each foot crossing over the path ever so slightly to create a more exaggerated swing and sway to the hips as she glided towards him. She moved her pathway ever so slightly to brush by his chair, tracing her fingertips up his forearm to his shoulder, then round behind him as she circled his chair to the other side.

As her fingers trailed the length of his other arm and away, she walked to the center of the living room, giving him his second magnificent view of her from behind that day. She paused dead stop to look over her shoulder as she had seen models do on television, before tossing her hair to head back to the dressing room.

"Wait, wait," Gray insisted. "I need to see more of you in this. Again please," he requested with a big smile in his voice.

She turned and looked him in the eyes and then down shyly as she said, "Yes, sir," in her most submissive voice and style. She repeated her runway walk towards Edward, but this time she moved very slowly and very softly, making each step a move towards a destination that Edward would want forever. As she approached his chair, she knelt between his open legs and placed her hands—one on each knee. Slowly, she leaned forward with her hands lightly running up Edward's trousers towards his hips.

Leaning into him with her sparkling earrings dangling forward like magical fishing lures, she reeled Edward into her feminine softness. Her lips softly brushed his cheek as she whispered into his ear, "Anything else I can do for you, Mr. Gray, while I'm down here on my knees, sir?"

She looked directly at him with a very naughty smile, and Gray responded, "Don't look at me in that tone of voice, Ms. Hart, unless… you really mean it." She could feel Edward was more than a bit aroused. His toned muscular body was tense and locked tight. He was breathing a little hard when he finally spoke slowly and deliberately, "What I want right now, is for you to give me the softest and then the deepest kiss ever, Angelica."

Still leaning over him kneeling, she whispered, "Your every wish is my command, sir," as her voice reached the deepest areas of his primal male mind.

She kissed his ear softly as she spoke, then his cheek as she made her way to his waiting lips. Softly, she traced over them with hers at first. With both of her open hands she cupped his face and pulled him fully to her. Gray let her lead with her full and soft lips until now. Then he encircled her back with both of his arms and pulled Angelica forward to lean fully on top of him. She kissed him passionately while his strong arms pulled her, pressing deep into him. Her breasts ached to burst from the elegant gown but somehow remained restrained. Gray's hands made their way to her heart-shaped ass that he had been watching since she first arrived. He simply could not resist cupping her in his strong hands any longer.

She was still kissing him, but in smaller, shorter, sweet little finishing pecks on his lips as she lifted up slightly between kisses to see his eyes. He was looking up at her beauty and her softness. Her playful sexy energy oozed from every inch of her as she smiled, saying, "Want to see what real trouble looks like, sir?"

"I can hardly wait to see you in trouble, Ms. Hart," Gray said with playful certainty in his voice. Angelica slowly slid across his lap to tease him one last time, as she gracefully rose from being on top of him. Her outfit was now slightly askew, and it was obvious that Edward was fully and completely rock-hard and erect. She smiled, looking from his hardness back directly into his eyes—smiling mischievously.

She turned and did her runway model walk back to her dressing room door, where she turned partially to look over her shoulder to see him watching her like a big cat hunting its prey, to say, "Hold that thought, sir. I will be right back," and then she was gone.

Edward groaned to himself, "What have I gotten myself into?" and then laughed out loud just a little. *Another glass of wine while she is changing might be just the right distraction to get his still-aroused manhood back to normal somewhat*, he thought as he headed to the wine bar.

Angelica was racing to get ready for her return. She didn't want her "audience" to cool off, so she hurriedly changed like you see the models do on television in a live fashion show. Shoes came flying off, but with care, and this time she stripped completely, including no bra or panties. The black sequin dress was backless, and it plunged almost to the top of her butt cleavage, so it was really designed to be worn "commando" style. *Sharon Stone would have liked wearing this in her movie Basic Instinct*, she thought as she slithered into the tight but somewhat stretchy material. It fit her like a glove but was actually super comfortable. The black Louboutin shoes with their signature red bottoms were accented with just a hint of red on the open toe—a nice touch. She just loved them the minute she first saw them. And this was the dress to match if ever there was one.

She leaned in to check her makeup and hair as she added the sparkly black earrings. Now, where was the bright red lipstick that matched? It was hiding somewhere in one of the little bags she searched for and rummaged through. She smiled with just a touch of devilish delight as she added the bright red lips to the next show for Mr. Gray. *He was in trouble*, she thought to herself.

"My turn to lead the conversation a bit," she whispered with newfound confidence looking in the full-length mirror at what was an infinitely sexier outfit than the elegant champagne gown in the first runway show.

She opened the door and posed like Jessica Rabbit with her hip arched to one side. Edward was not in his chair. He had moved to one of the two large white leather couches leaning back with both arms opened wide, laying across the back of the couch on either side. This gave Gray's full commanding wingspan, six-foot two, an impressive dominant look sitting dead center of the couch.

Angelica turned her sexy on as she walked, hips swaying confidently towards Gray. His eyes undressed her, looking down from the skin-tight black sequined dress to her hips. The skirt split on one side, showing her leg almost to her hip, making her legs look longer, and Gray looked longingly at them. But mid-room, she stopped dead center and put her hands on her hips with elbows wide, showing a pose of confidence and power. She looked at him in the eyes for one heartbeat before turning slowly to reveal the back of the dress, which plunged all the way down to the top of her canyon.

Gray's heart skipped a beat as Angelica bent over slowly. Her back arched as she reached almost 90 degrees with her torso flat level to the floor. She looked backward to wink at Edward to say, "Oh, I thought I dropped my keys." Rising slowly, she walked just past Edward, almost within reach, and circled behind the white leather couch to find the spot directly behind him. Bending forward, her long, baby-soft blonde hair flowed across Edward's neck as she leaned to whisper in his ear. "Maybe you can help me find them, sir?" she whispered in her best imitation of the very innocent Jessica Rabbit cartoon character.

She heard his deep voice respond with, "I'll help you search as long as it takes," encircling his arms around her to pull her closer to him from behind the couch. "Here, come sit next to me for a bit," he invited her.

Still, in her supermodel runway walk, Angelica slinked around the couch to take her place at his side and asked, "So, which did you like better for your big event in Tampa?" She slid closer to Gray, who was still enraptured with her private modeling show.

"You look amazing in both of them," Gray offered, "but they are very different looks."

"The lady at Saks said we can return one of them if you would like after you see them on," Angelica offered her genuine thought of cutting the cost of the shopping spree down by a good bit.

"No," Gray replied promptly. "Definitely keep them both. It is black-tie fundraiser season, and there will be lots of other opportunities. You'll need more than just these first two dresses for the season. Most women prefer not to wear the same dress twice in the same season, unless we are at an event out of town in New York, Miami, or Washington, D.C., for example, where no one will have seen you wearing it before."

"You're kidding!" she said, astonished. "Dresses this expensive and to wear them only just once. That seems crazy to me."

"Well, you did an amazing job of picking two great evening gowns to start with," he complimented her. "People will remember you in either dress, but for very different reasons," Gray said and chuckled as he looked longingly into her fire-engine-red lips.

"I'm so relieved that you like me in them and that you're happy, Edward." She confessed, "I was so worried about it the whole time I was shopping and especially on my way here."

"You did great. I am very pleased so far," Edward said, building a bit of suspense. "But it seems to me that there was a second part to the shopping homework assignment," Gray said, looking expectantly into Angelica's smiling eyes.

CHAPTER NINE

Hard Limits

As they concluded the fashion show of the black-tie evening gowns, Gray, of course, was enquiring if she had bought some sexy outfits to model for his private viewing.

Angelica beamed, excited to see Edward's response to what she had in store for him. "Yes, sir. Of course! When would you like to see me in them?" she asked, toying with him just a bit.

"I think you know the answer to that, Angelica," Gray said, looking steely as he instructed her, "Please bring the rest for private modeling to the Red Playroom. I will see you there in just a few minutes. I'm going to change clothes myself."

"I will be right there, sir," she said softly with a hint of excitement in her voice as she went off to slip out of her evening gown. She chose an exquisite black lace body suit from Dolce & Gabbana. After slipping into the very slinky and flattering lingerie, she covered it with a robe hanging in the bathroom and went to the Red Playroom door to wait.

She arrived ahead of Edward and felt uncomfortable going in without him, or at least without him giving her permission to enter his private domain. So, she waited just in the hallway outside the Playroom door.

Gray did not keep her waiting long, thankfully. He arrived in all-black yoga pants, a workout shirt, and padded workout gloves. The kind of gloves you might use to lift weights. She couldn't help admiring the shapes of his muscular arms and shoulders as he said, "Thank you for waiting for me. Let's go inside," as he unlocked the heavy door to the red room.

"Come stand in front of the dresser mirror, please," he asked Angelica, who complied. Gray settled in close behind her, looking over her shoulder in the mirror. He leaned into her ear, and she heard his deep, sexy voice say slowly, "Now it's time for you to show me what you brought for me to see in private, Kitten."

Angelica didn't know why her voice suddenly trembled a bit as she said, "Yes, sir." He had that effect on her when he leaned in close, and she could feel his masculine power. Her hands shook as she pulled the belt of the black satin robe open slowly, about to reveal the sexy black lace beneath. Only a few minutes ago, she had been so confident modeling the black sequin backless dress and feeling her feminine power. But there was something about being alone with Mr. Gray in his Red Playroom. His darker energy was palpable when he transitioned automatically as they entered his lair.

"Now, don't keep being a tease. Be a good girl and show me what I have to look forward to." The way he spoke to her could weaken her as the black satin robe fell off her shoulders and to the floor. His eyes were ablaze, looking at her shape. The outline of her naked body was shown through the black lace—the points of her breasts, the curves of her hips, and the look of those still fiery red lips. "Open the round box on the dresser, as you did last time, Angelica."

Still a bit shaky, her hands reached for the round antique box lid and lifted it open. Inside, awaiting discovery, was a collar with a series of small stainless-steel spikes every inch or so, plus a thin round loop in the center. His deep voice inquired, "Have you ever worn a collar and a leash before?"

"No, sir. Never," she whispered, still shaking.

She heard his calm voice, encouraging her forward, "I would like you to try it on for a bit to see how it looks and feels on you, Kitten. Would you do that for me?"

"Yes, sir," she replied as she reached down to take the leather collar. She held it up in front of her, looking at the gothic binder in the mirror, and saw how the buckles might work.

While she studied how the collar was designed, she heard him offer, "May I help you put it on?" as he reached around her from behind with both arms.

"Yes, please," she replied, relieved.

Gray took both ends of the collar and encircled Angelica's long, elegant neck with her first collar. He buckled it, leaving room for two fingers to fit between the collar and her neck. It was the perfect fit for safety and comfort. "Next is the leash," he explained, walking her through the ritual step-by-step.

He reached into the round box and withdrew a long silver leash with a retractable latch clip on one end and a leather loop on the other. Gray turned Angelica to face him to attach the leash to her collar. "There," he said with a look of satisfaction on his face at Angelica's completed transformation in the black lace bodysuit, now with the appropriate collar and leash for his submissive.

There was admiration for her in his voice, as he complimented her. "Take a look at how sexy and beautiful you are. And those are two very different qualities," he added. She loved pleasing him and never tired of hearing his adoration and compliments, especially considering they were coming from him.

Looking at herself in the mirror in the dim red lighting, she saw a glamorous character from a movie. Her reflection showed her transformation with her bright red lips shining as the only color next to the black lace and Edward behind her in all black as well. She looked into his eyes through the mirror—gazing back into hers.

"Remember, your two safe words are yellow and red, but I doubt you will ever need them with me," Gray reminded her.

"Yes, sir. Thank you, sir," she said gratefully. He always knew just what to do to make her feel safe. The trembling passed, and Gray added, "One more thing. Last time you wore the beautiful lace blindfold that is still here in the black bag if you like. But I ordered this new one, especially for you. It is made of black silk with very soft padding inside. Here, feel it," he said, pulling the new blindfold from its clear plastic package.

Angelica listened to Gray's voice as he told her of yet another item that he had ordered specifically for her. She loved being the center of his attention and that he was thinking of her, even when she was not there, as she reached out to take the newly arrived blindfold, saying, "Oh, it is so soft!" Angelica smiled.

"It is from Alaska, where the sun comes up and never sets for a few months, and some people who live there have a very hard time sleeping with daylight, so they wear these."

"I love it!" she said, stroking the uber-soft material.

"Would you prefer the black lace which allows you to see easily through it? Or would you feel comfortable trusting me to guide you while wearing the new black silk blindfold?" Gray asked.

Angelica thought about it before speaking and asked, hoping to follow his lead, "Which would you prefer, sir?"

"I would be fine with either choice, with a slight preference for the black silk as another small step forward in your training," Gray explained.

She shared openly, "I'm totally fine with the black silk. I trust you and feel comfortable with everything you do."

"Thank you," Gray said, appreciating her meaning as he helped her slip into the blackness of the silk blindfold. Its elastic bands adjusted to be snug but comfy, and it even had a silk cloth piece that sealed perfectly around her nose blocking out all of the light. She was completely and totally in his world.

Holding on to her shoulder, Gray gently guided her with his words and hands to first sit and then lay on the red bed, placing her in its center. He lay down near her so he could speak quietly and in the lower register of his voice.

"Are you comfortable, Kitten?" he asked.

"Yes, sir. Very," she replied smiling, "But I literally can't see a thing."

She heard his reassuring voice and edged closer to him, as he spoke to her, "Just listen to my voice. Feel my touch on your arm and shoulder as we talk for a few minutes. Okay?" Gray encouraged. "I want to talk about your hard limits. Are you familiar with that term?"

She heard his question but was not sure what he was asking. But Angelica had never been someone who felt the need to pretend to know about something when she didn't, so she simply replied, "No, sir. Not exactly. What does that mean—hard limits?"

"Well, we will talk about two kinds of limits for just a few minutes. There are some activities that I may suggest like the blindfold or the collar, that you are open to trying now and are completely OK with. Other ideas you might respond to by saying they are soft limits, which means you might be open to trying them someday, in the future, when we are further along in our relationship. And finally, hard limits are things you absolutely and positively know that you do not like or ever want to try and experiment with. Does that make sense?"

Angelica was listening closely to his voice as he described soft and hard limits. It was a bit intimidating. Just the sound of "hard limits" conjured up scary images in her mind. "Yes, I think I understand the difference. But do hard limits mean things like you wanting to hurt me?" she whispered back softly, afraid of what the answer might be.

"Thank you for the question," he encouraged her wanting to know more. "Let me answer your question with some specific examples. So, I will mention a few activities and would like you to express how you feel about exploring them with me. You may reply 'yes, no, or maybe one day' regarding how you feel about trying them. Would that be okay with you, Angelica?" he asked, seeking her consent for the very personal discussion.

"Yes, sir," she replied listening to his voice from her dark and blindfolded world.

"Excellent. I appreciate your openness to discuss limits," he encouraged her. "To begin, here are the first ten."

"The first ten!" she said, surprised. "How many are there? I can't even think of ten different things to try."

Gray gave her an affectionate and gentle squeeze as he continued. "There are a vast number of opportunities to explore," he shared gently, but you never have to do anything you do not enthusiastically choose. Here are your first ten. One–gentle spanking."

"Yes," she said instantly.

"Two–role-playing."

"Could you explain, please?" she requested.

Gray elaborated, "Role-playing may or may not involve costumes, and we assume other identities such as a schoolteacher or a boss and secretary or a nurse, etc."

"Oh. Definitely yes," she smiled.

"Three–soft bondage, such as silks scarfs around your wrists."

"Yes."

"Four–hard bondage, such as rope or handcuffs that lock."

"Maybe later," she said with hesitation.

"Five–harder spanking such as with a flog or paddle."

"Maybe, but probably no," she said. I have never tried that."

"Six–anal sex."

"No."

"Seven–gentle anal sex with small toys to help gradually ease into it."

"I don't know, maybe one day. I find the idea scary," she hesitantly offered.

"Eight–choking."

"Maybe," she said. "If you are gentle. The idea of your hand around my throat is a turn-on, but I have never tried actual choking," she said.

"Nine–sex in public places."

"I'm not sure. Can you explain a bit?"

He elaborated, "Sex in a place where we might be discovered; somewhere risky with high adrenaline and intensity."

She replied, thinking aloud, "I don't know. It sounds kind of exciting. So, maybe."

"Ten–hand signals."

"Explain, please," she asked.

"It is a common practice for a Dominant to use hand signals when training their submissive. It gives us a non-verbal way of communicating here in the Red Playroom at first, but later even when we are in public or in front of vanilla friends or family who may not understand our lifestyle."

"I like that. Yes."

Angelica was relieved when they reached number ten. Some of the items were a bit scary and "out there" but not extreme or as bad as she might have worried about, especially now that they talked about them.

"I'm very proud of you for being open to discussing all this. It wasn't needed or necessary before now, but before going any further, I wanted us to open the dialogue of communication a bit further," Gray explained. "How are you feeling now?"

"Excited. A bit turned on. A bit curious and nervous, too, I think," Angelica rattled off quickly.

His reassuring voice guided her as he said, "Lots to be excited about. Nothing to be scared or nervous about. Now just listen to my voice and take a deep breath and hold it for me." She did so—holding it, waiting for his further instruction.

He soon guided her to relaxation with, "Now release and exhale completely. Good job, Kitten! Now, repeat this once more for me." Angelica complied.

She heard his guidance on her journey deeper into his world continue with, "Excellent. Now, as you exhale, feel all of the worries of the hard limits discussion leaving your body. All the worries are gone now. You look so beautiful. And so frigging hot right now. You should see yourself blindfolded with your collar and leash on, draped in that exquisite, black lace lingerie lying on this red satin bed."

She felt her heart starting to race again, imagining the scene in her mind as she listened to Gray's description. He gently unbuttoned the front of her lingerie exposing her gorgeous breasts. She felt his mouth on her lips first, and then on her neck, and then finally on her aching, waiting breasts. He slowly licked them rhythmically while holding her gorgeous body in his strong hands. "Ahh," Angelica groaned and swiftly arched her back, as he gently sucked her round swollen nipples, but then paused to observe her thighs. "Please don't stop," Angelica begged as she pulled his lips onto her nipples. Edward smiled and bent down as he continued suckling her nipples, and he slowly ran his fingers through her thighs. Angelica was trembling like a fish who had just been pulled from the water. He slowly kissed each of her breasts just once more, before moving his kisses down her body. He took his time roaming across her stomach and finally to her thighs. His strong hands cupped and squeezed her buttocks as she opened them wider on the Red Playroom bed.

Her nipples were red and looked plumped as he rubbed them with his fingertips. He spread her legs wider and touched her delicate lips and slowly worked in between her legs. She started feeling goose bumps all over her body as he moved her hips up. As she was being stroked hard, she moaned in pleasure and felt swept away, intoxicated.

He stroked her hard as she moved seductively like a snake on the satin sheets moaning his name. Replying in his deepest voice to guide her deeper, he said, "I want you to close your eyes and think of your most unfulfilled deep desires and touch yourself gently with your favorite vibrating toy," he said, placing the powerful Magic Wand in the palm of her hand. "Stroke yourself as if you have never been touched before in your whole life," he whispered in her ears.

She groaned as she rubbed herself gently and then harder against the toy and felt as if she was trapped in a dream of ultimate seduction.

"I will show you a new world but don't forget to ask permission before you climax, Kitten. You don't want to get into trouble with Mr. Gray."

"Yes, sir," Angelica's voice trembled as she edged closer and closer to her ultimate joy.

He caressed her body with eyes full of great lust. Edward gently stroked very gently inside her with his fingertips while Angelica was trembling, holding the toy pressed outside her.

"Sir," she gasped. Unable to speak for a moment, she finally begged, "May I cum?"

"Say please!" Gray demanded.

"Please, please, sir," she urged desperately.

"Yes. You may cum just once," he said as he released her.

She screamed in intense pleasure while holding on to the steel frame headboard tightly as he pleased her body and let her shine through a whole new sensual experience full of intensity and discovery.

Angelica lay still, locked from the intensity still flowing through her. She breathed in gulps of air as her body wound down from the high-pitched waves she had felt over and over again. She was finally calming down from a heart that had raced wildly and now slowly returned to a steadier beat, but still pounding in her chest.

It was the most adventurous night yet for their newly forged bond, and it left her speechless. Gray had opened some brand-new doors yet to be explored with his hard limits conversation—some that she was about to enter. His world was taking Angelica to new levels in every part of her life, especially after so many years of unsatisfied sensual desires in her past but not anymore.

CHAPTER TEN
Cinderella's Ball

Angelica's legs stirred, rubbing against the soft silky feel of Edward's Egyptian cotton sheets in his king-sized master bed. She had spent the night with him after her adventures in the Red Playroom the night before. Far too exhausted to drive home last evening, she did not even remember falling asleep. She stretched like a big cat in the huge bed and turned her head to find Edward missing, replaced by a note on his pillow left for her.

Up early for meetings in the office. Help yourself to coffee and juice in the kitchen or anything you might need. May I pick you up at 5:30 for the drive to Tampa for our special event? Text me later when you know your schedule and availability. Smiles from Edward PS: You looked absolutely amazing last night in your "Fashion Show" and beyond words afterward...

Her face beamed reading Edward's note while lying in his bed even though she was a bit sad to have missed him before he left for the office. It was still fairly early, and the morning light was just coming up. She turned over on her side to look out at the ocean for just a few more minutes before coffee.

This was a dream life. The ocean was so beautifully peaceful. She could faintly hear the waves gently breaking with their steady rhythm every ten seconds or so. No wonder she slept so soundly and deeply here. Edward's entire world had a rhythm and power to it. Even the soundtrack playing 24/7 from the ocean itself seemed to feel just right.

Heaven, she thought as she finally got up to head for that coffee. Walking across the sweeping living room alone, she realized Edward had entrusted his entire home to her which gave her a good feeling. She felt the weight of the thermos-style stainless steel coffee pot that Edward had left full and waiting just for her. As she poured, the great aroma wafted upward, and she smiled. She loved the smell of coffee. But most of all, she loved that he had made it just for her.

She looked at the time and started gathering up all the bags and boxes from the shopping spree. Time to rush home and get ready for her half-day at the office. She had made arrangements to leave early on Friday for the special event in Tampa with her very own Mr. Gray.

After loading the car, she locked his front door behind her as she headed out. Her heart was racing as she pressed the gas pedal. Tonight, she had a date with destiny, and she could hardly wait for the fancy gala event and to see Edward again!

She needed to run home to shower and get ready as she began planning her day in her head and what she would wear to the office. No need to worry about lunch today as she would be out of the office by noon or 1 o'clock at the latest as she had arranged. It was a beautiful drive home with not a cloud in the blue skies, but she kept the car top up just to make sure none of the treasures from the shopping spree came flying out of her convertible as she sped across the bridge. Sarasota was just waking up, and a new chapter was waiting for her.

Racing to get ready for work and literally zooming through calls and projects all morning at the office, she counted the minutes until she could leave to go get her hair and nails done at Ana Molinari's salon which was her favorite place to get really made up for a special evening like tonight. The day would be fully packed to get ready for the big event. All over Tampa Bay, hundreds of others were getting ready for the big black-tie affair that evening. But for Angelica, this could be the first of many such special events in this new world if all went well for them tonight. She hoped Edward would want to invite her for more such evenings. She so wanted to look perfect for him tonight.

The closer the clock counted down to time for Cinderella to go to the ball, the more nervous and anxious she felt. The anticipation and a hundred little worries were simply killing her inside. But all that was laced with images of her and Edward together at the event as she imagined it on a movie screen in her mind, which played over and over. Most of all, she never wanted it to be over with her and Edward. The way he made her feel in and out of the bedroom was brand new, and she almost ached when she thought of him.

Her day marched on, and work was finally ready to release her to another world waiting just outside. She dashed to the spa first, and she was glad to be on time for her nail appointment because she had just enough time for all the magic that afternoon. First, she had to choose which dress to wear. Edward had left it up to her to select. If she wore the champagne gold gown, then a French manicure would be the ticket. But if she was going to wear the black sequin "maneater" backless number with the red bottom Louboutin shoes, then fire engine red nails and lipstick would be the choice.

"Your hottest red," she told the nail tech as they began with feet and toes in the swirling foot bath. Following her pedicure came the matching manicure table across the room. She loved watching the color go on with just a touch of gleam even after they dried. The color would certainly make a statement.

Next, her long blonde hair had an appointment with Samantha, the only person she trusted to touch her color. She had a terrible experience once before, and so had many of her girlfriends, with someone ruining their hair with color treatments over the years. Imagine that happening on a day like today. Oh my god, that would be the worst imaginable way to ruin the big event just hours away.

Samantha smiled as she sat down to first take a look in the mirror and asked, "So, tell me all about this big event tonight!"

Angelica smiled, radiating with excitement. "Oh my gosh, Samantha, where do I begin?" Samantha began getting Angelica ready for a bit of a color refresh, touching up her blonde highlights.

Angelica said, "I was on a dinner date last week with a blind date."

Samantha interrupted, "You met him on a blind date?"

Angelica shook her head ever so slightly while Samantha was doing her color magic. "Well, no. Not exactly. Wait until you hear what happened."

"The blind date was a bit of a horse's tail, and I knew by the time we sat down for dinner that I had no interest in dating this guy. But when he left me at the restaurant dining table to go to the restroom, it happened," Angelica said, painting the scene for her.

"What happened?" Samantha asked, now finally finished with coloring Angelica's locks.

"This very tall, dark, and handsome man gets up from the bar and walks directly over to me. Then, he has the nerve to sit down in my date's chair!"

"You're kidding me! What happened next?" Samantha said, entranced by the intrigue of the bold stranger.

"He said, looking right into my eyes and smiling, 'I want you to get rid of this guy and come back here and meet me,'" Angelica said, trying her best imitation of Gray's deep male voice.

"Oh my god!" Samantha laughed incredulously at the very forward approach.

"That's what I said!" Angelica blurted out. "But he was so charming and handsome, and he wasn't strange about it or weird. He was just looking at me with those deep blue eyes and repeated his request as my date returned."

"So, what did you do?" Samantha asked.

"I didn't do anything, my blind date did," Angelica recalled, shaking her head wearily. "He acted like a total ass blaming me for talking to other men. I didn't do anything. I was just sitting there minding my own business when Edward came over."

"So, is that who you are seeing tonight, this Edward fellow?" Samantha asked.

"Yes. Edward Gray," Angelica said nonchalantly.

"Wait. Do you mean 'the' Edward Gray?" Samantha asked. "The billionaire philanthropist from Longboat Key?"

"Well, I could tell he has some money, but I don't know anything about the billionaire part. And yes—he lives on Longboat Key," Angelica said, still in her unassuming tone.

"Honey. Edward Gray is the most eligible bachelor on the west coast of Florida," Samantha informed her. "He is quite the catch. And you have a first date with him tonight. That's so exciting!"

"Well. Actually, we have been seeing each other almost every night since we first met," Angelica confessed. "He is a very focused man."

Samantha gushed over her while finishing her color highlights. "I am so happy for you, Angelica. And I want to hear all the juicy details!" she said as they switched over to the hairstylist chair for some minor trimming.

"Oh, Samantha, I'm dying to tell you, but I can't," Angelica said, remembering her Confidentiality Agreement. "I gave my word I wouldn't."

"Oh, you can tell me anything honey, I won't say a word," Samantha encouraged.

Angelica was dying to tell someone about Edward, the Red Playroom, the Agreement, the shopping spree, the way he made her feel in and out of the bedroom, and how she loved being the center of his attention. His powerful male energy and tonight's black-tie affair were almost too much to resist.

"You promise?" Angelica asked in earnest, as though secrets told to a hairdresser are safe in any small town—especially one like Sarasota.

"Of course!" Samantha leaned in to hear the juicy gossip and details as she put the final finishing touches on Angelica's long, gorgeous hair for the black-tie event.

Angelica's first transgression of Edward's trust occurred that day, but more was to follow.

CHAPTER ELEVEN
The Black-Tie Affair

Angelica wrapped up at the salon and spa at four-thirty, and Edward would be there to pick her up in just an hour. She raced through traffic, glancing at her watch as she sped home to slip into the black backless gown and get ready. "Don't be late!" she said to herself out loud. Some habits just seem to die hard.

She was too busy getting ready to think straight, but her excitement level was growing and glowing inside of her. Her fashion show for Edward in the black dress was the proof she had hoped for that this sexy gown would have all eyes on her that evening, and she hoped Edward would be pleased with how she looked for him. This time with full makeup, hair, and nails, she was complete.

At five-thirty sharp, her doorbell rang. Edward, dressed in his black tuxedo with diamond cuff links and button studs, feasted his eyes on the new super-model-looking version of Angelica. He smiled, looking at her again in the black sequin gown, but this time with the little black purse with the gold chain dangling from her shoulder. He stood there speechless, drinking her in.

She smiled unassumingly at her handsome date, and said, "Ready?"

Edward drank in her beauty for just a moment, before speaking to state the obvious, "Gorgeous! You are absolutely gorgeous, Ms. Hart!" He offered her his right elbow to escort her to the waiting Cadillac Escalade. Gray's driver, Taylor, was waiting with the rear doors open for them. Edward, always the gentleman, helped Angelica gracefully glide into her rear passenger seat and closed the door for her. Then he walked around to his side to join his stunning date in the back seat. Gray introduced their driver, Taylor.

"Good evening, Ms. Hart," Taylor said politely.

"Nice to meet you, Taylor," she replied. And off to Tampa they went.

"Having a driver is a good idea," she said to Edward.

"Yes. I don't drink and drive ever," Gray shared. "Plus, it may be a bit late by the time we get home."

"Remind me again, where is the event this evening?"

"The Straz Center for the Performing Arts," Edward replied. "It's close to Olde Hyde Park near downtown."

"I'm so excited! I've been counting down the hours all day."

Gray looked at her once again. Her leg peeked out of the gown from the long-split skirt. The curve of her ample breasts hinted at the feminine mysteries that were hidden just beneath with every breath she took. "I should have brought more bodyguards with you in a dress like that," Gray chuckled.

"You are the only bodyguard I want, Edward," she cooed softly to him.

The ride to Tampa was smooth and flew by as they spent the hour on their best behavior in front of Gray's driver, who was able to overhear all but whispers they might share.

Arriving at the Straz was glamorous. The sun was just setting, but the spotlights out front were already shining their beacons of light upward to the coming night sky. They were part of the tribute to the vast array of local luminaries and celebrities arriving in a procession like a junior version of the academy awards.

"When we arrive at the entrance, just wait for me to open your door. Taylor would do those honors typically, but this way, he can drive away as soon as we are clear for the line of limos and vehicle drop-offs behind us," Gray said with the voice of experience.

"Of course." Her heart was pumping hard at the approach to the Straz' grand entrance as their driver pulled to a stop at the red carpet.

Gray opened her door and offered her his hand, and cameras were clicking away as the two of them made their way into their first society event entrance. Gray was calm and confident as they glided up the walkway, but Angelica's heart felt as though it might leap from her chest if it beat any faster.

Once through the grand doors of the Straz, they were instantly greeted by trays of champagne flutes in the hands of white-gloved wait staff. Classical music floated through the air from a string quartet playing live on a round stage in the corner. There were two large bars on the main level, but the gathering crowd was disbursed on the open balcony floors above.

"Perfect place for networking and socializing," Edward said with Angelica clinging to his right arm. They moved through the room with ease, each holding a champagne flute in their free hand for the occasional toast and photo opportunity.

Food began floating by as well, with a procession of gourmet goodies and delights to try in bite-size temptations. From caviar-crusted seafood to salad bites, and from short ribs to desserts, there was an endless supply of chef creations. Angelica dabbled carefully, not wanting anything to do with a sauce that might spill on the expensive gown.

As the night got underway, Edward did a fair amount of handshaking and introduced Angelica as his guest to everyone that stopped by to greet him. He seemed to know everyone, but perhaps more notably everyone seemed to know who Edward Gray was. There was to be a short program of the Straz' season highlights featured shortly.

Angelica leaned into his ear. "If you don't mind, I need to use the ladies' room before we go sit down," she whispered to Edward.

"Of course," he said. "I will meet you at… the bar?" he said after thinking about the easiest spot to find in the busy crowd.

"Yes. Perfect," she replied as she smiled and turned gently to walk to the restroom. Edward and many others watched Angelica walk, hips swaying gracefully in that backless dress that plunged down to the top of trouble. Edward shook his head, smiling slightly as he headed to the bar for a real drink.

At the bar, he ordered, "A Tanqueray Gin and Tonic—double with lime," from the bartender as he waited for Angelica to return. His drink came and went, but still no Angelica. He glanced down at his watch, and it was now time to be seated. Most of the other couples were starting to flow into the auditorium of the Straz.

He wondered if Angelica was okay. At least fifteen minutes had gone by. Although sometimes these events do have long lines for the bathroom, he reasoned with himself. An event coordinator walked through the room, striking a chime with a wooden tong to make the traditional series of tones signaling time to be seated for the show.

Still no Angelica.

He thought it would be best if he made his way to the restroom and waited just outside the entrance doors for her. As he turned the corner, he could see clearly across the large Straz lobby to the second bar. And there at the bar was Angelica talking to another man. It appeared that they were talking very intimately.

Feeling his back tighten and his blood starting to boil, he immediately began walking directly towards them from far across the Straz. He observed the other younger man reach up and gently touch Angelica's long blonde hair. And yet, she did not recoil or move away. Then the interloper leaned into her ear and whispered something, and she seemed to chuckle and then laugh out loud.

Finally, and this was the straw that "broke the camel's back," she stood still leaning on the bar as the other man put his hand on the middle of her back, exposed completely naked by the sexy black gown, and he watched in disbelief as she allowed him to slowly slide his hand down to the very lowest part of her back— dangerously close to her barely covered derriere.

He stopped about six feet from them as the awkward moment continued to unfold. "Angelica," he said in a strong voice. She turned to see the hurt and anger in his eyes.

"Edward." She looked at him in a bit of surprise. "I was. We were…" she stammered. "This is Keirlen. He plays for the Tampa Bay Buccaneers," she finally fumbled the words out.

The tall athlete at the bar didn't reach to extend a friendly handshake but rather looked at Edward as one predator to another with a half grin as he had been pawing at Gray's date in a hot black dress.

Gray glared back at the football star, known around town for his way with women and often in a bit of trouble over it. "It's time to go," he said curtly, offering his elbow to Angelica.

"Nice chatting with you," she managed quietly as she turned to leave with the one who brought her to the Straz. Angelica explained, "I'm sorry. I was just waiting at the bar as you said," sensing that Gray was angry at what he found.

"I think it's time to leave," said Gray. "I've had enough of the Straz for this evening."

"You mean we're not going to stay?" Angelica queried. "They are just about to start."

Gray texted his driver to pull up front. "Perhaps you would like to stay with your new date instead?" he said, looking at her with his mouth tight and eyes focused.

"It wasn't my fault," Angelica stammered. "I was just standing there waiting for you at the bar like you said."

Gray cut her explanation short, interjecting, "Flirting with strange men is not just standing there, Angelica. I saw what I saw walking over to you from across the entire lobby. And you weren't exactly looking for me, were you?"

She tried to minimize the damage done, adding, "Well, we started talking while I was waiting. That's all."

Gray opened the Straz doors for Angelica; this time, the smile had gone missing from both faces. The Escalade was just pulling up, and this time Taylor quickly circled around to open Angelica's door. Gray went to his door without aiding Angelica unlike earlier at home. The driver closed her door in Gray's absence and then climbed into a silent SUV to chauffeur the now estranged couple home on what would become a long ride back to Sarasota.

Gray did not offer any explanation to his driver for the early departure. The two simply sat in the back in silence. Angelica's mind was racing. Her heart was in her throat.

She wanted to plead her case further, but she found Gray's intense energy intimidating when he was angry. She had never seen this side of him before.

They were halfway home when she finally summoned the courage to ask, "May I speak?"

Gray shook his head slightly and replied, "Best not to talk right now."

Angelica bowed her head submissively and continued squeezing her hands together, rubbing thumbs back and forth against each other. She knew Gray had assumed the worst when he walked up. She wasn't sure how long he had been standing there. What had he seen and heard? She didn't know what to do or what to say. She was not used to socializing with famous and celebrity people, and when the NFL star talked to her, she didn't mean to do anything wrong. But Gray had walked up, right as the guy put his hand on her back, and she knew it probably looked way worse than it was in her mind.

Oh crap! she thought to herself. *There has got to be a way to fix this.*

The driver backed the Escalade into Angelica's driveway as he had earlier that evening when they picked her up. Gray told his driver, "I will get Ms. Hart's door for her." The driver nodded the unspoken instruction for him to simply wait in the vehicle.

Gray opened her door but did not extend a helping hand for her to exit the big SUV. She stepped down carefully in her new designer shoes. He extended his elbow to take her to her door. The first piece of civility since they left the Straz.

"Can we talk, Edward?" Angelica asked with a pleading tone in her soft voice. "Please?"

Gray responded with a resoluteness that left little room for interpretation, "No. Not tonight." He added firmly, "Let's talk in a couple of days. I need to cool down first … or…" He paused. There was a moment of dead silence.

"Or?" Angelica said, seeking more explanation.

"Or, I might say some unfortunate things that can't be unsaid," Gray explained. "Good night, Angelica."

Her hands were shaking as she fumbled to unlock her front door as Gray returned to the waiting SUV. She looked out the now-open doorway and watched the taillights of the black Escalade rolling away. He was gone.

CHAPTER TWELVE

Pleading Her Case

Angelica was stunned and now left alone moments after Edward had left her in his silent rage. She closed her front door and looked around her house. All was completely quiet, except for the first few sounds of her sobbing then deep, hysterical crying as she said aloud, "How could this have happened?" All the way home from Tampa, her mind had been racing thinking about what to say to fix this. But Gray had given her the silent treatment all the way home. She would have preferred it if he had hollered and raged at her—anything but silence.

She wept on the couch for several minutes as she felt her energy draining out of her. And then a new steely resolve began forming. She was not going to lose Edward over a misunderstanding. Letting him cool off for a couple of days could surely spell a full and final goodbye, she imagined.

I should drive there now and make him hear me out, her mind raced in desperation. She quickly changed clothes from the sexy black dress, putting everything neatly back in the hanger bags, and gathered all the elegant eveningwear, shoe bags, and boxes to return to Gray. Loaded with all the gorgeous designer wear, she grabbed her keys from the bowl by the front door and raced to her car, forgetting to lock up behind her. She would show him that she didn't want his money. In an act of selflessness—she would give it all back to him just for one moment for him to hear her out. Her mind was racing a hundred miles per hour, thinking precisely what she should say. She had already rehearsed this a dozen times on the ride home from Tampa but never had the chance to speak.

It's now or never. She clenched the steering wheel as she pressed on the gas in her sports car. The miles to Gray's home clicked behind her as she raced to recapture her place with Edward. She ached inside. She had not realized how much she cared about him and how devastating it would feel to lose him—not his money or station, but Edward, the man.

Racing faster to Longboat Key, she said aloud, "I will make him see how I really feel." She was determined to do whatever it would take to get him back. It was just that simple.

Angelica slowed down for the long ride out on Gulf of Mexico Drive as the local police were known for freely handing out speeding tickets for any amount over the limit. It was all she could do to drive this slowly, feeling her heart pounding. Her blood pumped hard as she finally pulled into Edward's circular driveway.

The house was dark except for the outside floodlights. And there was no sign of the SUV in the circular drive. She had been watching for it on the only road out to Longboat Key to see if Taylor, his driver, was on his way back from dropping off Edward. Perhaps he was inside with all the lights off? Unlikely, she thought, but it was worth it to give the doorbell a try.

She opened her car door and got out of her convertible, gathering up all the shopping bags and boxes to present to Edward. *Seeing her there returning all his generous gifts would be a surprise statement*, she thought. She rang the bell and waited.

No answer. Oh no. What if Edward had his driver take him out for a drink or two? Crap, she had not thought of that until now. She rang the doorbell again. And then a third time. *Surely, Edward would not have returned to the black-tie event in Tampa solo without her? Or would he?* Her resolve returned, and she would wait for him no matter how long it took.

Her resolve would be tested for almost two hours.

Gray's driver pulled into his circular drive just before midnight, carefully pulling in behind her red sports car. The entire front of Gray's oceanfront estate was awash with the bright headlights of the SUV which revealed a crumpled figure sitting on the ground leaning back against his front door, surrounded by a pile of shopping bags and boxes.

"Good night, Taylor," Gray's voice came trailing through the night air. Then, slowly, and carefully, the SUV backed out of the drive and pulled away as Edward walked slowly and deliberately toward her.

"I waited for you," Angelica's voice cracked.

"Yes. I can see that," he acknowledged without emotion.

"I just want you to hear me out," she cried. "Can't you at least do that for me, Edward?" she begged him adding one more, "Please?"

"Not tonight. I've had a few drinks," he stated calmly. "And, as I said earlier, let's talk in a few days," Gray reminded her.

"I brought you all the dresses and shoes back to you to return. I don't want them without you. It's not your money that I care about, Edward. I'm scared. I'm scared of everything. Scared of going to your black-tie event tonight. Scared of talking to those rich and famous people. Scared of needing to fit in. But most of all, I'm scared of leaving here and never having this feeling again the rest of my whole life—the way I feel when I'm with you."

She gulped for air—then exhaled deeply as the tears rolled down her cheek. Edward looked into her eyes as she looked up at him, still sitting on the ground in the pile of bags and boxes she brought to return to him as a sign, as an offering seeking grace.

Gray spoke calmly and firmly. "I saw what I saw with you and the ballplayer at the bar, Angelica. You let him put his hands on you, first on your hair and then all the way down your back," he described with emphasis. "You seemed to be leaning into his advances and never pulled away. You certainly were not looking around the room for the date who brought you."

"Just let me come inside and talk, Edward," Angelica pleaded, still seated on the ground blocking his front door.

Gray turned from her and headed to the garage doors a few steps away, and she heard the words, "Not tonight." Then, as Edward entered the side door by the garage, she listened to the click of the door locking behind him, and he was gone, once again.

Feeling defeated and rejected as she sat there, she rose to her feet, rang the doorbell, and knocked. Repeatedly. She called his name out loud through the door. "Edward, please," she cried out. "I just want to talk," she pleaded with the door. She continued over and over for more than a half hour with the occasional knock and doorbell, but to no avail. She surrendered to the iron will of the man she so wanted to win back.

She cried most of the way home but finally had nothing left. Exhausted, she climbed into bed and would not remember falling asleep, which she did—exhausted from the day.

CHAPTER THIRTEEN
This Ends Now

Gray woke early, which was his habit, even after getting home late. Before making his morning coffee, he could not resist looking out the curtains of his large front windows to see if Angelica's car was still there. Relief flowed through him to see it was gone. He opened the front door and was surprised to see all the Saks Fifth Avenue shopping bags and boxes sitting neatly on the ground just outside his door where Angelica had been sitting the night before. She had left them all behind.

Edward gathered the elegant bundles and brought them inside to a waiting white couch that welcomed them. Gray needed his coffee. He had drunk cognac at a downtown bar before coming home, which always made him sleep hard. As he drank in the smell of the coffee brewing, he replayed the scene at the black-tie gala, the ride home, and then the late-night pleading from Angelica.

He hated drama. Even worse, he hated letting his walls down and being vulnerable. Last night was a fresh reminder of what it could do to him if he allowed someone like Angelica completely inside the safe and sacred walls he had learned to build for himself. Everyone knows love can hurt, but Gray was excellent at building walls to keep people out or at least at a safe distance.

But he just couldn't leave her alone. Angelica was already on his mind as he took his coffee outside to think. "Why can't I just forget her already?" he criticized himself, even as he thought of calling her to wake her up and talk. Instead, Gray paced the length of the pool with his morning coffee. He wasn't done yet, and against his better judgment, he simply could not wait for a couple of days to pass for him to cool down.

Angelica woke from a deep sleep to her phone ringing. *What time is it?* she thought to herself. She looked at the clock, and it was only half past five in the morning. *Damn. Who would be calling at this hour?* Then she saw the screen on her phone, and her eyes popped open wide. *It's him!* she thought as she picked up her phone, just missing the call from Edward. She instantly hit redial and called him back immediately.

"Well, that was a quick return call," Gray said condescendingly. He was clearly still in his defensive posture mode from the night prior. Angelica apologized in her still sleepy early morning voice and said, "Sorry I missed your call. I was still asleep and didn't get to it in time."

"If you still want to talk, I have decided to meet and listen, provided you agree to my terms," Gray told her in a matter-of-fact tone.

She replied hopefully, "I really appreciate it. That's all I really wanted."

He added, "I still think waiting a couple of days would be in both of our best interests, but if you want to talk today, we can meet for breakfast or lunch."

Angelica encouraged him more warmly as she woke to this good news and said, "Could we just talk at your place? I don't mind the drive."

He flatly replied, "No. As I said—my terms and conditions." Gray reminded her, "I don't want any drama like last night with you ringing my doorbell and knocking on the door until late. That was not appropriate, nor is it invited to happen again."

"I'm sorry. I just really needed to talk to you and for you to hear me."

Gray said, "Well. I will hear you out, but someplace public where you won't cause another scene. Let's meet at the Ritz Carlton for brunch downtown."

"Alright. What time do you want me there? Or are you picking me up?"

Gray wrapped up the early morning call in his calm, business-like tone and said, "See you there at 11 o'clock for brunch, Ms. Hart."

She started to say goodbye and was really looking forward to seeing him and talking, but he was already gone. While she didn't get the warmth and fuzzies from Edward that she was yearning for, at least he would see her and talk. She had a chance!

Angelica rolled onto her stomach, pulled the pillow back over her head like she had done when she was little and wanted to sleep in on a Saturday morning. But she couldn't go back to sleep. Her heart was pumping faster with the anticipation of seeing Edward, and she had no choice but to get out of bed for coffee and start picking what to wear to brunch. It was hours away still, but her mind was racing.

Gray arrived early at the Ritz Carlton for their brunch reservation at the Jack Dusty restaurant. The view inside and out on

159

the terrace looked over the intercoastal waterway and was always easy to enjoy with their unrivaled service. The valet greeted him by name as a faithful regular, "Good morning, Mr. Gray. Great to see you again, sir."

"Thank you, Mathew," Gray replied. He knew most of the valets and bartenders by first name at his favorite places, this being one of the most notable. "I'm expecting a guest, a special guest in a red Nissan Z convertible sports car in about an hour. I need your help with some special arrangements after the valet parks her car. Can I count on your discretion?" Gray looked directly at the valet for his level of attention.

"Yes, sir. You can count on me and the team to arrange whatever you might need, sir."

"Excellent," Gray replied, continuing with Mathew for a few more minutes of instructions.

Across town, Angelica was just finishing getting ready, checking her makeup in the mirror. She was excited to be meeting Edward at the Ritz Carlton. She had only ever been there once before. She thought to herself, *An exquisite place for a kiss and make-up date.* Otherwise, he could have just picked anywhere for a place to talk. She finished getting ready and grabbed her keys to head out the door.

Gray had finished making all his arrangements at the Ritz and was waiting in the marble lobby of the hotel when Angelica pulled up. He could easily see her bright red sports car approaching the valet. "Good morning, Ms. Hart. Welcome back to the Ritz Carlton," the valet said, warmly greeting her.

"Oh, my goodness. How could you have remembered my name? It's been such a long time since I was here last." She smiled at the valet, Mathew, who had his special instructions.

"It's important to us to remember our special guests, Ms. Hart." Mathew added, "Enjoy your brunch," which was the dead giveaway that the valet had been instructed to greet her by Mr. Gray. She liked that Edward had spoken to them about her even more than the idea that the valet might have remembered her somehow.

A uniformed doorman opened the large wooden door to the Ritz Carlton lobby, and about 20 paces away from her, Edward stood feet shoulder width apart with his arms crossed. If he didn't look so damn handsome, he could be the head of security the way he was standing which was a bit intimidating to Angelica.

Gray watched her glide gracefully and smoothly across the lobby floor directly to him. Her blue eyes looked straight into his for a few steps, with Angelica smiling into his stone-cold face. Then, her eyes looked downward more submissively to the floor in front of her as she walked the last few paces to stand in front of him. Finally, she gazed up at his eyes again seeking any sign of softening or hope.

Gray reached out his hand to take hers, a bit less formally than offering her his arm to hang onto, which she always liked. But feeling his big, warm, and inviting hand also felt good on many levels. She was glad to have his touch and breathed easier as he guided her into Jack Dusty.

"Mr. Gray, your table is ready. Right, this way please," said the restaurant host, greeting them. And, without a word from Gray, they were whisked away outside to a table on the terrace with a view of the water. Their table had been specially arranged to be a bit secluded from the rest of the other tables for privacy. The only other table in this section had a small white "RESERVED" sign. One that would never be used as it would turn out, at Edward's special request.

Always the gentleman, Gray pulled out the chair for Angelica with the best view of the water. The waitress approached and introduced herself and took their drink order for mimosas. And finally, they were alone.

Edward leaned forward, "To begin, a couple of ground rules. First, when one of us speaks, the other will listen however long it takes without interruption. This is a sign of respect and the only good way to be heard and understood. Is that fair?"

"Yes. I like that," Angelica replied.

"Excellent," Edward said, relaxing back into his chair. "Since you were wanting to talk late last night so eagerly, would you like to begin?"

"Yes." Angelica started by saying, "First, thank you for meeting me in person, not just over the phone. And thanks for inviting me to the Ritz Carlton. This is a lovely place for us to talk over brunch. I really appreciate all that you do, Edward. I want you to know—I do not take it for granted," she added earnestly.

Gray nodded but did not speak as agreed upon. However, the waitress briefly dropped off their first of several mimosas and parted with a happy "Cheers!" which seemed like a good idea, so the two clinked glasses before Angelica resumed. "As I wanted to share with you last night, Edward, at the big gala in Tampa, when I came out of the restroom, which seemed to take forever because the line was so long, I didn't know which way to go because it was my first time at the Straz. So, I asked one of the ladies in line for the restroom which way the bar was. Two of them pointed simultaneously to the bar where you found me. I didn't know there was more than one of them." Angelica paused to take another sip of her mimosa.

"So, when I got to the bar and asked for another glass of champagne, I had only been there a minute when that fellow Keirlen came up and introduced himself. He then said that he saw I had arrived with Edward Gray, so I thought you two were friends, or at least he knew who you were. He said he thought I was beautiful and that 'Mr. Gray was a very lucky man.' When he said that last part, he reached over and touched my hair just a bit. So, we only talked for two minutes, and all but the last few seconds, I simply thought the ballplayer was someone who knew you. Finally, he said something very inappropriate, and I didn't know how to react, so I was caught very much off-guard and just froze."

Gray was beside himself, wanting to interrupt, but he had set the rules, so he leaned forward and raised his hand like in a classroom.

"Yes?" Angelica said, smiling at Gray's polite hand raised to speak as though she was the teacher calling on him.

"What did he say at the end that was inappropriate?" Gray asked intently as he moved closer to her, on edge.

"I would rather not say," she stammered a bit. "I don't want you to be mad at me or have your feelings hurt anymore."

"Angelica," Gray said with intensity allowing no further answer evasion.

"Ok, but don't shoot the messenger."

Angelica gulped her mimosa and continued, "After he said Mr. Gray is a very lucky man, he leaned over and put his hand on my back and said, 'If you ever get tired of dating a guy in a business suit and want a real man—anytime you want—just say the word.' And that's when his hand started down my back. I half considered throwing my champagne in his face when you rescued me. Instead, I heard your voice say, 'Angelica,' and I was relieved you found me," she said finally, getting it all out in the open.

Gray was leaning back in his chair, shaking his head in disgust, not at Angelica now, but at the situation and the gall of the ballplayer to speak to Angelica that way. Still, Gray remained silent.

"I have more to say to you later on, Edward, but I would like to pause for a bit and answer any questions you might have for me openly and honestly," she offered in a kind and sincere voice. "I have nothing to hide from you about last night or anytime."

Gray thought before speaking, still processing the scene from the night before.

"So, was that your entire conversation with the ballplayer?" Gray asked, looking directly at Angelica to read her eyes and body language, which he was skilled at.

"Yes, sir. That was everything, one hundred percent," she replied without hesitation, looking directly back into Edward's blue eyes.

Gray nodded, accepting her reply. "You should know that it looked terrible from the outside as I walked across the lobby at the event last night. You seemed to be gravitating towards the ballplayer. At least that is what the body language looked like to me."

"But it was so loud there I was just trying to hear what he was saying at first," Angelica blurted out in defense.

Gray held up his hand to stop her from interrupting and said, "It's not your turn." She nodded and leaned back in her chair to listen again.

"As I was saying, it looked different from behind you with you moving closer to the ballplayer. Then as I was still walking to get to you and he touched your long blonde hair, to my eye, you did nothing to resist or pull away."

Angelica wanted to tell him that that was when the ballplayer said that Mr. Gray was a very lucky man, which she took as a compliment but not weird or inappropriate, but she kept it to herself.

Gray continued, "But by the time I got close enough to the two of you for you to hear my voice, I saw him put his hand on the middle of your backless dress and start to slide his hand down towards your ass. All the while, you did nothing which would likely be interpreted by most men as 'silence means consent.' Can you understand how that might look to me?" Gray paused, looking at her with his intensity reaching a peak again.

Angelica paused thoughtfully. "Actually, I cannot imagine how it must have felt for you, but I can imagine how I would have felt if I were you. Just based on what you saw, I would have been hurt. I would have felt betrayed. I would have felt unappreciated for all you have done. I would have felt undone," she rattled off, thinking about it from his point of view. "But know this, Edward, I would never do anything to betray you, not in my words and certainly not in my actions." She teared up as the words flowed across her lips. "You have treated me better than anyone ever has."

Gray further interviewed Angelica. "Now that you understand a bit of what that felt like, if you had to do it over again, what could you have done right then and there to clear the air between us?" he asked, still looking into her eyes for clues.

She thought about it momentarily and said, "I should have done one of two things last night—right when you walked up." Gray leaned in, listening to her revelation. "I should have said out loud, with him hearing every word of me telling you, as my man and my date for the evening, every single thing that had happened in those two minutes before you walked up. Or, I should have walked to you privately and whispered the same thing in your ear with him still standing before us."

"And what would that have done for me?" Gray asked her.

"Honestly, it probably would have pissed you off and caused a scene which I would have hated," she said, thinking aloud as she went. "But at least you would have known the truth," she replied.

"And what would that have done for us, as a couple?" he asked.

Angelica paused to think. No man had ever asked her questions like these before, but the answers were coming to her now and she added, "It would have made us closer. It would have demonstrated my loyalty to you and alienated the asshole ballplayer." She realized as she said the words what that could have meant. Her eyes welled up again, and she began sobbing uncontrollably. Edward reached over to place his hand on her shoulder. Angelica said through her sobbing, "You don't understand, Edward, what my life was like growing up." She said short bursts of words between gulps of air and sobs. "When I was little, my mom would get a belt if anyone broke a glass or left something out of the refrigerator on the counter where it would spoil. And she would ask my two sisters and me, 'Who did this?' And if it was your fault, you were the one that got beaten." Angelica was still fighting to get her words out in short bursts between sobs that arose whenever she thought of her childhood abuse with the belt. Her body shook a bit as she tried and gulped to inhale.

"So last night, when you called my name," Angelica managed, "and I turned around and saw how angry you were, I froze inside. I felt scared of you and didn't want you to think it was my fault." She sighed finally.

"I can see that now. I think prior trauma can do that to anyone, Angelica. Everyone links up or anchors certain things as their triggers. Then, when something happens, our brain just takes over, and we tend to react like when the trauma happened in the first place, especially if it was when you were little," Edward spoke with empathy and greater acceptance now.

"But Angelica, if I have you in my life that means being with me in public and private. In that case, I need to know that if someone ever approaches you, touches you, or even just says inappropriate things to you, that you will, at the very least, immediately communicate everything that is happening to me to protect you. The role and responsibility of a real man is that of a protector. But I cannot be that man in your life if you do not trust me and to trust our bond so completely that you know to bring me the facts unfiltered. If you are silent and hope it just goes away on its own, that's where real problems begin," Gray lectured her in a friendly, fair, but firm voice. "Do you understand, Angelica?"

"Yes, sir," she replied, looking down at her hands submissively. She felt relieved to hear his words. She loved it when Edward said, "If I am going to have you in my life. If you are going to be with me..." Joy was filling her heart again but still with angst. "What should I do exactly?" she asked, seeking more of his guidance. His ownership of her and her world was what she sincerely wanted from Edward and to feel safe in his world again.

"First of all, if you are mine, and any man lays a hand on you or speaks to you inappropriately, he will have to deal with me. And if you are mine, then I will burn the world down to keep you safe," Gray said, jaw clenched, looking into her eyes with fierce intensity. When he was in his fierce mode, he was scary and intimidating, to be sure. "But if it looks like you are the initiator and flirting with another man, the problem now is between you and me. And that's what I thought I saw last night."

"It is not as simple as a discussion here over brunch," Gray added. To overcome years of trauma and conditioning, the anchors and triggers embedded in you from childhood will require some deep work to reprogram how you think and feel in any situation. I can teach you, but you will have to give yourself over to me on a much deeper level than just sexually, Angelica." Edward proposed, "I'm talking about total mind, body, and soul commitment."

"I would do anything for you, Edward," she replied without a moment's hesitation. "Anything you ask."

"Let's get some brunch now. But afterward, we will be putting that to the test, Angelica." As he spoke those last words, she could see the gears of his mind still working.

CHAPTER FOURTEEN
The Training Begins

Brunch on the veranda at the Ritz Carlton Sarasota was beautiful. The view over the water was spectacular. But most of all, Angelica felt an overwhelming feeling of renewed hope. She loved how Edward had finally listened to her side of the story from last evening. From total sadness and despair to now being back at his side caused a bit of lingering heartache inside. The feeling of having your entire world whipsawed can drain anyone, especially when layered with a few rounds of mimosas.

Edward looked at her intently and said, "I have something to pick up from the front desk. Wait for me here, and I will be right back." As he rose from his chair, he momentarily placed his hand on hers. His fingers lightly traced her forearm as he stepped away from their table.

Angelica nodded and murmured, "Yes, sir," as he passed by her, and then she was left alone on the veranda.

She thought about their conversation at brunch and how she felt heard but most of all, how safe she felt when she was with him and liked being at the center of his very powerful and laser-focused attention. She daydreamed about his eyes gazing into hers and how he wanted to be her protector. But seeds of worry crept into her mind as she sat there basking in the Florida morning sunshine. *What did he mean by 'we will put that to the test after brunch?'*

Gray returned shortly, carrying what would become the answers in his hands. "I signed the brunch check to our room, Ms. Hart. Follow me, please," he requested.

"We have a room?"

"We do now," he said, holding up the Ritz Carlton card key folio. In his other hand, he carried a large gym bag, the kind with two loop handles with black leather trim. He pressed the lobby button to call the elevator from the gold and bronze-colored marble wall. The elevators were very shiny stainless steel which acted like a mirror reflecting Angelica's radiant face and long cascading blonde hair. Gray's eyes traveled down her tanned sexy body, looking into the imperfect reflection in the shiny elevator door until it opened.

Gray gestured for Angelica to step inside first, and then he turned to swipe a black card that read "Club Level" as they started up to the 8th floor alone in the elevator car. Gray momentarily dropped the gym bag to turn and face her. She breathed hard as she felt his power pressing into her. Her back was pinned against the elevator wall as he crushed his mouth angrily into hers, then once more but softly as he said, "Just remember, Angelica. You never have to do anything you do not choose."

She breathed heavily as the elevator doors opened and whispered, "Yes, sir." Angelica could see behind Edward that an older, conservatively dressed couple was waiting for them to exit so they could enter the elevator car. Angelica cleared her throat politely and smiled at Edward, "hinting" that they might have an audience.

Gray smiled back at her but lingered just another moment, gazing intently into her eyes as she was still pressed against the elevator wall. Then, slowly he turned and scooped up the black gym bag in one hand and Angelica's hand in the other.

Angelica heard Gray's booming and friendly voice greet them as he said, "Top of the morning to you." The somewhat uncomfortable couple looked away in silence watching this unfold. The wife of the older couple seemed to smile just a bit, either finding some humor or simply remembering their younger days when passion overruled everything else around them.

Edward led Angelica as they turned to their right out of the elevator into the hotel's Private Club. There were couches and tables all along the 100-foot-wide expanse of floor-to-ceiling glass and sliding doors that opened to a grand water-view balcony. On display were delicious foods of all types, including an assortment of irresistible small desserts. The private bar was in the back, but the staff would bring you anything you desired. Gray picked up two champagne flutes and poured them each another glass to take to their room.

"Which way to suite 814?" Gray asked the uniformed concierge at her desk by the entrance. "Right this way," the concierge said as she rose to her feet with a smile and guided Edward and Angelica to a private, almost secret entrance at the back of the Club Level. When she opened the door for them, it revealed the Club Level hallway and suite 814 immediately connected to the club. Their suite was somewhat separated from all the other rooms on the Club Level.

"How convenient!" Angelica said, smiling broadly at their private access to the club.

"I asked for the best suite for privacy," Gray confessed, "and it looks like they gave us the perfect one. Thank you for showing us the way."

"My absolute pleasure," said the concierge, who discreetly bowed out of the conversation.

Gray's card key opened 814, and as they entered Angelica could see the beautifully appointed room and light marble bath with its glass walk-in shower. Their view and balcony were completely private and separated from the rest of the 8th floor. A giant king-size bed awaited them with a padded upholstered headboard. Angelica smiled as she looked around her, surrounded by elegance, and said, "I just love our room!" then added softly out of curiosity, "But why didn't we just go to the Red Playroom at your home?" Not that she minded him taking her up the elevator to a romantic suite at the Ritz.

Edward placed his hands firmly but gently on both of her shoulders to fully capture her gaze with his, as he spoke to her deeply, "The last time you were at my home, late last night, was not a great memory for either of us," he said thoughtfully, "and that energy would still be a bit of a cloud over us if we were pulling in my driveway right now. I believe this might be the best place for us to start a fresh new beginning."

Angelica thought about the wisdom of his words and envisioned the twinge of awkwardness that would likely loom over them both if they were pulling into his home just now. She nodded and said, "I can see that. Of course, you are right Edward, and thank you for all of this." Then she gushed, "And it is so beautiful!" She walked across the suite and looked out the window at the spectacular bay view.

Gray laid the large black gym bag on the bed, and she heard zippers opening it wide. From inside, he produced a black Japanese silk robe. He held up the hanger and gave it one light shake so the robe unfurled softly. Then, turning to her, he made his first request.

"Ms. Hart, I would like you to step into the bathroom and change into this for me."

Angelica looked back into his powerful gaze, now focused intently on her as she stood framed by the huge bay view window. She cleared her throat slightly and looked downward demurely and replied in her softest voice, "Yes, sir." She took the robe from his hand with only the slightest of glances upward into his firm gaze and smiled softly at her Dominant, before vanishing momentarily into the bathroom. As the door closed behind her, she felt her heart racing with anticipation of what might lie just ahead with Edward. She remembered his rage and pent-up anger from the night before. Would he vent all that fury on her? After all, she had been innocent and hoped he believed that. She took a deep breath and began slipping out of her shoes.

The bathroom was elegant, with a clean, minimalist design. It made you feel like an elevated experience just walking into this world. Her heart was pumping with excitement. She loved that Gray had thought to bring her robe with him—just in case he wanted her again.

She opened the bathroom doors to return to him wearing nothing but her black silk robe and her wide-eyed look of innocence at her discovery. On the bed was an assortment of whips, paddles, floggers, and restraints of various types. Gray had "raided" his Playroom and packed an away bag for the day for them. So apparently, he had planned ahead that morning, before hearing her explanation of how the events had unfolded at the ill-fated black-tie affair. She hoped that his faith in her was restored, but swallowed hard, unsure of what was in store for her.

Gray was putting on a pair of padded leather gloves, the kind that weight lifters use that have the fingers left completely open but the palm and back of the hand wrapped in black leather with a sturdy wrist strap. He spoke to her without eye contact as he tightened the wrist straps on his black leather weight-lifting gloves. "Today, we will begin your more advanced training, Angelica."

She could feel something tightening in the pit of her stomach. She swallowed hard and asked, "What does that mean exactly?"

Gray paused, smiled slightly, and replied, "Bondage and impact play. Remember your two safe words, 'yellow' and 'red.' You are in control at all times. However, if you say 'red,' then your training is over and you are free to leave and go home," Gray said with a direct and final tone that could mean many things.

She asked, eyes wide and unblinkingly, "Well, may I ask a question? If I say 'red,' would that mean the end of us?"

His deep and commanding voice said, without pause, "That would just depend on how committed I feel you are to your training and how far you are willing to go to show your devotion and dedication to me and our partnership, Angelica." Gray answered in his sure manner, adding, "You did say you would do anything at all for this to work. Yes?" He turned to look into her eyes for her reply.

She said timidly, "Yes, sir. I would."

"Well, you can tell me, but I would much prefer that you show me," Gray concluded as he walked around the bed and picked up a pair of black Velcro wrist restraints. They are similar in function to handcuffs but with no key required. Instead, they connect to one another, as a restraint, with a simple stainless-steel turnbuckle.

"Will you wear these for me?" he asked, always seeking consent for bondage play.

She heard her words start to flow out of her a bit more naturally now and said, "Yes, sir." She felt herself begin the mental journey of letting go. Breathing deeply and slowly, she let her energy settle, by choice, into her session with Edward as he applied one of the Velcro restraints to her wrists.

She heard his deep and compelling voice guide her forward with his next request, "Turn around, Angelica, with your back to me." Without words, she obediently complied, adding her required acceptance after her back was to him by whispering softly, "Yes, sir."

She felt him leaning into her ear to speak in his deepest register, which always made her shake and tremble, and then heard, "Now, place your hands behind your back for me."

Taking a deep breath as she prepared to be fully bound by him, she clasped her hands behind her back as she shakily spoke her devotion, "Yes, sir."

Angelica felt Edward's hand masterfully connecting her two wrist restraints, so she had both hands bound behind her back. Feeling vulnerable, she took a deep breath again and relaxed into his voice as instructed. Placing a pillow on the floor at the foot of the bed, he instructed her forward and said, "Next, kneel down on the pillow and then bend forward over the bed, so that you are face down for me."

Angelica replied, "Yes, sir. But I need your help to kneel." She felt his strong, gloved hands holding her shoulders firmly for balance, making it less awkward to kneel and bend over without the use of her hands. With his help, she ended up kneeling softly on the pillow and then found herself head down with her gorgeous heart-shaped derriere fully exposed to Edward to do as he pleased.

From her peripheral vision, which Edward had allowed her to keep with no blindfold thus far, she saw that he selected the black suede leather flogger from the display of toys and instruments on the bed.

Angelica heard his steady voice guiding her further on her journey as he said, "In this next level of your training, I will introduce you to impact play. You may discover that it is much more pleasurable than it appears to the outside viewer. It may look simply like punishment or pain. But actually, it can be very sensual and erotic." He continued, "I intend to replace the anchors and triggers you have in your mind with a new set of connections."

Angelica's blood was pumping hard. Her fear level was rising to hear his words about her abusive childhood. The trauma had been so unbearable she had left home at age seventeen. *That will not be as easy to replace as Gray might think*, ran through her mind.

She felt Gray's leather-gloved hands lifting her silk robe, exposing her naked derriere. She had chosen to wear no undergarments under her robe for him in case he wanted her open and accessible to him. Gray laid the length of the black robe well onto her back, covering her cuffed wrists, now bound tightly behind her back.

But what happened next was different than what she had feared most. She felt the lightest touch of the flogger with its many long strands of suede leather strips ever so lightly tracing patterns across her baby-soft skin. Down the back of her thighs, he lightly stroked her and then back up to her heart-shaped derriere. "You look beautiful," Gray assured her. "You should see how gorgeous you look at this moment."

She gushed upon hearing Edward's praise. How she longed for it and had worried she would never hear it again. "Thank you, sir," she said, turning her head ever so slightly to speak.

"Next, you will feel light steady strokes across your buttocks. You may find the sensation remarkably pleasant with zero pain at all," he encouraged as he began circular motions with the flogger that rotated like a windmill above Angelica's derriere. It turns out he was right! Every stroke of the flogger against her skin made a spanking noise, and indeed it sounded like she was getting an ass beating of the highest order. But in fact, it did not hurt in the least. "How is that pressure, Angelica?" Edward asked, seeking her feedback.

"It's fine, sir. In fact, it doesn't hurt at all, as you said," she replied happily, relieved that it was nothing like the belt whippings of her childhood.

Gray returned to the light, soft touch of the flogger across her light pink skin now. A heightened sense of feeling gave her goose bumps across her skin. Down and back up, the back of her thighs became intensely sensitive now. And then—whack, whack. Gray spanked Angelica across her ass, first from the right and then backhanded from the left. Two full-on strikes of the flogger across her bum. "And how did that feel, Angelica?"

"Nothing!" she said with surprise. "It makes a huge scary noise but doesn't hurt at all. That's amazing, actually," she added.

Gray laid the flogger down on the bed in clear view of Angelica so she could see he was finished with the instrument, at least for now. He caressed her baby-soft skin with partially leather-covered hands. His exposed fingertips traced across her backside and down the back of her closed thighs, which he gently opened as he said, "Spread for me." As she opened her knees wider for him, she felt her heart racing, aching for his touch.

Edward's hands gently ran up the inside of Angelica's thighs which trembled at his touch. She inhaled with a light gasp of joy as his fingertips lightly grazed her lips, just barely touching her center of joy. He observed and said, "As I had hoped, Angelica, you are completely and totally wet right now just from feeling the touch of your Dominant's flogger against your skin."

Angelica blushed, being so open and exposed and vulnerable to him. Having him stroke her revealed her growing pleasure and the pressure of excitement mounting inside. His deep voice compelled her forward yet again. "We need to go deeper, much deeper in your training, Angelica," Gray proclaimed. "Are you open to continuing further?" he asked, seeking consent once again.

"Yes, sir," she said without pause. "All green lights. More, please," she added with complete enthusiasm and a bit of surprise in her voice.

Next, Edward selected a long whippy black riding crop with a red heart embossed on the receiving tip. "Your next level is the soft tip of a riding crop. It can also feel light and erotic like the flogger, but in masterful hands, it can deliver a light amount of sting. On a scale of one to ten, one being low and ten being high, you might feel it as a one or two today." To prepare her, Gray said, "Are you ok with proceeding still?"

"Yes, sir," she answered, signifying the sound of her readiness for submission to a deeper level of trust. She would let Edward set the limits as she took her next deep long breath. Already the riding crop tip was lightly stroking her skin. Angelica arched her back to entice Edward to take her with his manhood. But his steady hand kept the focus on the riding crop tracing first the outside and then later, ever so lightly, up the inside of her thighs, but never any contact with her sensitive mound of pleasure. He made sure to steer completely clear of impact play there regardless of the device in hand.

She ached with anticipation. When would the riding crop strike with a bit of surprise and force like the flogger? This stroke? No. Gray kept teasing and stroking and caressing with very gentle rapid "taps" on her butt cheeks, so they became rosy pink, but still no pain and no powerful strikes as he lured her into total concentration on her sensations.

Then it happened. The humming of the big Hitachi Magic Wand started vibrating. She would recognize that sound anywhere from the Red Playroom. Edward gently pressed the soft, flexible head of the wand into the center of her pleasure, and she felt the surge of its intensity coursing through her body.

"Ohhhhhhh!" she cried out.

"Does that hurt you, Angelica?" he asked, pulling the wand away slightly.

"No, sir," she moaned. "More, please," she added, begging him to continue.

This time as Edward added the vibrating wand to the center of her pleasure and gently pressed in, Angelica felt the return of the riding crop tapping and stroking her derriere and thighs. It was almost overwhelming.

She heard his deep and sexy voice compelling her to move for him, saying, "Now, Kitten, rock back and forth for me gently against your toy." Gray instructed, "You do not have the use of your hands to guide the toy, so you must guide your hips back and forth against it. Do you understand?"

It was the first time he had called her Kitten all day. It was her very favorite term of endearment and made her gush to hear him say it as he guided her forward, and she instantly called out, "Yes, sir." Her hips began rocking back and forth against the powerful toy.

"But, remember my two rules, Angelica." He forewarned her, "Don't you dare climax without getting permission first? Do you understand?"

His words only made matters worse as she instantly felt her first wave as her core trembled uncontrollably. She struggled as she replied, "Yes … sir." She ached as she twerked her hips against the toy while Edward was positioned behind, guiding her almost like a jockey riding his horse, but without touching or sitting on her. He was enjoying the view of Angelica's bucking hips against the wand while he whipped her with the riding crop to run and twerk faster. He could see and hear that she was getting close to ecstasy.

"Please, sir, may I cum?" Angelica said, seeking his approval. Gray's response was one sharp stroke on each side of her ass with the riding crop. The crop stung just a bit but mixed with the intensity of the orgasm wave, which was just cresting, it was barely noticeable to her. If anything, it was pushing her across the edge faster.

"Beg louder!" his full deep voice demanded.

"Please!" she begged. "Please, please may I cum?" she shouted loudly.

"You want to cum for me?" Gray asked the desperately squirming and bucking Angelica.

She cried out, "Yes!"

"Ok, you may cum just once." Gray released her finally, only to see Niagara Falls erupt from inside Angelica. She was awash in her pleasure juices like never before in her life. Her climax seemed to go on and on, and with it, Edward continued whipping her ass, hips, and outside of her thighs to encourage her to thrust harder as his trousers finally dropped to the floor.

Angelica was still trembling from head to toe in the aftershocks of her most intense release ever when she felt his hardness enter her in one long and very deep stroke. There he was, buried deep inside her to the bone, just feeling her trembles around his manhood. He removed the toy and dropped the crop, and placed his leather-gloved hands on her shoulders and then slowly down her silk-covered back that was violated only the night before by the ballplayer at the event in that hot sexy backless dress. Downward his hands traced to pull the robe away, revealing her cuffed hands behind her back.

Gray released her cuffs so she was free again. His hands rested on her lower back where the sexy black dress had drawn every man's eyes the night before.

"Do you remember the feeling," Gray spoke as he was buried deep inside her, "of walking across the crowded room last night and the heat of men's eyes, perhaps women too, looking at you in that dress?" he asked in earnest.

"Yes, sir," she confessed.

"Many of those men went home last night and fantasized about you. Perhaps they made love to their wife or girlfriend. Or they just stroked themselves fantasizing about what it would be like to be right where I am right now," Gray said, sharing the minds of men with her. "Did you know that, Angelica?"

"No, sir," she managed as her waves were subsiding now. "Not like that exactly."

He instructed her in the ways of men further. "It's true—they do. Remember this feeling always, Angelica," said Gray, still buried deep inside her. "It is just you and me against the world. If ever again, it goes beyond just looking or if anyone violates you in their words or actions, you run to me. Do you understand me?" said Gray with an angry thrust of his hard cock.

"Yes, sir. I promise I will," she cried softly, still reeling from the emotions of the past twenty-four hours and now her most intense climax with Edward.

"You belong to me now. All of you..." Gray proclaimed. "Do you understand?"

"Yes, sir. And I want only you," she said, crying softly.

Hearing Angelica's devotion pouring out of her, he finished her training with one last admonition, "If you want this bond to last, then you must learn to trust your Dominant with all things. Immediately. No exceptions. No exemptions. Understood?" His words echoed in her mind and soul as she felt him kissing her softly on the back, still buried inside her deeply.

She whispered to him as her voice and energy floated, feeling lightheaded. She needed a moment to rest saying only, "Yes, sir. I promise."

Edward gently withdrew his length from her, telling her to climb up on the bed and rest. With a warm gentleness returning to his voice, he said, "We are going to spend the entire day in bed here, only answering the door for room service."

Angelica's eyes opened wide for a moment as she thought to herself, *All day long in bed in our suite at the Ritz Carlton with Edward Gray? Making love over and over? I hope I can keep up with his expectations.* She worried just a bit but smiled at what a lovely predicament to be in. She was his again.

CHAPTER FIFTEEN

The Morning Glow

Morning came at the Ritz Carlton, and with it, the sweet bliss of spending all night with Edward, wrapped in his arms. His caress had awoken her once in the night when she thought no more sexual energy could be left in either of them, especially after the long day of advanced training Edward had begun, with her being bound and flogged and taken over and over that day.

But once more, in the wee early morning hours, he found her a willing recipient of his between her open and aching thighs. He had taken her gently in the middle of the night with a softness she dreamed about. Afterward, he whispered, "I just can't leave you alone," before they both dozed back off to sleep.

She looked around the hotel suite, but no Edward anywhere. She found a note on the pillow, with a plastic room key next to her saying, "Meet me in the Club Lounge if you are hungry. Bring the card key to get in. Your Edward."

She smiled at his pillow note and got up to get dressed and join him. Neither of them had packed an overnight bag, so her only option was to dress in the same outfit as the day prior.

She ran her fingers through her hair like a few strokes of some primitive hairbrush to make herself look halfway presentable. She was not as well put together as two nights ago at the gala, but perhaps Edward would overlook her imperfections in the morning glow. She took one more look in the mirror, Club Lounge card key in hand, and shrugged her shoulders. Off she went to find Edward.

She was relieved that the Club Lounge was not very crowded; just Edward sitting on a couch with a beautifully decorated table in front of him and a few other couples and one family spread sparsely around the lounge. *Not a huge audience for her early morning look,* she thought, thankfully. Edward looked up and smiled as she walked to him.

"How did you sleep?" he asked with a warm smile.

She smiled. "Great! Except I had a dream about you in the middle of the night, and it woke me up."

He moved closer to hear more about it. "What was your dream about?"

"Well, we were here at the Ritz Carlton in our suite, deep asleep, and you woke me up first with your hands and then making love to me slowly and gently. It was so nice, it woke me," she snickered a bit, pretending that she dreamt about his nocturnal mischief with her.

"I had the same dream," he confessed. "Only in mine, you were the one who started it all."

"Oh?" Angelica said, sitting next to Edward, snuggling into him to steal a sip of his coffee.

"Yes," he continued. "It was all your fault, lying there looking so beautiful like an angel on the pillow next to me. I just couldn't leave you alone."

"I see. So that makes it my fault?" she said playfully, reaching down to his lap to discreetly grab a handful of Edward in public.

He didn't move away but rather looked her in the eyes and said, "Careful, Ms. Hart, that you don't get more trouble than you can handle. We do have the suite for several more hours, you know."

With her aching loins and tired body mindfully needing a day of rest, she slowly and gently let go of the playful grab of his goods.

She smiled at him before looking downward demurely, whispering to him, "Yes, sir. I will behave."

Edward smiled at his Kitten. Secretly, he liked this playful spunky side of her. It made her unpredictable and definitely harder to control when she was not wearing cuffs or a collar and leash during playtime.

A worthy adversary.

Gray shared, "I've been up since 4 a.m. and didn't want to wake you in the suite, so I got dressed quietly and came over here for an early morning coffee."

"That was thoughtful of you, but you could have stayed in the suite. There is a coffee machine in there, and I wouldn't have minded."

"You needed your rest, and I like to think quietly and read in the early morning hours, so the Club Lounge was ideal. I had the entire place to myself for quite some time."

"Well, that's good then," she chimed in.

"So, I have been thinking this morning that we need an additional Agreement going forward, Angelica," he said. "One that outlines my expectations of you and yours as well, such as your hard limits and other conditions that are important to you."

Angelica listened to his request for more paperwork, and commented, "But we already signed the Confidentiality Agreement."

Edward nodded. "Yes, I agree. But that does not cover situations like when we are out in public, such as the Straz black-tie event or your newly commenced advanced training, which absolutely needs to continue," Gray said, thinking out loud. "I really want your consent and permission for that in writing. I think that would be best for both of us."

Angelica thought about the security of a long-term Agreement with Edward and perhaps, even more, and said, "All right, Edward. I trust you, and if that is important to you, then I am fine with that." She said agreeably, "What do you need me to do?"

He suggested, "Give me a couple of days to have it drawn up, and we can go over it together at my place."

Angelica leaned into him. "If I say ok to everything now, will you feed me? I am famished!" she said, smiling into her soft kiss on his cheek.

Edward beamed basking in her early morning glow, helped her up off the couch, and said, "Let's go see what they have for us." His arm circled her waist in a familiar walking hug to the bountiful breakfast baskets lining the countertop. Skillets of delicious foods on warming plates smelled amazing with a view of the ocean from the top of the world. Angelica thought to herself, *I might just be able to get used to this. Heaven.*

After their Sunday morning coffee and breakfast at the luxurious and relaxed pace of the Club Level Lounge, it was time to check out and head for home. Despite Edward's earlier playful threats of a few more hours of submissive training, the day and night before had drained them both. A day of rest might just be needed before they resumed.

They returned to their love nest suite for Edward to gather up all the toys and tools of Angelica's advanced training session. The black satin robe was carefully placed on top of everything, folded neatly. The sound of zippers sealed the black leather case for a discreet exit from the five-star hotel. "Should we call the valet to bring up our cars?" Angelica suggested. *A practical, time-saving idea*, she thought.

"I believe you will find that they kept both of our cars out front for us," Edward replied.

"Oh. I guess being a VIP comes with many perks. Not that I am complaining!" she said playfully, pulling Edward's arm just a bit.

The elevator ride down from the Ritz tower was less eventful than on their way to their angry make-up sex session the day prior. But both smiled as they entered the same elevator car. Angelica tilted her head into him as Edward leaned over and kissed her forehead tenderly. She thought silently to herself, *What a difference a day makes*.

The walk across the marble lobby saw a busy morning with guests arriving for Sunday brunch and others checking out to fly home after a vacation retreat to Sarasota from all over. It was a cross section of different lives interconnecting in the busy lobby of the most iconic hotel in the area. One would never have guessed about Edward and Angelica's story after seeing the two of them gliding normally across the lobby.

As Edward predicted, their cars were out front waiting silently for them to return as if they had just arrived. Gray raised his hand slightly for one of the valet attendants. Mathew from the day before was not in sight. As the uniformed valet approached, he said only one word: "Gray." And with a nod, the valet was gone.

"Won't they need our valet tickets?" Angelica whispered in his ear. But her very logical question was answered with the quick return of the valet with both sets of car keys. "We kept you both right up front, Mr. Gray," the valet gushed in the very typical Ritz Carlton style of service with excellence.

First, Edward walked Angelica to her car, locked securely with its convertible top up and kept safe overnight, under the watchful eyes of the valet team. She saw her backseat was filled with all the boxes and shopping bags from Saks Fifth Avenue, the very same ones she had left lying at the front door of Edward's oceanfront estate two nights ago as her penance to earn back his favor and trust. She looked at him with surprise when she saw them.

Angelica turned to face him, placing her hands on his muscular chest, to plead her intent once more and said, "I wanted to return those expensive dresses and shoes to you. I didn't care about them. All I want is to be with you."

Edward encircled her waist in his arms. "I bought them for you as a gift. Regardless of how our brunch conversation yesterday had gone, I wanted you to have them always."

She opened her mouth to thank him profusely but managed to get out only one word, "I...."

But Gray's index finger gently silenced her. He looked deeply into her soul and said simply, "I know." Replacing the gentle touch of his hushing finger to her lips with his, he kissed her tenderly, softly lingering as they held each other with a longing embrace after their goodbye kiss. He helped her into her car and, always the gentleman, closed her door.

Angelica's eyes welled up with joy at the feeling of being under Edward's protective gaze, still looking into her eyes briefly through the car window before he turned to go. She was consumed with how he looked after her—even when she was not looking or aware. Her heart hoped to find an eternal place in his world. Whatever that would cost her is the price she was prepared to pay.

Hers was a feeling that soon would be tested, yet again. She started her motor for the morning drive home.

CHAPTER SIXTEEN

The Agreement

Arriving home from her night of marathon make-up sex with Edward found her, once again, retrieving the shopping bags and boxes from her car. Perhaps not as gleefully as when she had first brought them home from her VIP shopping spree, it felt different laying them on her bed this time. It was a sign from him that he would have wanted her to remember him and to think of him for years to come—even if he had broken things off at brunch the previous morning.

She didn't want to think about that, but apparently, he had set that in motion upon her arrival at the Ritz Carlton. Ever the chess player, he was Mr. Gray, after all, but perhaps it meant the connection with her mattered more to him than a bit of revenge recapturing the prizes from Saks.

She was exhausted and needed to sleep. Kicking off her shoes on the floor by the bed, she laid down next to the shopping bags. They symbolized him watching over her, and she liked drifting off to a much-needed nap next to them. The bags were comforting somehow, but not as much as having his great smell and warmth next to her the night before.

Hours passed before she awoke to see the afternoon sun streaming in her window. The long shadows gave clues that it was already late Sunday afternoon. She thought, *Oh my goodness! How long was I asleep?* Looking to find her alarm, she discovered it was almost 4 o'clock. Her body and mind must have needed rest after the past two days' stress and emotional roller coaster. She stretched and thought about getting up, but not just yet.

She reached for her phone to discover two missed messages from girlfriends and one from Edward, which said simply, *Hope you are home safe. Let me know when you get this?*

She said aloud, "Oh shoot! That was from this morning." As she raced to reply, she texted, *Just woke up from a long nap. Apparently, someone wore me out with advanced training yesterday.* She added a smile emoji to her late but playful message to him, hoping it would help make up for the lateness of her reply.

Edward promptly responded, *Glad you got some rest. You needed it. Are you available after work Monday to discuss our new Agreement?*

She happily replied, *Yes, sir. Of course!* She was relieved to have confirmation that he wanted to move forward with her long term. An Agreement, she felt, meant a commitment from Edward to her, and a huge step forward from the crisis narrowly averted after the black-tie affair in Tampa. *Where would you like to meet?* she added.

Let's meet at my office building downtown at 5:30 p.m. after work. I will email you a copy of the Agreement beforehand to review.

Angelica thanked him via text and closed her eyes for a few more needed minutes of rest.

The impressive glass and marble office headquarters of Gray Global Enterprises were his ultimate home court advantage, as if he weren't intimidating enough anywhere she would have met with him. But the high-rise glass tower downtown was certainly his impressive domain to finalize his negotiations with Angelica.

She left her work just before 5 o'clock Monday. She had no time to run home to freshen up, so she touched up her makeup at the office before heading over to meet him. She had worn her best office dress that day—a tight black skirt and white silk top with one strand of pearls. Well, imitation pearls, but they looked nice with the matching earrings resulting in a classic look.

She arrived promptly in the lobby waiting area and was about to give her name to the incredibly attractive, but older receptionist when she was asked, "You must be Ms. Hart, yes?"

Angelica replied politely, "Yes, ma'am."

The receptionist nodded to her and said, "I will let Mr. Gray know you are here. Would you care for coffee, water, or anything to drink?"

Angelica shook her head and smiled. "No, thank you. I'm fine."

The receptionist pressed a button on her high-tech headset and said into the curved glass microphone, "A Ms. Hart is here to see you."

Angelica looked out over Sarasota Bay from the lofty perch of the penthouse office view. She could see the boats cruising out for sunset as they had done every day since she was little growing up. How much Sarasota had grown since those days, as had she—with the passage of a few decades.

Edward came out of his double-door office at the end of the hall to greet her. "You look stunning as always, Ms. Hart." He waved for her to join him as they walked past his huge conference room to his office for their meeting.

Angelica complimented, "Impressive office, Mr. Gray."

He replied modestly, "Thank you. It's a good location for my work."

Angelica added, "I love the view of Sarasota Bay, and you have your choice of sunset views from either here or at home."

Edward nodded in agreement and invited her to sit in either one of the over-stuffed chairs or a couch in his office. A good place for informal meetings, Gray found it to be a much more intimate setting than the conference room, and he had closed many of his deals here.

They chose seats angled next to one another for ease of reviewing the paperwork together. "Ms. Hart, if you would like, let's begin with your comments or questions about the paperwork I sent over."

Angelica pulled out a printed copy of the Agreement she brought with her, complete with her handwritten notes in red ink. She felt prepared this time. "Page one is fine. No changes."

Edward commented, "Excellent!"

"Page two, Section 7 says 'The submissive's behavior while in public shall at all times meet the approval of the Dominant, whether the Dominant is present or not.'" She asked for clarification, adding, "How will I know what behavior meets with your approval?"

Gray replied, "Training, along with full and open communication as we discussed on our Saturday brunch."

She nodded, moving on.

"Page three, Section 12: 'The submissive shall submit to any sexual activity requested by the Dominant and shall do so without discussion other than those activities listed in the Appendix: Hard Limits.'" She added, "Turn to the Appendix Soft Limits. Find Anal Sex."

Edward looked down at his copy of the Agreement, saying, "I'm with you."

Angelica continued, "Strike it out please. Strike out Anal Sex."

Edward inquired, "Are you sure?"

Angelica said, "Yes." She continued, "On the same page: 'Is the use of sex toys acceptable to the submissive?' Vibrators? Okay. Dildos? Fine. Butt plugs? Absolutely not."

Edward accepted and said, "Consider them gone."

Angelica inquired, "Who else knows about this Agreement? This is very personal information."

"My staff knows only what I choose to tell them. I prepared the paperwork myself personally. So, we have total privacy around the terms of our Agreement."

Angelica, feeling relieved, said, "Thank you for that. Also, on page five, some terms need clarification."

Edward explained, "Ball Gag and/or Suspension Hanging— that is the art of Shibari rope bondage from Japan."

Angelica was uncertain and said, "I've never been tied up before. Is this important to you?"

Edward explained, "It is for your absolute pleasure. And mine."

Angelica's eyebrows raised a bit as she sighed, "Really?"

Edward encouraged, "Something to consider?"

Angelica decided to concede this one for Edward.

"'Is bondage acceptable to the submissive?' I'm good with rope, leather cuffs, and Velcro cuffs, but let's agree with no metal handcuffs. That gives me the creeps."

Edward complimented her, "May I just comment on how impressed I am with your level of detail in reviewing the Agreement? And in the spirit of collaboration, I will offer you a special concession. How about we add one section to the Agreement to be drafted by you? Something you would like to see in our plans for the year ahead that is not currently addressed in the Agreement—whatever you want within reason, of course."

Angelica smiled and said, "I like that idea very much. Thank you. You're very kind."

Edward added, "I want you to be incredibly happy, Ms. Hart. So much so that you will not want to end our Agreement. If you let me, I would like to spoil you rotten, where no one else will ever compare to the life you could have with me."

Angelica smiled and said, "While I appreciate your gifts and generosity, it isn't why I am doing this. Edward, you draw me here like a moth to the flame. May I think over the rest of the Agreement?"

Edward replied, "You really want to think it over? We both know you want this as much as I do."

Angelica looked at him coyly, trying to undermine his confidence in his powerful office. "Maybe I do. But this is a lot to commit to."

Edward moved closer to her, wanting the paperwork done and completed between them and said, "Ms. Hart, what would have to happen for you to sign today? I hear your words, but everything that has happened in these past few weeks tells me you want this. Even now, your body, your eyes, your voice—all are telling me you are ready now. Then there is how you are breathing at this moment, while I look at you."

She felt flush as he looked into her eyes and confessed it all to him right then and there. "Yes. You know me well, Edward, on some levels. But men just don't know or understand the secrets of a woman's heart. Do you really want to know what goes through my mind? Or, why I wanted to be your submissive?"

Angelica leaned back in her chair and gazed deeply and intently into Edward's eyes, who —for once—was at a loss for words. "Just this once, let me take you on a bit of my journey and why I am with you, Edward."

She took a deep breath, and began, "What does it feel like to belong only in your hands as my Dominant?" She looked down from his eyes shyly as she spoke and looked at her knees. "Time suspends," she continued. "I find myself floating somewhere toward the heavens with you." Struggling to finish, her voice trembled hearing her own words as she said, "But most of all, my mind will shut the entire world out as I only want to hear your voice and feel your touch."

Edward reached out with his warm hand to cup her chin and lift her eyes back to his. Now looking deeply into his crystal blue eyes, she confessed, "My submission to you takes me to a dream, Edward—from which I never wish to awaken."

Her eyes welled up looking back at his gaze as he looked into her soul. Angelica felt her heart pumping. Her blood rushed.

He owned her now. She was simply his for the taking. Angelica consented, "So, yes, I will sign your papers, Edward. What do we do next?"

He leaned in a bit closer as he explained the next steps for her. "I would make the changes we both agreed to on the paperwork, and we would move across the room to my office desk to sign and initial the changes. But, before you sign, I would help you out of that little skirt of yours."

Angelica replied, breathing hard, "Oh really?"

Edward continued the preview of what lay just ahead and added, "I would want you bent over my desk while you sign with me just behind you."

Angelica, feeling emboldened, asked while smiling at him playfully, "Is that a good idea, Mr. Gray? Wouldn't that make the contract invalid because of unfair pressure to get me to sign?" She opened her knees with her skirt facing Edward so he would be tempted to glance and discover if she wore panties.

Edward answered, "It's called coercion, but in this case, just think of it as a memorable closing for the paperwork, a tradition we might wish to repeat each year when it is time to renew our Agreement."

Angelica played with her pearl necklace, toying with it and Edward for a moment, before inevitably caving in. "I'm ready to sign."

Edward hurried to make the few changes they agreed to and marked them for each to initial. Then he stood and confidently walked over to the large desk where he worked most days and laid the paperwork flat for signatures, next to a large custom engraved gold pen.

"Right here?" she asked, bending over only slightly.

"Yes," Gray said, unzipping her skirt from behind. As it fell to the floor, he used his hands to bend her over further, so her face was nearly touching the document. "Here, have a closer look, Ms. Hart."

As she felt the first firm slap of Mr. Gray's hand on her perfectly heart-shaped bottom, it was clear this closing might go on well into the evening hours.

CHAPTER SEVENTEEN

The Getaway

The next day, Edward called Angelica to suggest celebrating their new one-year Agreement. He had to go back to Washington, D.C., on business for a few days and asked if she could join him. If it were possible for her to take off work on Friday, he would have her back home by Sunday afternoon. It would be their first trip out of town together, and while not an obligation for her to join him, he would welcome her company if she would like a weekend getaway.

Before Gray had even finished speaking, her mind was racing with excitement. She could hardly stand to let him finish talking. "I would love to!" came her enthusiastic reply. "Let me check on getting someone to cover me at the office for Friday, but I am sure I can make it work."

"Excellent. Just let me know by tomorrow to confirm, and I will make all the arrangements."

Her heart was racing with excitement—flying away with Edward Gray for the weekend! *Hooray! was an understatement*, she thought as she smiled, beaming, feeling her adrenaline rush at all the possibilities. It might feel like a little honeymoon for their new Agreement and commitment for the year ahead—dinners out and, best of all, sleeping next to him. His smell was intoxicating, and the thought of Edward's muscular body getting out of the shower, or as he was getting dressed for his meetings, or at dinner with her, or, better yet, the thought of him getting undressed for her at night or even in the middle of the day had images whirling in her mind.

She made a few phone calls to discuss the details of her Friday off. She never took sick or vacation days, so it wasn't like she didn't have time off coming. It just took a bit of juggling on her part because no one ever had to cover for her before. She was the reliable one that was always there.

She texted Edward within the hour and said, *I'm all yours for the weekend!* As she hit the send button, she was all smiles.

It was only moments before she heard back. *That's great news! If you would like to head out Thursday after work, we could have dinner on the flight up to D.C., just the two of us.* Edward invited.

Angelica loved the romantic idea of flying off to Washington, D.C., with him and was bubbling over to reply, *Love to!*

So, the trip was set in motion, and with it, all the many little details she needed to take care of to get ready to go away for a few days. Angelica started stressing, thinking about all she might need for the trip. She wasn't sure if she would be accompanying Edward on any of his meetings or what she needed to bring to wear. She wouldn't have long to wait for Mr. Gray to lead the way as she had grown quickly used to.

Call me after work, and we will discuss the plans for the weekend, including a bit of the schedule and details. Edward added, *I look forward to hearing your voice and sharing a preview of upcoming events. Pun intended.*

She smiled at the "coming events" which was misspelled in her dirty little mind, corrupted, of late, of course, by her very own

Mr. Gray. She could not wait to learn the details from him after work. She had traveled a little bit before, but only once outside of Florida when growing up. Travel on the Edward Gray level and style would be in another league, she imagined.

He had invited her to call him, so the minute she got into her car to leave the office, she phoned him up with energy beaming from her voice with excitement. She heard his deep voice as he answered, "Hello."

In return, she simply gushed, "I'm so excited! I just can't wait for Thursday to get here!"

Gray chuckled out loud, hearing her overflowing with pent-up energy. "We're not going to Paris or Rome, sweetheart," Gray said teasingly to remind her. "It's just a business trip to Washington," he said.

"You always go on these business trips, so it may be no big deal to you, but it is super exciting to travel anywhere for me, especially since you are taking me!"

"Fair enough, Kitten." He laughed and added, "I'm glad you're willing to accompany me. It's sure to be more fun with you there."

Angelica wanted Edward to be looking forward to it as much as she was and added, "I will make absolutely sure it is!" she promised with a sexy flirt in her voice. "I will try to make it irresistible for you to bring me every chance you get when you go out of town. Perhaps one day I will become your indispensable personal assistant that can keep you stress free while you are out taking over the world, Mr. Gray."

"Hmmm," Gray grunted. "That's not a half-bad idea, but you might have to serve as an intern and audition for that role in the

Red Playroom for hours and hours, Ms. Hart. Are you sure you want the position that badly?"

She smiled as she pulled into her driveway and parked to continue the conversation, still sitting in her car and added, "I like every position that my Dominant puts me in, sir. So far, I haven't found one that didn't feel better than the one before."

Gray laughed out loud over the phone. "Someone is in a big energy mood tonight. All of this is bubbling out just from the invitation to D.C. for the weekend?"

Angelica gushed, "I don't know, but I haven't been able to stop thinking about the trip all day. Perhaps I am in love with the idea of being away on a trip with you, Edward. Maybe I love the idea of travel now that you have suggested it to me. But I'm sitting in my driveway, still in my car, daydreaming about it as we speak. Tell me all about the trip, please!"

"Okay, calm down a bit," Gray said, still laughing at her glee. She sounded like a youngster on Christmas morning opening the presents, with the kind of excitement that she was exuding over the phone. He added, "To begin, we fly out Thursday evening after work."

Excited about the trip with him, she interrupted, "What time is our flight, and when do you need me to be there?"

Gray cleared his throat slightly and replied, "Well, the flight leaves when we get there, Kitten. We are flying private, not commercial. There is no security line to go through, and there is also no charge for your luggage or parking either at the jetport, just so you know."

Angelica was still processing what Edward had just explained to her. "So, this is like a private plane, not like a regular airline?" she asked.

Her new life began unfolding a bit further as Gray answered, "Yes. A private jet. It's called a Gulfstream 650."

"Well, aren't we Mr. Fancy Pants?" she teased her wealthy Mr. Gray. She knew he had money, but he never showed off his wealth. He had always been quiet about it. She remembered what her hair stylist had told her about the "Billionaire Edward Gray," but she didn't believe half of what she heard around the rumor mill.

Gray retorted back playfully, "If flying private feels too fancy, you could just stay home, and I promise I will send you a postcard from D.C., Ms. Hart." He laughed as he paused for her reply.

"No," Angelica said very steadily. "No, no, after some deep thought, consideration, and careful reflection, I have decided that we are okay with flying private this weekend, Mr. Gray," she said laughing, giving her playful, tongue-in-cheek retort. "Just as long as you tell me it is safe," she added, giving her one and only concern. She had only flown a couple of times before and never on a private jet.

His deep and reassuring voice continued. "It is the safest and best way to fly. Especially these days with all that is going on with the airlines," Gray commented in a business-like manner in which he made most of his decisions. "Besides, both of our pilots are former major airline captains after they got out of the Air Force flying fighter jets. So, we are in exceptionally good hands in the air, Ms. Hart."

"Sounds amazing!" she conceded, after hearing all the details.

He continued, "Here is a bit of a preview of our trip plans. Wear what you have on from the office for the flight so you can come straight to the plane from work, Angelica. We will have dinner on the flight up. It will just be the two of us on this trip. When we land, our driver will take us straight to the Ritz Carlton in downtown D.C."

Angelica asked, "The entire plane just for the two of us?"

"It will be a nice experience, and I look forward to our time alone on the flight up," he added with a bit of sexual energy for her to think about. He continued, "On Friday, while I have my daylong set of meetings, I have made you a reservation for a full day at the spa and salon. They will bring your lunch and whatever you would like to drink for a very relaxing day. It will feel like a vacation."

Angelica responded, "It would be a lot more fun if you could join me, Edward, but I understand you have to work."

"I will call and check on you and how your day is going a time or two, Kitten."

"Promise?" she asked. She liked the idea of him checking on her during his business day. Even a bit of his attention when they were apart was energizing to her.

"Absolutely," Gray confirmed and added, "That evening will be a first for us, a business dinner with a father and son whose business I just bought recently. The father is retiring, and the son was not quite up to the challenge of taking over his father's big business, so the son is newly working for me now. A delicate situation if you think about it."

Angelica felt like this was a big step forward having Edward trust her to be in a meeting with his new business partners in D.C. Wanting Edward to know, she said, "I will do anything I can to be helpful, but I don't want to mess up or say anything that would be out of place. Perhaps you can tell me more about them on the flight up to D.C.?" she asked.

"I will do my best, Ms. Hart," Gray said with his flirt on, "perhaps while you are sitting on my lap without your panties on for most of the flight. That turbulence could come in handy," he added, laughing. She gathered from his tone he was kidding—but not kidding about the sitting on his lap part.

Gray finished with her favorite detail and said, "But Saturday is ours. There will be no business over the weekend this trip other than possibly a phone call or two here and there. Saturday is our shopping day for the new apartment in Washington. I'm going to challenge your inner interior decorator a bit to add some ideas. It is already furnished with the basics, but it needs some style and personal touches. Plus, I would like to get you a new outfit each time we travel. In this way, you can add some memories to your closet wardrobe from any travel you choose to join me on this year," he offered temptingly. She loved the idea of outfits from all over the country—from their travel trips to remind her and him of memories they had made together. How romantic!

Gray interrupted her daydream. "Sunday, we fly home after brunch. It should be a nice long weekend."

"Nice?" she asked about his obvious understatement. "It sounds absolutely amazing!" she said with her excitement flowing through the phone, making Edward smile. He loved the power to make Angelica gush, both in and out of the bedroom, and playing with her gleeful girlish energy with his every word and touch.

Angelica made his inner lion roar, and because she was so emotionally legible, she made him feel like the man he most wanted to be—a difference maker. Her hero.

Bursting with questions and still filled with excitement, Angelica rattled off, "What should I bring to wear? I don't want to be too plain or too fancy for the business dinner, Edward. And what about the rest of the time? Can you give me a few clues?" She smiled as she went in rapid bursts over the phone. Eager with anticipation was perhaps an understatement.

"Three things I need you to do for me. First, go see Sandra at Saks again for just the right cocktail dress or two, then second, stop by Dream Weaver on St. Armand's Circle where you will find some one-of-a-kind options there for sure."

Interrupting him mid-sentence, Angelica said, "Oh, I've heard about Dream Weaver but have never shopped there before. It's not exactly in my price range," she added, realizing she had cut Edward off mid-way through. "You said there were three things. I'm sorry to interrupt. What else?" she paused.

Gray let a moment of silence go by to emphasize her interruption when he was speaking, not to be encouraged often before he continued. He finally resumed, "The third and most important preparation for your trip, Ms. Hart, is tomorrow evening at my home. It is time to continue your training with the introduction of two new elements: First Position and hand signals." He paused for the inevitable questions.

"So, you know I have to ask," Angelica said slowly to draw out the information from him. "What is First Position?"

Gray replied, ever the voice of mystery and intrigue on her journey, "Get your shopping for our trip done, Ms. Hart. Go do your part to help keep the economy running, and I will show you what the next level of submission training looks like tomorrow evening." Finishing, he added, "And yes. I will be feeding you as well, so come hungry if you like great Italian food."

"Yes, sir," she said, the response coming across her lips ever more easily as time moved on with Edward. As she hung up, Angelica was beaming with excitement about everything like the clothes shopping for the trip and getting her hair done again. She would have to tell her confidant at the salon what was happening this week with Edward. She was more intrigued than nervous, but a bit of both about "First Position" and the training tomorrow night. He did say it would be "the next level."

CHAPTER EIGHTEEN

First Postion

As soon as she hung up with Edward, her car headed straight to Saks at UTC Mall in Sarasota's upscale Lakewood Ranch area. She never liked to have the valet park her older car at the mall. Even though it was a flashy red convertible, it was getting up there in miles, and she was always a bit nervous about having the valet take her car. Especially since they were often parking the Ferraris, Mercedes, Rolls Royce, and other incredible high-line cars that were everywhere in Sarasota, especially in Lakewood Ranch. So, she parked in the main lot near Saks and quickly went in to see if Sandra, her shopping guide from before, was working.

Her luck continued, finding Sandra beaming to see her favorite new client back so soon. "A little bird told me that someone has a big trip coming up this weekend!" Sandra sang in a little melodic, enchanting sing-song way that added to the smile Angelica was already sporting.

Angelica put her hands around Sandra's elbow to reconnect with her shopping star partner. "Yes! I'm so excited, but I need your help again," she said as her brows furrowed. "There's a business dinner. It is important, I believe," she added.

"Well, you'll need a cocktail dress then," Sandra said. "Edward said the dinner is at the Willard Hotel in D.C.—very conservative, historical, and fancy," Sandra added.

Angelica marveled, "You always have the inside scoop, Sandra!" Laughing, she said, "What would I do without you? I'm so glad you were here today. It is our first trip together, and I want to look perfect for him."

Sandra offered a fun idea. "You know it would be thoughtful of you to surprise Mr. Gray with a gift for him on the trip. Something that you picked out, especially for him."

"Oh! That is a great idea," Angelica said, beaming. "And I would like to pay for that separately with my own money," she added.

Sandra coached her gently and said, "You could. But don't worry about the money as much as the thoughtfulness of what you select. Mr. Gray has exquisite tastes. He only buys the best, and he has an excellent eye," she said laying down a bit of a challenge for them both.

Angelica suggested, "What about a tie? He said he will be wearing a suit to dinner Friday evening."

Sandra beamed and said, "Perfect! Let's head to the men's section, and I will recruit some help if needed."

Gray always wore dark suits, black or midnight blue, with white or blue shirts. His remarkable blue eyes kept Angelica glued to him the first night they met. She said, "If by any miracle they have a tie with some of the same shade of blue as his eyes, that would be hard to beat."

"And that would make it very personal and special coming from you!" Sandra added. "Let's go look!"

Out of the hundreds of ties at Saks, none they pulled out had just what Angelica was looking for until she found a fantastic gold and red paisley tie with an accent of deep royal blue that reminded her exactly of the magical color in Edward's gaze. "This is it!" said Angelica as she held it up towards the sky like the Golden Fleece she had discovered as her prize. "And it is the softest silk I have ever felt. Feel this, Sandra," she requested, carefully offering it over for her to touch.

"He will just love it, Angelica!" Sandra agreed as she nodded her approval and smiled. She added it to the growing pile from their second shopping spree together.

The two had shopped and tried on so many outfits it was too late to try and get to St. Armand's Circle and the other great store Edward had suggested today. On her way home, she gathered up her next round of shopping bags and boxes from Sandra at Saks to dream about the trip coming up on Thursday. She noticed that she was getting more comfortable with this unlimited shopping budget in Mr. Gray's world. The pangs of guilt at the checkout register were still there just a bit, but not as much this time.

On the way to her car, she thought about that, but it did not take the wind out of her sails. So, her mind turned to this First Position training that Edward previewed for her briefly on the phone. She was curious, but he offered no further details.

Ever the curious researcher, as she was the night they first met when Gray told her to get rid of her date and come back to meet him, she had done a good bit of homework before putting herself at risk of meeting a total stranger. She now parked in her driveway and gathered all the shopping bags inside and onto her bed, adding a bit of excitement to the décor. She loved opening them and laying all the "spoils of war" out on her bed to see when she got home. There was something about getting a new outfit; it just made you feel good.

She went to the kitchen and poured a glass of white wine, and her curiosity got the best of her. Sitting down with her wine, she Google searched "BDSM First Position" and hit enter. The results opened a new world, and so did her jaw when it dropped open.

There were many articles and videos about the subject, and it was apparent if anything had a "First" position—it probably had more. And in this case, BDSM had lots more positions, but what got her attention most of all was under the subject heading "Slave Training."

"Slave Training?" she said out loud as she took another gulp of her cold wine. Her mind was racing further down the pathway that she was already on. *Is this what Edward wants from me?* she thought. *To be his slave?* The hard limits section of her contract came to mind. Maybe she would need her safe words after all. Gray was not a man that was used to hearing the word "no."

What if she couldn't do or be what he wanted from her? Now her mood shifted from the joy of shopping for the trip to being nervous and a bit afraid of the advanced training tomorrow night in the Red Playroom at Gray's oceanfront estate.

Angelica tossed and turned all night. First Position in slave training rang in her mind, as her imagination reeled about what this "next level" with Mr. Gray might entail. Her research into his First Position training revealed many articles, websites, and videos about the BDSM world and slave training. Some of them were much more extreme than she was prepared for.

"Is this what he wants from me?" she kept asking as her mind searched for answers. She awoke the next morning, tired from lack of sleep, but already nervous about seeing him this evening. She had been reticent today and avoided texting him, half afraid of the answers and half wanting to be with him in person to talk about it. But for now, she needed some extra coffee to get through the workday.

But the hours ticked by, and a bit sooner than she would have liked, it was time to leave and get ready for her evening with Mr. Gray. *What was the worst that could happen?* she thought. She could simply ask him to let her out of her one-year Agreement. Plus, their prior discussion was about her hard limits and her safe words. After all, if he honored those parts of their arrangement, she could offer First Position all he wanted tonight. Maybe?

She left work and drove to St. Armand's Circle to the high-end exclusive store Edward had recommended, Dream Weaver. In a way, this is what Mr. Gray had been doing to her all this time— "weaving" dreams of a life so unobtainable and so extraordinary that it would make it hard for her, or any woman, to say no to Mr. Gray. So, she walked through the door to peek at the most exquisite designer clothes she had ever seen. Those who shopped there were likely less concerned with the price than simply having something that no one else would be wearing—one-of-a-kind and very chic.

So maybe a little slave training was back on the table as she picked out one outfit that would likely become her favorite thing in her closet. As they rang up her latest shopping purchase on Edward's Platinum card, her apprehension of advanced training in Edward's Red Playroom began growing in the pit of her stomach. She had always felt safe with him, but she was less than an hour away from her date with destiny. She put her new prizes in the trunk of her car so she could leave the top down on her Nissan Z for a short drive along Lido Beach. It was almost sunset, and she loved this time of day on the water. Just the feeling of the ocean breeze against her face and flowing through her hair always seemed to set her free. She thought about Edward and their upcoming trip this weekend which was still going to be exciting and full of first experiences.

As she turned her car around to head toward Gray's home on Longboat Key, she decided to turn her mind and energy around and go to him with an open mind. After all, he had earned her trust on many levels. She wished he had talked to her more to prepare her mentally. Her mind had raced all night and much of the day today in anticipation. The conflict within her was really about the words "slave training." She hated that label or expression, she rationalized. Even though, slowly but surely, she wanted to belong to him more and more however high a price there might be.

Once again, her car made its way to Edward's circular drive, and she found herself with her finger about to ring his doorbell when the front door opened magically before her. Edward's free hand and arm made a grand sweeping gesture, palm up, inviting Angelica in as he welcomed her. "Good evening, Ms. Hart," he said with a gracious smile.

She walked straight to Edward, dropping her purse on the ground to free both her hands to wrap around his neck. She pulled him tight to her and held him close. He could feel her nervous energy and quickly sensed something was wrong. Gray wrapped his strong but gentle arms around Angelica and welcomed her warmly without speaking. The two just stood there inside his doorway, silently clutched in an embrace unlike any other until now.

He stroked her long hair and down her back with an energy he hoped would comfort her as he broke the long silence and said, "Is everything ok, Kitten?" She replied with a bit more silence, nuzzling her nose and lips into Edward's neck, still holding him tightly. Then, after another moment or two, she was finally ready to speak to him.

"I am a little nervous about tonight, Edward. Maybe even scared just a little bit."

For once, Gray was at a loss for words. He had no idea what had brought this on, especially after how they had been intensely and passionately together each time. He invited her eagerly and said, "Please come on in and tell me all about it. Start at the very beginning, and don't leave anything out." Gray gestured for her to join him in the kitchen as he closed the heavy front door behind them.

Angelica sighed as they walked together with his arm encircled gently around her waist. "I knew I would feel better the moment I saw you and could hear your voice, Edward."

Gray gently pulled her closer and probed further, "Tell me what is worrying you, Kitten."

Angelica began sharing her story as Edward poured each of them a glass of her favorite white wine. "I went shopping at Saks for our trip yesterday after we spoke on the phone, just like you instructed. Sandra was amazing as always, and everything went great there." She paused, and he could see the clouds forming over her forehead as her eyebrows furrowed closer together when she said, "But I Google searched First Position training out of curiosity. I just wanted to see if it is a thing, and if so, what it is about." Angelica paused momentarily to find the courage to continue.

Gray intervened, sensing what she might be uncomfortable talking about. "And what did you discover when you did your search?" he asked in a calm, quiet voice coaxing her to continue down this path a bit further for him as he handed her a glass of wine.

Angelica said, "Thank you," as she took the glass from Edward, thankful for the momentary distraction before she plunged into the more challenging conversation ahead.

"BDSM Slave Training," she finally blurted out, relieved to have shared her worry. She continued and added, "The results went on for pages and pages with websites and videos and blog articles." She described her eye-opening journey and said, "It was more than just a little bit intimidating; the whole idea of 'Slave Training,' potentially starting with you in the Red Playroom tonight, Edward." She paused and took a long and much-needed drink of her wine but felt relieved to have it finally out on the table.

Edward reached over to Angelica gently and stroked her hair and then caressed her cheek with the back of his fingers softly as he spoke to her. "First of all, Angelica, thank you for sharing your worry and concern with me," he said gazing at her with those hypnotically blue eyes she could always get lost in. He continued, "But most importantly, one of my first principles is simply this— you never have to do anything with me that you do not enthusiastically choose." Then he gently cupped her chin in his warm and inviting hand for emphasis and said, "Do you understand?" He paused for her reply as she looked back into his powerful gaze.

After only a heartbeat of a pause, she said softly, "Yes, sir."

Gray took her wine glass back momentarily to set it down on the kitchen's granite countertop so he could wrap her in his arms and hold her close once again. With her body pressing into his but still looking into her eyes, he added, "I wondered why you were so quiet all day. I heard hardly a peep from you. I only had one text from you all day. I certainly wish you had called me right away or at least texted me if you had any questions or concerns about anything related to us but especially things having to do with our Dominant and submissive world. I know this is still very new to you, Angelica."

She was relieved to hear his response and gushed, "I know I should have. It kept me up tossing and turning all last night, worried sick about slave training with you tonight," she confessed.

Gray smiled warmly at her once more, looking into her eyes, as he asked her to turn around with her back towards him.

Angelica turned around first and then said, "Yes, sir," having already complied. Gray further guided her, "Now, Kitten, lean your head back into my chest, please."

"Yes, sir," said Angelica, the words oozing out as she leaned back and into him. Now resting on his muscular frame, a slight smile began spreading on her face as she added, "You always know just how to make me feel comfortable again, sir."

He replied, "Which is one of the things we talked about at our brunch on Saturday, if you recall. So, when there is a problem when we are out in public, with anyone you meet, what are you supposed to do right away, Kitten?"

Angelica thought about their deep conversation after the horrible episode at the black-tie affair in Tampa and how angry he had become when first he felt betrayed. But he listened to her, and they had become much closer in their bond when they could talk openly and fully about everything. She paused and then replied, "I am supposed to come to you with any kind of problem, big or small, so that nothing can ever come between us, sir."

Edward stroked the outsides of both her shoulders and down her arms as he said, "That was very well said, Angelica. I am impressed with how you put that."

"Thank you, sir," she replied, smiling. She loved to hear his words of affirmation for her.

Then Gray gently confronted the trust with her. "But did you do that yesterday or today?" he asked.

"No, sir," she replied and added, "I let fear get the best of me again."

Then came the obvious question from Edward, still hanging in the air. "And how did you feel the moment you were in my arms and talking with me?" he inquired, already knowing full well what the answer would be.

Angelica exhaled deeply before answering, still leaning back into Edward, feeling his reassuring strokes and his powerful but patient energy. "Relieved. I felt the stress and worry run out of me, Edward, the moment I felt your touch and heard your voice."

His hands moved from stroking her arms and shoulder to now gently roaming across her ample round breasts as he spoke into her ear in his deep voice. "Let's agree not to let the labels you discover on a Google search or anyone else's opinions define us. Let's agree that a Dominant and submissive relationship requires exceptional communication," he said as her eyes slowly closed, feeling her aching breasts starting to bud up against his gentle strokes. Gray added, "And finally, let's agree that building trust at our deepest darkest levels can only truly last if we test it always and often."

Angelica arched her back slightly to press her breasts into Edward's hands more fully, but they slipped downward across her tight toned stomach to the top of her hips. Her skirt was no match for his fingers on a mission to find her mound. Saying each word slowly for emphasis, he probed with his voice, "Do you understand, Angelica?"

"Yes, sir," she gasped, feeling her moist excitement rising as his fingertips expertly found their mark.

He rewarded her with several soft but rapid strokes before his invitation for more. "That's my very special Kitten. I was hoping you could come with me to the Red Playroom so I can teach you a new little ceremony that I think you will be very excited about. Plus, I ordered something new for you to wear tonight and to bring on our trip this weekend."

Angelica gasped, "Yes, sir!" as Edward gave her several more light little strokes inside her now completely creamy panties before gently releasing her to get ready. She swept her wine glass off the kitchen countertop to bring with her as she grasped Edward's hand in hers and started literally pulling him toward the elevator to the Playroom.

Gray laughed out loud. "Well, someone is an eager beaver now all of a sudden," he said about the complete and total change from apprehension to excitement in Angelica. Only Edward's touch and voice could flip all her switches on inside of her. Her biggest fear deep down inside would be ever losing him.

She walked briskly to the Playroom door, where she dutifully waited for him to open the locked entrance to their alternate world. Gray opened the heavy wood door and gestured for her to enter. Inside, the lights were already red and dim with the pulse of Enigma music playing. Angelica set her wine down on the drinks bar inside the Playroom door and asked him, "What would you like me to do first?"

Edward returned to his position, standing just behind her, to remind her body and pumping heart of the sensual energy they had moments before. Angelica responded to the feeling of his hands on her shoulders and neck as if they were her innermost reaches.

Guiding her mind, he said, "First, let me explain the purpose and meaning of First Position. Without that, it becomes much less significant," he explained. "Each time you come to the Playroom, or if I ask you to go to the bedroom and prepare for me on our trip this weekend, I would like you to change into your robe or very sexy lingerie. Then, by yourself, come to the foot of the bed precisely in the center please," he said, encouraging her to move to that exact spot.

He continued, "Now, I would like you to climb onto the foot of the bed kneeling with your knees apart about shoulder width for good balance. Then, just relax sitting on your heels for me. Can you try that for me, Angelica?"

"Yes, sir," she replied dutifully and climbed onto the bed on her knees and sat on her heels just as he described.

Gray encouraged her and said, "Excellent! Are you comfortable?"

"Yes, sir, thank you for asking," he responded and was happy that he was checking on her well-being.

Edward probed further to be sure. "No knee or back issues that would cause you any discomfort to sit in this position for perhaps two or three minutes?" he asked, seeking her consent.

She replied, "It feels fine now, but if it ever becomes uncomfortable, may I request to change position, sir?"

Gray smiled at her understanding. "Thank you for the question, and yes, you may ask or use your safe words anytime as communication is always encouraged," he said, adding one final bit of instruction. "The final touch to First Position is placing your hands on each of your knees with your palms facing upward." Gray added, "This last gesture symbolizes that you are open and available to your Master which is a high honor."

"Like this, sir?" Angelica asked, looking for his approval.

Gray looked at her, sitting obediently on her knees, with her gorgeous heart-shaped derriere resting on her heels, palms upward resting on her knees, symbolizing her open readiness to please him in any way he might wish within her hard limits they had agreed to, of course. He leaned into her neck and ear to speak quietly in his deepest voice. "You look perfect," he confirmed to her, and unable to resist, added, "You are so coachable!" Angelica smiled and loved that he was so pleased with her for something as simple as kneeling on the bed. But, of course, the way he described it as a high honor, she was now starting to see why it was such a big deal to him. It was an unspoken symbol of her devotion to him.

He led her forward from here and said, "In just a moment, I would like you to go across the hall and change into a new sheer robe that I ordered for you. It is for you to wear this evening and bring with you on our weekend trip. Tonight, I would like you to wear nothing but the sheer robe for me. Once you change into it, I would like you to return to the Playroom by yourself. This time, I will not be here just yet. Please get into First Position for me and wait for your sir's arrival. Do not turn or speak when you hear me enter and close the door behind me. Simply wait in First Position for me. Can you do this very special ceremony for me?"

Angelica felt the bond growing deeper with Edward, with their expanding secret world. The special ceremony was now hers to give only to him, as she said with a soft whisper, "Yes, sir…I am happy to do this for you if it pleases you." She added, "May I go and get ready for you now?"

Gray kissed her softly on the cheek and released her with a simple, "Yes."

Angelica climbed gracefully off the bed and rushed to the bathroom, anxious to see what Edward had ordered especially for her to wear that evening. But even more, she was still tingling and ached with excitement to feel his touch again, to feel the waves of pleasure that only he could bring to her. Her voice trailed across the hallway as she went. "I will hurry, sir!"

He was smiling as he left the Playroom door wide open for her return and walked the long hallway to his room to change clothes.

Angelica discovered the bathroom lights were already on but dimmed to about fifty percent brightness for her. The most elegant midnight blue lace robe was hanging behind the bathroom door, awaiting her discovery. Angelica smiled as she held the long and flowing fabric in her hand. The material was the most delicate complex pattern and varied throughout the garment. *So very elegant and sophisticated like my host and sir, Mr. Gray*, she thought as she began undressing, eager to see what it would look like.

It did not disappoint. Angelica looked stunning in the sheer robe, and while it did not leave much to the imagination, it added a touch of class and chic fashion to her gorgeous figure draped inside. After one turn to peek at herself from behind in the mirror, she left to head back to the Playroom and take her place in First Position for her sir.

Kneeling on the bed with knees shoulder width apart, she thought, *Now sitting down on my heels, resting and hands on my knees, palms up. Simple.* But as she waited alone in the Red Playroom, her anticipation grew. She felt her heart pumping harder with nervous tension as she symbolically offered herself to her sir. There was something powerfully primal about giving herself to Edward—like this. She would not have long to wait.

She heard the quiet jiggle of the doorknob as Edward entered the Playroom and closed it behind him with a clear and solid "click" as it shut. He did not speak as she maintained her pose, her gaze transfixed straight ahead. Next, she heard Edward removing something from one of the dresser drawers. Then she could feel him standing directly behind her.

Leaning into her ear slowly, his deep and sexy voice broke the silence as he said, "May I touch you?" He always requested her consent.

"Yes, sir," she said nervously, still feeling tension and excitement growing between them while in First Position. Gray touched her long blonde hair first. He stroked and ran his fingers through it before moving it to one side to bare her neck. Next, he reached his hand around her, placing his leather-gloved grip firmly on her throat, not squeezing or choking her at all but firmly taking control of her with his hand as he said, "Are you going to be a good girl this evening... and do what Mr. Gray tells you to do?"

Her body had tensed up the moment he walked in the room, but with each step he took, with the arrival of his mighty hand wrapped entirely around her slender neck and now his deep voice seeking consent in her ear, she trembled as she spoke shakily, "Yes, sir." He felt her breathing hard and the shakes from her nervous tension rising.

Before relieving the pressure, he decided to add to the fire and said, "I'm going to take my time tonight. I want to make you ache and quiver and then beg me over and over for permission before I let you finally cum for me tonight. I want to take you there, to the very edge of bliss and relief, only to bring you back down, then build you back up to your limits and hear you beg for permission again and again. But tonight is about learning the power within your loins like never before. I want you to climax so hard for me tonight that you shake and cry, not in pain, not from sorrow but crying out from pleasure as you have never, ever felt before. It is called 'edging,' Ms. Hart, and I want you to do your best not to let me down." He added, "Do you understand me?"

Still quivering with tension and anticipation, Angelica said shakily, "Yes, sir." She was in sweet agony, not from sitting on her heels in First Position, which was easy enough, but from his power over her soul with his voice and touch. She was shivering like she was outside on a freezing winter's day in that sheer robe, even though it was cozy, warm, and safe inside. She shook as she answered, "Yes, sir. I will do my best, sir."

She felt his hand loosen and then release her neck with instructions. "Put on your black silk blindfold," he said as he laid it across her open palm.

Still trembling with anticipation, she replied, "Yes, sir." The blindfold was uber soft and padded for comfort, with an elastic band to keep it securely in place. She slipped it on and was suddenly immersed in total darkness in his world, guided only by his voice and touch.

Gray moved closer to her ear, guiding her further, and said, "Next, I want you to lean completely forward with your head down and that gorgeous heart-shaped ass of yours up." She complied and felt him lift her lace robe up and onto her back, so she was fully exposed and available to him. "Excellent," he said, encouraging her when she was head down and ass up for him. His warm hands caressed her hips and then down the outsides of her legs before lightly tracing the curve of her inner thighs back up to her very moist and aching center. She longed for his touch. She daydreamed about his voice and how he guided her, but to have him explore her this vulnerable and exposed had her heart racing with anticipation.

With his hands guiding her hips, he instructed, "Now roll to your side and then fully onto your back for me." Gray's voice was gentle but firm. She complied with the help of his hands so that she would open to him. With her knees bent and spread wide open for him still near the edge of the bed, Gray knelt on the floor before her so that her mound was at eye level with his voracious appetite. She always loved it when Edward asked, "May I taste you?" seeking her consent.

"Yes, sir," was only a whisper preceding her first moan. She ached aloud with the arrival of his talented tongue. Then, softly, and delicately, he traced her lips to the top and gently pulled her slightly more open with his fingertips. Gray exposed her most sensitive area as his tongue circled and flicked endlessly. She was full of anticipation and nervous energy from a full day of worry about First Position training. Her pent-up energy and stress about slave training were finally released as those emotions and tensions came flowing out of her almost instantly.

Angelica twisted on the bed, gripping the red satin sheets with both hands and urgently cried out and pleaded, "Please, sir, may I cum?" Gray replaced his tongue on her clit with just the tip of his finger to keep the stroke alive and her tension at the edge of release so he could speak and tease her as he said, "Already?"

"Yes, please!" came the second request from Angelica as she lifted her head off the bed, slightly trembling with the first waves of her climax already rushing through her body.

The permission she had begged for came finally from the only voice she longed for. Edward released her with, "Yes, you may cum long and hard for me."

He replaced his finger strokes with his tongue, stroking her fully while he inserted the tips of two fingers into her creamy and aching pussy. He stroked her G-spot gently with his fingers while keeping her peak alive with his tongue repeatedly. He orchestrated the strokes of his fingers and tongue so perfectly timed with the rhythm of the waves crashing through her that she felt that he was part of her. Their energy was powerfully in tune, again and again. Her waves crashed through her until it was so overwhelming, she had to stop. Finally, it was too much as she held her hand up in the gesture of "stop" with her palm towards Edward and mumbled "red" in a loud aching voice.

Edward stopped stroking her instantly and gently placed the palm of his warm hand on her mound to help wind her down. Then, grounding her with his energy, his voice said only, "Breathe. Just breathe."

Her body was still locked tight from the intensity of her climax, but the unbearable intensity had now passed, and she felt her heart still racing.

He watched over her with care and said, "Are you ok, Kitten?"

Angelica breathed deeply but shakily once before she could speak. "Yes ... sir, but it was so intense this time. You kept going when I was already at my very peak. It was just a little too overwhelming," she explained feeling drained but warm and glowing now.

She heard him rise from kneeling and move next to her on the bed as he requested, "Come up further on the bed towards the pillows and lie next to me." She complied and found his chest and shoulder with her head to nuzzle next to him, arms and legs wrapped easily and instantly to cuddle with her sir. "Safe from the world is how I feel when I am with you, Edward," she said softly.

He squeezed her gently and asked, "Feeling back to normal now?" She pressed her nose into his ear to whisper, "I'm still floating, sir."

Gray was happiest when she was content. He encouraged her progress and said, "I am very proud of you, Kitten. You have come such a long way in such a short time."

She loved hearing his words of affirmation and positive energy about anything big or small. But mostly, it was how he spoke to her kindly. She felt cherished by Edward, which powered her devotion to him.

Gray shared a revelation and said, "You felt different tonight. Did you notice what happened?"

Angelica quickly responded, "It was much more intense!"

Gray nodded in agreement and added, "It started when you assumed First Position. It was your complete and total submission for the first time. It was a letting go of control and, with it, everything that distracts the mind. It felt as if you were completely and totally mine."

She added with excitement in her voice, "And when you had me put on the blindfold in First Position, it took me to another level of being owned by you," she described.

Curious to know, he asked, "How did that feel?"

Angelica thought about it for a moment. "A mix of excitement and nervous energy, but when you began touching me and, oh my god, when you did oral," she paused to think of another word, "Amazing! Simply amazing." She kissed him over and over on his cheek as if saying "thank you" with her little rapid kisses playfully.

He smiled and reached over to lift the blindfold from her eyes and up slightly on her forehead so she could see for a few minutes. "Better?" he asked with her vision now restored.

She quipped, "I'm actually starting to get used to the blindfold now. I just have to follow your lead because I can't see a darn thing." She smiled with a beautiful gaze at Edward.

"Well, I need you to see for a few minutes," he continued as he slowly stood up from the giant red bed in the center of the Playroom. He walked over to the wall where a wooden and wrought iron rack held a series of floggers, paddles, and riding crops. Gray selected the black flogger with soft suede leather strips bound to a black handle wrapped in leather. Lifting it from its hook on the wall, he returned to the bed and asked, "Remember this?"

Angelica's eyes widened a bit at the arrival of the relatively large black flogger now in Gray's hands and answered, "Um, yes, sir. From our make-up sex at our hotel suite." She could feel the butterflies of nervousness returning to her stomach again.

Gray intervened with encouragement and said, "There is nothing to worry about. Here, feel the soft suede leather strips," as he handed the flogger to Angelica to hold.

"This particular flogger is very high-end and is specially designed to make a lot of noise but does not hurt at all nor does it leave any marks." Angelica ran her fingers through the soft suede leather strips but was not convinced that the big flogger would not hurt if she were truly whipped. Gray, sensing her apprehension over the intimidating-looking flogger, reached over and took it from her and said, "Please allow me to demonstrate on myself."

Lying down next to her with one knee bent to expose his thigh as an ample target, he swung the flogger with full force. Upon striking his leg, the flogger made a surprisingly loud cracking sound like that of a whip on flesh. Gray looked her in the eyes and said, "Nothing. It didn't hurt a bit," he added. "Now, some floggers, paddles, and riding crops you see hanging on the walls can sting a bit. But others like this one are specially designed for impact play training," he explained.

Angelica was feeling a bit more comfortable and even a little curious after seeing Edward demonstrate on himself without so much as the slightest twinge on his face when struck by the flogger. Then, finally, he asked her, "Would you turn over for me and lay on your stomach, Angelica? I want you to feel it lightly for yourself, and you will see what I mean."

She immediately turned over, lying flat so that her bare bottom and legs were exposed. Still wearing the lace robe covering only her upper body, she offered herself simply and said, "I trust you, sir."

Gray dangled the flogger in his hand high above her back and lightly traced the outlines of her shoulder blades and spine very softly. "Most people don't understand impact play," he said. "They think it is just about pain, but it can be very sensual." He lightly and delicately ran the soft suede across the back of her legs, down to her calves and the soft soles of her feet and toes. "How does that feel?" he asked.

She smiled. "It's nice, almost like a backrub with a feather," she said, laughing lightly.

Gray said in encouragement, "Exactly! But then, the intrigue builds because you never know when you'll get a little love tap." He swung the flogger gently, giving her the first of a series of little spanks on the bottom. Then, asking her promptly, he said, "Did that hurt at all?"

Angelica enthusiastically said, "No, not even a little bit!" She was a bit relieved to discover that it was just as Edward promised. He continued and said, "Now, Kitten, pretend you have been a naughty girl today, and I am going to give you five spanks on the bottom. I want you to count them out loud for me each time you feel the flogger, ok?"

She felt adventurous as she complied, "Yes, sir!" Gray, without hesitation or delay, delivered the first stroke of the flogger as lightly as he could. Angelica counted out loud, "One!" The next swing of the flogger Gray made ever so slightly with more force. "Two," she counted aloud.

Finally, Gray said, "Just a tiny bit harder this time." He eased the power up to medium and a louder "whack" was heard as the suede strips of the flogger found their mark on her backside.

"Three!" Angelica shouted with playful and fun energy. She was growing bolder as she became more comfortable. Gray added more speed as he swung, and a louder strike was heard over her voice, as she called out, "Four!" As he had been alternating butt cheeks between each blow, he now moved down to the top of her thighs for the last and final swing, which made the loudest sound as it struck, and Angelica said, "Five!"

Gray instantly asked for her report. "How much did it hurt, Kitten?"

She looked up at him, smiling, and said, "Zero. Not at all!"

He looked into her eyes, happy to see all smiles and added, "But it sounded like you were getting a heck of a flogging, didn't it?"

She nodded in agreement and said, "Yes. It sounded like you were whaling on me, but it didn't hurt."

Gray lay down next to her to discuss it further and said, "I would like your permission to add flogging to playtime occasionally. Only some of the time. Otherwise, that would get boring and routine."

Angelica said, "I would be completely open to that now that I've tried it a second time. I was afraid of impact play before. It seemed strange and scary, but now I think it is kind of hot and sexy."

Gray was pleased she was so open to experimenting and smiled at her progress, then added, "Remember our 'make-up sex' as you called it at our hotel suite? Picture this, one day, during playtime, we repeat that scene when I am inside you, doggy style, and I have given you your favorite vibrating toy to hold magically in the right spot. Imagine you are just at the edge of climaxing, perhaps almost as intensely as you just were a few minutes ago. And right as you ask for permission to cum, I add the flogger across your backside with each stroke, me pounding you out as you climax over and over again," he said to her with intensity.

As Edward described it, Angelica was seeing the scene come to life in her imagination, and she confessed, "I am getting so wet again just thinking about it, sir."

Gray ended with, "Can you imagine the intensity that would give both of us?" He smiled.

Angelica wrapped around him and asked, "How can I please you right now, sir?" She looked at him with her seductive bedroom eyes and voice. He stroked her hair and caressed her face softly.

"You have given me the greatest gift already today, Kitten," he said, complimenting her. You have gone to the next level of trust and surrender with how you gave yourself to me today—waiting for your sir in First Position, being blindfolded, and then opening yourself to me so completely like never before. You transcended today to the next level in my world." He kissed her softly. "Nothing more for today, Kitten, as you have been stressing all day and are tired from a lack of sleep I can see in your eyes."

Angelica nodded, admitting he was right, and said, "And the way you made me climax today drained me like you wouldn't believe."

"I don't want you driving home tired and exhausted, Kitten. Come to my room and sleep with me tonight."

Angelica's face lit up at the invitation to sleep wrapped around him and she asked, "Can we leave the door to the balcony open just a crack so I can hear the ocean waves? I slept so soundly last time, hearing the breakers' rhythm rolling in as I slept in your comfy bed."

He replied, "Of course." Edward reached out his hand to help her up and out of the Playroom bed. As they walked across his huge home to the master suite, he said, encouraging her, "Let's go get you a good night's sleep. You need to rest up the next few days because I have you completely to myself for three full days and nights on our weekend trip."

Angelica squeezed his hand and asked, "Oh? Should I be worried, Mr. Gray?" playfully teasing him.

He replied, "That depends on how well-behaved you are, Ms. Hart." With a smile that hinted of more to come, Gray added, "I am bringing the flogger and a few other toys on our trip."

Angelica giggled loudly and enthusiastically, channeling her newly blossoming inner kinkster and gushed, "Don't threaten me with a good time, sir!"

CHAPTER NINETEEN

The Homework

The rhythmical sounds of the ocean waves breaking on the Gulf of Mexico gently filled the morning air. It was always that deep percussion as the waves broke, followed by a softening sizzle that faded away as each wave inevitably gave in to make room for the next. It was a song that had played for millennia that filled the room and Angelica's first morning stretch. She wiggled her toes under Edward's silky Egyptian cotton sheets, which felt just one shade above excellent in incredible softness. She sighed out loud, looking around to find him but, of course, he was gone already. Ever the early morning riser and alpha entrepreneur, his note on the pillow where his head had watched her sleep pre-dawn wished her "Good Morning" and invited her to help herself to anything in the kitchen.

She loved getting Edward's written notes in the mornings when she had been invited to sleep over on a few rare occasions. But this one had a unique twist and said, "Call me after work. I have a homework assignment for you to prepare for our upcoming trip." She smiled with instant curiosity about what it might be as she stretched one more time before getting up for work. Something about that bed and the ocean waves invited her to sleep in forever if she could. *Duty calls*, she thought, glancing at the clock and the need to get home, shower, and get to the office. *Only two days to go before their trip*, she thought, walking through Edward's palatial home. *What this home needs is a couple of dogs*, she thought as she walked across the empty expanse of the living room. *Something to add warmth and that feeling of home.* The Keurig machine filled the room with the aroma of freshly brewed coffee for the ride home. She loved that everything felt back to normal between the two of them, if normal can describe what it feels like being with a Dominant like Edward. Her unfounded fears and worries about Slave Training had melted into his voice, guiding her last night. They had bonded on a deeper level. She had given herself to him entirely. Now, wearing nothing but his white linen button-down dress shirt, she was in his kitchen making coffee. It was her favorite makeshift pajamas when she slept over with Edward. What a fantastic way to start a Wednesday.

It was quite a rush to drive home, get ready, and then get to her property management office. Sometimes she felt like she was catching every red light when she was in a hurry. But she finally made it only a minute or two late which was a good feat of magic, given the logistics of getting home and then back downtown. She had never packed an overnight bag when Edward invited her to his place for an evening date, but that would save a lot of time and having to race around in the morning on a workday. She didn't feel it was her place to suggest the idea as she did not want to "assume" that she would be invited to stay over in his world. Perhaps the opportunity could come up to discuss it on their trip.

Work flew by with nothing consequential to deal with, and she looked forward to leaving the office right on time for her call with Edward. But mostly, she looked forward to hearing his voice. Plus, there was an added bonus of her homework assignment she had been curious about all day. As she locked up the office and headed to her car, his text arrived, signaling that she would not have long to wait. *Call me when you are available to talk. Edward.*

Angelica smiled and teased him playfully in her text reply. *I am always available to you, sir.*

Her phone rang almost immediately, and as she answered it, his voice came through clear and calm as he said, "I thought I would test the words of your last text, Ms. Hart." Her pulse quickened as only it could with his voice. There was something about Edward when he was in his Dominant mode. His voice changed to a subtle but significantly different gear of tone and slow, measured pace such that each word was clearly heard and understood. It worked if it were his design to keep her hanging onto his every word.

Instinctively, she replied to his greeting, "Yes, sir, I am here for you always."

The deep voice responded, "Good answer, Kitten. I like it most when we are together in person, where I can see your eyes, touch you, and feel your breath. But we cannot be together every moment of the day, and that is the purpose of your homework assignment tonight."

Angelica felt flush hearing his words about their deep connection and energy together. She smiled instantly as she heard him describe precisely how she felt being at the center of his attention and responded, "Thank you, sir. It makes me happy, more than you will ever know, when I please you."

Gray said, "As we are flying out to D.C. tomorrow evening, I have to work late at the office wrapping up paperwork and loose ends and then get home to finish packing for the trip. So, I won't be able to see you this evening in person. However, I have taken the liberty of ordering you dinner. It is being delivered at about 7 p.m. to your home, and once you have had dinner and are all packed and settled, call me for your homework assignment this evening."

"Edward, you have no idea how it makes me feel that you think of me. That you thought to send me dinner on a busy day to take care of me means the world," Angelica said, speaking in a serious tone now with a sincere and earnest ache in her voice. What she did not say but felt in her heart was that it meant more than extravagant shopping and an unlimited clothing budget. She loved his attention and care most of all. So, instead, she said only, "I will text you tonight when I am all packed."

The unspoken words of a heart aching went unsaid as she hung up, still sitting in her car in the office parking lot. She sighed as her engine started a bit slowly. For some reason, it took a second attempt for the machine to roar to life. *I will have to get my car checked out when I return from Washington*, she thought. The red sports car was no match for the speed of her racing mind wondering what Edward had ordered her for dinner. He always loved surprising her. Most of all, she had been thinking about what she needed to pack for tomorrow's long weekend getaway trip with Edward.

Her car pulled into the hair salon at the last minute for a quick stop on her way home to get some travel-size hair products. It was an excellent excuse to see her friend and confidant, Samantha, who would be dying to hear all the juicy details about the weekend trip with Edward. Despite signing the Confidentiality Agreement, Angelica simply could not resist telling at least one of her friends about heading off on a private jet to Washington, D.C.!

When she walked into the salon unexpectedly, Angelica smiled broadly and saw Samantha give her a discreet little hand wave as she was finishing up with her last client. Angelica gathered up a few of her favorite hair products in travel size while she waited for Samantha to be free to talk. She was secretly beaming inside to tell her the latest but could hardly wait for her to ring up her client and be free to speak. Samantha was a beautiful blonde herself and was no stranger to dating and the ways of men. Angelica loved getting her advice, especially since she was one of her friends who had known the most about Edward Gray and his vast business and financial reputation when Angelica first met him.

"Hey there!" Samantha said, beaming as she walked over to give her a friendly hug. "I wasn't expecting you today, was I? Your hair still looks great!" she added, touching Angelica's long, flowing blonde locks, and admiring her work. Angelica held up the hair products and handed the travel-sized bottles to Samantha. "No, I just stopped by to pick these up for a trip and see you for a quick minute."

"Sure, let me ring these up for you," Samantha said, smiling. "Where are we off to?" she asked nonchalantly in the tone you might expect for small talk at the salon.

Angelica paused, and the biggest smile crept over her face as she whispered, "Can you keep a secret?" She leaned in towards Samantha across the register as she spoke.

It took only a heartbeat for Samantha to pause and look at Angelica with widening eyes as she said with hushed excitement, "Oh my gosh! You two are going away somewhere? First the black-tie event and now travel. Is this getting serious?"

Angelica's smile said it all, but Samantha wanted more. "Tell me all the juicy details!" she urged as she took Angelica's card, which still read Edward Gray, Platinum American Express, across the front.

Angelica looked around the busy salon with customers and other staff milling around close to them and said, "I'm dying to tell

238

you, but I promised to keep it confidential. I'm not sure if I can talk here. Perhaps I can call you later?"

Samantha intervened and said, "Better than that, how about we grab a quick drink next door, and you can tell me all about it? That was my last client, and I can head out now if you are free."

Angelica agreed with one caveat. "Ok, but just one drink. I have to get home to pack yet."

Samantha nodded in agreement and said, "Just let me grab my things."

The two blondes walked the short half block and across the street, to a great little Italian place called Caragiulo's which had been in downtown Sarasota for two generations. The smell of fresh Italian bread and delicious plates of food on their way to tables filled the air. It was one of those places where if you weren't hungry when you arrived, just wait a few minutes. Angelica and Samantha made a striking pair of blondes at the bar for anyone passing by on the sidewalk looking into the charming bistro. They each ordered a Grey Goose Cosmo, but only after Angelica started discussing the trip with Edward.

"So, we had our first fight after the black-tie event last weekend," Angelica said, offering the news about the drama first. "Why is it that men blame us when other men are flirting or hitting on us?" she asked Samantha for her sporting opinion about the topic.

Samantha smiled. "Oh honey, don't get me started," she said, laughing out loud as their Cosmopolitans arrived. "Cheers!" she added. They clinked and resumed their quiet huddle to get to the big news.

Angelica shared the story about the stress of the short-lived breakup and the painful details of the silent ride home from Tampa. But when Angelica relayed how she went to his home late at night to beg him to listen to her, Samantha interrupted her and advised, "Oh, sweetheart, never beg a man to take you back or to make up. It can open some bad doors and roads you don't want to go down," she said.

Angelica listened to her sage advice but added, "Well, it's too late now for last time, but I hear you."

Samantha, wanting all the details, egged her on and said, "So things must have worked out somehow?"

Angelica's smile was a dead giveaway as she described how they "kissed and made up" all the next day and night at the Ritz Carlton and confided, "I think we actually bonded and were closer after what happened. But I don't ever want to go through that again."

All caught up on recent events, Samantha inquired about the trip next. "So where is Mr. Gray taking you? What's up with this trip all of a sudden?" she asked with excitement, smiling with encouragement to get all of the scoops.

Angelica took another sip of the Cosmo, which was going down very smoothly, and began, "Well, Edward bought a company in Washington, D.C., and has a fancy closing dinner scheduled with the former owner and his son this Friday. So, he asked me to join him and be his dinner date, plus have a long weekend in D.C. with him."

"That's huge!" Samantha exclaimed. "He trusts you to be in front of his business associates at an important function." She recognized it instantly. "That shows how much he trusts you."

Angelica had thought about that somewhat but had not framed it in her mind as a sign of great trust by Edward until she heard Samantha word it that way. So, thinking more deeply now, Angelica added, "I guess you're right."

Samantha shared, "From what I hear about Gray around town, he never lets any woman into his inner circle. So many have tried, and they all crash and burn. He is one of the most eligible bachelors in South Florida but always remains very aloof, unobtainable, if you know what I mean?" Samantha warned her friend, hoping she would be careful and not get hurt.

Angelica thought about her sobering words while finishing her Cosmo. "Thanks, Samantha. That is good to know, I think."

Then, Samantha inquired, "When are you two love birds flying out?"

Angelica smiled on a much more positive note and said, "Tomorrow night, right after work!" She perked up thinking about the trip just twenty-four hours away.

Samantha said, "You'll be flying first class and enjoying life to the max. I'm more than a bit jealous!" She laughed out loud and added, "Want one more Cosmo before you go?"

Angelica looked at her watch and said, "Thanks, but I can't. I have to get home to pack. Edward has ordered dinner delivered for me at home while I am packing tonight, and I need to get going. I don't want to be late."

Samantha shook her head with envy and commented, "This is really getting serious with you two."

Angelica pulled out her card again to cover the drinks and said, with a little wink between friends, "My treat." Both of them knew full well that Mr. Gray was treating happy hour.

Leaning over to whisper one last secret reveal, Angelica said, "Samantha, one last thing. I thought we would be flying first class on an airline too. But we're not. He is flying us up to D.C. in a private jet." She covered her whisper with her hand by Samantha's ear for added privacy.

"No way. Holy shit!" Samantha said loud enough for a few others to hear. Her face was still in disbelief as her friend was suddenly turning into Cinderella at the ball before her very eyes.

As Angelica signed the check for the drinks, she parted ways with her friend, giving her a hug but wondering if jealousy might spoil her friendship with Samantha.

As she drove home to start packing, her mind kept thinking about how Samantha had reacted to her newfound life of luxury with Edward. And what about her other friends? Might they see this sudden leap of lifestyle and be less than supportive, perhaps secretly even hoping Angelica might crash and burn as Samantha had forewarned? Her mind kept going over the happy hour conversation and wondered, *Perhaps this is why Edward wanted her to sign the Confidentiality Agreement?* Perhaps the wealthy had to deal with this sort of thing all the time, or worse? She would think about it later, she resolved as she pulled into her driveway. Time to get inside and start packing!

She smiled as she breezed through her front door, excited to start getting ready for her weekend getaway with Edward. In only twenty-four hours, she would zoom away with Mr. Gray to our nation's capitol. Her adrenaline surged each time she thought of it. She was filled with pre-vacation excitement on the eve of the trip.

She poured herself a glass of white wine and started to get organized. First, the suitcase was laid wide open on the bed, ready to receive its cargo.

She would, of course, bring all the new items she had just purchased for the trip at Edward's suggestion, plus the sexy lingerie she had bought but not worn for him yet. She smiled as she put them piece by piece in her suitcase, each in a separate dry cleaner's plastic bag—a little travel trick to keep things from getting wrinkled in the suitcase she had read about online.

The doorbell rang just as she was about to start on her bathroom toiletries and makeup. *The food is here!* she thought, realizing how famished she was. She raced to the door and, as she had hoped, it was her delivery from Edward with two big bags of goodies from P.F. Chang's downtown. She loved their food and thanked the delivery driver, asking if she could tip him. He held up his hand and said it was already taken care of. She smiled as she set the bags on her kitchen counter and tore them open to reveal the goodies. It was fantastic sushi and Japanese hibachi with stir-fried vegetables, filet mignon, and lobster.

Angelica plated her first course on a nice dish and sat down at the barstool in her kitchen with her glass of wine. She didn't realize her hunger until she smelled the fantastic food. She loved sushi and dived into that first with the chopsticks in hand. While she ate, she texted Edward, *My amazing dinner just arrived, and it is so delicious! Thank you so much!* She added emojis for hearts and kisses to Edward.

Gray was not much of an emoji type of guy texting but smiled to see her enthusiasm and simply replied, *I'm glad you liked it.* He added, *It is a preview of coming attractions as our hotel in downtown D.C. is newly remodeled with an Asian theme that is quite beautiful. So, enjoy, and text me later when you finish packing for your homework assignment.*

As Angelica munched on her crisp ginger salad, she replied, *I will, I promise!* After wolfing down dinner quickly, she washed her hands and returned to packing for the trip. She was proud that she got everything she needed into one suitcase and one little carry-on bag. She wanted to avoid showing up at the airport looking like she brought too many suitcases. Gray would think she was "moving in."

She looked at the neatly packed bag with everything perfectly organized and ready for the trip. The only thing left was to close the suitcase up, but she preferred to wait until the morning to do that just in case she thought of any last items she wanted to bring along. So, she texted Edward, *I'm all packed and ready for our trip!* Smiling, she hit the send button.

Her reply came quickly, which she always loved, and he said simply, *Will call you in just a few minutes.*

She poured herself another glass of wine and started turning down the lights and locking up her home for the evening to get ready for Edward and homework. She was eagerly curious to see what this assignment would be. When the phone rang, she beamed and said in her most flirtatious voice, "Well, good evening, Mr. Gray."

Edward chuckled at her somewhat over-the-top greeting and retorted, "Sounds like someone is already in-flight to Washington without the plane! Glad to hear you are in a good mood."

Gushing like it was Christmas Eve, she said, "Yes, I am so excited about our trip tomorrow! I can hardly wait! I loved the dinner from P.F. Chang's, Edward. In a kinder and sweeter voice, she added, "That was so very thoughtful of you."

In his easygoing tone, Edward replied, "You are very welcome. It was my absolute pleasure."

Angelica's curiosity could wait no longer as she asked, "So what is this homework assignment you have for me?"

Gray replied, "Thank you for the question." Clearing his throat lightly before he began, he said, "First, to be clear, I want to share the purpose of the homework before we get into the details. Would that be all right with you?"

She replied, "Of course."

"In thinking about you and some of the uncertainties and fears you have, some of which go way back to childhood and perhaps a bit of abuse or trauma along that journey, I would like some of your homework to be dedicated to self-care as a positive healthy and whole person, Angelica. I think you will like this assignment a lot. Would you be open to exploring that for a few minutes for me?"

Angelica was still not sure what Edward meant exactly, just yet, but replied, "I trust you Edward, and I would do anything for you. Tell me more about it."

His deep voice said, "Thank you. And trust must be earned over a long period of time. But tonight, I want you to invest in trusting and appreciating yourself. So here is the homework assignment. It is called the Mirror Exercise, and it has three parts. First, I would like you to take a hot shower or a bubble bath, whichever is your favorite ritual when you want some downtime. Then afterward, use cocoa butter or whatever moisturizer you love to make your skin feel cared for from head to toe. Think of it like a mini-home-spa date experience.

"Step two: Put a chair in front of your full-length mirror in your bedroom and sit so you are facing looking directly into your own eyes. Get comfortable, for the homework will take about fifteen minutes, and it works best if you turn the ringer on your phone off.

"Step three: I want you to say what you most appreciate about yourself aloud. What do you most admire about yourself? What you are most proud of about the person that you are? And if you feel uncomfortable saying these things, imagine it is me saying them to you for you to hear. Lastly, I want you to complete the fifteen minutes by saying aloud what are the things in your life that you are most grateful for. Do all of this while looking directly into your own eyes in the mirror."

Edward paused from his description of the Mirror Exercise to ask Angelica if she had any questions.

Speaking slowly, she asked timidly, "I've never done anything like this before. What if I feel weird or uncomfortable?"

Encouraging her, Edward said, "You deserve to hear these things about you, Angelica. And most people have low self-esteem. Most people feel that they aren't worthy." He paused before he added, "You are rare. You are exceptional. And you are worthy. This is a good first step in building you into a more confident, stronger Angelica."

Her eyes lit up as she listened silently to Edward's words.

Edward asked, "Are you still there, Angelica?"

She sniffled, "Yes, sir."

"Why are you crying, Kitten?" he asked quietly.

"Because no one has ever talked to me this way before." Now the tears were welling up bigger and rolling down onto her cheeks.

Gray said in his deep and reassuring voice, "This is homework for me, Kitten. And imagine it is me there with you, cherishing and encouraging you. Imagine they are my words, not just your own, and be brave and bold with your praise for the full fifteen minutes, if you can. Will you do that for me?"

Angelica smiled and laughed a little with the crying still in her voice as she replied, "Yes, sir."

Edward said, "You're my good girl, and I am proud of you. Please text me when you finish your homework, ok?"

Exhaling, she said, "I will." She set the phone down on the bed and looked at the door to her master bath and thought to herself as she sighed, *Why couldn't he ask me to do something easy, like another O.M. session? Bubble bath*, she thought to herself. *Definitely going to be a bubble bath tonight for the homework.* She exhaled with the tears still blurring her vision and got up to start running her bath with her favorite lavender bath beads. *He did say to make it like a home spa date with him*, she thought, so she lit a candle in the bathroom and got another glass of wine. As she slipped out of her office clothes and put them away, she saw her bath was nearly complete. Time to sink in and relax.

Soaking in the bubble bath with music, a candle, and a glass of wine is a pretty tough assignment from Mr. Gray, she thought with a smile as she surveyed her bathroom and looked at her wet, glistening toes sticking up through the bubbles. She had always loved bubble baths, especially when she was little. She breathed deeply and exhaled as Edward had taught her to relax. She smiled warmly in the bath but was still uncomfortable with the coming Mirror Exercise.

What if I just told Edward that I did the homework assignment, which was nice? she thought. *How would he really know?* She lay in the bubble bath, trying to figure out ways around the rest of the homework. Then, finally, she decided to think about something else, like the trip. For that, she was genuinely excited.

When Angelica exited the bathtub, with lavender bubbles gurgling down the drain, she toweled off slowly and took her time. She loved cocoa butter, which Edward knew, and filled her cupped palm with several pumps of the butter from the bottle on her bathroom counter and, rubbing both palms together, got prepared to coat her legs first. Again, she took her time and did every part of her except her back which was hard to reach. Afterward, she slipped into her pink robe. She brushed her teeth and did everything to get ready for bed, except for the final homework assignment.

She got her comfortable chair and positioned it just in front of her full-length mirror as Edward had requested and thought about it for one more moment before sitting down. Again, Angelica looked at herself in the mirror. But this time, she looked at herself, not as if she were brushing her hair or fixing her makeup. She really looked. She looked into her own eyes for a good full minute. It was a different feeling; almost odd, really looking herself in the eyes.

She thought about what Gray had asked her to do and said out loud to her reflection, "Edward wanted me to tell you that you are amazing. You are beautiful and exciting to your man. You are kind. You are a good person. You take care of everyone at work. They count on you, and you are always there for them." Her voice drifting into the night, she added, "You are a good friend to others. And, you are worthy."

CHAPTER TWENTY

Wheels Up

Angelica woke up sleeping next to her fully packed but still open suitcase. Her sleepy eyes barely opened to the sight of the bag. She smiled, remembering what day it was. Travel day! Her eyes searched for the time on the digital clock by her bed, which told her it was only half past five in the morning. *Oh, good. I can sleep in a bit longer*, she thought as she wrapped around her pillow, imagining it was Edward snuggled next to her in their hotel bed over the weekend just ahead. The smile grew bigger with her eyes wide shut, but now her mind was racing with the idea of pulling him closer and wrapping around his muscular frame and having him to herself for three whole days. *Oh my!*

Angelica gave up. There was no going back to sleep now with her adrenaline starting her mind to race already. She picked up her cell phone to look at her screen and discovered one text from Edward, from the night before, asking how her homework assignment had gone and then saying, *Sweet dreams*. After that, she didn't even remember going to sleep. After those few glasses of wine and the hot bubble bath, she had been very relaxed, but then the Mirror Exercise had done her in. She did the full fifteen minutes in front of the mirror as Edward had asked, crying several times. Afterward, she crawled into bed and was out like a light switch had gone off.

She was a delicate soul that rarely heard those words, the ones that tell you how great you really are except maybe her grandmother on their talks, just the two of them, when she was little. She was her grandmother's favorite, and they had been very close. She still missed her.

Knowing he was always up early, she texted Edward, *Good morning! I'm up already making coffee.* She was hoping to surprise him that she was up early and that he might be proud of her for being an early riser like him.

Angelica's phone buzzed with his reply. *Good morning, Kitten. You're an early bird this morning!* She smiled at every little acknowledgment she received from Edward. They were her oxygen. He continued, *Are you looking forward to flying off to D.C. this evening for our trip?*

Was this the understatement of the year, or what? Her coffee was brewing as she replied, smiling, just giddy with excitement on pure adrenaline this early with no caffeine helping yet. *I simply cannot wait to spend time with you!* She sent her message while beaming. She only wished she had a magic time machine, and it could already be this afternoon. How she wanted it to already be time to go to the airport and be transported into another world with Edward.

He held her captive with his final note as he added, *I'm off to the office to wrap up some important work before we go. But I'm already counting the hours until we fly away together.*

Angelica's biggest smile peeked out as she read his last line. She finally took her second sip of coffee and thought instantly, *Counting down the hours? I will be counting the minutes! Time to shower and get to the office early.* She could get a head start and make her day zip on by!

Try as she might to get Thursday to fly by, it simply would not. She watched the clock too often and time seemed to stand still. But finally, as it always does, four-thirty in the afternoon arrived, and Angelica left the office as if shot out of a cannon. The Sarasota-Bradenton airport was only five miles from her downtown office, but it would not get any closer soon. Her car wouldn't start. She turned the key for the fifth time. "Oh no! Of all days for this to happen." She looked at her watch and wondered if she should call Edward or just call an Uber. She hated to bother him, especially since this was a bit embarrassing to her for some reason. So, her passion-red Nissan Z just sat there dark and depressed in her office parking lot.

She remembered Edward's words to her when he said, "Whenever there is a problem, come directly to me without delay with total transparency." So, she gathered up her courage and gave him her report via text, *I've just left the office, but my car won't start. Should I call an Uber? I don't want to be late!* She sighed as she pressed the send button. Finally, the problem was off her plate. Now it was shared by the two of them. She waited in suspense for his text reply, which did not come.

Instead, her phone rang. Seeing it was Edward, she tentatively answered, "Hello."

Gray was in a booming mood and instantly changed her state with his playful reply. "Hello, ma'am. I understand you just called for the Edward Gray Uber service. We happen to be just leaving the parking garage of my building downtown, only a few short blocks from you. We can be there to pick you up in about two minutes if that might be helpful?" he said with an energetic, upbeat tone.

A relieved Angelica laughed out loud at his fun bit of comedy at the situation and said, "Why, yes, that would be absolutely lovely!" She was thankful and smiling at his playful response and added, "I will see you soon!" She didn't have long to wait.

She recognized the same black Cadillac Escalade and driver from the black-tie event in Tampa pulling into the parking lot just moments after their call. It pulled right up next to her vehicle, and Edward and his driver exited to help her aboard. Waving to their driver, Angelica said, "Hello again, Taylor."

Greeting her more formally, Taylor said, "Good afternoon, Ms. Hart." He reached into her open trunk to grab and load her bags into the SUV.

Edward gave her a quick but firm hug, almost lifting her off the ground, and a quick kiss before opening her door for her. "Ready to go see what Washington, D.C., is up to?" he said nonchalantly, his smile revealing his shared excitement.

Angelica managed a quick "I am!" before her door closed. Edward circled around the SUV to join her on his side.

The driver closed the automatic hatch and slid into the driver seat and said, "On our way."

Angelica felt relieved and excited that her momentary car issue had not become a major calamity. "Thank you both for rescuing a damsel in distress. I don't know what I would have done without you two gallant gentlemen coming to pick me up."

Gray said, "A problem shared is half the challenge, as you can now quickly see." He smiled, acknowledging that she had trusted him with her predicament.

Taylor followed Gray's lead and said, "Never a bother at all, Ms. Hart. Happy to pick you up. Do you think it might be a dead battery or something else?"

She replied with a slight shrug and said, "I have no idea, actually. It was just completely dead this afternoon."

Gray nodded and offered, "If you don't mind leaving your keys with Taylor, he can have it looked at tomorrow while we are away and hopefully fixed good as new when we return."

Angelica was bashful to accept the offer for help with her car and said, "Oh, I don't want to impose. Besides, you already went out of your way to pick me up this afternoon."

Edward's practical logic was undeniable as he said, "It will need to get fixed sooner or later. It might as well be while we are out of town, and you don't need your car. Yes?"

She thought about it and could find no plausible arguments to debate his offer. "Well, if it is not too much trouble…"

Taylor, overhearing the discussion, chimed in, relieving her worry and said, "It will be no trouble at all, Ms. Hart. I know one of the guys at the Nissan dealership, he is a good friend, and I'm sure they will be happy to help."

As Angelica handed her car keys forward, she said, "Thank you so much!" She always felt safe with Edward, but now she felt even more profoundly that way. Going through a crisis together, even a little one, makes you feel closer. All the stress had left her body, leaving only relief and euphoria. What a great way to get to the airport, and what great company to be with! She was almost glad that her car wouldn't start now. And it would not be left at her office parking lot all weekend until they returned. *Even better*, she thought.

Taylor pulled the full-size, long-body Escalade into the Rectrix Airport parking lot at the Sarasota jetport entrance. Angelica pressed her face to the SUV window to ogle at the sleek, streamlined jets of various makes and types. Each looked prepped and waiting for their passengers to zip away whenever ready with no schedules to check and no security lines requiring you to remove your shoes and be probed and searched. Private aviation was a different lifestyle. Angelica smiled shyly at Edward as this was his world, not hers.

Sensing her fish-out-of-water dilemma, Edward offered, "Let's get checked in, and I will show you around a bit if you like."

She nodded silently and waited for him to arrive at her passenger door. The door opened to a new world as Edward's warm palm was there to help her step down and she said politely, "Thank you."

Edward slipped his arm gently around her waist to keep her close to his side as they walked towards the double doors of the jetport. The sounds of plane engines in the background of various pitches and speeds were heard as some were winding down and others were taking off.

Gray opened the glass entrance door to the jetport for Angelica, which held a small lounge with comfortable oversized leather chairs and a refreshment center, plus a wall of electronics and avionics equipment for the private pilot enthusiast to browse. Edward guided her to the check-in counter manned only by an older gentleman, wearing a leather flight jacket covered with patches and insignias of various types, who looked like a veteran pilot who lived in this world. Greeting them, the older man said, "Hello, Mr. Gray."

Gray nodded his head and respectfully replied, "Good afternoon. Here to check in with you."

The jetport manager pulled out an iPad for Edward to sign in with. After a few clicks on the tablet, the gentleman said, "Mr. Gray, your Gulfstream 650 is fully fueled, and your pilots have already completed their preflight check-in and filed your flight path with the tower. You and your guest can load and board at your convenience. I will radio your pilots to let them know you have arrived."

Gray nodded and added, "Thanks for the great service. We'll see you back here Sunday." He squeezed Angelica's side slightly once, indicating it was time to head out. They rejoined Taylor who had loaded all their bags from the SUV to a rolling jetport cart, and the three of them headed towards the waiting white Gulfstream.

As she looked at the sleek, swept-back-looking lines of the 650, Angelica said with giddy excitement, "It looks like it's going fast even just sitting there parked on the ground!" Curious, she said, "If you don't mind me asking, what does a jet like this cost, Edward?"

Gray was never someone to talk about what he owned or how much things cost. It was not how he was raised, nor did he feel the need to impress anyone with what he had. His eyes narrowed, and his lips squeezed into a narrow line before he replied, "This model runs around 65 million dollars new, but most clients like me use fractional ownership where we pay for flight hours used, not the entire plane. It is much more cost-efficient that way."

Angelica, processing what he said, asked, "Kind of like a time-share condo?" Wide-eyed, she hoped she got the concept.

Agreeing with her quick and accurate analogy, Edward smiled and said, "Exactly like a time-share."

Taylor met the copilot just outside the baggage compartment on the tarmac, and the two began loading the baggage into the Gulfstream, which could have held much more cargo than they were bringing aboard. Angelica now realized packing for the trip didn't need to be limited to her one suitcase. *Mental note for the next time.*

Gray guided her to the sleek stainless steel and white staircase leading them into the plane and said, "Ladies first."

She climbed the ten steps upward to enter the jet, and there she was greeted by a lovely redheaded flight attendant in uniform who greeted her with a warm smile and said, "Welcome aboard, Ms. Hart."

Angelica smiled and said, "Thank you. You are so pretty!" She always complimented other beautiful women. She turned and looked across the most luxurious and opulent interior with light tan leather seats and couches, which looked ready to comfortably hold fifteen or more people. She was surprised at the size of the jet for just the two of them.

The attendant, sensing Angelica's hesitation, added, "Sit anywhere you like."

Angelica paused, waiting for Edward to arrive and guide her. In a deep voice, he said, "Good morning, Crystina."

"Great to see you again, Mr. Gray. Good to have you aboard. Please get comfortable in your seats, and I will be over momentarily to take your drink and dinner orders."

Gray nodded and led Angelica to the two oversized first-class style seats connected without an aisle separating them and gave her the window seat. They were just settled in when Crystina arrived with her smile again.

"Care for a drink before takeoff?" she asked them, acknowledging them each individually with her eyes.

Edward looked at Angelica and asked, "Care for a glass of wine, champagne, or a cocktail?"

Now hearing the full bar menu, Angelica requested, "How about a mimosa?" She smiled as she thought of their recent brunch at the Ritz, which had led to her daylong next level of training.

Looking into his eyes with a twinkle, she smiled, and Gray, getting her subtle reference, said, while gently squeezing Angelica's hand, "Two mimosas, please,"

She leaned into his ear so that the flight attendant might not hear her and said, "This is so impressive, Edward. I knew it might be fancy, but I had no idea!" Her eyes were still wide from taking it all in as the sound of a champagne bottle popped in the Gulfstream's small, but well-appointed kitchen galley and bar.

Looking into her eyes, Gray smiled only slightly, never the boastful braggart, and said simply, "I'm glad you approve, Kitten. But the most important part of this flight to Washington is who is sitting next to me."

She felt his warm admiring gaze for a long moment before Crystina returned with the mimosas for each and said, "Cheers! I will be back after takeoff for your dinner orders." Nodding graciously to them both, Crystina returned to the front to notify the pilots that they were all aboard with seat belts on and ready to roll.

The captain's voice came over the PA system from the front of the flight deck. "Good evening, Mr. Gray and Ms. Hart. This is Captain Charles Gross joined up front by Co-Captain Michael Bailey for this evening's flight. We will be taxiing and preparing for takeoff shortly, and I will return later in the flight to provide you with an update. If you need anything, just let your exceptional flight attendant Crystina know, and we will see you on the ground in under two hours from wheels up to wheels down. So please sit back and enjoy. We have a clear night with 72 degrees in Washington, D.C., so you should arrive on time with a smooth flight this evening. Captain out."

Angelica, squeezing his arm with one hand and raising her champagne flute with the other, smiled broadly and said, "Cheers!"

Gray winked at her as they toasted, and he commented with a bit of humor, "Things could be worse." They both smiled and took a sip.

Edward changed his tone and asked, "Did you do your homework assignment for me? I didn't hear back from my text last night."

Angelica silently nodded a few times in the affirmative, looking down at her glass.

Gray waited a moment before inquiring further, "And... how did it go?"

She paused and answered, "I did everything you asked. First, a bubble bath and then the Mirror Exercise. I did the full fifteen minutes like you said." Angelica stopped there without further details.

Probing a bit further, he asked knowingly, "How did it feel?"

Angelica instantly welled up with a resurgence of the tears from the night before as she said, "I couldn't stop... crying."

Edward held her hand and said, "It's ok. Thank you for sharing that." Gray thought about their journey together to this moment, how they had met, and the many steps to here and now. "It gets easier." Angelica's eyes met his to listen to his meaning. He gazed deeply back at her and added, "When you are ready, try the Mirror Exercise again, and it will be different next time."

She heard Edward's words, and the tears were fading now, so she asked simply, "How do you mean?"

Gray looked at her knowingly and, with a kind voice, shared, "The next time, you will actually hear the words and be able to process them a bit. The third time you do the exercise and beyond is when it starts to happen." Edward paused, looking at her for a moment before looking away, leaving her hanging there.

As the plane started rolling in its preflight taxi, Angelica took the bait and asked open-eyed with curiosity, "When *what* happens?"

Gray paused for a heartbeat before moving closer to her ear to kiss her softly and whispered, "Before you start to believe," he paused once more, then added, "in the real you."

Angelica felt herself shake just once, but she quelled the feelings, not wanting to return to that state from last night. Not right now. And not in this place. She took one of those long deep breaths and held it briefly before letting it out slowly.

"Feeling better?" Edward asked with a gentle smile.

Angelica looked up to Edward with her eyes worshipping his protective male energy over her and simply affirmed, "Always, when I am with you."

She felt the warm squeeze of his hand on hers as the Captain announced, "We have been cleared for Manassas Regional Airport serving Washington, D.C. Please confirm cabin is ready for takeoff."

Angelica felt the power of the mid-size jet instantly pressing her back into her seat; not at all like a regular commercial airliner. The force was smooth but much more powerful. The feeling of acceleration was quick, as was the lift-off from the ground.

"Whoa!" said Angelica, smiling, as they lifted the first few hundred feet off the ground in just seconds.

Edward added, "Now, that's a jet!"

Angelica laughed out loud at the rush of power, speed, and relief, letting go of her memories of the homework assignment. She looked out the oval jet windows at the beauty of Sarasota Bay. It was only a short time until sunset, and she could see all the boats on the bay, literally right where she grew up as a little girl. It all came rushing back to her, growing up in her sleepy small town with many hopes and dreams. But Sarasota had grown up a lot since those days. Perhaps it was her turn?

CHAPTER TWENTY-ONE

The Capitol

They landed at Manassas Regional Airport, just a short drive from downtown D.C. There was a fantastic vista of the capitol's nighttime skyline as they descended to land. Angelica loved the grand and incredible view of the capitol buildings and monuments from the air. Her heart began racing again as the excitement continued. "I loved our flight up, and the dinner was simply amazing! I didn't know airplane food could be so delicious," she said, smiling about their private flight.

"Well, that's probably because it wasn't airplane food, Kitten. It was custom-ordered gourmet, catering selected just for us. I am glad you were pleased," Edward said, winking at her with a bit of a playful smile.

Angelica, smiling gratefully at this attention to their every detail, added, "Well, that certainly explains it."

As their G-650 taxied up to the jetport, she noticed out the window that they were not the only sizeable private jet on the tarmac. They were clearly in a different world from Sarasota and now on the bigger stage Gray liked to operate on.

The Captain's voice came overhead for the final time. "Thank you for flying with us this evening, Mr. Gray and Ms. Hart. We hope you have a great weekend in Washington, D.C., or wherever else your travels might take you. We will be parked at the Manassas jetport momentarily."

Gray looked over at Angelica, who was studying the fleet of other planes and the airport lights. "Ready to go, Kitten?" he said, holding his hand out for her.

Angelica looked thoughtfully at him with big innocent eyes and suggested, "Shouldn't we be polite and wait?"

Edward looked quizzically at her and asked with a slight shrug of his shoulders, "For what?"

She smiled and, with a nod towards the back of the plane, and said, "For everyone else to get off first?"

Gray shook his head smiling and said, "Let's roll."

The Captain greeted Edward and Angelica personally as they exited the Gulfstream. As they descended the stairs from their jet, they saw their driver was waiting to greet them, holding a "Mr. Gray" sign on a backlit LED screen. Gray raised his hand only slightly to gesture the driver over, who promptly responded, rolling a luggage cart behind him.

Angelica looked back at the flight attendant who was still at the top of the jet ladder, waving goodbye. Angelica waved in return, and said to Edward, "The crew was so nice, and the entire flight was simply amazing! I see why you like flying private so much."

Gray circled her waist with his arm comfortably, as they both were starting to grow accustomed to, and walked her to their next awaiting ride in a large black Suburban SUV. She liked the feel of his arm around her waist and the feeling of Edward keeping her safe and right by his side. She may not have grown accustomed to all the luxury and jet travel yet, but his arm around her waist felt safe like no home she had ever known.

It was no accident that the drive into Washington, D.C., was impressive, if not even intimidating. The scale and enormity of the buildings and monuments were designed by the early leaders of the young republic, newly separating with their independence from England, to represent a great power emerging. The entire metropolis of D.C. was designed and built at enormous expense to create the world's most fantastic home court advantage, a strategy designed to impress world leaders visiting the newly minted America when negotiating trade deals and treaties. The empire capitol was all fancy stuff for a nation often living in simple log homes or squatting on lands that had never seen roads before. You might even call it the most fantastic game of "fake it until you make it" ever successfully pulled off on the global stage. So, Angelica's wide-eyed gawking and pointing as they drove into town was not a testament to the charm of her slight naivety, but to the founders' vision who designed this evening's drive into Washington to amaze. And it was still working its magic.

Their driver, updating the two of them, said, "We are arriving at the Washington, D.C., Ritz Carlton, located less than a mile from the White House and famous Dupont Circle. Mr. Gray, will you be needing the car service any further this evening, sir?"

Edward looked over at his excited and wide-eyed Angelica, awake and percolating with newfound energy, and gazed down her body to her waiting hips and legs. Edward's deep voice said calmly, "No, that will be all, but thank you for checking. We will be staying in this evening."

As Gray's hand slipped over onto Angelica's inner thigh, she felt a knowing squeeze of what lay ahead. Instantly responding to Gray's hand on the inner slope of her thigh, she placed both hands over his, briefly pressing him to linger then sliding them ever so slowly upward. Looking longingly into him, she opened her thighs ever so slightly then smiled and moved his hand away before they were discovered.

Just at that moment, the uniformed valet opened her door to greet them. "Welcome to the Ritz Carlton!"

Before they exited the SUV, Gray whispered in her ear, "You're a tease."

Feeling sure and full of herself for getting a rise out of the all-powerful Mr. Gray in the limo, she had that confident girl power smile as they walked into the opulent hotel lobby. She was already immune to all the glitz and glamour of Washington at the moment, as she looked straight ahead, feeling Edward's gaze admiring her curvy, feminine frame. Doing her best Marilyn Monroe-style walk right through the hotel lobby, she turned heads left and right as they arrived, while not openly flirting with any other men. She did not want to have that misunderstanding ever again. She used her peripheral vision to see how many eyes admired what the fortunate Mr. Gray had his arm around. Perhaps this was her chance to restore the balance of power in their universe just a bit.

As Edward was busy with the front desk checking them in, a group of Japanese businessmen arrived at the check-in desk next to theirs. Angelica could feel their appreciative gaze looking her over from a distance. She had felt that heat many times before. Men were always looking at her at the grocery store or a restaurant or club when she was with friends. Men seemed to be poring over her, inch by inch, perhaps fantasizing about having their way with her. She waited until Edward had their room keys and all the luggage details were settled before making her move.

"Ready to go, Kitten?" said Edward, as she turned fully towards Gray, pressing into his chest, and glancing over her shoulder to the onlooking Japanese businessman. Catching him still staring at her, Angelica flashed a condescending smile for an instant, as she caught the interloper looking at her backside. Then, channeling her inner Marilyn, she turned to Edward, kissing him softly on his cheek and said, "In case I forget to tell you later, I had an amazing time tonight."

Gray blushed for the first time she could remember. Then, clearing his throat as they walked to the lobby bar, he said, "Not that I don't appreciate the attention of the most beautiful woman here, but may I ask what that was all about, dear?"

She wrapped his arm tightly around her waist as they walked across the marble lobby to the bar. Confiding in her man, she said, "Men look at me everywhere I go. It doesn't matter the time of day or what I'm wearing. They just do, and it gets annoying. So here I was with my powerful man, and they were still doing it, and I wanted to make it clear that I belonged to Mr. Gray. And when I glared at the guy, so he knew he was busted for staring at my backside, he looked away like a coward." She explained, "I would never have the courage to do that if I were alone or at home where we might run into them again. But here we are, out of town, and I feel so safe and secure with you that I finally had the courage to put a stop to it just once in my life."

Edward looked at her with new eyes. He had never thought about what it must be like to have men ogling you or making uninvited comments everywhere you go. He thought about what she had shared before he asked, "How did it make you feel?"

Smiling brightly at him, she said, "Powerful. I hope you don't mind?"

Shaking his head and laughing ever so slightly, Gray said, "No. Not at all, especially since we just arrived in Washington, arguably the global seat of power. And power belongs in the hands of those who can wield it. If not you, who?"

They entered the gorgeous and elegant bar filled with solid royal blue leather couches. The room looked majestic paneled in dark blue wood with ceilings that soared. Edward seated Angelica on one of the bar stools and stood next to her while they were promptly greeted by the attentive bartender. They watched as he mixed their craft cocktails with some style and flair. All the while, the growing sexual tension between Angelica and Edward continued taking its new twist.

Sensing Angelica was feeling her oats this evening, he leaned closer while waiting for their drinks and asked discreetly in her ear, with a sly smile, "Are you going to be a good girl and do what Mr. Gray tells you this evening?"

Glancing at him with a new seductive "I could tear you up maneater smile," she leaned into his ear and inquired, "What if I don't want to be a good girl tonight? What if I feel a little bratty?" She looked into his surprised gaze with her smile lingering. As her hand circled behind him to squeeze his muscular, toned ass, she leaned into his ear and with a sexy, sultry voice whispered, "Are you going to bend me over and just settle for punishing your submissive? Or are you going to take a chance on letting me rock your world for a change?"

Edward sat down at the barstool next to Angelica's to conceal his sudden, rock-hard arousal. Surprised by his newly discovered vixen, he cleared his throat, but for a rare instance, he did not speak.

Sensing her opportunity, she pressed her advantage over him a bit further, leaning in again and asked, "What's the matter, sir? Cat got your tongue?" Just as her hand slid up the leg of his trousers to find him fully engorged and aching hard, she gave an entire handful of his manhood a firm but playful squeeze. Right before their drinks arrived, she released him to turn nonchalantly back to the bar; perhaps a bold move in the 5-star hotel full of guests.

Edward, managing to smile, responded moderately, "Let me recover for just a minute or two, and we can continue this conversation upstairs."

Angelica turned towards Gray, sitting sideways on her bar stool, and replied, "Oh? Do you want to cool down for a minute or two? What if it stays rock-hard all night, Edward? Don't you want to see just a little peek of what's inside these sexy panties you bought me? You paid for them. You might as well find out right here in the lobby bar. Want to bet if they are creamy-wet already or not?" Picking up his hand from the bar and drawing it towards her aching pleasure mound, she added, "Why not come feel for yourself."

Edward allowed her to guide him all the way to her already moist panties for one brief stroke upward, but it was enough to feel her warmth and wetness before he pulled away. Edward said, still slightly startled by this newfound facet within Angelica, "I see you have discovered your inner 'switch.'" He turned to his drink for a moment to gather his composure.

Angelica whispered closely, "What does 'switch' mean?"

While Edward took a good drink of his gin and tonic, he explained, "A switch is someone who can change back and forth between a Dominant and a submissive."

Angelica thought about that for only a moment before she responded, "No. That's not me at all. You will always be the

267

Dominant, Edward. No, ifs, ands, or buts about it. It's just that I am in the mood to seduce my man tonight. Is there anything wrong with that... sir?" She leaned into him like his Kitten again. Ok, perhaps a Kitten in heat.

Edward didn't need long to think about the possibilities before he told the bartender, "Check, please." And then he moved closer to Angelica and whispered, "I see you are topping from the bottom this evening, Ms. Hart. But what this could add—is intriguing."

They found the elevator forgivingly close to the bar, so Edward didn't have to cover up his condition for long. Angelica stood before him to provide additional "cover" as needed until the empty car opened. They got in, and Gray pressed their floor number. As soon as the door closed behind them, Angelica hugged him fully, pressing her breasts into Gray. "When we get to the suite, I want us to start in the shower together. Would you be willing to do that for me, sir?"

Gray cleared his throat and said, "I think that would be a great place to start after the long flight. I think clean is... sexy."

Their door opened, and they walked side by side with Edward pointing the way, literally and figuratively, to their corner suite. As they walked, Angelica whispered, "You know what else is sexy?" Gray looked at her, waiting for the dangerous answer in his condition. "Me washing you with shampoo from head to toe," she replied as he groaned. As the door to their suite swung open, they could see their luggage had already been delivered to their room. They had a large dining table that could seat six in an open living room with dual couches. The two wide-open French doors revealed the separate main bedroom with a bronze padded headboard that was the length of the entire wall.

Acknowledging her request in the elevator, Gray said, "Why don't you unpack just a bit, and I will get the shower started for us."

Angelica loved her newly discovered effect on Edward and urgently wanted that to continue into the night. She only needed two things out of her bag, bringing her robe and toiletry kit into the bathroom. There, she was happy to find him getting the jets of water flowing from an overhead "rainforest" style showerhead.

Edward turned to see Angelica undressing and watched her move slowly, now only in her bra and recently stroked panties. She smiled, gazing into his eyes as she slowly, seductively walked the few steps between them until she was pressed gently and softly against him. "Let me help you out of this, sir." One by one, she undid the buttons of his dress shirt revealing his toned and muscular chest and abs. As the shirt slipped off, she neatly hung it on the nearby wall hook.

Returning her attention to his belt and trousers, she softly reminded him, as she said, "Seems you were having an awful time with these tight trousers at the bar, Edward." She playfully smiled as she unbuckled and unzipped his pants and then slowly knelt at his ankles to help him step out of them. Angelica folded the trousers and laid them neatly on the toilet seat, while still kneeling in front of Edward's fully bulging royal blue silk boxers. Next, she gently rubbed her hands up his legs and across his boxers, intentionally brushing against his thickness on her way up to his waistband. She rose slightly to be mouth level with his hard greatness as she slowly, sensually pulled the boxers downward just an inch at a time, revealing him as she went. Angelica teased with the prospect of her slightly open full lips awaiting his throbbing, aching member, but a brushing with her fingers was all he received.

He ached at barely missing the full entry of her waiting mouth—that might have been.

Finally, she asked, "Step out of these for me, please?"

Gray removed his feet from the boxers so they could take their rightful spot on top of the neatly folded trousers.

Angelica rose gracefully, turned her back to Edward, and asked, "Would you mind terribly helping me with my bra?"

Wearing only the champagne-colored, elegant bra and panties, Gray swallowed as he undid her bra clasp. She gently pulled her bra partly off but still covered her ample, beautifully shaped breasts. Then, she turned around to face him, looking into his eyes before slowly lowering her bra. She was curious to see how long Edward could manage to keep his gaze in her eyes. His struggle quickly ended as his eyes drifted downward, drinking in her beauty. While Edward remained transfixed, she slowly slid her panties down and off one foot at a time, placing both on the growing pile of clothes just shed. She pressed the soft skin of her breasts and budding nipples into Edward as she leaned into him, while pulling the glass shower door open with her free hand, and asked, "Shall we, sir?"

Once inside the spacious, oversized walk-in shower, Angelica got two hands full of shampoo first and began covering her breasts and abdomen with the slippery sudsy results. Then with both of them standing just inches away from the powerful water stream, she began slowly transferring all of the shampoo from her body to his. First, she rubbed sensuously from side to side and then added more shampoo for her torso's up and down motion against his. Next, she slowly circled behind Edward, refilling her hands with the slippery foamy agent, and began washing his back with her breasts and hands.

Edward stood rock-hard and still with his full manhood at attention while he received her gentle strokes and rubs, serving him without asking.

She refilled her hands one last time with shampoo and asked him gently, "Lift your arms for me, please?" He did, and Angelica reached around Edward from behind to wash his chest and abdomen. Finally, after what seemed like an eternity of torment, she finally grasped his thick cock and balls gently and slowly washed him with frothy, slippery foam. With each long, deliberate stroke she made, she whispered into his ear the things she wanted to do to him. Things she dreamed of feeling with him. What she wanted from him for hours and hours into the night. Then Angelica turned Edward around to face her with the water streaming on his back. She kissed him softly, passionately, full on his hungry lips, and then down his neck to his chest. Angelica gently plucked at his nipples as she slid her lips across his sexy abs, kissing and nibbling at him as she went. By the time Angelica was kneeling in front of him with water jets pounding, it was all that Edward could do to keep from finishing in the shower. She swallowed him slowly and sensually with her plump, full lips—stroking him deeply with her throat only a few times to feel him reach his peak of readiness.

She stopped to look up at him, kneeling in the shower with the water cascading over them both. She looked pure and magical as she led him. Her energy was supple and feminine, and she moved slowly and with a grace unlike his. Angelica asked if they could move to the bedroom.

Edward nodded his consent and turned off the hot, steamy shower. Each dried the other off as part of their sensual care ritual. She served him first, toweling him front to back, including his still-engorged manhood. Then Edward returned the favor, as part of their new ceremony, hoping to find a way to match her slow and sensual touch. Now finally dry and blissfully clean, she took Edward's hand and led him to the bed. In the other hand, Angelica carried a bottle of Argan oil from Morocco that she had packed for the trip from home. She laid a dry towel on the bed, asking Edward to lie face down for her. He did so without speaking a word, apparently enjoying this newfound seductress energy in Angelica.

She covered her body generously with the delicious-smelling Argan oil and climbed onto the bed straddling Edward, who was awaiting her arrival, still lying face down. She lay fully prone with her oily breasts and stomach on his toned muscular back. She began slowly, sliding up and down in long gliding strokes, massaging his body with her breasts Nuru style. She asked, "How is that pressure, sir?"

"You feel amazing!"

She turned over on her back and slid her oily, firm butt cheeks up and down his, so they were "back-to-back," slipping and sliding with the oil. She soon rolled back to him with her breasts leading the sensual sliding massage, and with it, she finally said, "I would like you to turn over on your back for me next."

Edward did so gladly, aching to feel Angelica with his manhood. He was not to be disappointed. Her breasts made their way, slipping up to press full onto his face, gently touching before sliding all the way down his chest and then back up to his waiting mouth. But she continued on the next stroke, much further down him until her breasts gently brushed his thick and rock-hard core. Her mouth was temptingly close with her soft full lips available. But instead, Angelica interlaced her hands, covered in the oil, and did a magically effective job of stroking Edward to his edge with both her hands. Slowly, with long deep strokes, each time simulating what it would feel like inside of her. Over and over, she slid her hands to the sensitive tip of his head only to race back down the shaft and start the subsequent slow rise again.

When Edward could no longer control himself, she stopped and straddled him with her oily thighs to finish her teasing journey of agony and relief. She heard him groan aloud as Angelica settled with her magical mound and creamy wet lips just over his shaft, sliding ever so slightly forward and backward, right on the spot. It was all she could do to keep Edward from penetrating her fully yet, as they were both so slippery. But she wanted him to ache and feel himself at heaven's gate. Angelica wanted him to lust for her more than anything or anyone ever before.

It was that moment when Edward called out an expression she had never heard him utter. "Please!" he said in his full voice as he reached for her hips with his hands to guide her open and swollen pussy onto and all the way down his mighty shaft.

Angelica gasped out loud as he entered, both of them already in the first wave of their mutual and simultaneous climaxes. Feeding off one another's energy, he forcefully guided her hips with his hands. Angelica arched her back and rolled her hips to make each long, snakelike stroke a full and amazing experience for both. Finally, Edward's core locked up, and he said, "Wait. Wait!" He breathed hard and added, "Don't move."

Angelica paused, stroking even though she was still trembling from the last few waves of joy and ecstasy, and asked him before reaching out to touch his face, "Is everything OK?"

Edward breathed in deeply and exhaled completely before he answered, "Yes." He breathed again and added, "It was just ... so intense."

Angelica slid her hips up and down his still-hard shaft one last time in torment before leaning forward to kiss him softly. Then, she relaxed her whole body into him and sighed. She floated upwards toward the heavens, as she laid her weight on him, feeling his energy still inside her and his every breath, in rhythm with hers.

Edward's hands moved to hold her face so he could see her eyes. As they both smiled, she spoke first. "Thank you for allowing me to show you my feminine side; to bring my softer tantric energy to mold into your bold, stronger, Dominant side. I didn't know if you would allow me to go there," she said, pausing to blink as she gazed at him.

He reflected a moment before speaking. "Angelica ... apparently, there is another whole world I've been missing. Perhaps we are stronger together than we are apart," he said as he finished kissing his newly discovered tantric lover, thinking to himself, *I must have more.*

As they fell asleep, Angelica wrapped naked around him, under the star-filled, velvety night of Washington, D.C., our nation's center of power was newly theirs as well, they discovered.

CHAPTER TWENTY-TWO

The Willard

Angelica awoke, still half-dreaming, under towels and the blanket Edward had draped over her. Drifting off to sleep after making love with Edward left her glowing. What a contrast to the choker and leash still plentifully available in his Red Playroom. She smiled as she stretched and felt her morning come alive. Both worlds of sexual intimacy were exciting but in entirely different ways. She hoped that, perhaps, Edward would be open to exploring her sensual tantric energy again sometime.

No note was lying on the pillow next to her, so in her early morning voice, testing to see if he was still there, she called out, "Edward?" She heard a chair sliding back as Gray rose in the living room to come to her. The French doors opened to reveal him wearing a smile plus a luxurious black robe from the hotel.

"Good morning, Kitten. I didn't want to wake you, so I was up early working a bit and getting ready for my meetings today."

Angelica patted the bed beside her, signaling she wanted some company. "I didn't hear a thing. I must have been sleeping hard." Edward sat next to her on the edge of the bed, reaching down to stroke her blonde hair framing her face. She said, "Don't look at me! You're already up and groomed and looking gorgeous. My hair is still in bedhead mode." She smiled and laughed, pulling one of the soft luxury pillows over her head for a moment.

Gray used her momentary lack of vision to pin her down and tickle her sides mercilessly. Angelica jumped like a fish fresh out of the water, squirming with a shriek. "No, no! I will get you for that, Edward Gray!" she said as the tickling subsided after only a few nice convulsions.

Reminding her, he said, "You have spa reservations all day here at the hotel. So, you have to put up with them spoiling you all day and plying you with food, wine, or champagne while doing every service you can imagine. Do you think you will be able to stand it, Kitten?" Gray smiled playfully at the question.

Angelica pouted her face and said, "It won't be as much fun if you're not there. Can't you come with me?"

Gray leaned down to kiss her on the forehead. "Have to work, sweetheart. Big business, and tonight is our formal closing dinner with the Williamsons—Jim and Rob," he reminded her.

"What time is dinner?"

Edward said, "We should leave here at about half past five. Café du Parc at the Willard Hotel adjoins the White House, which is close—just a few blocks away."

"All kidding aside, Edward, I hope your meetings go fantastically. Don't worry about me. I am quite sure I will survive the day at the Ritz Carlton Spa!" she said in a playful voice that summoned her poor, poor victim mode in jest.

Gray leaned down, kissing her sweetly before getting dressed in his business attire. She heard his voice trailing off as he went into the bathroom to get ready. "You rocked my world last night, Ms. Hart."

Angelica pulled the sheet over her head with half embarrassment and excitement. Loud enough to be heard around the corner, she asked, "So you liked it a little?"

Gray's deep voice came from the bathroom. "No," he said, before his face appeared around the corner to look her in the eyes. "I didn't like it. I ... loved it! I'm going to want that about ten more times, please?" he said, smiling as he disappeared into the shower.

Angelica sighed, lying in the luxurious bed. She reached over to slightly open the heavy dark curtain to reveal the blue sky over Washington, D.C., and smiled as she said, "I'm here."

After 15 or 20 minutes, Edward reappeared in his boxers, getting ready to slip on his midnight blue Brioni suit from Italy and alligator shoes and belt. She loved drinking in his manly frame with her eyes and how his dreamy body moved. He looked sharp and very clean-cut in whatever he wore, but today was a special day. Angelica cleared her throat, holding a box with a bow she retrieved from her suitcase while Edward was showering. "I know it's a special day, and I have something for you," she said sweetly.

Gray looked over at the box and gift bow and repeated, "You got something for me?"

"Yes, sir, I did!" she said, smiling.

Gray walked over wearing only his slacks and unbuttoned white linen shirt with his sexy chest and abs still showing. He thanked her as he received the rectangular tie box and opened it. To his surprise, he discovered the most elegant silk paisley tie with rich burgundy red, gold, and cobalt sky-blue touches. It was sharp and sophisticated like him.

Angelica said, "I had to get it the moment I saw it. I think it will set off your amazing blue eyes."

Edward smiled and held it up in the mirror by his face. Complimenting her while getting dressed and including the new tie in the ensemble, he added, "I think you have quite exceptional taste, Ms. Hart."

Angelica asked, "Did you mean good taste in men or neckties?"

Gray didn't miss a beat while tying a perfect Windsor knot on the first try with the new silk tie. "Why both, of course," he said, winking at Angelica who was still hopelessly trapped in bed without a stitch of clothing under the sheet and blanket.

Coming over for one last kiss from his princess before he was off, he said, "I will meet you here in the suite at five sharp to head down for one drink and then to dinner."

"I would rather kidnap you all day in bed, but I will meet you here at five, and I... will be ready!" she said, smiling at her hero in midnight blue—out to take over his next business conquest.

Each day was busy and fulfilling but at different ends of the spectrum while Angelica recharged her mind, body, and spirit in blissful spa day magic from her 90-minute massage, followed by a facial before lunch with a lovely white wine. Then after was the wind-up to prepare for the big dinner with nails and hair to perfection.

Conversely, Gray was working on the growth of his business, supercharging his balance sheet and portfolio of income streams. When growing companies, he always found the most significant challenge to be people. He motivated and inspired them to do the right things to move the mission forward. But Angelica found bonding with people to be easy. She made friends with the entire staff at the Ritz Spa. She felt royally treated and genuinely "adopted" by a few of them. Angelica hoped she would get to return there one day, just to see the people again.

The five o'clock dinner event was rapidly approaching, so she returned to the suite to give herself plenty of time to get ready without her usual rushing and stressing. Tonight was to be a huge deal.

She knew that Edward would be wearing the midnight blue suit and tie she had bought him, but she was so excited to wear the champagne gold evening gown she had purchased on her first shopping spree. It looked so gorgeous on her as it fit like a glove. It was much less revealing than the backless black sequin dress and more elegant and refined. She hoped Edward would like to see her in it and that it would be the perfect choice for Café du Parc, the fancy French restaurant. If ever there was a time and place to wear an elegant evening gown, this was it.

She turned on some of her favorite relaxing music on her iPhone, while it charged, to keep the pink bubble feeling from her spa day going. She felt amazing and wanted the blissful energy inside her to never end. First, she laid out her makeup and chose soft pink lipstick to match her French manicure and the champagne gold dress. *Perfect*, she thought. *Not too daring. Very feminine and sophisticated. Edward would want to kiss those lips.*

She selected a very sexy, cream-colored bra and panty set to wear that evening. The top was a super sheer, lacey, quarter-cup bra that left the top half of her nipples partially exposed and would be irresistible to Edward, or so she hoped when they returned to their suite after dinner. The bottoms were a matching lace pair of panties, barely covering the entrance to heaven with three straps on each hip, creating a high V-line, flattering look. Wearing this lingerie under her much more conservative-looking evening gown would be her secret weapon when she looked at Edward all evening. Every girl needs a secret superpower.

It was finally time for the pièce de résistance, the champagne gold gown. She had it hanging in its unique zippered garment bag from Saks Fifth Avenue in the closet since they arrived to let any wrinkles fall out. She removed it carefully, looking at all its elegant detail. It made her blood race just holding it in her hands. Edward had not seen this since the fashion show in his living room, but she remembered the look in his eyes at the sight of her plunging neckline. Finally, she slipped into a gown Cinderella would love to have met her prince in.

Just a touch of her favorite Dior perfume behind each ear, and she had to take one more look in the mirror before the knock came at their hotel suite. Edward opened the outer door, and his deep voice drifted into the room. "Housekeeping," he said, smiling and pretending to be hotel staff as he entered. The French doors had been closed while she was dressing, so this was the moment for her big reveal. She walked to the center of the outward swinging doors and then pushed them both open simultaneously and voila!

Gray stood there speechless and stunned. Yes, he had seen the dress once before, but never with Angelica looking runway ready in her full hair and makeup. She looked like she belonged on the red carpet at the Academy Awards. He finally uttered, "You look devastatingly divine and devilishly delicious all at the same time!" His smile was a mixture of pride and lust looking at her radiant beauty.

Angelica played humbly and said, "Oh, this old thing?" She referenced her dress with her hands, smiling playfully. Then she added quickly, "Edward, thank you again for this amazing dress! I feel so special wearing it out for you tonight." She wanted to ensure he knew how much she appreciated him getting her something this remarkable.

Gray took one more long flowing look down her body, poured into the champagne gold dress, and added, "Whoever designed such a stunning gown hoped, most likely dreamt, it would one day be worn by a woman as gorgeous as you, Angelica."

She welled up inside, seeing his admiring eyes and hearing his words wash over her. The feeling she got looking into Edward's gaze at this moment was the dream she had always waited for since she was little and to be truly cherished by a real man of the highest values like Edward. She looked away, dabbing her eyes. "Don't make me cry, Edward," she said as she fought back the wave of tears in her eyes and added, "I will be right back."

Angelica disappeared momentarily to touch up her makeup and dab her still-moist eyes with soft tissues. She took one last deep breath and grabbed her tiniest clutch purse before returning. "I didn't bring my phone. Is that ok, dear?"

Edward looked at Angelica with a glowing smile. "Everything that matters is right here with us. Of course, it is ok," he said. "Let's go."

Their elevator ride to the lobby of the Ritz Carlton was joined by a younger couple, perhaps on a first date to someplace fancy. They wore nice, ordinary Friday night clothes but nothing like the elegant attire worn by Edward and Angelica. When the young couple got on the elevator, they suddenly stopped giggling and tried to behave in front of such fancy company. With a warm ice-breaking smile, Angelica looked at them, holding hands full of new "first date" energy, and said, "You two make a great-looking couple."

Both youngsters smiled nervously, and the younger girl returned the compliment. "So do the two of you, and I just love your dress!" the girl said, smiling directly at Angelica.

Edward tapped her on the hip, secretly smiling as they remembered their elevator escapade a week ago. Angelica thanked her for the nice compliment, and the doors opened, and the fleeting elevator friendship was gone.

"That was very nice of you in the elevator. You made their night," Edward remarked, smiling as he acknowledged her grace with people.

Angelica inched closer to Edward and whispered, "They are probably giggling and laughing about it now." She smiled, remembering getting grown-up compliments when she was just their age. Finally, they arrived at the bar and sat next to the same bar stools where all the naughty, flirty trouble had begun the night before.

A different bartender was on duty this evening. *Perhaps a bit of grace in that*, Edward thought. "Two glasses of Dom Perignon champagne, please," he ordered.

The bartender nodded and said, "Right away, sir."

Angelica squeezed his arm and nodded to the barstools where she had tempted and tormented Gray with her eyes, words, and hands when they had just checked in. Smiling teasingly, she whispered discreetly in his ear, "Did you want me to be a good girl or a bad girl this evening?"

Edward thought about the options, seeing them play out in his mind, before responding. Turning slightly toward her, he smiled with a bit of grit in his voice and said, "Let me get back to you on that a bit later, Ms. Hart."

Angelica took a breath and thought, *How could he make me feel so flush just with the sound of his voice?*

The champagne arrived, and Edward handed one of the crystal flutes to Angelica with a toast. "I would like to celebrate two evenings with one toast," he said. "The night we met when you kept me waiting for hours, to this evening and all of them in between. So here is to you, my princess." The chime of the beautiful crystal champagne flutes when they clinked their toast was a beautiful marker to the romantic words from Gray. Angelica thought about the night they met, how he had offered to send her and her wrongful date each a glass of champagne, and the journey from then until now as she sipped her glass of bubbly.

"May I propose a toast?" Angelica requested. Edward nodded approvingly as he listened. She raised her glass ever so slightly as she said, "I had a dream of you. You were handsome and powerful. You were brilliant but kind. You were always the one I had hoped for in men, but you never came to me until now. So here is to my dream of you, since I was five, and all the years you kept me waiting until now." Angelica's lips and voice shook just a bit as she got the words out, trying to smile into his gaze.

Edward looked into her eyes as she raised her glass towards his to clink once again. But instead of toasting, Edward paused a moment drinking in her words and cupped her chin to look at her. He thirsted for her, drinking her in instead of the champagne, kissing her softly once before he said, "Thank you for that."

They finally clinked glasses to toast, thoughtfully gazing into the magic of each other's eyes. After one more sip, Angelica excused herself to go "powder her nose," a chance to compose herself, once again, before they left for dinner. Gray had signed the check to their room and was ready when she returned. He invited her to take his arm and said, "Our driver is waiting to take us to dinner."

As they walked across the gold and cream-colored marble floor of the Ritz Carlton lobby, Angelica asked, "Did you say it is only a few blocks to the restaurant?"

Gray shook his head and replied, "No, more like a mile or so."

Angelica paused and said, "Could we just walk? It is such a lovely night out, and I've been in the hotel all day."

They stepped out of the hotel lobby doors to the waiting black Suburban SUV and the same driver, Patrick, who had brought them from the jetport the evening prior. "Good evening, Mr. Gray," Patrick said.

"Good evening. We are headed to the Willard Hotel for the Café du Parc restaurant. But we would like to walk the last two or three blocks if you don't mind?" Gray replied as he opened the door for Angelica. He circled the vehicle to join her, and they were off. Angelica was beaming as she took in the historic buildings on either side as they went.

D.C. is beautiful at night, and as they pulled onto 22nd Avenue, their driver stated, "I will pull over shortly to allow you to walk the last few blocks as you requested. As you walk straight ahead, the Willard, which opened its doors in 1818, will be straight ahead on your right. As you walk, if you look off in the distance, you may see the Thomas Jefferson Memorial, and as you turn to the right at the Willard, you will find the grand entrance of the Willard and Café du Parc just a few steps beyond." Patrick pointed ahead and to the right as he continued. "Just three blocks in that direction, sir."

Gray nodded his appreciation for the directions and said, "The lady was hoping we could walk. Would you be so kind as to follow us?"

Patrick responded, "Of course, Mr. Gray."

Gray helped Angelica from the SUV onto the sidewalk, and they began their short stroll to dinner on foot. Angelica beamed, walking in the cool night air. "Thank you for this. But if it is so close, why does Patrick need to follow us in the SUV?" she asked.

In a low voice, Gray said, "He is an armed bodyguard. Plus, we have him reserved for the entire evening for the return ride back to our hotel."

Angelica's eyes widened as she prodded him a bit further. "Armed bodyguard?" she said quizzically.

Gray nodded. "It is a big city."

The two made it safely, with the SUV following at a modest three miles per hour, keeping a watchful eye over them.

They turned right onto the sidewalk in front of the Willard to see the red-carpet entrance for a procession of cars carrying dignitaries and fancy guests to and from one of Washington D.C.'s most iconic hotels. The regally uniformed doorman of the Willard tipped his hat to Edward and Angelica as they walked past. They arrived at the courtyard patio and concrete steps leading up to the fancy European-style entrance to Café du Parc. The elegant glass door hosted its name etched into the frosted glass entrance set in the dark mahogany wood frame.

Edward opened the door for Angelica. They were greeted inside at a host stand with a gentleman in a black tuxedo and two female hostesses on either side in simple but elegant black cocktail dresses. "Good evening, Monsieur and Mademoiselle, welcome to the Café du Parc," he graciously said with a slight bow. "The last name, please?"

Edward replied simply, "Gray."

With an uplifted voice, the maître d' said, "Ah! Monsieur Gray, a great pleasure to meet you and Mrs. Gray." As he bowed again, Angelica squeezed Edward's arm gently at the "Mrs. Gray" presumption by the host, who continued with his greeting. "Your other two guests just arrived moments ago and are at the bar awaiting your arrival. Shall we gather them up on our way to your table, monsieur?"

Gray said, "That would be perfect, thank you." And away they went.

Edward held her arm more firmly in his, so she would have a solid, stable anchor in her high heels as they navigated down the two short sets of very wide, dark wooden steps that descended to the main bar and dining room.

At the bar, Edward greeted the father and son team, James and Robert, whose business he had recently acquired. "Please allow me to introduce you to Ms. Angelica Hart."

Both men stood and smiled graciously to say hello and shake Angelica's hand. Next, Edward gestured to the waiting maître d' and said, "Shall we head to dinner?"

Instinctively, before they had to ask, the maître d' said, "Your drinks will be brought over to your table," as he circled his hand once in the air for the bartender's attention, "and added to your check. Follow me, please."

The maître d' whisked them away to one of the best tables in the restaurant, set for the four of them dead center in the one large alcove window that looked outside. From the balcony level, their table overlooked the Café du Parc Garden terrace full of umbrella tables and thousands of white twinkling lights in the trees. "Messieurs and mademoiselle, please enjoy your dinner with us this evening. It is our honor to have you here with us."

Angelica cooed as they were seated. "What a beautiful view!" she said, looking out the floor-to-ceiling bay window framed with elegant royal blue curtains and their gold tied-back ropes the thickness of her wrists.

Jim, the elder and retiring father of the two Williamsons, said, "Edward, first, I want to thank you for inviting us here. The Willard Hotel is famous, but I have never been here before in all my visits to Washington. It is quite the place!"

As promised, the bartender arrived to promptly deliver their two drinks from the bar and offered to bring any other cocktails. Angelica asked for a Grey Goose Cosmopolitan and Edward his usual Tanqueray Gin and Tonic with lime.

"Jim and Rob, it is my absolute pleasure to host dinner this evening, and my apologies for being just a bit late. This is Angelica's first trip to D.C., and she wanted to walk a few blocks and feel the city's energy," he said adoringly.

Jim Williamson had a friendly grandfatherly-type smile and turned to Angelica, speaking in his easy-going style. "I like to walk too. But, unfortunately, no one seems to take the time anymore for simple pleasures." He patted Angelica a time or two on the back of the hand as he nodded knowingly and said, "Everyone seems to be in such a hurry to get where they are going, they miss the journey sometimes."

Angelica beamed at Mr. Williamson, who had chosen to partner with Edward to begin his path to retirement, and enjoyed the kind wisdom in his words. She said, "Thank you, Mr. Williamson, for understanding and a bit of grace for my making us late." She smiled adoringly at him.

He immediately replied, "Mr. Williamson was my father, God rest his soul. You should call me Jim." He smiled and nodded to her like a newly adopted granddad.

Edward watched with pride how Angelica made friends so easily and a positive impression on his new partners, especially Jim, who was the founder, CEO, and lifelong steward of the company he was being entrusted with. Angelica was a good partner and asset socially, in any setting, he observed. Not that that was his primary reason for inviting her to join him, but a nice bonus, nonetheless.

Their new round of drinks arrived, and they took to task pouring over the menus as their waiter told them of the incredible unique creations of the chef for that evening. Finally, Edward asked the waiter to continue. "My guests are here at Café du Parc for the first time. Could you be so kind as to tell them about some of the regular items on the menu that people just rave about?"

The waiter said, "But of course. My pleasure, monsieur. Our Boeuf Bourguignon may be the best beef stew you will ever have in your life. For the salad course, our Salad Niçoise is amazing. Then there is the dish for which the French have been most copied around the world—our French Onion Soup—which tastes like the source of all life itself. Our fresh catch of the day is the Sea Bass which is finished in a light French crème sauce with capers, and our number one dessert, of all time, is the Chocolate Torte which is very light, not heavy."

"Oh, my," Angelica blurted aloud softly, hearing the choices. Everyone agreed, chiming in with nods and yeses around the table.

"Give us a few minutes. I will place my dinner napkin back on my plate when everyone is ready to order," Edward suggested to the waiter as a unique signal.

"Excellent, monsieur!" said the waiter, smiling. He liked Edward's invention of the "we're ready" signal.

After a bit of chatter about the menu options and the grand style of Café du Parc, they all placed their orders with their attentive waiter. Edward asked his guests if they would enjoy wine with dinner. Both Jim and Rob nodded enthusiastically as long as Edward made the selection. Edward ordered a bottle of red and white wine for the table, a beautiful bottle of red Bordeaux and a light Pouilly-Fuissé, from their exquisite French wine list, both "great choices," according to the waiter.

As the bottles of wine were opened, a small tasting of both was poured for each of them to try. Gray nodded to the waiter, a bit of a signal for a special delivery, and raised his glass of red wine to toast. "I would like to celebrate this evening with a toast to the merger of New Vest Technologies with Gray Enterprises. I believe that together, the future is bright for each of us and, most of all, for your people and the company," Gray said. "To our future together," he toasted.

As Angelica raised her glass of white wine to toast with the men, she could see Rob's and Jim's eyes getting larger as they elbowed each other with surprise.

As they clinked glasses, a rolling table covered in a burgundy tablecloth arrived carrying a long rectangular base on which sat an ice sculpture of their "New Vest" company logo. The ice sculpture was lit from beneath with LED lighting, which highlighted the beautiful fissures and carvings in the ice. The servers placed the ice sculpture directly behind Jim and Rob as guests of honor. Rob spoke first and said, "Edward, this evening was a great idea, but the ice sculpture is extraordinary. It means a lot to us, especially my dad, after 30 years of building this company."

Jim was overwhelmed seeing the company he built from the ground up being honored by Edward this way. Handing Edward his phone, Rob asked, "Would you mind taking a picture of us in front of it?"

"Of course!" Gray replied and began taking a few photos of the proud father-son team as they marked a new era in their lives and their company.

Jim Williamson asked, "Edward, would you come and join us in the picture?"

Angelica quickly volunteered. "I'll be glad to take the photos!" she said, smiling as Rob's phone made its way around from Edward to her. As Edward rose to stand next to Jim, Angelica sensed that Rob felt uneasy seeing his place next to his dad in the business being supplanted by Gray.

After taking a few photos, Angelica suggested trying one more picture with each holding their wine glasses. They all liked the idea instantly, and now with each armed with a glass of red wine, she encouraged them and said, "This will be a 'Three Musketeers Cheer.' I say 'all for one,' and you say...?"

All three men in unison cheered, "One for all!" A couple of the neighboring tables applauded the special event cheer as though it were a birthday, anniversary, or any special occasion that marks the passing of a milestone in life, which tonight was.

After dinner, Edward and the men shook hands before dispensing with the formalities and giving each other their first hug as new business partners. Jim hugged Angelica briefly and said, "You got the right name, young lady. You are an angel. Keep an eye on Edward for me, would you? I'm counting on him to do great things."

Angelica smiled. "I promise."

The black Suburban pulled up, and Edward opened the door for Angelica. She waved to Jim and Rob, who waved back, smiling at her as Edward circled the SUV to join her. And then they were gone.

Edward asked Patrick, "Before we head back to our hotel, could we see a short nighttime driving tour of the capitol and a few of the monuments?"

Their driver replied, "Of course, Mr. Gray."

Edward turned to Angelica and asked, "What did you think?"

Slowly and thoughtfully, Angelica said, "Well, the business was good. They both loved the ice sculpture that you had made for them. I can't believe Rob wanted to take it home in the back of their pickup truck so he could show his wife and kids!"

"And the waiters loaded it onto the truck for them. Unbelievable!" Gray said, shaking his head while chuckling.

"You don't realize your impact on people, Edward. To you, this was just another day. Another business dinner. But to Rob and especially Jim, this was an important 'marker,' a life moment they won't ever have again," she said.

Edward thought about her words for a moment. He didn't have a ready response for once.

Admiringly, looking at her hero who was sitting silently, Angelica softened her delivery and said, "I thought what you did for them was very special. I know they will remember it always, Edward, and I was proud of you." Gray looked away out the side window as they passed the Washington Monument. It was convenient timing to hide his face for a moment of composure. Angelica knew how to read her Mr. Gray.

They toured the Lincoln Memorial next with a guided tour and a short history lesson from their driver, Patrick, giving Edward a welcome break from the conversation. "The Smithsonian Museum is actually home to 21 museums and a national zoo." Finally, they wrapped up a close-up drive-by of the White House, which was only steps away from the Café du Parc restaurant. Patrick said, "During the early colonial days, the first capitol was in New York and later Philadelphia, and did not officially move to Washington, D.C., until 1800. While they were building an appropriate capitol building for Congress to meet, the early first sessions of Congress were in the Willard Hotel, the nicest building available back then. So, the word 'lobbyist' comes from the lobby bar of the Willard, where the 'lobbyist' would wait for congressmen to leave their sessions to try and get trade deals done with the federal government. That's how we started as a nation, right where you were having dinner this evening, Ms. Hart."

Angelica sat mesmerized, hearing all the history of D.C., and imagining what those early days must have been like before hardly any of this city was even built. Then, as she looked out the window of her ride back to the hotel's grand entrance, she said, "Amazing. Simply amazing!"

The doorman greeted them on their return. "Good evening, and welcome back to the Ritz Carlton," he said as he tipped his hat to both of them.

CHAPTER TWENTY-THREE
Careful What You Wish For

Angelica sighed as she slipped from the SUV limousine onto Edward's waiting arm to walk back into the hotel lobby. Again, she was deep in thought, this time ignoring the admiring eyes of everyone at the hotel as she returned from dinner in her gorgeous gown.

Edward, sensing her unusual silence, asked, "What are you thinking about?" He watched her face for a response.

She continued looking ahead but slightly downward, thinking still as she said, "I'm wondering… what it must have been like for them here in 1800, over two hundred years ago with no technology and candles and gas lamps. I mean—primitive. Yet, they built all this."

"It was certainly a more primitive time, but men have always been and will always be primal on some level," Gray said. "It is just our nature." Finally, they arrived at the lobby bar for a nightcap.

"I know what the word 'primal' means sort of, but what do you mean when you say that men are primal in nature," she asked, sliding onto a barstool Edward had pulled out for her.

Gray sat next to her as he motioned to the bartender and said, "A Grey Goose Chocolate Martini for the lady and a Hennessy XO cognac neat for me, please."

Turning back to Angelica, he forewarned, "Are you sure you want to hear this?" Edward looked at her with narrowed eyes, his lips pressed into a thin flat line.

She curiously said, "Yes, I want to hear."

Gray picked up his cognac and took a whiff of the pungent aroma from the snifter before taking a drink, and said, "What makes us the way we are after hundreds of thousands of years of evolution is that only the strongest survive. Therefore, only the strongest are selected by women when they look to select a mate, and men must be ready to fight, kill, or even burn the world down to compete for the woman they want. And then do it all again to keep her safe and yours." Gray leaned into Angelica's ear, speaking of the base, primal instincts of men. Continuing, he said, "It may not be what you want to hear in a civilized society today, but that is the way it is."

Angelica felt herself responding to Gray's passionate description, especially the fire in his voice when he said he would "burn the world down" for his woman. She asked, "Is that what you thought when we first met, and you came to sit in my date's chair at the restaurant?"

Gray smiled slightly as he took another drink of cognac and signed the check to their room. "I looked at you. I saw how you moved. Every inch of you oozed with feminine energy, and your dowdy date did not deserve you. I had to let you know that I wanted you." Edward paused and said, "Like I want you right now." Gray looked down at the elegant gown hiding all her feminine secrets.

Angelica was aroused and turned on by this primal side of Gray, the way he was looking at her like a big male lion, king of the jungle. She took the chance of teasing the lion and said, "Do you like what you see down there?" She caught his eyes drinking in her breasts and her hips that were poured into the fancy gown.

"Only that I want to fuck you into the middle of next week." Gray took her upper arm and pulled her to stand up facing him and added, "Perhaps a little demonstration of primal would give you a deeper understanding of what I mean. Let's go." With a bit of force, he guided Angelica towards the elevator.

She had not felt this kind of aggression from Gray before, which filled her with fear and excitement. Her heart raced, and her adrenaline surged as they walked with urgency towards the elevator bank, Gray still holding her arm hostage, as he took her away. Then, Angelica asked, "Do you want me to…"

Interrupting her, he said, "I want you to listen, and do as you are told."

"Yes, sir," she replied obediently. The elevator door opened, and they stepped into the empty car. When the door closed them alone inside, Gray grabbed a fistful of her long blonde hair and pulled her head backward, exposing her fragile neck. He leaned down passionately and kissed and sucked on her neck and throat while his free hand squeezed her whole breast to the edge of almost pushing out of the gown. He ravaged her until they stopped on their floor, and he released her hair to grab her arm again, taking her briskly down the hall to their suite for a date with her dark and primal destiny. She was shaking with nerves and unexplained excitement of what might lie ahead, as she had never seen him this worked up before.

Gray opened the door to their suite and instructed, "Go undress down to your bra and panties. Nothing else. And be waiting for me in First Position on the bed. Do you understand?"

Angelica trembled. With Gray still firmly holding her upper arm, she said shakily, "Yes, sir." He released her arm with a slight push to start her walking to the bedroom. Her mind was numbly racing as she closed the French doors behind her.

She heard Gray say only, "Careful what you wish for."

She was still trembling as she took the elegant champagne gold gown off. It was so delicate, a striking contrast to the primal animal she had somehow unwittingly summoned from deep inside Gray. Now, she felt she had no choice but to stay the course as she laid the gown to rest on its hanger and put the designer heels away. She looked in the mirror at the girl she used to be before Edward, before all the shopping and the glitz and glamour. She chose this path, whatever may come next.

Onto the bed she climbed, kneeling, with knees shoulder width apart. Sitting on her heels resting with her hands on her knees, palms up towards the ceiling, she waited openly.

Gray didn't knock on the closed French doors to the bedroom in their suite. Instead, having waited long enough for his prize to be ready and presentable for his pleasure, he opened both doors and entered the bedroom of their suite, his lair, already stripped naked from his clothes and carried only the black gym bag full of contents from his Red Playroom. Already rock-hard, fully aroused, and ready for his waiting Angelica, he dropped the black leather bag on the bed next to her with a "thud." She gasped from her mounting tension.

"What's the matter, little Kitten?" Gray asked in the deepest register of his voice. "Afraid to come out and play all of a sudden?"

Angelica sat frozen in silence, not sure what to say. Then, finally, Gray reached around from behind her with both hands on her throat and pulled her upright and against his chest while standing behind her. His erect manhood pressed against the cheeks of her gorgeous ass as he again asked, "Cat got your tongue all of a sudden?"

Angelica said, "No, sir, I am here for you."

Gray let go of her throat and said, "Good girl." As he reached for the black leather gym bag, the zippers opened. He withdrew a thick black collar with spikes and a wide leather loop in front from inside the bag. This collar looked much more substantial than the first one she had tried at his home. She heard his next command as he said, "I want you to wear this for me, and do not remove it without my permission. Is that understood?"

"Yes, sir," she responded promptly, wholly resigned to her submissive role now. She leaned her neck forward and moved her hair away so Gray could place the collar on her. The buckle closed the leather collar around her neck very securely. Next came the pair of leather weight-lifting gloves with padded palms and fingertips cut out. This went on Gray one glove at a time while she patiently awaited his instructions. Next, Gray removed a long, thick, steel leash of much heavier gauge steel links, the kind you might use if you were walking a Rottweiler or more giant breed dog.

Gray instructed, "Sit up straight." As she lengthened her spine and neck, he attached the leash to her collar with the heavy clasp. Finally, he removed four Velcro cuffs from the bag, one restraint for each wrist and one for each ankle. Angelica's palms were waiting face up as each wrist took its turn, getting snugly attached with a Velcro cuff. Next, Gray said, "Lean forward on your elbows, ass up."

"Yes, sir," she said and was instantly on all fours for her Master to freely attach the Velcro straps to each ankle.

Gray said, "Excellent. Now, remember your safe words, Ms. Hart. However, remember, if you say red, playtime is over, and it is time for us to check out and fly home, ending our trip together. Do you understand?"

"Yes, sir," she replied quickly.

"Good girl. Now I want you to be like a good little kitten and get down on the floor on all fours—hands and knees. Will you do that for me?"

"Yes, sir," she replied, climbing off the bed to assume the position on all fours, with Gray holding her leash wrapped firmly around his hand and wrist.

"That's a good kitten," he said, encouraging her. "Now, let's go for a little walk on the leash around the room for me," Gray instructed her.

"On all fours, sir? Or should I stand?" she asked for clarification.

"How do kittens walk?"

Angelica replied, "On all four paws, sir."

"Good answer, now let's get going," Gray replied as he gave her ass cheeks a pair of spanks with his leather-gloved hand. Angelica began moving instantly, crawling around the suite on her leash on all fours. "Good kitten, good kitten." Gray added, "If you ever get tired of crawling on all fours, you may stop and rest in first position on the floor."

Angelica paused and sat up in First Position as crawling on all fours was hard work. Gray walked before her, still holding her leash, and instructed, "Open your mouth for me." She did. "Open it wider," Gray said. She did. "If you are not going to crawl and need to rest, you need to be of service and suck on your Master while resting. Do you understand?"

"Mmmm hmmm," she mumbled in the affirmative, as her mouth was full of rock-hard cock. Gray stroked back and forth with long deep strokes until it was almost more than Angelica could take. Her gag reflex had kicked in as he pounded into her.

"Is my little kitten needing a break from oral for a bit?" Gray asked after he withdrew and tightened the slack on the leash taught, pulling her towards him.

"Yes, sir," she said as she gulped for air.

Gray commanded, "Crawl back to the bed and climb back up in First Position facing the headboard."

"Yes, sir," she said, crawling as her Master had instructed and climbing back to her starting position, kneeling on the bed. He reached into the gym bag again, withdrew a brand-new ball gag, and removed it from its plastic packaging. He washed the ball gag with bottled water, wiping it dry before putting it in her mouth. The elastic strap to the black ball gag attached it securely in place.

Gray instructed, "When wearing a ball gag, to say 'stop' you may tap me twice to 'tap out' or you may utter the sound for 'N' twice in close succession if you need to stop for any reason. Nod your head 'yes' if you understand."

Angelica nodded her head "yes," a signal she was prepared to proceed.

Gray said, "Now bend over again and put your head on the bed."

Angelica complied.

"Now reach both hands between your knees for me," Gray said.

She did, and Gray grasped hold of each of them and connected her wrist restraints to her ankle restraints such that she was now in total hard bondage, bound for the first time—head down and ass up; Edward's favorite position for Angelica's heart-shaped derriere. He left her fully exposed in this vulnerable position, but she could watch his every action as there was no blindfold in play today. At least not yet. He withdrew the black suede leather flogger and the vibrator from the gym bag and showed them to her.

Gray said, "Nod your head if you recognize each."

Angelica nodded her head in the affirmative.

"Now one of these is for pleasure if you are a good kitten and please your Master," he said as he turned on the Magic Wand for a two-second reminder of its powerful vibration. "The other," he said, holding up the flogger, "is for punishment when you disappoint your Master." He finished with a powerful swing of the flog, hitting the bed at full force with a loud wallop. "Nod your head if you understand," Gray said, bending over to look into her eyes which were widened now after the swat on the bed with the flogger.

Uttering the most she could manage with the ball gag, Angelica nodded "yes" and mumbled, "Mmm hmm."

Gray returned to stand directly behind her, turned on the vibrating wand, and pressed it fully onto her creamy wet mound.

Her lips were aching with excitement after his powerful buildup and forceful primal energy took complete control of her. She widened her knees on the bed to be more fully open as her eyes drifted shut. Her moans were coming through even though the ball gag muffled and throttled their sound. Angelica was instantly twitching and aching to cum but could not ask for permission as her eyes popped open wide, not knowing what to do. She made all the noise she could, trying to speak with the ball gag in, but to no avail.

"Is someone trying to ask for permission to cum?" he asked as he slid his fingers inside her to stroke her G-spot, continuing to press her center of intensity with the wand.

Angelica's head nodded violently forward and back for "yes."

Gray said, "Oh. My poor little kitten. All tied up and nowhere to go except to cum on your Master's cock." He removed his fingers and slid all of his rock-hard manhood inside of her and added, "You may cum one time."

Angelica's ship had already sailed as she came and came on Edward's long thick joy buried deep inside her.

He removed the toy to free his hands for the flogger, but instead of spanking her with it, he slid it around her waist like a belt holding on to each end so he could pull her into him and bounce her ass up and down on his rock-hard cock over and over again.

Bent over and restrained, head down and ass bouncing over and over, she rode him. Angelica came so hard she could not breathe, and the ball gag was starting to restrict her breathing. She became scared about breathing. She did not want him to stop, but she had to breathe.

Finally, Angelica felt desperate and had to tap out by tapping his thigh with her hand tied to her ankle.

Per his safe words, Gray stopped immediately and detached Angelica's wrists from her ankles. She quickly reached up to remove her ball gag that was blocking her breathing and took a deep gulp of air. Then, she exhaled and breathed again, gasping for air as Gray came to lie next to her on the bed for aftercare.

He put his arm around her and asked, "Are you ok, Angelica? Is anything hurting?"

She lay in his arms for a moment before speaking to continue catching her breath and finally said, "I'm fine, nothing is hurting. I just could not breathe when I started climaxing with the ball gag," she explained. "I was starting to panic about not being able to breathe."

Edward had returned to his usual persona and comforted her gently and asked, "Feeling back to normal now?"

She smiled and replied, "Yes, sir. I hope I didn't disappoint you."

He smiled, stroked her hair gently, and said softly, "You never disappoint me, Angelica."

She looked deeply into his eyes and whispered, "I came really hard. I was so turned on by your primal, fierce energy. I don't know why, but you just had me shaking the whole time." Looking down from his eyes, she said, "But you didn't cum."

Cupping her chin to pull her eyes back to him, Edward said, "That's no big deal. We have the whole weekend ahead of us with no more meetings—just the two of us."

Angelica snuggled into him and buried her face and soft hair against his chest.

"What if we pretend this is like a honeymoon weekend and just not leave the bedroom except to answer the door for room service? Then, we can take turns with you showing me more of your tantra, Nuru massage stuff, and perhaps a little bit more of my

BDSM world, except no more ball gags," he said with a playful smile.

"All weekend, just the two of us in bed, a real BDSM – Tantra – Kink weekend? Oh my... I think that sounds like the best invitation I have ever received!" she said, giggling. "But you promise, no more ball gags?" She held up her index finger to anchor the point.

Edward kissed the tip of her finger playfully, over and over, as he said, "One hundred percent guaranteed."

CHAPTER TWENTY-FOUR
Return To Paradise

Angelica woke Sunday morning to a rare sight. Edward was still in bed next to her asleep. She looked at his lean, muscular tanned body. He wore only his thin yoga pants, no shirt, revealing his tight, toned physique from his daily gym routine. Well, every day, except for yesterday when they stayed in bed all day together as he had promised. She had been his workout, and he had been hers. The two of them remained in the hotel suite, from brunch in bed to dinner and a movie. He had placed the "Do Not Disturb" sign on the door, and other than requesting lots more towels and bottles of water, the housekeepers did little more than giggle when one of the two lovebirds opened the door for the provisions. Room service was allowed to make meal deliveries with their rolling carts, draped with a neatly pressed white linen tablecloth, into the living room only, as the bedroom had an assortment of ropes and restraints, toys, and lingerie in varying arrays of disrepair. That room at the Ritz Carlton might never be the same again.

She liked watching him sleep peacefully. He didn't move. He didn't snore. He was her prince with all his strengths and flaws, his gifts, and imperfections. She saw only her Edward. Leaning over, she risked kissing him softly on the forehead while he slept, and lightly ran her fingers through his deep brown hair with a few flecks of grey for that distinguished salt-and-pepper look.

Gray stretched like he was pulling out of deep sleep. When he finally opened his eyes, he lay there looking at her. A

305

mischievous smile crept onto his face as he reached over to grab Angelica, pulling her giggling and squirming over on top of him. His hands ran down her back and across her toned backside.

Angelica cried out playfully, "No more!" She could feel his manhood growing thick and aroused yet again. Pleading, half-kidding, and laughing after their full-day marathon of sex from Friday night and all day long on Saturday, she cried out, "Get that thing away from me!"

Edward rolled both of them over so that he was on top, pinning her easily. "Are you saying 'uncle?'" he said as he smiled with his disarming charm. Then, he added, "Don't make me tickle you again."

She replied with both hands up on the pillow in a sign of surrender, "OK. I give up. You win!"

"Let's get some coffee sent up while we pack. We'll have Sunday brunch on the jet ride home. Sound good?" Edward asked nonchalantly.

Looking at him, Angelica slumped and replied, "Is that like even a normal conversation for you, Edward?" Then, half-mocking him in her best Edward Gray imitation, she said, "Let's have coffee sent up. We'll have brunch on the jet on the way home."

Finally, he smiled, looking her in the eyes with equal parts of love and lust, and said, "You know, Ms. Hart, you are still not too big for a proper spanking if you don't behave."

Angelica squirmed and flirted, channeling her best Marilyn Monroe for him, and cooed, "Oh really? A wise girl knows her limits, Mr. Gray. A smart girl knows she has none."

Edward said, "I think I want a photo shoot done of you Marilyn Monroe style and have that quote put on the large, framed print made for the Playroom. Would you do that for me sometime, Kitten?"

Smiling as she got up to head to the bath, Angelica replied, "Whatever makes you happy—tickles me to death, sir. In her first subtle instruction to her Master on starting his new day, she said, "I'm turning on the hot water for the shower if you want to join me after you ring up for that coffee, sir." *He didn't even catch it, did he?* she thought as she smiled, turning on the rainforest showerhead in the luxurious Ritz Carlton, D.C., for one last time.

The ride to the Manassas jetport was smooth and uneventful. Angelica was still enjoying the sightseeing from the SUV limo as she had been "sequestered" by Edward most of the weekend in their hotel suite. She hinted as she said, "I hope to get invited again sometime when you return to D.C. I would love to do some touristy things like visiting museums or galleries. There is so much history and amazing things to see here."

He inquired, "What did you like most that you saw or heard about on this first trip?"

Angelica replied, "My favorite thing about Washington, D.C., was seeing it with you. You make everything special and exciting, Edward. If I came here again with you, perhaps the Smithsonian Museum while you were working and in your meetings. The spa was a dream day for any girl, and I loved it, but I would probably go to as many museums as possible. There are so many of them! Plus, I still owe you that interior decorating project for your new condo here, Mr. Gray."

Gray responded, "Duly noted."

It was a short drive to the jetport, and no sooner than the skyline of D.C. was fading away behind them on their drive than they were pulling into the regional airport loaded with private jets. Edward said, "Last flight, we were upgraded to that Gulfstream 650, for no extra charge, as it had just landed in Sarasota, and they needed to move it to Washington, D.C., for a large group. So, we will likely be on a different plane going home."

Angelica commented, "Well, that makes sense. I was going to ask why you got such a huge jet just for the two of us. I thought you were just showing off for me, and I felt both good and bad about it."

He commented, "I should have explained that then, but it just didn't come up."

Their driver pulled into the jetport, and they went inside together on the way up for Edward to register with the flight master. He was an old veteran with thick white hair who had seen all kinds of presidents and prime ministers flying in and out of D.C. As he looked at his screen for reservations, he waved Edward over and asked, "Who might you be?"

"Gray. Edward Gray."

The flight master nodded and said, "I see you right here, Mr. Gray. Your Cessna Citation Ten is fully fueled and ready. We are just waiting for one more of your crew to wrap up another flight now. So please have a cup of coffee or juice, and we will be right with you as soon as he checks in for your flight."

Angelica cozied up to Edward in the lounge with her arms around him and asked, "Do you ever get used to this?"

He thought about the question but wasn't sure of its meaning and asked, "Can you elaborate on that?"

Sighing, she said, "This life you lead is very high profile. Extremely high power. Very full of fancy stuff." After a pause, she added, "What do you do to unplug and relax?"

Edward thought about her question and said, "I think I relax most when I'm working out. My mind gets clear, and my heart is pumping. I feel best right after that."

Chiming in, she smiled and said, "Those are endorphins, and they are really good for you, but that's not unplugging, that is jacking up your metabolism to get a natural high. Would you ever consider taking a walk on the beach with me or just listening to a meditation session together?" She smiled at her second influence on her Master of the Universe that morning. And as far as she could tell, he still didn't catch on to her gentle guidance. "No pressure, nothing fancy, just us unwinding together. Just an idea."

Edward nodded and said, "Maybe. Let me think about it."

Angelica leaned closer, with a seductive smile, and whispered, "What would have to happen for me to convince you to try either just once?"

Gray said, "That, I do not have to think about very long. If you agreed to join the Mile High Club with me, on our flight home, I would do either or both with you."

Angelica asked curiously, "What is the Mile High Club?"

The flight master called them. "Mr. Gray, your crew is ready for your flight whenever you want to board. Your luggage has already been stowed and secured for you, sir."

"Thank you, let them know we are on our way," Edward responded as he took her hand in his for the walk to the plane.

"Edward, you didn't answer me." She was intrigued to know more.

Gray spoke quietly in her describing what is required to be "officially" a member of the Mile High Club.

Angelica's eyes widened a bit, and she put her hand over her mouth as she laughed and said, "No way. Are you kidding me? And people actually do that?"

Edward nodded as they climbed aboard.

The Cessna Citation 10 is a mid-size jet seating about ten people, so it is still a big plane, to be sure. It was beautiful and luxurious like the Gulfstream, but with lots of burled wood and white leather seating. The aircraft had two club sections, each with two seats facing forward and two facing backward, for meals, meetings, and conversations. Edward led them to the second club section, further back in the plane for more privacy.

Angelica looked sheepish, thinking about Edward's request to have sex once they were high in the sky. Flying at over thirty thousand feet in the air while doing it would qualify them as Mile High Club members.

She looked at Gray and asked plainly, "Do you do this with all your girls, Edward? Is this how you impress them with a ride in your private jet?"

Her tone was a bit off-putting, but Gray replied unblinkingly, "Actually, you are the first woman I have ever trusted to bring on a business trip or introduce at an important business dinner. So, this is a bit of a first for me as well, Ms. Hart." He spoke quietly and steadily, gazing directly into her eyes. Something told her he was speaking the truth, and she softened.

"Well, I still don't know about doing it with people watching."

Edward replied, "And if I arranged for total and complete privacy with just the two of us in the cabin, would you consider the idea then?"

Angelica felt her adrenaline flowing at the thought of Edward's powerful energy inside of her, high in the air, flying five hundred miles an hour in a sleek, sexy-looking jet. Finally, she said, "Well, the idea is kind of hot and sexy, but I don't want to put on a show for the crew. I would be totally embarrassed."

Edward smiled as his mental gears were already at work to arrange their privacy. "Leave it to me, Kitten."

Midway through the flight home, their lovely flight attendant came back to check on them and delivered two more champagne mimosas, which Gray had gone forward to order moments earlier. Then, she asked, "Is there anything else you two might need right now before I take a short mid-flight break?"

Edward and Angelica innocently said, as she looked down at her feet shyly, "No, we're fine."

The flight attendant added, "I shall be back at my station in about fifteen minutes or so if you should need anything else." She then turned to head up front, where she drew a dark privacy curtain, and was gone.

Angelica leaned over and whispered urgently to Edward, "Did you tell her what we were going to do?"

Gray said calmly, "Absolutely not. I told her we had something urgent and confidential to discuss and needed a few minutes of privacy. She asked no questions and simply said, 'Of course.'"

Angelica's face turned flush as she still felt shy and under the moment's pressure. Both were now seated in window seats with an aisle between them.

Edward leaned towards her in his deep voice and said quietly, "I have a fantasy running through my mind of you taking off your panties in your seat to give me a little show, Angelica. Then, you come over and kneel in front of me for a minute of magical oral ecstasy. After which you turn and face forward, and slowly, very slowly take a seat straddling me reverse cowgirl style on my lap. In this way, we have all four hands free, yours and mine, to roam and stroke your body while we fly high in the air." Offering an alternative, Gray said, "Or, we could just sit and talk for fifteen minutes."

Angelica giggled aloud. "Well, since you put it that way..." she said as she unbuckled her seat belt and lifted the armrest out of her way to turn sideways, facing Edward. She slipped her sexy white panties off, sliding them down her legs before tossing them over on his lap, and said, "A little memento for you to keep, Mr. Gray."

He watched her as she began slowly, gently stroking her lips. Angelica slunk down in the seat with her legs splayed open and apart. Her breathing came harder as she closed her eyes. She wanted so badly to please him and tease him. For him to see what lengths she would go to—just to be his everything.

Gray responded instantly across the aisle, watching Angelica's sensual show just for him at 30,000 feet. He unzipped his trousers and slid them partway down, revealing his already thick and engorged excitement. He began stroking himself for her to see as he commanded, "Come to me."

As he reached across the aisle with his mighty arm, she took hold of his hand and was swept across the aisle to kneel at her Master's feet. She bowed her head onto his lap while keeping her fingertips between her legs, stroking both of them with the same rhythm. Edward's back arched as she applied her magic deeply with her plump full lips.

Gray momentarily lifted her head from his manhood and onto her feet before spinning her around to face the front of the plane. As he bent her forward, she felt him place both hands on her gorgeous heart-shaped ass, guiding her home repeatedly, and she slowly bounced on his rock-hard cock. The danger of being discovered, the threat of turbulence and possible injury, and the risk of sex in a semi-public place with people just a few feet away was intoxicating.

Angelica felt her first waves of ecstasy coming over her as her legs began to shake and she feared that they might hear her cry out. She must not cry out. She must not. Those thoughts gave way to a small cry for help. "Please, sir, may I cum?" she uttered in a faint voice.

Gray would not relent his pounding as he demanded, "Say it louder!"

She was shaking and begged, "Please, sir, may I..." Whispering only the last word, she added, "cum?"

Satisfied with her efforts to please him, he said, "Yes, cum for me while you ride me hard."

She let everything she had left in her go. Stroke after stroke on her Master's forceful will, until her legs collapsed from shaking and she sat on him fully, his seat, now wet with her juices. She collapsed onto Edward. "Oh my, that was intense…" she whispered, still hoping to remain undiscovered.

Angelica was suddenly startled, as she heard the captain's voice crack loudly over the P.A. system. "This is your captain speaking, we are seeing some potential turbulence up just ahead, and we will attempt to climb above it, but please check the security of your seat belt and remain seated for the next few minutes for safety." Angelica and Edward looked at each other and burst into hushed laughter.

She sprang off Edward and returned quickly to her seat to buckle up. Edward asked for the brunch napkins as he needed to dry off after her showering him with her love. It took Edward a bit longer to recover and refasten his trousers, and a bit of turbulence started to buffet the cabin before Gray finally returned to the safety and security of his seat belt.

He exhaled and looked over at Angelica. They both smiled briefly before bursting out laughing once again. They had made it. It felt like they were now officially "partners in crime," adding another special secret to their growing list of firsts and rare, exotic trysts.

Second, only to that, was the view of Sarasota Bay from the air as they descended through the beautiful blue-sky morning to their return to paradise. The blue-green water was so clear and transparent it did not look real. People travel worldwide to spend their rare and treasured vacation days on the sugary soft, white mica quartz sandy beaches. Visitors had often returned home to vow to move there, or at least marvel at those who got to call it home. It was easy to get the picture and perspective of so much natural beauty from the air.

Edward and Angelica held hands across the aisle on the landing as he said quietly, "Welcome home, Kitten."

She smiled. "It was so exciting to go away with you on a trip, but it also feels nice to be home, doesn't it?"

Gray nodded, smiling. "Yes. I agree. Travel almost always feels that way."

Taylor was waiting at the Rectrix jetport to greet them with the black Escalade and said, "Welcome home, Mr. Gray and Ms. Hart. The SUV is running with the air conditioning on if you would like to go be seated. I will be there shortly with the luggage."

Gray said, "Thank you, Taylor. We will take you up on that." Moments later, the hydraulic lift gate of the Escalade opened to swallow their luggage, and they were on their way home.

Taylor asked, "How was the trip, sir?"

Edward said simply, "Excellent. Washington, D.C., is still standing. We didn't do any damage, so they have agreed to let us return anytime."

The driver smiled and nodded at the news as he pulled out of the jetport to take Angelica home first.

Leaning forward a bit to hear the update, Angelica asked Taylor, "Did the Nissan service folks have any luck figuring out what was wrong with my car?"

He replied, "Yes, ma'am. They sent their tow truck over to pick it up at no charge. But unfortunately, it was not the battery. It was the alternator that recharges it, and they needed to order that part. They said it should be here this week."

Angelica gratefully said, "Thank you so much for getting it looked at. At least now I know what the problem is. That was very nice of you."

Taylor nodded and added, "My pleasure, Ms. Hart."

Angelica held Edward's hand in the back seat as they had just done on the flight landing and said, "I can just take an Uber for a day or two. Not a big deal."

Gray nodded agreeably. "Or it could just be time to get a new car," he said nonchalantly, never telegraphing the arrangements he and Taylor had made over the phone that weekend.

She said, "I haven't car shopped in years. I wouldn't even know where to begin." However, she would only have to look so far as they soon turned down her tree-lined street and pulled up curbside to stop as a new car blocked their path in her driveway. It was a red convertible Aston Martin Volante, one of Edward's premiere vehicles in his collection from home, that he had asked Taylor to bring over and park in Ms. Hart's driveway. It was absolutely gorgeous, and Angelica was stunned. She slowly looked over to Edward, who simply nodded. No. It was not a mistake or a neighbor parking there by accident.

Gray said, "With your car out of commission, I thought you might need some transportation. Let's go take a look."

Taylor discreetly handed Gray the keys to the Aston Martin as he exited the SUV to come around and open Angelica's door. She was still a bit awestruck and was at a loss for what to say.

Taylor unloaded her luggage while the two walked around the gorgeous design of the elite British sports car. Describing the lineage, Edward said, "They've been building these by hand for

316

over a hundred years in England to feel like a race car, so be careful when you hit the gas pedal, Kitten. She's quick."

Angelica looked at the gorgeous interior as she opened the driver's side door to peek inside, and said only, "It is the most beautiful car I have ever seen! This is too much, Edward."

Handing her the keys to her new world, he simply said, "Just sit inside and see what it feels like."

As she climbed inside, she said, "I think 'wow' about sums it all up! Can we go for a drive in it?"

"Go ahead after we put your luggage inside. But unfortunately, I need to catch up on work today after our long weekend in D.C., but one evening soon for a fun drive, OK?"

Taylor was waiting at her front door to deliver the luggage inside, if needed. Still awestruck, Angelica climbed gracefully out of the Aston Martin. "I can take the luggage from there. Thank you so much, Taylor," she shouted to Taylor on the front porch and added a wave goodbye.

"Thank you for the generous loan of your beautiful sports car, Edward. I will be cautious with it. Trusting me with it for a few days is so nice of you."

Edward gazed into her beautiful eyes as he held her waist in a gentle goodbye embrace and added, "Who said anything about it only being yours on loan?" He leaned in to kiss her softly, then gently pulled her full lower lip into his mouth, his thoughts lingering for one last time on their trip together. Edward left her breathless and speechless, and his black SUV and its driver took him home.

When his taillights had turned the corner and were gone, her heart ached. Still standing by her suitcase outside, she closed her eyes to help hold on to her memory of Edward for a moment longer. How he smelled. How he felt on their first trip together. Especially how it felt sleeping in his arms. The only thing remaining of him was parked in her driveway.

She opened her eyes again, seeing the shiny red reminder that she was his. *Oh, my...* she thought.

CHAPTER TWENTY-FIVE
A Girl Like Me

Angelica was still shocked at the red Aston Martin convertible in her driveway. She rushed to put her suitcase and bags inside, and her adrenaline and blood were pumping with excitement to take it for a spin. As she closed and locked her front door, she turned and paused just to look for a moment at the magnificent beast parked in her driveway. "Ok, calm down," she told herself as she raced to get in the high-end British supercar. "Note to self. Good luck with that!" After all, James Bond drove an Aston Martin, and the speedometer went up to over two hundred miles per hour. Holy moly!

She slid behind the wheel, and the moment she pressed the "Start" button on the dash, the over five hundred horses under the hood made themselves known. It did not sound like her Nissan— not even close. She gently backed the Aston out of her driveway and babied it forward. In moments, she found herself heading downtown to take an extraordinary drive in the new wheels. She was unsure what Edward meant by "who said it was a loaner?" She hadn't asked. *But did he intend for her to drive it for a while longer than just the repairs on her car? Maybe even long term? Certainly, it could not possibly be a gift, could it? This would be way too much to give away, even for him*. Nevertheless, it was an impressive machine. She noticed a few eyes watching her red convertible with her blonde hair streaming as she drove, and it was hard not to feel super-charged behind the wheel of so much elegant class and incredible power.

She half-hoped one of her friends would see her in it and was half-deathly afraid of having to explain it if she did. How do you explain the unexplainable? She remembered her good friend Samantha's warnings about Edward Gray and not to get her hopes up too much. "Crash and burn" might be the end result, and Samantha had wanted her to be forewarned before it was too late. A torrent of mixed emotions was flooding through her. This was all because her car didn't start last Thursday, making her late for the airport. *How did all this happen anyway?* She decided to think about it later and enjoy the cruise around Sarasota at a new level. It wasn't hard to smile from ear to ear.

A few hours flew by as she toured St Armand's Circle and Lido Beach. She thought of Edward and how to say thank you to someone who is at such a completely different level. There needed to be more than a text or even a phone call. *I have the perfect idea,* she thought. She pulled over to a cute little gift shop on the Key. But she wanted to write more than a thank you card, she wanted Edward to know how much he meant to her. So, she bought a card, a fancy pen, and some lovely stationery. Then, she headed back to Lido Beach to park while sitting in the car watching the sunset.

Angelica wanted to tell him everything. She took the chance, the high risk, of pouring her heart and soul into the letter. And, once she moved the ache of her heart onto the written pages, she drove to his home and discreetly slipped it in his curbside mailbox. She was able to make the discreet delivery without getting out of the car and drove away undetected.

Giving him his space after being together 24/7 on their trip was best, she thought. But she wanted him to check his mailbox tonight, so she texted him, *Dear Edward, I wanted you to know how much I appreciate you and all that you mean in my world, so there is a note in your mailbox, waiting to be read by you... XO, Angelica.* She paused before hitting the send button as she drove.

The letter she had written to Edward had started as a simple thank you and had taken her a couple of hours to finish. She shared what he meant to her and how her life had changed since he had come into it and described her hopes, her fears, how she sees him and asked him to guide her as to where she fits into his life. It was the conversation you have in high school when friends ask you if you two are "going steady or what?" It is the always dreaded "DTR" conversation or defining the relationship. She knew they had an Agreement, but she wanted more and felt that Edward did too.

Gray was outside watching the sun go down. It had been an intense and highly pleasurable weekend with Angelica, but he recharged his batteries best alone. It had always been that way for him. The solace and solitude came at a price. But he preferred being happy and alone to miserable in a toxic relationship with lots of drama. And is there any other kind of relationship? From the male perspective, it can be daunting.

The giant orange sun ball had finally disappeared, and he went inside to pour another glass of red wine. He saw the text from Angelica and discovered he had a "special delivery" waiting for him in his mailbox. He smiled and retrieved what he expected would be a nice, polite thank you card from his mailbox. But, when Edward opened the envelope, he discovered the long handwritten letter from Angelica instead. He thought, *Oh no, here we go.* As he headed back inside, he was already worried about what might be in store as he read the letter.

My dear Edward,

I miss you already. A thousand thank yous would not be enough to say how grateful I am you invited me to join you in Washington. That you entrusted me to be by your side at your important business dinner. And now, with your wildly exotic Aston Martin, which I am fearful of getting the least little smudge or scratch on. I drove it slowly to Lido Beach with the top down and the wind in my hair, thinking of you the whole way, how you are with me, how you treat me, and how proud I am of how you treat everyone around you. You are that rare man I have dreamed of since I was a little girl, my hero who is brave and powerful, brilliant, and kind, but that dream would have never come true if I had never met you.

I am at the beach now, hearing the waves roll in, and each one of them makes me think of you. On waking up those few mornings, I awoke sleeping in your bed and hearing the breakers rolling in on the Gulf. I feel the safest when I am there with you. So, please don't be mad at me or upset or disappointed when I say the next thing to you. I only mean it from the heart. So, you should know it's not your cars and jets or shopping that make me feel this way about you, Edward. If all that were gone tomorrow, my heart would still belong to you. You see, I had a dream of you my whole life.

I smiled, watching you sleep this morning; a rare sighting of my Edward not up hours before dawn on yet another big conquest. I was struck by how beautiful you are. As I ran my fingers through your hair, I thought of you as a vision that I can never find in anyone else, and it is at times like this that I know what my purpose is in life.

I am here to love you, Edward, to be held in your arms and you in mine and to protect your guarded heart as much as you have proven to protect mine. I am here to learn from you and to receive your love in return. I am here because there is no other place but you for me.

Today as you left to return to your home by the sea, I stood watching with a breaking heart as you slowly drove away. I find myself straining to remember everything about you the moment you leave. But soon, always too soon, you are gone again. I bow my head and cry and cry, aching for you. Just you.

So that is the thank you note I'm writing to you on this day, to say thank you for the greatest gift of all you have given me. Just you.

With all my love and devotion,

Angelica

"Men don't cry," Edward said to himself as his eyes blurred from the tears fighting to form on the battlefront within. He sighed, got up from his white couch, and walked to the bar to pour himself a cocktail, seeking insulation and protection from the feelings welling up inside him reading her words. He was supposed to be the best at keeping his distance from romantic, emotional connections based on his painful past. But, somehow, Angelica had slipped past the guards at the gates to his heart. He took his drink outside to the pool and looked at the ocean to think. But when he saw the breakers rolling in, his thoughts returned to her.

He gathered his composure before reaching out to Angelica with a text and said, *Can you talk?*

A moment passed before she replied, *Always.*

Edward phoned her up, and she picked up on his first ring with a cheerful but reserved "Hello." She felt cautious about how far she went in her letter and wanted to hear him speak first.

He spoke in a kind but careful tone. "First of all, thank you for all that you wrote in your letter, Angelica. I was very flattered to read all of it. But I think it is important that we talk about your expectations of me. And with us."

Angelica replied, "I just came back to Lido Beach."

Edward smiled, relieved that she had not driven all the way back home yet and added, "Oh, so you're just ten minutes away from me then. Care to come here so we can talk?"

Angelica said cheerfully, "Sure! I'm on my way."

Edward stopped himself as he was just about to say "drive safe," his usual conversation when she was on her way to him, but he didn't want it to sound like he was worried about the Aston Martin, so he just added, "See you soon."

Angelica was so happy that Edward wanted to see her and talk in person. A text or phone call to "talk" would have been a big letdown after what she had written to him. So, she did not speed but took her time deliberately, driving slowly back out to his home. Seeing the outline of his massive oceanfront estate drawing near, Angelica took a deep breath as she was about to pull in, yet once again.

Edward paced the whole ten minutes until she arrived in his circle driveway and parked in the exact spot she had the first night when she drove him home. That had been the fateful night they met, and he asked her to drive him home after she got rid of her date, only to come back hours later to meet him.

In a way, Mr. Gray had called this meeting and summoned Angelica into his world. The question for him to answer was: "What are you going to do now?"

Angelica looked sheepishly down at her shoes as she rang Edward's doorbell. She had poured her naked heart into her letter. It was his to pound into the ground if he chose; she had nothing to protect her and nothing to hide behind when the door opened. Her heart was laid bare already.

Edward graciously but carefully invited her in. It was not a rush to passionate hugs and romance as much as a careful walk across rice paper. "Please come," Edward said, leading her to the white couches. Angelica was glad he wanted to talk in person but was trying her best to keep her heart from pounding any louder lest Edward might hear it.

He spoke first. "Thank you for what you wrote. And I know we just signed a one-year Agreement and made our plans around that, but I can tell from all that you poured into your letter that you want more," he said with a pause, looking at her, inviting her to speak.

Angelica smiled, relieved. She thought that Edward understood. "Yes, I do, Edward. I hope you aren't upset with me."

"Of course, I'm not upset with you. How could anyone be upset after reading that letter? What I would be willing to do is provide you with a generous allowance so you would not have to work anymore, unless you find something that you are passionate about or want to pursue. And I will look for more opportunities for us to travel together. I can have an abundance of retail shopping clerks all over town waiting for the chance to spoil you anytime your heart desires!" he said with a kind smile, hoping to put a jovial and positive spin on his increased financial support for Angelica. "How does that sound?"

There was a long pause as Angelica looked down at her knees to think before she spoke. She knew that whatever she said next, she would need to be totally sure of. "That's a very good offer Edward, for a girl like me. And a couple of months ago, before I fell in love with you, I would have said 'sure, that sounds great.' But now I want... more."

Gray paused to think. "I understand wanting more and negotiating for more. I'm one of the best there is at it. The question, Angelica, is how much more?" he asked as he gently placed his warm hand on top of hers.

Angelica's eyes were blurred from tears as she tried to explain, "I'm not negotiating for more money or things. I will return the Aston Martin. I just want my Z back when it's ready. It's not any of that, Edward. I'm in love with you, and that is all I want."

Edward asked, "What exactly?"

She looked at him with her aching eyes and managed to speak with only the smallest quivers and shakes in her voice. "I want my childhood dream. My dream of you..." Angelica said, looking down and sobbing quietly as Edward tried to console her with his arm around her shoulder. Slowly standing up, she said, "I'm sorry. I promised myself I was not going to cry. I should go."

Edward, for once, did not know what to say. He was out of his element. Lost in a world he wanted but was desperately afraid of. He was floundering as they walked to his front door together. Angelica grasped the doorknob and opened it slightly before Edward put his hand up, blocking her momentarily. "Wait! Wait..." he said, pausing, grasping for the words to say next. With a bit of quiet desperation in his voice, which she had never heard before, he urged her. "Don't leave like this, please. Stay the night with me?"

Angelica paused and looked into his eyes for just one moment before looking down as she spoke. "I can't. It would break my heart, Edward… I have to go," she said as she gently opened the heavy, oversized door without help or hindrance from Edward this once. He watched her walk to the convertible sports car through the window. She started the powerful engine and sat there idling for just a breath or two to collect herself. And then she was gone.

CHAPTER TWENTY-SIX

The End

Angelica made it halfway home until the sobs overcame her. She pulled over to a small side street to let it all out, to cry until no more tears were left, at least for now. It left her exhausted, empty, and drained.

She pressed the button to restart the Aston Martin engine. It was time to finish the lonely drive home. This is when her thoughts of "second-guessing" began. Ideas of what she had done wrong started racing through her mind. She would likely blame herself for anything wrong. She was always the first suspect her mind would seek to round up to accuse in the blame game.

What could I have done? How could I have done things differently?

She would not ache alone in the solace of her pain that night. That long sleepless night was playing out for them both.

Gray paced his enormous home in torment. He went to the door of his Red Playroom and looked inside the empty chamber filled with memories of her. The walls were lined with floggers and paddles and secrets. His whole life had been secretive by keeping the pressures and passions of his life locked away behind those closed doors and the other doors locked inside of him that no one ever saw.

Looking one last time across the red satin bed of his Playroom, he closed the door and said aloud as he tried rationalizing to himself, "It's lonely at the top." His world would toss and turn all night until finally, just after three in the morning, he gave up as he sat in the bed that felt empty for the first time ever. He needed his space to recharge. It was when he did his deepest and most profound thinking as a man and a leader of others. But now his Achilles heel had been struck, and as every armor has its weakness—she was his.

He walked alone from his master bedroom to sit outside by the pool. Watching the ocean waves, he heard the music of the sea breaking rhythmically. But this morning, their sound would not be the only powerful thing breaking. Edward Gray closed his eyes to search his soul for the answers—one last time. And then again and again across the hours just ahead.

Across town, Angelica's alarm went off a second time. She was still exhausted from the trip and even more so from crying herself to sleep that never seemed to come. She hit the snooze alarm one last time to lay there buried under her pillows.

Finally succumbing to the persistence of the alarm, she got up and trudged to the kitchen to make coffee. She would need more than one as she struggled to prepare for the waiting property management office. She definitely could not just blow off work. The last thing she needed, especially now, would be to lose her job. She felt flat and empty inside, making her second cup of coffee while she got ready for a dreaded Monday full of maintenance calls and the usual flurry of details and problems for her to handle.

Angelica sighed as she locked her front door for the ride to work in the red Aston Martin, a painful reminder of the path she chose to leave. Love wants to be sung as a duet, not a lonely solo, she painfully learned last night at his doorstep. But her heart still ached for her love lost, for her Edward. She steeled herself to prepare for the drive to work and said out loud, "Don't cry, just drive."

But all that changed in a moment as she approached the Aston Martin. There was a shape waiting inside the red car for her. Sitting in the driver's seat were two dozen red roses, with an envelope bearing only the word "Kitten." Only one person had the other key to the Aston Martin, and only one person in the whole world called her that. She felt her adrenaline surge, and her mind raced as she opened the car door. Moving the gorgeous flowers and greenery to the passenger seat, she ripped open the envelope to discover his letter to her…

To my dear sweet Angelica,

I don't know how to begin except with my beginnings; how I got this way and why I am so hard to reach, it must seem to you. It was how I grew up in a home where the only thing that mattered was performance. The only measure that would get my father's approval was straight A's or excelling at sports. If ever there was one report card with all A's and one B+, my father would ask, "What the hell happened with that B?" That was all I knew.

I grew up in a home with two "alpha" personalities; both my father and mother were this way, and the fights were constant and never-ending. This was pretty daunting to the five-year-old that still lives inside of me. I didn't wish to live that way; that was the only model of love and marriage I was given. The pattern was imprinted on me from my early days.

So, I performed. I conquered school, business, and money but nothing else. I am still seeking that validation in some way to this day from my father and mother—all these decades later. Locked away in a world where that is all that matters, as I was taught.

That is why the "Arrangement" is safe. That is why the Red Playroom has been my hard limit. That is why, until you, I have kept my heart in check and my head in charge of me.

My darling Angelica, we live in a harsh world of cynical competitors. My toughness on the battlefield comes from a pure and powerful light where I will burn the world down to win, and men look in my eyes with no doubt of my resolve. So, they ultimately step aside every single time. But I have no weakness nor softness in my world—except now—with you. I am embarrassed to tell you that you have reached me in a way that no one else ever has, and many have tried.

I am afraid not of you, my angel, my Kitten, but of me. I do love you now, but I am afraid. Because of one question, I am terrified, petrified, and mortified of what this love could grow into.

If this grows a hundredfold, what would I do if I lost you then? That would be the end. It would most certainly destroy me. I am not built to handle any of this. So, my sweetest Angelica, this, for me, has always been the high price of loneliness. It is why I have always kept the walls built tall around my heart until you.

Last night, I felt an emptiness in my soul without you in my arms. I find myself searching for words to explain it to you. I know it is impossible, but I cannot help myself. If I lost you now, my search for someone like you ever again would be a never-ending quest that is doomed to fail.

So here I am with you, hopelessly and helplessly exposed and full of hope for love to be returned. And along with it, full of the fear

331

that one day, it will no longer be—may that day never come. Even as you read this, I am now waiting impatiently for your reply.

With all my love, Edward

Angelica's eyes welled up with big crocodile size tears. Her sides shook as she wept, reading the story of Edward. Then, hearing his heart, she clutched his letter to her chest against the ache she felt to her core. "He does love me!" she said aloud.

She smiled through the tears streaming down her face until the dark cloud arose. A large and foreboding black shape appeared in her driveway and pulled up directly behind her. She caught only a glimpse of it in her rearview mirror. So, she opened her car door for a better look behind her only to see it was him.

Edward Gray stepped slowly and gracefully from his black Tesla. He was dressed as he was that night she first met him, in his black tuxedo, with no tie, with a few buttons open, revealing just a bit of his chest hair. Edward smiled and waited for her to come to retrieve the one single long stem red rose he held waiting in his hands for her, and her alone.

The End of Book One

Thank You!

for reading

"The High Price of Loneliness"

Please Leave A Review For VIP Access To

BONUS

CONTENT

Curated Digital Content For My Readers

PS: If you take a moment to send me a screenshot of your honest review, I would like to send a "Thank You" along with **Bonus Content,** including videos and curated digital experiences to help bring this story to life. Plus, you will receive access to my "Reading Room," where I personally read selected chapters with the emphasis on the "Author's Pen." (Sometimes, it's not just what you say, but how you say it.) You'll also find a few "behind the scenes" insights into the real-life inspirations behind the story.

Need help with screenshots? Simply Google it for how-to tips, or write me a short personal note telling me about the review you've recently posted, and I will trust you at your word.

Thank you for reading this personal note *and stay tuned for more of this trilogy!*

Edward Gray, Author (Reviews@TheHighPrice.com)

Made in the USA
Columbia, SC
22 September 2023

23217319R00205